PEOPLE ALONG THE SAND

M000012499

PEOPLE ALONG THE SAND

A NOVEL

RACHEL KING

Copyright © 2021, Rachel King
All rights reserved. This book or any portion thereof may not be reproduced or used
in any manner whatsoever without the express written permission of the publisher
except for the use of brief quotations in a book review.
First Edition 2021
ISBN: 978-1-950843-48-0

Parafine Press
5322 Fleet Avenue
Cleveland, Ohio 44105
www.parafinepress.com
Cover and book design by Meredith Pangrace

To JD

PART ONE

1.

Leah stood at the kitchen island waiting for yeast to activate in warm water at the bottom of a tin bowl. Through the front windows of her bakery, mist fell through fog, the weather lit by porch lights. The yeast frothed; she broke eggs. With a wooden spoon, she stirred in cinnamon, sugar, butter, salt, flour, and raisins. She poured the mass from the bowl, pulled it toward her, and pressed it down with the palms of her hands.

She made blueberry muffins; oatmeal, chocolate chip cookies; and honey, orange-peel scones. She stepped around the kitchen, firm and graceful, a dance with ingredients and implements. Baked goods, cooling on cookie sheets and metal racks, crowded the counters. Bowls, spoons, and spatulas filled the double-barreled sink. By the time she'd washed the dishes, the muted morning competed with the porch lights. She unlocked the front door and switched the lights off. She stood on the porch, smelling overgrown mint below the steps. A logging truck rattled by on the nearby highway. A ship horn blew farther off. The fog had thinned to ribbons and clumps, but the mist endured. It came at her sideways, wetting her arm. A crack of dawn did not happen here, she thought, but rather a gradual fade from darkness.

Back inside, Leah sliced cinnamon-raisin bread. The bell above the door rang. Without turning, she arranged samples on a plate. She recognized Sandy's heavy breathing before she heard her voice.

I could've swiped a few doughnuts and been home by now.

Leah popped a bite in her mouth, turned, and held the plate across the counter.

Sandy threw one in and wiped her fingers on her long cotton skirt. Good, she said. Very good. I'm telling you, you need to sell your product elsewhere.

I don't have time for that, Leah said. Sandy loved to give business advice, though her cluttered antique shop, open erratic hours, hadn't made a profit in years.

Those students could drop it off in Florence or cart it to Eugene. Sandy examined baked goods in the display shelf, touching the glass above her favorites like a child.

Leah poured coffee from the percolator and gently set the porcelain mug across the counter. In the winter, that might work. In summer, I can't keep up with the baking.

Hire someone. We're not as young as we used to be.

Speak for yourself. Sandy was pushing sixty, over fifteen years older than her. Baking alone gave Leah joy, and running the shop did not wear her out. Grief wore her out, but moving away might help with that. For the past five months, ever since her husband, Micah, had died, she'd wondered whether she should lease a storefront inland. She noted Sandy's smudges. The muffin or the scone? she asked.

You could use the students in the shop. I bet they'd work for free.

Most free labor is lazy labor.

Sandy shook her head. Those students adore you. Love can be a great motivator.

You sound like a hippie.

Thank you. I was born forty years too early.

Leah imagined Sandy in one of the Vietnam protests she'd read about in the newspaper. In a photo, protestors marched shoulder to shoulder, raising signs or fists. Sandy would be that lady who pushed her sign in the face of a suited man passing by. Leah grinned and tapped the back of the glass.

The muffin, Sandy said.

Leah placed it on a porcelain plate and slid it across the counter. Sandy gave her two quarters. Leah didn't give her change because she knew she didn't want any.

Sandy sat at a table beside a front window. The fog and mist had dissipated. A cloudy sky remained. As she ate, crumbs fell from her mouth, to her chest, to her lap. She lit a cigarette and looked at a framed photograph. A chain-link fence created a perimeter on the beachside of a five-story hotel. A wooden sign attached to the fence read "Keep Out." Other photos on the walls were of bakeries in Portland or on the coast.

Leah stepped to the island and touched the loaves. They were cool enough. She carried them to the display case.

Where'd you get this photo? Sandy asked.

Leah looked over. One of the students. I do use them, see?

Sandy laughed, her cheeks ballooning. Crumbs bounced from her skirt to the hardwood floor. You're really getting into this beach stuff, aren't you? I'm saving my protesting for the war.

Maybe this'll lead to all kinds of political involvement.

Never saw you as much of an activist.

Maybe I've caught the students' enthusiasm. Leah pulled a leather notebook from under the counter and opened it next to the cash register. She thought of Laura, the college student who two months ago had taken her to the Eugene chapter meeting of Citizens for Oregon Beaches. One of the goals of the organization, for all Oregon beaches to become public land, had resonated with Leah. On Mondays, her day off, she'd attended more talks. She'd asked precise questions. The political terms became intelligible.

So what's the news? Sandy asked. On the beach stuff?

Leah looked up. Last week some representatives drafted a bill.

What did it say?

It wants to reserve the public's rights to the dry sands all the way to the vegetation line.

That's a big step.

It is. But who knows if it'll reach the floor, let alone pass? In the notebook, Leah listed ingredients she needed. *Blueberries.*

Raisins. Butter. Brown Sugar. Her thin, cursive words rose slightly across the unlined paper.

Sandy took a drag and squinted out the window, where a black sedan was parking against the curb. Marilyn's here, she said. Tim too.

Leah nodded. If she wanted to make soda bread tonight, she thought, she'd have to buy raisins at the general store this afternoon.

The door opened and Marilyn stepped in, her eyes downcast. Her son, Tim, followed, his eyes searching behind the counter.

Good morning, Leah said. She smiled.

Marilyn looked up and grasped the counter. Its coldness startled her.

Tim smiled without showing teeth. He mussed his hair and reached for a sample. Leah pushed the plate forward. They stood eye to eye across the counter. Do you have that album? he asked. Mom said you had an album for me. Leah squatted, and from a shelf underneath the register, she pulled out a record sleeve and handed it to Tim. Thanks, Tim said. He studied the cover while he chewed.

Marilyn was examining the baked goods. Those blueberry muffins? she asked.

Yes, Leah said.

Five cents more than last summer.

It's off-season for blueberries.

So the price'll drop midsummer?

We'll see.

Marilyn's directness reminded Leah of how she spoke to her own suppliers. But today, while Marilyn talked, she squeezed her hands together. Her tone was more serious than usual.

You can't go back down after a price raise, Sandy said. It's like the government. Never stopped a program once they started it. She finished the muffin and licked her fingers. Like that beach thing, she said. You think they'll just take to the vegetation line. Soon, the government will own the whole town.

I'll take a dozen muffins, Marilyn said.

And a maple bar, Tim said. He'd come for the record, but if he could manage a maple bar too, he might as well.

Three maple bars, Marilyn said.

Full house? Leah asked.

No vacancy, Tim said. He took another sample.

Strange for April, Leah said.

Strange in this weather, Sandy said. I've seen my place packed in April but on sunny weekends. Maybe people want to see if the beach is worth saving.

Maybe, Leah said. But most people don't know we're trying that.

Weekends in the spring have become busier every year for the past five years, Marilyn said.

Five years? Sandy said. Last May was rainy as hell.

I just looked over the records. At our motel, Marilyn added. It might be different at your place.

Sandy squinted as though trying to see the past and took a drag.

Leah loaded three maple bars into a paper bag and handed it to Tim. He slid into a chair at a table in the center of the room, fished out a bar, and, as he ate, examined the record's back cover. His face scrunched, concentrating. Leah folded a flattened cardboard box into shape and loaded in muffins.

Sandy's small eyes focused on Leah. Some of these people own the tidelands, you know, she said, if they bought it before 1913. She tapped the photograph's frame.

Leah closed the box and gave it to Marilyn. Yes, I heard, she said. If the land becomes only public, hopefully those people will receive compensation.

Marilyn handed Leah a crisp five-dollar bill.

You don't even like maple bars, Leah said.

They're for Jackson, Marilyn said.

As Leah handed over change, she caught Marilyn's eye. You're buying your husband two pastries and none for yourself? Leah thought. Marilyn looked out the window. Light pressed through a cloud and shot a rainbow across glass.

Like they did for the interstates? Sandy said. Her legs sprawled as she leaned forward. Give them money and throw them out?

No one is being thrown out, Leah said. You know better than that.

Someone has to argue the other side, Sandy said. I think the beaches should be public. But does public mean ownership by the people or the state?

The people, Leah said. The whole idea is to preserve.

The government's really preserving the national forests around here, Sandy said sarcastically. Those loggers at Joe's were telling me about it last night. Let's hope the beaches become more like national parks. She smashed her cigarette into a wooden ashtray and brushed crumbs from her chest. And people will be kicked off a *section* of their land, and that's the truth. She went to the counter and handed Leah the plate and mug. I should head to the shop. Marilyn's problem will soon be my problem. She nodded at Leah. To be continued.

Anytime, Leah said.

Good to see you, Lyn.

Have a good one, Sandy.

I intend to. Sandy looked over Tim's shoulder. Dylan, eh? We'll have a protest in this town yet. She started to sing "Masters of War." Her voice was loud, scratchy, and off-key. Her hands waved side to side with each phrase.

After Sandy shut the door, Leah smiled. Her friend would probably mention the photo to every person who browsed her antiques. Publicity, Leah figured, both for The Sweet Seller and the beach cause.

Tim, please take the muffins to the car, Marilyn said. I'll be right out.

Tim placed the record sleeve on top of the box and the bag on top of the record.

Did you thank Leah? Marilyn asked.

I thanked her, Tim said. You heard me.

If the students leave any other records around, I'll let you know, Leah said.

Sure thing, Tim said. He pretended to balance his load as he walked out the door.

Leah retrieved risen dough from the top of the stove, brought it to the island, and beat it down.

I wish he were going to high school this fall, Marilyn said.

You tired of teaching him? Leah asked.

I've taught him almost all I know. Or all I remember anyway. What kind of bread?

Plain old white. Bookkeeping too?

Jackson doesn't want him involved in that.

Leah divided the dough, cinched each loaf over, and placed them in cast-iron bread pans. Why not? she asked.

He thinks he's too young, Marilyn said. She sampled the cinnamon-raisin bread.

Leah placed the dough-filled pans in the still-warm oven for their final rise. She poured a splash of coffee and handed it to Marilyn, who drank it in one gulp.

That's good. Wish I could bake like that.

You know I'd show you.

I know. Again, she wrung her hands.

What's wrong, Lyn? Leah rested her elbows on the counter and leaned toward Marilyn. The coolness felt good. Burn scars splotched her forearms like birthmarks.

Jackson decided to build the new units, Marilyn said.

When?

When the rainy season lets up.

No, when did he decide? Leah asked. Marilyn and Jackson had been arguing over whether to expand for months. But before, Marilyn had said, it had always been he wants this and I want that—not he decided.

Last night.

Marilyn saw herself as though observing from above. She sat at the table off the kitchen and edited an essay of Tim's. The scent of their tuna supper lingered. Jackson, with quick but heavy footsteps, ascended the stairs, and holding paperwork and a thermos, approached her. He smelled like the forest; wet earth and spruce trees. I've decided to start the new units by the end of May, he said. He set the paperwork on the table. She set the pen down. They hadn't discussed the new units for a week. We're going to the bank on Monday, he said. I want you to do the cost estimates by then. His eyes searched for hers; she looked at the stack of wrinkled paper. He walked into the kitchen. The thermos clicked against the bottom of the sink. He returned to the sitting room and turned on the television, its noise forcing her to leave and edit downstairs. They hadn't spoken since. Now, Marilyn realized that she'd been waiting for this moment, when she could tell Leah. The pressure in her head subsided.

Leah poured her friend another swig of coffee.

I need to get back, Marilyn said. Guests will want muffins.

Your rough estimate didn't give him pause? Leah asked.

No. If he actually read it. She again drank the coffee in one gulp. We're going to the bank on Monday.

For a loan? Leah asked. So soon?

I don't want to.

Send him alone.

They might have questions. He wouldn't know what he's talking about.

Leah took Marilyn's mug from the counter and went to pour more.

No, Marilyn said. I need to go. She glanced out the window. Tim sat in the sedan's passenger seat, his feet crossed on the dashboard, his eyes on the album cover.

I'm free after work, Leah said. Come by then.

OK. Tim can check in guests, I guess.

Jackson lets him do that?

Sometimes. Won't let him take their money.

You want a scone? On me. Leah put one in a paper bag. For later.

Thanks. I'll call before I drop by.

Sure thing, said Leah, imitating Tim.

Marilyn smiled. Her long dark hair slid over her shoulder as she turned. Leah watched her step into the car and speak to Tim. The boy took his feet off the dashboard and said something, pointing at rays of sun. Leah drank the coffee she'd poured for Marilyn. She twirled a strand of hair while they drove down her residential street and turned onto Highway 101. She took out a broom and dustpan and swept up Sandy's crumbs.

2.

Marilyn and Tim passed the Oregon Coast Bank; Dame's Fine Chowder; Kalapuya General Store; Lollipops, a sweet shop; and Joe's, the bar. Many of the houses and the rest of the commercial buildings, including The Sweet Seller, lay on a grid between highway and ocean. Once south of town, the highway closely paralleled the sea. On their right, black jagged rocks sloped into the water; on their left rose a hill forested with spruce and hemlock, patches here and there leveled from clear-cutting.

As Tim had pointed out rays of sun, he'd said he might go exploring. Marilyn imagined him ducking in and out of caves, his pockets wet from damp agates. She remembered when she and her younger brother, Dave, had explored the woods around their hometown, Toledo. They spent days following creeks, picking berries, swimming, hiking, and fishing. She wished Tim had a sibling or close companion. During the summer he'd bop around with regular summer guests, but during other seasons, he was alone. He himself didn't seem to mind, but lately he'd spent more and more time in his bedroom listening to music, and Marilyn had become worried for him. Because their local junior high was thirty minutes away and the bus didn't service their area, Marilyn had decided to homeschool for seventh through ninth grade. Now, at the end of the first year, she wondered whether her decision had been a mistake, and that because of these years of isolation, he'd be the oddball in high school.

They turned right into The Wave, the southernmost property in Kalapuya. The motel name was painted in white block letters on a wooden sign at the highway edge of the property. A board that said "No Vacancy" hung off the bottom. Marilyn stopped and asked Tim to hop out and flip it over.

Rain's starting again, he said as he slid back inside. He rubbed his palms against his jeans.

The mist wasn't heavy enough for Marilyn to turn on the windshield wipers. They needed to create a slower setting, she thought, specifically for coastal mist.

They drove by Jackson cutting firewood in a grassy, open area. With his beard and flannel, he looked as much mountain man as motel proprietor. Rainwater rested on his forehead and red cheeks. He was bringing down the axe and didn't look up.

The entryway sloped to the dark brown motel that sat above rocks and the sea. Marilyn pulled alongside a rectangular building that held an office and lounge on the bottom floor and the family's apartment on top. Three rows of guest rooms circled this building like an angular horseshoe. The most coveted rooms were on the western side, a few dozen feet from the rocks. Here Jackson planned to build five more units on top of the current five units. The motel would then have a total of twenty rooms.

I might give you a writing prompt on one of those songs, Marilyn told Tim. So listen carefully.

OK, Tim said. As though he wouldn't listen carefully otherwise, he thought.

But first go help your dad with the firewood.

Mom—

You have the whole day after that. Go on.

OK. Tim got out of the car and opened the office door and ran through the office and up the stairs two at a time, his thin hair bouncing. He wanted to put the record in his room away from the rain.

Marilyn, holding the box of muffins, closed the office door, then walked by a window box, empty except for dirt, and entered the lounge, where the motel maid, Annie, was reclining. Marilyn placed the muffins on a silver tray, then cut them in half. The pieces, leaning against each other, filling the tray, comforted her. For now, for today, The Wave was running well. She filled up a mug of coffee from the dispenser and felt hungry for Leah's scone, but didn't want to return to the car to fetch it, because then she'd settle into the office where she had to budget for the addition they didn't need and didn't have money for. She sat on the couch kitty-corner from Annie, who had her eyes closed.

What d'you think of all these people? Marilyn asked.

Annie opened then closed an eye. I think it's more work for the same paycheck, she said.

I can understand that. You need my help? During the busiest times, on weekends in the summers, Marilyn helped Annie clean rooms.

I'll be OK. Least they aren't all over the place at 7 a.m. Only seen two. We've got the weather to thank for that.

Marilyn sipped the black coffee. Rain blew against the window. Across the room, Yahtzee, left out by a guest, sat on top of an oak table. Above the table, built-in bookcases held *Reader's Digest* books and board games. In the corner stood an out-of-tune piano, middle C chipped, brown paint flaking. Marilyn went over to pick up Yahtzee, feeling grateful for a full house of guests. During winters, the few travelers hardly soiled their sheets and left in the muted coastal winter dawn. Jackson said that the new units could make up for their losses during winters, but the preliminary estimates said otherwise. Maybe in thirty years, Marilyn told him. Then Tim'll reap what I sow, Jackson said. What if Tim doesn't want to run this place? Marilyn wanted to ask. Instead, she said they needed the money for Tim's education. If he wants to go to college, he can earn his way through, Jackson said.

Tim walked by the window carrying an armful of firewood. Marilyn noted his short sleeves that wouldn't protect him from splinters. He opened the woodbox outside a corner unit with his knee and rolled the firewood off his arms. He dropped the lid, ducked his head into the rain, and jogged toward the office.

Marilyn washed her mug, the hot water caressing her hands. The warming weather made her thankful to be done with winter. During the darkest months, gusts casually tossed up twenty-foot waves. Most days, on the beach, you couldn't stand up straight against the wind. Few people had summer homes here on the Central Coast, so far from the Willamette Valley.

What's wrong with us, Marilyn asked, to live here year-round? I need the job, Annie said. I can't speak for you.

Annie could probably land a similar job in Salem, Marilyn

thought, where her sister lived. As for her, her marriage tied her to this place. Jackson's father, while out logging alone, had broken both arms and legs, spent two weeks stuck in the woods, and after he was rescued and recovered, opened The Wave. It began as an inn with inexpensive boarding in the row of units facing the sea. Later, he added both wings, which they were still paying off. When she'd asked Jackson why his father had built here, he'd said that this area needed an inn. His father had had a nose for such things, just like how as a solo logger, he'd known which mills needed timber. And Kalapuya still needed a motel. Besides the new hotel being built on the north end of town, The Wave was the only place to stay.

Marilyn turned toward the door, resolved, if not ready, to do the estimates. I'll bring over more coffee in an hour or two, she said. Doubt this'll last them.

Annie stood and ran her hand down the wrinkles on her white dress. From the closet behind the recliner, she pulled out a cart off which hung a mop, broom, and duster. Marilyn held the door open as Annie rolled the cart outside, then shut the door behind them both.

In the office, cold air and mist blew through a window, open a few inches. When hot after physical labor, Jackson had a habit of opening it. Marilyn grasped the top of the window frame and slammed it shut. The pane of glass wobbled. She hated the bang, but if you weren't forceful, it would stick.

She dropped into the leather armchair, a Ryder family heirloom that Jackson's grandfather had bought with his first earnings from solo logging. She pulled the logbook across the desk. Two rooms had checked out, thirteen remained. When she heard Jackson on the stairs, she kept looking down but no longer saw the writing on the page.

I checked out two while you were away, he said.

Jackson examined local knickknacks for sale on a bookshelf. A wooden box of seashells and sand dollars, a row of purple and orange starfish, a few magnets, a few postcards. Marilyn stared out the front window. A young woman with two young girls crossed the street. One tried to spin in the rain, but the mother grasped her shoulders and pointed her toward the lounge. From above came the muffled sound of Tim's record.

I got maple bars, Marilyn said. She nodded toward the bag on the desk. She'd brought in the scone too, but her desire to eat had disappeared. The pressure in her head expanded.

Jackson pulled up the window a full foot. With all this humidity, he thought, the room could use the air. Rain scattered across his jeans and the checkered linoleum floor. He pulled out a maple bar and bit into it. Tim needs to gather more shells and things, he said.

He hasn't seen many shells this winter, Marilyn said. I'll ask him to grab a few starfish.

The tide would be at its lowest around one. Marilyn remembered when she hadn't felt the tides as acutely as the weather. The first couple years she lived in Kalapuya, she carried around a small blue pamphlet that listed the times for low and high tides. Jackson laughed when she examined it. Look out to sea, he'd say. If it's dark, just feel it. Because she'd grown up an hour inland, he called her a landlubber.

I think I might go to my parents' tonight, Marilyn said. She hugged her arms.

Are your parents OK? Jackson asked.

The floor's covered with rain, Marilyn said. She snatched a rag from the closet behind the office and, kneeling, wiped up water.

Jackson lowered the window. It's hot in here, he said. He took off his flannel and hung it on a nail. Sweat ringed his white shirt's neck.

Marilyn stood and slammed the window closed. She turned to him, wet cloth in hand. I'm not going for my parents, Marilyn said. I'm going for me.

Jackson leaned toward the logbook. Already eight rooms were booked for tonight. The busyness this weekend confirmed his decision to build the new units.

I'm worried about taking out another loan, Marilyn said. The pressure in her head lessened. She needed to tell him, she thought. She needed to make her worries known. A young couple walked hand in hand toward the lounge. Are you listening? she asked.

It's the first busy weekend of the year, Jackson said.

Tim can manage, Marilyn said.

No, he can't.

You and Tim can manage. Did you hear what I said?

Jackson turned.

I do the books, Marilyn said. I'm basically the accountant.

Who's at the desk this afternoon?

Me, at the beginning of check-in. Tim'll take over around four or five, when he gets back.

Back from where? He's here now. That goddamn music.

There's worse around.

I forgot you attend college parties. Jackson grinned, but Marilyn was looking away. A couple times she'd happened to be at Leah's among college students. Once, she'd returned smelling like pot. He meant it as a joke; his wife was far from hippie material.

Marilyn felt as though she could do nothing against his sarcasm but agree with his mocking, become angry, or ignore him. Only ignoring didn't spur him on. She stepped into the closet and threw the rag in a hamper. Do you know what we'd have to pay per month if we get that loan? she asked.

We don't have to pay on it immediately, Jackson said. He relaxed into the heirloom chair, fitting his arms into the armrests. An old man wearing suspenders and a mesh hat hobbled toward the lounge. The whole motel was waking up, yawning and stretching.

Jackson loved to watch it come to life. You're the accountant, not the manager, he said. I know what I'm doing.

The little girl who'd spun across the street entered the lounge, then hesitated. Children, like dogs, could sense conflict, Marilyn thought.

Can I help you? Jackson asked.

I need a towel, the girl said. Two towels.

You sure the sun won't dry you off? Jackson smiled.

The girl studied the rain, then shook her blonde pigtails.

Jackson went into the laundry room and returned with the towels. He squatted and held them out. Anything else, milady? he asked. She remained silent. Why, I bet you want to touch my beard.

The girl reached out and tapped his hairy brown chin. She grabbed the towels, squealed, and ran through the door.

Jackson was so personable, Marilyn thought. If people remembered the place and returned year after year, it was partly because of him.

Why do they need extra towels? Jackson asked.

Who knows, Marilyn said. Maybe one of the kids vomited. She'd seen it all: carpets and sheets and counters and bathtubs covered with food or vomit or semen. Sometimes, while cleaning, she dry-heaved from the nastiness.

Which room are they in? Jackson asked.

Seven, Marilyn said.

I'll give Annie a heads-up, Jackson said.

Great, Marilyn said. She was grateful that he called out the guests who left the worst messes. I'll run the estimates, she said, but I don't think it's a good idea.

Great, Jackson said. He was relieved that Marilyn had, for now, abandoned her soapbox. I'll take over the desk.

As she moved toward the stairs, Jackson stepped to the window and opened it. Marilyn saw him, but not wanting to deal with it, continued up the steps.

In the kitchen, Marilyn nibbled at the scone and looked out the window, west, over the units and out to sea. Dark gray clouds hung low above the dark blue water. Whiter clouds were high in the sky. During rain or sun, in any season, she found the view beautiful. The yet-to-be-built second-story units would block her sight of the ocean. Yes, she could walk above or on the rocks for a similar view, but she wouldn't be able to enjoy it while preparing food, washing dishes, or making tea. A muted light broke between the dark and lighter cloud layers while she finished her breakfast.

Marilyn walked through the sitting room and down the hallway, passing Tim's bedroom before entering her own. She shut her door but could still hear "A Hard Rain's A-Gonna Fall." Five and a half years before Tim could be drafted, she thought. This would be over by then. Both Jackson and her dad had served, but she balked at the thought of sending Tim. Carl, whose family stayed at The Wave biyearly, had left for basic right before his family's spring break visit. Because he was sixteen, his parents had signed for him. Marilyn didn't understand why people allowed their sons to join the army in lieu of high school, especially this year, when each week the number killed over there had increased.

Marilyn had watched the worry on her son's face when he watched the evening news. Yesterday, she'd reminded him that Carl was still in training: he wasn't over there yet. Tim had shrugged but relaxed; he didn't admit those rare times she read his mind.

Marilyn lifted a mustard-yellow suitcase from the back of the closet, plopped it on the bed, and tossed the lid open. *Lady* indeed, she thought. Initially, Jackson addressing her as a lady had charmed her; after ten years of being called *girl* as a waitress, the word *lady* felt refreshing. But Jackson could use the word derisively, too. A lady wouldn't understand, he'd said more than once. Or, a lady's way of thinking complicates the problem. There weren't any good or bad words, she'd decided, only positive or negative tones.

She tossed two skirts and two blouses into the suitcase, then paused, her fingers in her hair. She wasn't sure whether women thought differently than men; many times, she caught herself planning far in advance, like her father. And even if they did, if Jackson went with her advice, in the long run, life would be *less* complicated. They'd have less debt, more money for Tim's education, and maybe they'd be able to afford an annual vacation. And that view. Although she'd miss it as much as the money, she hadn't mentioned it to Jackson. Since her husband didn't love the ocean, she thought he'd listen to money concerns over sentimentality. She put a necklace, bracelet, and three pairs of earrings into a silk travel box.

On one of the rare clear days in January, while she and Jackson had walked hand in hand above the rocks, Jackson, for the first time in years, had said that he wanted to build new units. As he talked, his grip became firmer, while Marilyn wanted to pull away. She told Jackson that right now, she felt overwhelmed with their 1966 taxes. He said he understood and that they could talk more later. While they watched gulls swoop in and out of a cliff's lip, they discussed Micah, his death, and how Leah was doing. Her loss made them grateful for each other. They kissed overlooking the sea, like a young couple on vacation, and went home and made love. The office bell from a drop-in guest interrupted them. They played rock-paper-scissors to see who had to go downstairs. Marilyn lost. The flush in her dark cheeks and her breathless voice turned on the guest, a passing-through trucker.

When Jackson dismissed her, like he'd done in the office, she didn't feel like touching him. She packed three pairs of underwear—an old cotton, a new cotton, and a silky pair, Jackson's favorite. She remembered the first time they'd touched, on the day they met, while she sat on a woodbox, her legs wrapped around him.

Is this how you treat all stranded guests? she'd asked.

God, no, he said. You're the first.

First to be stranded?

Well, both, he said. He grinned. They continued kissing on the mouth, then away from it. The saltiness of the sea on his neck tasted foreign.

It had begun too passionately, she thought. That was the problem. She did this every few days, reducing their problems to one cause. This kind of logic, like figures on a balance sheet, calmed her. Then a contradictory memory would surface and she'd admit one incident didn't explain complexities. They hadn't had sex that first night. They dated for over a year before she moved to the coast.

One day a couple of weeks ago, she'd thought that leaving her hometown was the problem. She'd lived in a small town all her life and was accustomed to its eccentricities and jealousies, but she'd had to adjust to the ocean, its vastness and seeming omnipresence. Trees had enclosed Toledo. The ocean here was like a prairie of water, a flatness she had to turn from to retain equilibrium. Now its scents were like the scent of the Toledo sawmill; background only visitors noticed. And although she knew the waves were powerful enough to kill, and had killed her best friend's husband, she thought their breaking and lapping a comfort. Since she now loved Kalapuya, she'd concluded that their problems didn't stem from being here.

Jackson thought he had veto power because she'd married into the property. Maybe she should have encouraged him to move to Toledo, where they both wouldn't have had assets. If she'd encouraged too strongly, she knew, she and Jackson wouldn't have married, since Jackson and the motel were a package deal. She loved the motel and worked as hard as Jackson at it: at this point, he shouldn't have veto power.

She zipped up the suitcase and headed downstairs to the closet between the outer office and the laundry room, where she did the bookkeeping. She heard the song "Corrina, Corrina" coming from

Tim's room. The window was open, but Jackson had abandoned his post. They might as well be paying to heat the outdoors, Marilyn thought. The pressure in her head grew. She held her temples. She banged the window closed. The bottom pane shattered at impact. Glass bounced off her dress and onto the floor. Pieces lay below the frame, among rainwater. The shock had dissolved her head pressure. Her hands smarted from splinters. The bookcase and its curios remained intact. She went inside the closet-office and sat. One by one she pushed the splinters up and out with her thumbnails.

3.

On Tim's first listen, each song rolled through his head, the tunes and lyrics indistinguishable. On his second listen, he copied the lyrics into his notebook, each song a paragraph without line breaks, compact and claustrophobic. On his third listen, he began to internalize the lyrics and hear differences between the tunes in different verses.

He'd come to expect this deepening after each listen. It was like exploring an area in the woods; on each repeated trek, the landscape would become more familiar and nuanced. He saw mushrooms on fallen trees or the depth of the stream or where a woodpecker lived or places the undergrowth became too dense to traipse through.

After his fourth listen, he dropped the notebook into his backpack—small for him, since his mom had bought it before his year in fourth grade—grabbed his raincoat, and took the stairs two at a time to the office. The front desk was empty, the closet-office door closed. The light inside and out was dim; he couldn't tell whether the rain had stopped. A young couple holding hands walked toward the office. His mind returned to the music, the longing of the love songs an ache in his chest.

At the sound of the bell, his mom stuck her head out of the closet-office. You got this? she asked Tim.

Yeah, he said.

She nodded to the couple, shut the door, then reopened it. Watch under the window, all of you, she said. The pane broke. All three looked to the side, then stepped away. Your father will fix it, Marilyn said. She shut the door.

My god, the woman said. How did that happen? She pulled her skirt away.

Tim checked the bottom of each shoe for shattered glass. Only mud and sand filled the crevices.

Number twelve, the man said. He set the key on the counter.

Tim took the key and placed it on the number twelve hook on the board to the side of the desk. I hope you enjoyed your stay, he told the couple. Can I give you directions somewhere? A recommendation for a restaurant?

The woman smiled, amused. Tim sensed her as affectionate, not mocking, and smiled back. A red sweater accentuated her breasts.

That lighthouse south of here, the man said. Can that be toured?

Tim shook his head. That's privately owned, he said. There's Heceta Head Lighthouse—

We were there yesterday, the man said.

Thank you though, the woman said. We loved the view from our room.

The man opened the door.

Hope to see you again sometime, Tim said. July through September, there's little rain.

Outside, they held hands again. Tim watched them round the corner of the motel, then put on his raincoat. His mom stuck out her head.

Can you grab some sand dollars or starfish or something? she asked. We're running low.

Tim examined the shelf from a distance. OK, he said.

He went outside, cut through the space between two rows of units, and jutted onto the rocks and into perpetual mist. His tennis shoes dropped in and out of the crevices in the black rocks, stepping on barnacles and over small tide pools filled with dark green sea anemones until he lowered himself to the wet, brown sand. He wasn't cold. He didn't think of the temperature. He didn't think of the gray sea either. The ocean was like a sibling; something to play with, ignore, or yell at; something, above all, always there.

He crouched, searching for agates, and ducked in a cave into which shallow waves curdled. He'd collected the rocks for years, substituting the duller as he found ones with more facets or shine. A pastime he'd always done alone, then sometimes with Carl, and now, again, always alone, because Carl wasn't coming back, at least, he told himself, not for a while. A sunny day would be ideal, but he knew how to work in dimness. Agates were often found in or near rivulets that started on cave walls and flowed over sand and into streams that ran along the beach and into the sea. He shivered as he dipped his hands into water to grab a shimmering rock. He held it up. It was OK, he thought. He'd compare it to his ones at home. He pushed it deep in his pocket, wiped his hands on his jeans, and emerged from the cave.

At the waterline, purple and orange starfish suctioned low on a rock. Every third or fourth wave washed over them. Tim worked off a purple starfish, pulling first one leg, then another, until he could gently work off the belly with a finger. Waves washed over his hands. He pushed the starfish into his backpack, then finagled off an orange one. Unlike his father, who'd taught him, he never left a broken leg on a rock. He walked along the beach, feeling the starfish's bumpy backside and searching for sand dollars. No unbroken ones caught his eye. Planning to return to that line of beach, or maybe walk in the other direction, toward town, when the tide was lower, he scrambled up steep rocks, ducked under a Sitka spruce whose branches, contoured by the wind's constant battering, leaned toward the water, and walked along the grass line, still clasping the starfish. Its legs, which had twitched, now lay motionless. It would take a couple of days to dry. Then they'd sell it for fifty cents to some guest too lazy to walk a hundred yards from the motel and open his eyes.

The water and rocks merged, narrowing the beach to a few feet, then a few inches. Tim walked on muddy grass alongside rocks that rose and rose until the ocean was fifty feet below. Seagulls screeched. Two swooped toward the ocean, then out of sight. Tim had seen their nests in the crevices of a cliff face when Micah took him boating for his tenth birthday. Micah told him that people who fed seagulls bread, like tourists from the decks of Joe's or Dame's, caused the birds to rely on human food. By fall, Micah said, they became lazy and had more trouble finding food for themselves. Since then, Tim had been careful not to feed them.

The dense woods crept toward the rocks; soon Tim traipsed through the edge of the forest as often as the side of a cliff.

He was headed to an unlocked house that he'd entered for the first time during spring break. Last summer, he and Carl had crossed the property but never approached the house because Mr. or Mrs. Yager was always about the place. Now Mr. Yager lived in the lighthouse a hundred yards south. Tim wanted to ask his mom, his dad, or Leah when the old man had moved and why, but he also wanted to keep his discovery secret. Right now, he could go inside without disobeying orders.

As he approached the Yagers' cove, the rocks again lowered toward the sea. The lighthouse, the land, and the beach were private. Leah wanted all of the beaches to be public land, Tim knew. He himself hadn't formed an opinion. He liked that, right now, someday he could own his own beach, but he also liked to go wherever he wanted. Not that private property had ever stopped him from exploring. Moving inland, he skirted a patch of sword ferns and jumped a moss-covered log. He walked through knee-high grass to a two-story, shake-shingled rectangular house, opened the door, and stepped inside.

He went to the right, into the kitchen, and from a cupboard took down a tin of cocoa. The powder was clean; he'd sifted through for bugs when he'd discovered it. He ran water into a saucepan and heated it on the stove, then carried a mug of cocoa and his backpack to a couch in the front room and sat under the dustsheet that covered it. He sipped, feeling warmth in his stomach and limbs. If someone looked in a window, he thought, they wouldn't notice him.

Carl would have loved it here, Tim knew. His friend would make a fire in the fireplace and claim one of the bedrooms. Tim himself hadn't made a fire or been upstairs. The fire might alert Mr. Yager, and a ghost might live upstairs. Mr. Yager's wife had died; maybe her spirit lingered near her old bedroom. He and Carl had decided that ghosts didn't exist, but Tim would rather stay downstairs just in case.

The front door rattled. Trees swayed. Tim took out his notebook, flipped past the Dylan lyrics, and rested it against a knee. *She's a ghost without a care*, he wrote. He was writing a poem about the wind. He'd rather write a song—it sounded less sissy—but he didn't know how to play an instrument or write a tune. *Always searching for her sorrow, looking here and there,* he reread, *tearing through trees, swishing down chimneys, she's a ghost without a care.* He crossed out *trees* and wrote *firs*. He pulled the sheet off him to look out the window.

A couple house lengths away, beyond the overgrown yard, Mr. Yager crouched, his black poncho billowing, his beige floppy hat tilted down. Probably looking at a sea lion, Tim thought. Maybe a bunch of them. Last summer he and Carl had seen a dozen in that inlet. The poem forgotten, he wished Mr. Yager would go inside so he could take a look.

Drops of rain tapped against the tin roof of a shed. The old man turned toward the noise, then strode toward the lighthouse. His expression remained flat. Sandy had said that Elliot Yager had become a hermit, Tim thought. She'd predicted that he'd soon follow his wife and die. But his father had argued he'd always been a hermit. Who else but a hermit, his father figured, would spend his life as a lighthouse keeper?

Tim put up his hood and went outside. He glanced toward the lighthouse to double-check that he was alone. At the top of the inlet, he looked down. Three sea lions lay against one other. One lifted its head, looking at Tim with a black eye. Another drummed its flipper on the wet sand. Raindrops splattered on them and the sea. Tim stepped down a rock, toward them. All three rolled away from one another and scooted toward the water. Intent on touching a flipper, he jumped from three feet up. As he landed, a strand of seaweed caught a foot and he tumbled over, the wind knocked out of him. The sea lions yelped, a sound between a gull's screech and a dog's bark. Tim raised himself to all fours while they scuttled into the ocean. By the time he stood, Mr. Yager perched on a rock above him. His appearance startled Tim.

No sea lions where you live? the old man asked.

Not right by, Tim said. Water had seeped through the knees of his jeans and a patch on his thighs. Wet sand stuck to his palms and ankles. He climbed the rock, wanting to get his notebook and backpack and go home.

Did you know that cave goes back a hundred feet? Mr. Yager asked. Conrad, his son, had discovered the deep cave in high school. The boy had shared his discovery with Elliot—one of the only times the high-school Conrad had shared anything with his father.

No, Tim said. He stood a step away from the old man. There was a deep cave so close to The Wave that he hadn't known of? But ever since he was allowed to explore, his mom had forbidden him to go this far down the coast. Last summer, when Carl had asked, Tim decided he was now old enough.

The sea lions probably stay in there at high tide to remain dry, Mr. Yager said. I've done it myself.

Were there sea lions with you in the cave? Tim said.

No. I wouldn't want to be stuck in there with them.

I didn't know they were dangerous. Rain blew against Tim's back. He pushed his hands in his pockets and focused on not shivering.

Can be. Had to kill one years ago. Kept coming too near the house.

Tim's eyes widened.

Would you like to see its skin? It's in the lighthouse. Elliot had never invited a trespasser in, but this boy seemed so impressed, in such a naive way, that Elliot knew he'd properly appreciate it.

Tim wanted to see it, but he didn't want to leave the area without his notebook and backpack. He forced himself not to look at the house. OK, he said. But I need to be back home soon.

Mr. Yager turned toward the lighthouse, a square building attached to a square light tower, and Tim followed. In the anteroom, he pulled off his shoes and jacket and brushed sand off his hands and ankles. Mr. Yager nodded at an empty peg next to the outer door, where Tim hung the coat. From the other side of the inner door a dog whined.

Lana, Mr. Yager said. If I want to see sea lions, I keep her inside.

As Mr. Yager opened the inner door, the black, long-haired dog bounced both paws off his owner's thighs. She sniffed Tim's socks. Is she nice? Tim asked.

Best dog I've owned, Mr. Yager said.

Tim held out a hand. Lana licked it.

Inside, a fire blazed, a basket of shells decorated the mantel, and an armchair sat on either side of the fireplace. More than a dozen photos of shipwrecks hung across the walls. Tim stepped close. One ship leaned toward the sea near Cape Perpetua, the mountain south of Mr. Yager's light. Another ship was sunk deep into sand. A huge rock splintered another, while Tillamook Lighthouse blazed in the distance. Did you see these happen? Tim asked.

I saw some afterward, Mr. Yager said. He waved an arm toward the wall. A sea lion skin hung to the side of the front door. Firelight scattered across it.

Tim touched it. The smoothness he'd expected; the softness surprised him.

Don't get your oils on there, Mr. Yager said.

How'd you kill it? Tim asked. He imagined Mr. Yager throwing a spear and the sea lion letting out a deep death moan.

Shot it, Mr. Yager said. My wife joked that the bullet would bounce right off, Elliot said. Like sea lions had bulletproof skin.

Lana sat up, as though she knew Elliot was talking about her dead owner.

Tim remembered seeing the old man and his wife at Dame's Fine Chowder. His wife's face had even more wrinkles than Mr. Yager's.

Tim wanted to touch the skin again. Would you shoot another one? he asked.

Only if I thought it dangerous. I'm friends with the ones around here.

Friends?

Those three today. The big one's a bull, about ten. The cow's seven or eight, and the little one's two.

Tim was impressed; all sea lions looked similar to him. Maybe Mr. Yager studied sea lions like he studied songs, he thought.

Would you like chili? Mr. Yager asked.

OK, Tim said. The chili-infused air smelled good.

Mr. Yager went into the kitchen, Lana trotting after, head erect. Tim looped by the fire to warm his face, hands, and feet.

The kitchen had high cream-colored cabinets on either side, a table in the middle, and a closed door on the far side, which Tim guessed led to the light. An open door to his left revealed a room with a narrow bed and a desk, on which lay a notebook and pencil. The bed was made. Mr. Yager stood at the stove, stirring. Tim peeked out the window above the sink. The rain had stopped. Sections of the sea teetered on light blue.

You can see the ocean out my kitchen window, too, Tim said.

Mr. Yager poured chili into two brown pottery bowls. Best place for an ocean view.

My dad's gonna build a second story on the oceanfront units. Then you won't be able to see it.

That's too bad. But your father probably knows what he's doing.

Tim accepted the bowl and a spoon. Purple kidney beans and bits of beef spotted the food mound. Tim took a bite. Better than Mom's, he thought. And Mom's was good. Did Mr. Yager know his dad? he wondered. If not, how could he know whether his dad knew what he was doing? Tim ate more, and quickly.

Did you know this cove is private property? Mr. Yager said.

Tim stopped shoveling.

You do, don't you? If you want to visit, fine, but let me know you're around. I don't want trespassers all over my land.

Yes, sir, Tim said. If he had to tell Mr. Yager, he probably couldn't sneak in the house anymore. He sighed. If Leah gets her way, he said, the cove won't be your land.

Mr. Yager swallowed. Who's that?

The lady who owns The Sweet Seller.

And what does she want?

She wants to make beaches public land.

There's always a few like that.

Tim looked down. He ate the last bites almost frantically. She's working with people in the government, he said.

Elliot searched his memory for mention of that in the newspapers. He couldn't think of anything but that didn't mean much: his short-term memory had gone to the devil. He'd have to look through them again.

You think I could see the light? Tim asked. I've never seen one. Up close, I mean. He'd seen a couple from the car.

Didn't you grow up here? Mr. Yager asked. During his youth in Aberdeen, he'd loved to visit Grays Harbor Light.

Yes, sir, Tim said.

Mr. Yager shook his head. Come on, then, he said.

Lana followed them to the lighthouse door, where Mr. Yager told her to stay.

The stairs weren't spiral, as Tim had imagined, but short diagonal flights. The fourth flight opened onto a deck that surrounded the lamp. Tim walked around it. The top of the light was a cone, the bottom a concentric circle. Grooves covered the opaque glass from the top above Tim's head to the base at Tim's feet.

This light doesn't rotate, Mr. Yager said. Most do. All, now, in Oregon. Yaquina Head and Coos Bay were automated last year.

Automated? Tim asked.

It's electrical, Mr. Yager said. They don't need traditional lighthouse keepers anymore. Often they don't even need the light. Mr. Yager's eyes focused on the sea. Tim followed his gaze. Cape Perpetua loomed to the south; north, the buildings of Kalapuya nestled into the hillside. The deep-blue ocean stretched until the earth curved. Radio and radar can get ships through snow, sleet, rain, and fog, Mr. Yager said. They're remarkable devices. He thought of the memoir he was writing. Had he written that sentence or simply wanted to write it?

Tim wanted to hear stories, but Mr. Yager had retreated inside himself like his mom sometimes; physically but not mentally present. Tim turned to the light and tried to make out the massive light bulbs inside. He ran his fingers down a vertical crevice in the light, which must, he thought, be how you opened it.

Mr. Yager turned. Careful now, he said.

Is this how you open it? Tim asked.

Mr. Yager nodded. He didn't volunteer to show him the interior, so Tim stepped to the window and ran his finger along the top of the chest-level frame. Numerous cross frames connected tall rectangular panes of glass. Were there wrecks out there? he asked. Is that why you built this place?

There were wrecks, Mr. Yager said. But I got special permission to build it. The time in this lighthouse would encompass the last third of his book, he thought. Or maybe only the final fourth; he wasn't sure. Didn't you say you needed to get home? Mr. Yager asked.

I guess, Tim said.

Tim opened the door and hopped down the stairs. He waited in the kitchen for Mr. Yager, and together, they walked through the main room. The fire had waned. Mr. Yager squatted and moved the small pieces with a poker until they burst into flame. Tim opened the anteroom door and lifted a hand to Mr. Yager. Mr. Yager replied with the same gesture.

The wind had warmed. Tim skirted the edge of the rocks until he was out of sight from the lighthouse, then ducked toward the house. Inside, he grabbed his backpack and notebook and left, double-checking that the front door had latched.

When Tim rounded the corner of a rock and saw the next cove, he remembered he'd taken Carl here to search for agates the first day they'd met. Carl had seen them on display in the motel office and asked where they'd gotten them. I'll show you, Tim said. Carl followed Tim, but trailing. Sensing Carl's skepticism that a younger kid could show him anything new, Tim kept the closer caves a secret and led Carl to one of the farther ones. They arrived at this inlet near high tide, the ocean on its way out. Tim explained tides to Carl while they'd sat, legs dangling on an overlooking rock. As they entered the cave, the soles of their sneakers sunk into wet sand. It was an overcast day, and they had to step outside into light to examine handfuls of stones. Once, when Tim stepped out, a sneaker wave was approaching. He yelled Carl's name. As Carl crawled out, the wave was upon and underneath them, lifting their bodies. It knocked Carl onto the rocks. Holding grass with one hand, he grabbed Tim's jacket with the other and threw him ashore. The boys lay next to each other, gasping.

After that, Carl had taken Tim under his wing. They never spoke of the incident. Today, and often on his way to Mr. Yager's house, Tim would cut into the forest, bypassing this cave. Now, hugging the top of the inlet, he strode by. If he were desperate for agates he'd go in, he thought, but not until then.

4.

Elliot went into the kitchen, Lana at his heels. He scrubbed and rinsed the bowls and the pan, then took lukewarm coffee into his office that also served as a bedroom. As Elliot sat, Lana curled by his feet under the desk.

Elliot had halted in his memoir-writing earlier because he couldn't decide whether he wanted to include his family life with his wife and son. He'd included a first chapter on his growing-up years in small-town Washington State—the incessant rain, the childhood deaths of two out of four of his siblings, his high-school shop classes, and Grays Harbor Light, which had opened in 1898, the winter he was born. Besides his memories of the lighthouse, the other details were so hazy that he could have been writing about another person's life. His wife and son, on the other hand, were without a doubt part of his life, though Darlene was dead and Conrad was estranged from him and worked as a lawyer in Salem.

Writing the chapters on his life as a keeper at Tillamook Lighthouse had come easily. He had detailed the lighthouse's history and function in his first book on the history of Oregon lighthouses, but the place still fascinated him. Because the lighthouse stood on an offshore rock, supplies could be delivered only during certain weather and at certain tides. To transport supplies or men across the 130 feet between boat and lighthouse, they loaded them into a cage attached to a pulley. The lighthouse acquired a telephone a few years into Elliot's service, but the rock remained remote: in harsh winters, a boat couldn't deliver supplies or letters for up to seventy days at a time.

In his memoir, he related anecdotal day-to-day life more than the lighthouse's history and the keepers' duties. He narrated specific quarrels and moments of camaraderie, the ghost who blew out oil lamps and left doors and windows open, colorful Japanese glass fish floats that had drifted across the entire Pacific, and birds that killed themselves by flying against the lighthouse glass in both clear and foul weather.

He'd worked at Tillamook Light from when he joined the Lighthouse Service at seventeen until his marriage to Darlene ten years later. Because keepers' families weren't allowed on the rock, he requested a transfer. For the next twenty years, he was stationed near Coos Bay.

He remembered seeing Darlene for the first time on a foggy morning. She sat fishing alone, her legs dangling off a dock, her light-brown hair in a tight, high bun. He liked how she seemed simultaneously sporty and proper. Approaching her, he learned her story: she'd come to Astoria from Portland after she'd finished high school and had simply stayed on, working as a waitress at a café during winter and helping her aunt and uncle fish during spring, summer, and fall. Every three months, on his two weeks' leave from Tillamook Light, Elliot visited the café or her aunt and uncle's house.

It was a plain story, Elliot thought, special only to him. And if he wrote about the beginning of their relationship, would he have to write about all of their relationship? He didn't want—or wasn't ready for—that. The readers of this book would be the same people who read his first book, he figured. Most likely they wanted anecdotes related only to lighthouses. But to go from Tillamook Light to Coos Bay without mentioning Darlene seemed like a leap. Maybe a couple sentences would suffice.

He titled the next chapter "Transition." *In 1925,* he wrote, *after ten years on the rock, I requested a transfer. That summer, while on leave, I had gotten married, and my wife wanted to see me more than two months out of the year.* No, that wasn't true, Elliot thought. The idea wasn't hers, it was his. She'd encouraged him to stay on as long as he wanted at Tillamook Light; he'd been the one impatient for their lives to fully intertwine. At the time he wondered whether her leniency meant she didn't love him, but years later, when their marriage became claustrophobic, he'd regretted his haste: maybe she'd been right all along.

He struggled to remember most people—their names, their faces, their personalities, and his association with them—but about Darlene, he remembered too much. He put aside his memoir.

As he opened to the bookmarked page in Robert Bly's book, *Silence in the Snowy Fields*, Lana placed a paw on his sock-covered foot. Elliot petted his dog's back with his free foot and read two poems, one on a funeral, the other on a ferry ride across a bay. The first reminded him of his questioning the existence of an afterlife when he buried Darlene. The second reminded him of the highway bridge completed over the Columbia River the previous year, which had eliminated the final ferry crossing on the Oregon Coast Highway. Elliot had loved the coastal ferries. Bridges took you above the landscape and you could be indifferent to it; on ferries you had to feel the crossing. Bly wouldn't have noticed as much, or written this poem, if he'd *driven* over a bay: Elliot was sure of that.

In his notebook, he jotted down a description of sea lions. He wanted to make it into a poem, but he wasn't sure how. Where to start a new line confused him, and compared to the poets he read, he felt like his attempts contained too many arbitrary details and lacked any feeling of transcendence.

Elliot remembered the dead sea lion he'd found in front of his house. Its body had weighed over three hundred pounds, too heavy to pick up or drag. He'd called a friend in Southern Oregon and asked him the best way to skin it. Conrad had watched his father make incisions but turned away when Elliot dug in his knife. His son had never enjoyed hunting or butchering. For this reason, among others, he'd settled in a city.

Elliot had lied to Tim. He didn't know why, which bothered him more than the lie. He'd lied before; he'd once been an expert liar. He'd lied to evade, he'd lied to keep the peace. He'd ruined Darlene's trust for a time, and Conrad's, as far as he could tell, forever. But this sea lion lie seemed like a tall tale for children who enjoyed and even needed epic stories. Maybe Tim needed one, too.

Didn't a story of Tim's make him want to do something? Elliot thought. After staring at the wall, he remembered: look over newspapers. Pulling his foot from Lana's paw, he stood. He was content with the five paragraphs he'd written in his memoir before Tim's visit. As a young man, Elliot had rushed to finish woodworking projects, as though he only had a few months, or a few years, to live. Now, when he did only have a few years, or a few months, to live, he didn't feel the need to hurry at any task. He had confidence he'd finish his memoir before he died.

In the anteroom, newspapers were stacked, divided by month, and tied with twine. Elliot kneeled and searched. Water from Tim's jacket had dripped on the top newspaper in each stack. Logging politics, racial politics, and the conflict in Vietnam filled the most pages. Lately he'd skipped or skimmed stories on the conflict in favor of more local news. By meticulous searching, he found one short article, from August 1966, on the beach issue.

Cannon Beach Motel Owner Says "Keep Out"
Daniel Gordon, owner of the Surfside Motel in Cannon Beach, has upset some community members by cording off a section of the beach. According to him, he owns that section and wants only his guests to have access to it. According to others, the beach is public land.

Both he and others are correct. In 1913, Oswald West declared the wet sands a public highway. However, before that, some property owners had signed contracts that stated they owned the beach as a part of their property, and during the last fifty-four years, public and private entities have claimed sections of both wet and dry sand.

Some community members, notably the group Citizens for Oregon Beaches, want to pass a law that declares all beach—both wet and dry sands—public property. Texas passed a similar law, arguing that because the public has used the beaches for so long, the beaches de facto belong to them. Other citizens argue that they bought the beach, pay taxes on it, and it belongs to them.

Elliot's contract had stated that he owned the adjoining cove. He had certainly paid taxes on it. He searched back until 1965, but he didn't find any other stories on the issue. Most likely, Citizens for Oregon Beaches would accomplish nothing. On the other hand, the legislature could propose and pass a bill without it becoming a news story. It would be easier to try to stop such a bill than to deal with lawyers and lawsuits afterward. He might as well go talk to Leah.

In the main room, Elliot separated the three pieces of firewood with a poker. In the anteroom, he restacked the newspapers and put on his boots, coat, and hat. He kneeled and scratched Lana behind the ears and placed a hand on either side of the dog's stomach and gently shook it. Lana whined with pleasure and retreated to her large red pillow by the fire. Elliot tipped his hat to his dog and went out.

His truck started on the second try. He drove up a dirt road, firs on both sides, his house, uninhabited since Darlene's death, on his left. At the top of the ridge, he turned left onto the Oregon Coast Highway. The curves between his property and Kalapuya were so familiar that he could drive them with his eyes closed. Elliot remembered when much of the coastal highway had been beaches and you had to be adventurous to take the drive. Within minutes he'd passed The Wave and was entering the commercial section of town.

Cigarette smoke, probably from loggers, rolled from the cracked door of Joe's Bar. A family Elliot recognized sat on chairs eating ice cream in front of Lollipops. Two tourists stood on the sidewalk, showing each other starfish that they'd probably bought at some trinket joint. Too lazy, Elliot thought, to find them themselves. To wade in the cold water or walk on the beach in the rain. What was this, April? The tourists and afternoon sun felt like July. No doubt the sun was teasing, and by evening, rain would return.

He turned left and drove by a handful of one-story houses before pulling up to the curb outside The Sweet Seller. Darlene had made their own bread; they'd never been inside. On the rare times they'd driven by, Darlene had admired the year-round flowers. Now the yard was flowerless. Elliot took the cement path in five strides and the three stairs in one. A bell rang as he opened the door.

No one was at the counter. A middle-aged couple Elliot didn't know drank coffee at a window table, a paper sack between them. Leah, her hands covered in flour, stepped to the counter. Be with you in a moment, she said. She wondered what had brought him in.

Elliot circled the small room, examining photographs. Photos of bakeries in Astoria and Coos Bay seemed familiar, but he couldn't remember whether he'd been in them or passed by. He paused at the photo of a gated beach outside the motel. Leah was involved, he thought, like Tim had said.

What would you like? Leah asked.

Her hands were rough, Elliot noted, as though she'd worked for years outdoors. He thought it strange to pay for a cup of coffee, especially without ordering a meal, but he didn't know what else to have. He studied the baked goods on the display shelves. I'll take a cup of coffee, he said, and a loaf of bread.

Leah said she had only white bread left, and he said that was fine. She rang him up. I'll bring them out to you, she said.

I want to have a word with you, Elliot said, if you're free.

I am. I'll sit with you.

Leah couldn't think of what she had in common with Elliot, except that they'd lost their spouses that past year. He liked to live on the peripheral of a community, while she preferred to involve herself in one. She could give him sympathy for his loss, she thought. Like she and Micah, he and his wife had seemed very much in love.

Elliot sat in the center of the room, where Tim had sat that morning. Rays of light splotched his shoes and the floor. His eyes rested on the "Keep Out" sign in the photo and he frowned.

Leah brought out his coffee and bread, poured herself a cup, then sat across from him. She leaned toward him and asked how he was doing.

She hadn't asked as an acquaintance, Elliot thought, but as a friend. The intimacy unnerved him. Although Leah's spouse had also died, they'd conversed only a few times; they weren't friends.

The coffee was good; nice and dark. He took another sip. And their spouses' deaths weren't surprising, Elliot thought. Darlene had died from cancer. Micah had died in a boating accident. Although not as dangerous as logging, and not as dangerous as it used to be, seafaring wasn't working in a bakery. Every season, relatives and friends of fishermen and sailors should expect the worst. Near his hometown, at the bar at Grays Harbor, where sudden storms arose, many men, some his friends and relatives, died every year. To expect sympathy for something so predictable seemed selfish.

Leah waved at a neighbor who was walking his dog. It's very warm for April, she said.

It won't last, he said.

Their spouses and the weather, Leah thought. That's all she had. She'd ask after his dog, if she could remember its name.

Elliot squirmed. I heard you're, you're trying to get the beaches made into public land, he said. He'd forgotten the name of the organization.

Leah cupped both hands around her mug. Oh, that's why he's here, she thought. I support the idea, she said. I'm not doing much personally. Not yet.

What do you plan to do? Elliot asked.

They just drafted a bill, Leah said. They need public support for it. People writing letters to the legislature and whatnot. I'll probably do that.

They had a bill, Elliot thought. Not much else Leah could tell him. His cup was half full; otherwise, he'd leave. He took a large gulp, burnt his tongue, and grimaced. Why do you want to help? he asked. Her eyes were gray-blue and surrounded by crow's feet.

The bell rang as the couple exited. Leah took their cups from the deserted table to the counter. Why did she want to help? she thought. In her mind's eye she saw the beauty of the coast: the arch rock formations north of Brookings, the rocky inlets at Cape Perpetua, the high cliffs near Cape Foulweather, the long stretch of sand at Seaside, the wide Columbia River spilling into the sea. From a desire to share with others what she loved, she decided. Like when she'd given pastries to street children in Portland or when she gave these townspeople free samples or baked goods. She sat across from Elliot. I want everyone to have access to the beach, she said. Not only the rich or lucky.

Everyone does, Elliot said. Just not all parts of it.

I want everyone to have access to all parts, then. Each terrain has a different kind of beauty. Remove a few sections and people don't get the whole experience.

Elliot shifted his legs. He wasn't used to talking in terms of beauty.

Without a law in place, Leah said, people could claim more of the dry sand. A hundred and twelve miles are already claimed by private owners. Before long, the public might not have access to any of it.

I'm old, he said. As you know, I served the public for many years. I just don't want people traipsing across my land.

Just the beach. The land above would still be your land.

The beach, then. I don't want people there.

They probably won't. Not many people around here.

Not yet. A lot more people on the coast than thirty years ago. Look at Lincoln City.

Kalapuya's beaches are too rocky for it to ever be a large tourist destination.

I'm not so sure about that.

Leah wanted to somehow personalize the issue. Do you know Tim? she asked.

Elliot's legs pointed toward the door. Why did he continue in this conversation? he thought. He gulped at his coffee, heat be damned. The kid at The Wave? he said. Yes.

I want him and his kids to continue to enjoy the beaches, Leah said.

Elliot stood. My son works in Salem, he said. He knows people on the legislature.

Leah raised her eyebrows.

It was the wrong move, Elliot thought. Everyone knew he and

his son hadn't talked in years. He wished that he himself knew people in politics. I'm going to visit him tomorrow.

Good luck, Leah said. I hope for your sake you're able to keep your beach. Maybe you can be grandfathered in or something. His body's almost audible tenseness repelled her. She stood and picked up Elliot's cup.

She was agreeing with him again, Elliot thought. How infuriating. Unlike people he respected, she couldn't stick to one side. He stepped to the "Keep Out" photo and took it off the wall. He was hesitating whether to put it back or take it when Leah turned from the counter.

Her sea eyes settled on the photo, then on him. She crossed her arms. Elliot—, she said.

Elliot imagined the photo in the anteroom, above the newspapers, to the side of the inner door. He raised the frame. I have just the place for this, he said. He walked toward the door, grabbing his loaf on the way out.

Leah followed him outside. Elliot, she repeated. Give that back.

He slammed the truck door, started it up, and did a U-turn. He clenched the wheel as he barreled past the smug houses, past the idle people on the main drag, past The Wave, into his woods, where, feeling at home, he slowed down. He would visit Conrad, he thought. Or at least write him a letter. Though he doubted his boy would do him any favors.

5.

Leah and Marilyn were walking on a sandy path behind town. Waist-high dune grass blew on both sides. Above them the sky was a deep blue that on clear nights preceded black.

After Marilyn told Leah that she'd spent all afternoon working on the cost estimate and business plan for the new units, Leah asked Marilyn who did the motel's books before she and Jackson got married.

His dad, Marilyn said. He taught me The Wave's books. They were different than a restaurant's. But I already knew the basics.

Marilyn ran a hand over the top of the grass and remembered the hours under Phil's tutelage. They sat side by side at the table in the motel lounge. Tim swelled her belly. Phil laughed when she didn't know a term, though after a session it became clear that she knew more about bookkeeping than he did.

Never knew Phil well, Leah said. He limped, didn't he?

The pain from his logging accident never went away, Marilyn said.

They reached a rise. Below them rocks dropped into the sea. It was as deep blue as the sky now and darkening, except for whiteness where waves curled, which let off a kind of light.

I don't like the solo loggers I've known, Leah said.

Marilyn's gaze followed Leah's seaward. The line between sky and ocean was hard to distinguish. To take such risks, they have to pretend they're invincible, Marilyn said.

Maybe that's all loggers. But yes, especially them. The path narrowed and Leah took the lead. I admire your speed with numbers, she said.

It's the only thing I'm really good at. The only thing I love to do.

In high school, Marilyn had been the only girl in her algebra class. The old man teacher stood over her on the first day. She focused on the hair in his ears while he looked over her figure. You signed up for the wrong course, young lady, he said. No sir, she said. I need to test your skills, he said. He walked away and opened a drawer in his desk. I took an exam to get in here, she said. But not my exam, he said. He came back and set a paper in front of her and rested both hands on her desk. It was an algebra test, equations that none of them had learned yet. I'm good at math, she said. Ask anyone. Why don't you show me? the teacher said. But sir, she said. This is an algebra test. He slapped his hand on her desk and glared at her, his bushy eyebrows lowering. She is, sir, said a know-it-all. She's good at math. After a frown toward the know-it-all, the old man took the test and walked to the front of the room. Turn your textbooks to page three, he said. Under the sound of shuffling pages, Marilyn sighed. She later learned that the teacher was scared of the know-it-all's dad, who was on the school board. She'd taken geometry, trigonometry, and calculus without another teacher questioning her.

The trail was leading to a flat, open area and the frame of a two-story hotel. Come on, Leah said. I've been meaning to take a look.

They stepped over a row of Scotch broom. The frame stood where the beach thinned and dirt began.

Marilyn touched a vertical board, covered in windblown sand. She brushed at it as though brushing sand from Tim's cheeks. They should have waited until the rainy season stopped, she said.

But would they finish it before it began again? Leah asked.

They walked down the interior hallway, peeking into the same-sized rooms. Smaller than most of ours, Marilyn thought.

A little competition? Leah asked.

Maybe, Marilyn said. In the business plan, she'd argued that this new hotel would charge more than The Wave and appeal to a clientele who right now rarely visited Kalapuya, a clientele with disposable income. Lenders could argue for or against their expansion when a potential competitor was moving in. In the business plan, Marilyn had argued for, but she hoped the lenders would argue against.

They stood in a high-ceilinged communal room or lobby at the front of the hotel. Marilyn stepped over the front doorframe and looked at the structure straight on. It was a balloon frame, a construction using thin studs and nails. Many structures used this method now. She preferred mortise and tenon: heavy framing timbers carved at the joints so that they locked together; a slower method that allowed less variation but lasted longer. Phil had made The Wave's units in this way, one of his and Marilyn's only points of agreement, and Marilyn had used the mortise and tenon method in the cost estimate for the new units.

Marilyn turned toward the long dirt driveway that wound toward the highway so her hair would blow away from her face, toward the sea. The light had faded; she could see stars.

Leah stepped to Marilyn's side. I went into the kitchen, she said. Or what will be the kitchen. And let me tell you, I'm coveting my neighbor's kitchen right now.

Marilyn smiled. Do you want to walk back by the highway? she asked.

What're you thinking?

Just want to estimate which place is closer to downtown—The Wave, or this one.

They walked side by side down the driveway. Leah took three steps for every two of Marilyn's. On the highway, they walked single file, facing cars coming toward them. When they saw headlights, they stepped away from the road into brush. Two more cars came by, then it was silent, except for the sea and wind-rustling trees.

The Wave's closer, Leah said.

Hard to say, Marilyn said. Darkness makes the distance seem longer, you know?

As they approached town, music and voices trickled out from the restaurants and bars. They turned down Leah's street. They walked around the shop and entered the house through the backyard screen door. Leah turned on lights. Marilyn kicked off her flats, plopped on the couch, and tucked her feet under her dress. Mind if I crash here for the night? she asked. I'd rather stay in town than go to my parents'.

Not at all, Leah said. She went to the kitchen and put on water to boil.

Marilyn reached over the arm of the couch and moved the record player needle. Jerry Lee Lewis's debut album began. Marilyn started at the sound but left it on. She took a nightgown from her suitcase and went to the bathroom. By the time she returned, Leah had set a cup of steeped mint tea next to the record player.

Going to bed early? Leah asked.

Marilyn sat on the couch. Figured I'd get up with you, she said. She sipped at the tea. This is nice, thanks.

Leah nodded. Good album. You know it?

No.

You want to help with the baking in the morning?

I'll help, Marilyn said. I'd like that.

The women listened to the music. The upbeat tunes raised Marilyn's spirits; she liked the pounding piano. It made her think of Tim running down the beach in a hurry to find something important only to him.

After the first side finished, Leah secured the needle and took Marilyn's empty cup. I'll wake you, she said.

Marilyn pulled a cream-and-brown wool blanket from a basket beside the couch over her body and under her chin. Her dark hair spread against a couch cushion, the stitched outline of a bear stretched against her middle. For a long time, she didn't sleep. She was surprised, because she'd thought that here, away from Jackson, she would. But she did feel relaxed, awake and alone and not needing to think of what Tim or Jackson needed or wanted from her, that night or in the morning.

Leah seemed to not need anything from anyone. If she and Marilyn were together, they enjoyed each other's company. If Leah was alone, she seemed fine too. If Leah wanted something, to start a bakery or work for the beach issue, she did it. It was admirable, this self-sufficiency, but a little off-putting, too. Marilyn had felt closer to her friend since she'd come to sit shiva with Leah after Micah died, and Leah had cried, her head on Marilyn's shoulder. Leah told Marilyn that she waited until Marilyn arrived to cry. I needed you here first, Leah said after her tears stopped. And Marilyn admired that elegance, too—Leah's awareness and statement of her need.

Jackson and Tim had too many unstated wants or needs, ones she must infer in Jackson's case or formulate in Tim's. Marilyn didn't know whether she would help Jackson any further with the new units. She already made a quarterly budget—to which Jackson never adhered—kept the books, calculated income sheets and balance statements, and filed taxes. Today, in order to do the cost estimate and flesh out Jackson's sketch of a business plan, she'd called dozens of places and skipped supper. When she'd laid the papers in front of him, she didn't receive as much as a thank you. Leave those on your desk, Jackson said. I'll look at them tomorrow. She enjoyed the work and she wanted The Wave to be successful, but surely she wasn't being selfish to want appreciation? Or for Jackson occasionally to admit she had good advice?

To avoid all that, she focused on images the music had conjured: a dance from high school; her aunt Pearl's dramatic gestures; the foam and swirl of Devil's Churn, a chasm a few miles south. She fell asleep smiling and woke in the morning to her friend's small, leathery hand on her shoulder.

To Jackson, it seemed like someone was knocking on the office door. The clock on the bedside table said six. He lay tense but heard only the clock's ticking, the rustle of leaves, and the sea. Because he'd stayed up till midnight replacing the window glass in the office, he allowed himself to doze another thirty minutes. He then woke up and sat up. He'd never used an alarm. As a boy, he'd learned he could tell himself what time to wake up and he'd always wake up a minute or two before that time. He thought it a handy skill but kind of strange, too. Not something he brought up in Joe's Bar, among acquaintances.

Jackson sat blinking. He'd ended up on the right side of the bed. He and Marilyn had never designated sides. When younger, in the middle of the night, they'd crawl over each other just for fun, or they slept wherever they ended up after sex. Now, whichever one went to bed earlier lay on one side and the other took the other side, or lately Marilyn had slept on the couch. Muted light shone through the crack in the middle of the curtains. Jackson threw his legs over the edge and, grunting, pulled on a pair of jeans that he'd left on the floor.

The office opened at seven. Annie should have made coffee for the lounge, he thought. He slipped on a white T-shirt that was on top of the bureau and walked into the hallway and passed the boy's room. Two years ago, Tim would have been underfoot at this time. Now, if undisturbed, he'd sleep another two hours. Because they'd had another night with no vacancy, Jackson might send him into town for more baked goods. But by the time the kid walked there and back, half the motel might be awake.

Damn Marilyn, Jackson thought. This was the fifth Sunday morning since New Year's that she'd been gone. And she thought he couldn't count. He grinned and measured three tablespoons of coffee grounds into the percolator and set it on the stove. After unlocking the office door, he returned and poured coffee into a mug that said *The Wave*, with a crest of a wave behind the letters. What was Marilyn trying to prove? She didn't want the addition. So what? Sometimes you needed to gamble to secure your legacy or even to gain a few extra thousand a year.

Now he was sure he heard knocking. He went downstairs, cup of coffee in hand. The same small girl from yesterday stood outside looking up at the pane of glass. He opened the door. It was unlocked, he said. His first words aloud sounded scratchy. He coughed into an elbow curve. She stepped inside. Towels? he asked. She nodded. He retrieved five from the laundry room. Annie had said that saltwater and sand had covered the towels in this girl's room. Apparently, her family had gone swimming or wading in the Pacific Ocean in April. Whatever floats your boat, Jackson thought, though it was something only someone from away would do.

That'll tide you over, he said, bending to her level. You think you can carry all those?

She nodded, gave his beard a poke, and took the towels.

He stood and opened the door for her. Did you knock earlier? he asked.

She tilted her head, then shook it. Thanks, she squeaked.

He nodded and shut the door.

As a child, Jackson had heard such knockings frequently. Just a drowned sailor who wants some warmth, his dad used to say. Jackson never saw one, and as he grew older, he no longer believed in ghosts.

If any drowned man haunted The Wave right now, Jackson thought, it was Micah. He was the only the seafaring man who'd had a sustained presence there. Micah and Jackson were never close, but whenever Leah and Micah had come to The Wave for supper, the two men had had more than enough to discuss. Both had lived on the coast all their lives, and both loved the variety of challenges that defined their workdays. If you don't love your work, Jackson thought, there wasn't much point to living. Marilyn protested when he wanted to risk merely money, but Leah wasn't scared for her husband who had risked and ultimately lost his life.

Jackson rubbed his bare arms, stepped to the wall, and ticked up the heat. Marilyn kept the center building an icebox in order to lower costs, and they couldn't start a fire upstairs unless one of them would be around to tend it. Days went more smoothly when he took care of some tasks while Marilyn took care of others. When he was honest, he admitted he couldn't run the place as well without her.

He picked up her estimates from the closet-office and brought them out front and sat at the desk and put his feet up on it and smoked a cigarette and drank coffee. His eyes blurred whenever he glanced at the figures, but he knew he should check them as best he could. His stomach rattled.

In the lounge, he found half a blueberry muffin and Annie drinking coffee in the recliner. Jackson waved his hand at the tray. That all we got? he asked.

That's it, Annie said.

Many people come through?

Just that little girl, Annie said. Marilyn must not be used to a full house in April. If this was summer, she'd've bought fresh pastries by now.

Jackson bit into the muffin. She's not here, he said.

Why, where's she at? Annie asked.

But Jackson was out the door. He'd finished the muffin by the time he entered the office. He plopped in the chair and read through the supplies, equipment, and labor needed, and scanned the cost for each item. He reread the list. It didn't take a construction genius to see that the estimate used mortise and tenon, not balloon, the less expensive method. To throw off the estimate or because Marilyn honestly thought it better, he didn't know. She'd heard enough of his arguments with his father to know his own preference.

He picked up the phone and dialed her parents'. Richard, her father, answered.

This is Jackson, he said. Is Marilyn available?

You tell me.

She's not there?

Nope.

Linda there?

Yep.

May I speak with her?

One moment. She's in the garden.

Jackson didn't want to ask her father where Marilyn might be. Her parsimony mirrored her father's, and Jackson thought he might be her confidant.

Jackson's dad had offered Richard a half-price room after the family's car broke down a mile south of The Wave. Richard was offended by the offer, as Marilyn explained when she rendezvoused with Jackson in the lounge. He thinks you offered us half-price because we look like we can't afford to stay here, she said. They sat on the couch, their knees almost touching. He didn't, Jackson asked. That's just how he is. And that's just how my father is, Marilyn said. We can't force them to change. Jackson liked Marilyn's hands-off approach as well as her wide mouth and sleek hair. As long as their children get along, I'm fine with leaving them alone, Jackson said. He moved his knee to touch hers.

Jackson had described aspects of the war: the feeling of flying in an airplane and the taste of foreign foods. She asked about the workings of the motel in such detail that he didn't know the answer to all her questions. How many guests per night do you average in the off-season? she asked. Which months don't you make a profit? He liked that unlike some women, she didn't hide her intelligence. Before they went outside, so he could show her a rock through which seawater spouted, he glanced at her hand. He couldn't believe his luck; she wasn't wearing a wedding ring.

Jackson? Linda said.

Yes, ma'am.

You asking for Marilyn?

Yes, ma'am. She ain't with you?

Haven't heard anything for a week.

Jackson plucked at his beard.

Everything OK? Linda asked.

Fine.

When you find her, you tell her to call me.

Yes, ma'am.

Don't worry, Richard can't keep track of me, either.

Jackson chuckled, pleased that Linda was joking around. Richard would have been concerned and suspicious. When he visited The Wave, he was worse than Marilyn, raising his eyebrows at any new furnishings or necessary repairs. On the rare days of windless and warm summer weather, instead of relaxing on the beach like most guests, he stayed inside and read detective novels. Jackson was glad that Marilyn's parents hadn't taken her offer to move to The Wave in their old age. All right, Linda, Jackson said. I'll talk to you later.

Bye, dear.

Jackson stood up, then sat down and bowed his head. Married couples get in spats, dear, Linda said once. Spats were one thing. Your wife going off without telling you where was another. Marilyn, who was not forgetful, meant to not tell him. That's all there was to it.

He raised his head at the intense scent of sea salt. On the display case sat two new starfish. Did Tim not let them dry out? You'd think he was five sometimes. Jackson stood to move them but instead turned to the phone and dialed The Sweet Seller.

The Sweet Seller, Leah said. How may I help you?

Is Marilyn there?

Yes. You want to talk to her?

No thanks.

After hanging up, he went to Tim's room. The boy slept on his side, legs curled to chest, blanket and sheet on the floor. Tim, Jackson said.

The boy raised his head.

Why'd you put the starfish inside?

Tim rolled to his back and opened his dark blue eyes, the same color as Jackson's. We were out, he said.

They're not dead yet. You're gonna stink up the office. Take them outside.

OK.

And you're in charge of the desk.

Tim sat up and rumpled his silky, dark hair.

Same texture and color as his mother's, Jackson thought.

In The Sweet Seller, quiet, hungover loggers sat at tables, their jaws slack and eyes glazed. Townspeople, some dressed for church, stood around the counter. Jackson turned from the doorway and walked around the building to the entrance to Leah's house. He knocked twice. He imagined Marilyn in the shower, her wet hair long along her back. Or curled on the couch ignoring the knock because she knew it was him. She'd done that only once, on an evening in February when he'd forgotten his keys for the third time in three days. He'd gone downstairs and returned with the spare key from the laundry room and opened the door to find her sitting on the couch with a cup of tea, looking at the rain. Her dismissal had surprised, then gnawed at him, like the way his ankle ached in winter where he'd twisted it on the rocks as a boy. He pounded on the door with his fist and turned and walked around front and into the store. Someone had put on a record, something upbeat and jazzy. He didn't know much about music. Behind the register stood Marilyn. She wore a light blue apron over a dark blue skirt and a frilly white blouse, her hair in one long braid. For some reason, she looked more native today than usual, he thought. Because she was only a fraction Indian, he didn't usually notice.

Out of baked goods? she asked. She lowered her eyes and stepped behind the glass case.

I called your parents, he said.

Marilyn opened a bag and loaded in muffins. I told you I'd be back today, she said.

I had a question on the estimates.

Is a half dozen enough?

We need a dozen. Jackson looked around. The bell rang as an adolescent girl came through the door. Behind Marilyn, Leah washed dishes. What're you doing? he asked.

Helping Leah, Marilyn said. Another busy night?

A full house. Jackson studied her barely perceivable crow's feet and tight lips while she opened another bag and loaded in more muffins. Her large mouth seemed to have collapsed in on itself.

Good news, Marilyn said. We need all the guests we can get.

You could have told me. Now your parents are worried. To share his irritation that she wouldn't tell him where she was staying seemed too intimate, especially here in a public place.

I'm sure they're fine, Marilyn said. He was just mad she didn't tell him, she thought. To stay with Leah was a spur-of-the-moment decision that had nothing to do with him. He probably viewed it as some plot. She pushed the bags across the counter, took his cash, and gave him change. Chocolate chip, she said, if you wanted to know. She turned and dusted flour off the island cutting board.

Lyn, he said. He took the estimates from his back pocket and faced them toward her and smoothed them against the counter.

She turned. The creased sheet bothered her. If their presentation were neat, she thought, the bank would take them more seriously.

Do you think we won't use balloon construction? he asked.

I hope not, she said.

You know I like that method, right?

I like the other.

He leaned toward her. There are two of us. Someone has to make the final decision.

And that someone is always you, Marilyn said. Her hands wanted to unite and wring but she pushed them into her apron pockets. She looked over Jackson's shoulder at the adolescent girl and he stepped aside. The girl bought a loaf of sourdough and asked when they'd carry strawberry pie.

About three weeks, Leah said. I can't wait, too.

The girl smiled and tossed a nickel in the tip jar.

Jackson stepped back to the register. If you're worrying about cost, this isn't helping, he said. Because they had a finite number of days between rainy seasons, the speed of construction mattered more to him, but he was trying to meet her on her level.

Marilyn shook the tip jar. If you're worrying about a legacy, balloon isn't going to last as long.

It might need upkeep sooner. But you can spread out that money.

Why was he bringing up money again? Marilyn thought. Since when did he care so much about that? She bit her lower lip. I walked by that new hotel last night, she said.

I need you to rerun these estimates.

She glanced at the paper, then away. She wanted to tell him to hire someone to redo them. If she wanted anything to change, she couldn't keep giving in. Do you think expanding now is a good idea? she asked. When competitors are moving in?

Jackson ran a hand through his hair. Yes, he said. They'll attract a different clientele. Our rooms will cost less. You wrote that yourself.

You read the business plan?

He'd skimmed it and was impressed that she remembered to delineate The Wave's differences from the new hotel. Come on, he said, I need those estimates.

Marilyn placed a thumb on either side of the paper. Jackson removed his hand. Her dark eyes darted over the figures. Maybe she could do it all in her head, Jackson thought. It wouldn't surprise him. She put the paper below the counter under Leah's logbook to straighten it out. I'll call you later, she said. If she were going to say no, she thought, she'd rather not say it to his face.

Just bring it home with you this afternoon.

He walked toward the door through silence. The loggers had left; only a few townspeople remained. The record was over. He didn't know when it had ended.

Morning, Jackson, said Joe, the bar owner, who sat at the table closest to the door. His flat face and thin, straight body held a heron-like, quiet strength.

Morning, Joe, Jackson said.

At The Wave, Jackson walked by the office window. Tim's head lay against his arms on the desk. Jackson took a step backward, then inside.

Tim raised his head at the sound of the bell.

No sleeping on the job, Jackson said.

OK, Tim said.

I said no sleeping at the job.

Yes, sir. Tim clasped his hands in front of him.

For some reason, the pose escalated Jackson's frustration. When guests entered the office, a dual bell system rigged through the laundry chute would ring in the apartment; the boy could have listened from upstairs. Why'd you come down here? he asked.

Thought I'd fall back asleep and not hear the bell. Tim pulled sleepy stuff from the corner of his eye.

You sleep up there or stay awake down here. Got it?

Yes, sir, Tim said.

He tossed the muffins at Tim. The bags bumped off the desk, hit Tim's chest, and slid into his lap. Put those out, Jackson said. Cut them in fourths.

Tim coughed. Yes, sir.

Wash your hands first.

Tim nodded and stood, a bag in each hand.

Jackson left. The boy was going through an awkward stage. He remembered wrestling with friends at that age. Tim spent too much time alone. Jackson wished he were in school, but since Marilyn would have to drive him there and back every day, he didn't blame her for homeschooling.

He strode to the end of the center building and stood, hands on hips, in front of the oceanfront units. Four woodboxes, filled to the brim with firewood he'd cut, sat between the five doors. It was too bad they'd have to level the roofs, Jackson thought. They probably had another fifteen years. And while the construction lasted, guests couldn't stay in these units, the favorite and most profitable ones. Marilyn would have to call guests who'd reserved them and ask which units they'd like to switch to. If she were ever home long enough to get anything done, that is. Jackson smiled and pulled at his beard.

His grin dissolved as he focused above the woodboxes, on the four window boxes that held hard dirt, not yet loosened from winter. Marilyn usually loosed it before spring break and added some kind of mulch to enhance the soil. She'd plant annuals a couple weeks later. He'd mentioned the emptiness to her a week ago. Pay me and I'll plant them, she said. When he laughed, she said she wasn't joking. That's out of the question, he said. Why would he pay her for what she'd always done for free?

He walked around the units to the ocean side and looked up. He imagined the new second story intact. Guests could see waves against rocks not fifty feet away. He imagined a brochure, one photo from this angle of the new units, one from a window of a new unit of the sea. He smiled and turned. The sea was azure, the sky long wisps of clouds. The ocean as its own entity didn't enter his thoughts. Like emotions toward his little sister, who'd died in childhood of meningitis, intimacy with the sea was distant and needless. He thought of it only in relation to business. When Leah spoke of the beach becoming public land, he didn't mind, as long as such a law didn't include the main feature near The Wave, the rocks. If the law included only beach, the new hotel would lose one of its selling points. He'd seen their brochure, the structures hand-drawn since the place wasn't built yet. *Restaurant, pool, hot tub*, it said, *two acres of private beach.*

As he looked seaward, Little Faithful spouted. During the final years of his life, his dad had christened that crevice, where Jackson had taken Marilyn on the first night they'd met. The fissure, between top of rock and interior of cave, sprayed the most as high tide turned. Because the highest tides were in winter, most tourists missed its most intense performances. Our own private natural wonder, his dad had said after he'd watched Old Faithful on television. After they'd bought a television, his dad had become obsessed over the box, in awe of the invention and of the places it showed that he'd never been. He explained how television worked to any guest who'd listen. During his last few months alive, Phil stared at the screen for hours or days at a time, forgetting to come to meals or to say goodnight to Tim. Jackson found his dad's fixation strange and embarrassing. He wanted the end of his own life to be full of concrete work, not fantasies. Today Little Faithful shot high, over ten feet, and Jackson, who hadn't been on the rocks in months, walked toward it.

Jackson imagined that if the state took over the rocks, they might set up a tourist attraction here, like at Devil's Churn. Maybe they'd gate off the area; maybe they'd charge you fifty cents to park or to view. Little Faithful spouted again. Since his boyhood, he'd seen large patches of coast *preserved* by gaudy gates and historical plaques that cluttered the land. If tourists wanted to know history, they could talk to locals, he thought, and if they wanted to see natural wonders, any bartender or motel owner could point them in the right direction. People didn't need the government to designate importance.

On the next blast he felt mist. He swiped his shoe over the opening, as he had as a kid. Adrenaline flooded him. He held his shoe over the hole for five seconds, then ten. While he was counting to fifteen, a spurt of water hit his shoe, threw him in the air, and laid him on his back. Jackson caught his breath, then raised himself to an elbow, then checked his flannel for barnacle cuts. The chasm burped more water and he smiled. And that's how Tim found him, grinning and shivering, when his son came to say that a guest wanted to buy a postcard and he needed Jackson to handle the money.

6.

Leah swept a pile of crumbs and sand into a dustpan. Late afternoon light and shadow played across a table that Marilyn was wiping with a wet rag. All day it had been sunny. In between tasks at The Sweet Seller, Leah had noticed Marilyn studying a piece of paper. Now, she asked her friend about it.

Marilyn met Leah's eyes. The estimates, she said. Jackson wants me to redo them.

Did you do them wrong on purpose? Leah asked.

Used a method I knew he wouldn't like, Marilyn said. On purpose, yes.

Leah carried the dustpan to the back and dumped it. If you want, go ahead, she said. I can finish here.

OK.

Wait, Leah said. She opened the cash register and held out a ten-dollar bill. Thanks, she said.

You don't have to pay me, Marilyn said.

Come on, Lyn.

You were teaching me. It's a fair trade.

I'd pay a regular employee more than ten bucks, Leah said. You've worked almost twelve hours. Just take it.

Marilyn took the bill and pushed it into her skirt pocket. She twisted the rag and water dribbled to the floor. Frowning, she touched the drops with the tip of her flats. I don't know whether I'm going to fix it, Marilyn said.

Leah raised her eyebrows. Fix what?

The estimates. Marilyn hung the rag across the divider in the stainless-steel sink. I need to go farther away. My parents', maybe.

Leah began to sweep under the front counter. She could understand the desire to get away; for months she'd wanted to flee from the ghost of her husband. I'm staying in Newport tonight, she said. And going to Lincoln City tomorrow for Beach Bill canvassing. You can come if you want.

I'd like that, Marilyn said. Let me call Jackson. She took the estimate from under the counter and walked through the back door and into Leah's house.

Leah swept under the stove and around the island. Since Jackson had proposed the new units, she thought, Jackson and Marilyn had conversed mainly through confrontation. But maybe they'd had other issues for years. Leah swept out the pantry, tucking her broom into the corners and under the open metal shelves. More crumbs than usual, probably because Marilyn had helped. The morning lesson had gone well; Marilyn, who could focus and be precise, could make a good baker, Leah thought, although at the moment not a great one. She was too particular. Following a recipe for lemon scones, Marilyn would never think that maybe orange peel would work in it, too. She needed to use her imagination. But maybe that would come. In baking it was better to start out too exact. The college students Leah had allowed in the kitchen had too much faith in approximation. When she gave them a recipe to try solo, their bread wouldn't rise or their cookies would be too dense.

Leah placed the broom in the pantry and blinked her heavy eyelids. The past four weeks, she'd attended meetings every Monday, her day off, and she was tired. But soon the legislature would vote, and she could rest. The traveling had been a good distraction, too. On some Mondays, she'd packed egg-salad sandwiches with thick slabs of leftover Sweet Seller bread and had gone fishing with Micah. No matter whether the sky rained or the sun shined or the fog was dense, while on the water, they had their best discussions.

In the house, Marilyn sat on the edge of the couch, the phone in one hand, the ten-dollar bill in the other. While she talked, she smoothed the bill with her palm against the top of the side table. Tim knows which math problems, she said. And I wrote a writing prompt. On that Dylan record. It's on the closet desk. Marilyn's face was flushed, and the hand holding the bill shook. She lifted it in a wave as Leah passed.

Leah paid me, Marilyn said into the receiver. Ten bucks. Then, after a pause, No, not bad. Maybe I should work here.

Leah turned. Marilyn's face was a deeper red. Yes, yes, Marilyn said. Tomorrow before dark. She hung up.

Leah poured herself a glass of lemonade. You could just ask him to pay you, she said. Or pay yourself. You're the bookkeeper.

He might notice the extra money in our account, Marilyn said. She pushed the bill deep into her pocket.

Then you could tell him you paid yourself.

That wouldn't go over well. Marilyn ran her eyes over the estimate.

Leah put the pitcher in the fridge. Ready? she asked.

Marilyn nodded. Can we drop off the estimate at The Wave?

Sure, Leah said. Did you fix it?

Marilyn shook her head. I told him he'd have to use this one or reschedule his meeting with the bank.

The women drove up the coast. The sun lowered as they paralleled the miles of continuous beach before Waldport. By the time they entered Newport, pink and orange light filled the bay and sky.

They stayed with Ned, Micah's former business partner, in his house with sloping floors that overlooked the bay. Leah had courted Micah while he lived with Ned; when visiting, she'd felt her body pulled seaward in the front room and landward in the kitchen and joked that the men wanted to feel at home like they were at sea. Tonight, while she boiled water for pasta, the water in the pan tilted.

Ned, who was ten years older than she and Micah, had retired from commercial fishing after Micah drowned. He now worked as a fish grader at a cannery. Leah hadn't seen him since the funeral. The bags under his eyes sagged into his cheeks, and his reddish beard had grown. His deep voice cracked, as though unused to talking. He fried the women salmon on a cast-iron pan.

Not a bad idea, Ned said, after Leah explained the beach issue. But it doesn't much concern me. The ocean's my territory. You still running your shop?

Yes, Leah said. Business is good. She glanced at Marilyn, who was tossing salad, her dark hair covering the side of her face. If she could talk to anyone about her potential leaving, it would be Ned. Marilyn wouldn't spread the word but was less disinterested; she'd want Leah to stay, say that Kalapuya had become her home.

Ned turned off the stove. Ready when you are, he said.

They didn't speak again until everyone had dished up food and sat around the table. Leah buttered a piece of white bread from a loaf she'd brought. Marilyn said that the salmon had a rich flavor.

Caught them this morning, Ned said. He stabbed lettuce with his fork. Fishing is more relaxing when it's not my livelihood.

Sounds like something Sandy would say, Leah said.

That antique store owner? Ned asked.

Leah nodded. She doesn't need income from that place, she said. She has a family inheritance. Leah surveyed the pasta, salmon, and salad on her plate. I've thought more than once that you'd make a good couple.

Ned smiled, revealing crooked front teeth. I'm too old for such shenanigans.

That's what I say about myself, Leah said.

Come now, you're quite a bit younger.

Don't you start. Leah took a bite of salmon. The flavor reminded her of the many fish dinners that she, Ned, and Micah had shared. Ned should know better than to even hint she look for someone else.

Her eyes looked pleading, so Ned turned to Marilyn and asked about her son and the motel. Marilyn mentioned homeschooling but not her and Jackson's feud. As soon as she finished, she excused herself to the back room to call Tim. She wanted to say hello and give him his school assignments firsthand. She didn't trust Jackson not to forget something.

From a paper bag by her chair, Leah brought out three fist-size apple pies that she'd made in large muffin tins. The apples, from last fall, she'd stored in her cool basement.

Ned cleared his throat, then dug in. Still good, he said. You might even be getting better.

Leah sat across from him and picked at the sides of the crust. When she'd first moved to the coast, she missed baking and her sense of community in Portland. She made multicourse breakfasts and desserts for her and Micah, who invited Ned over to help eat them. Micah encouraged Leah to sell her baked goods at the local market or to find a space in which to open a bakery. Ned, who rented out houses between Newport and Florence, had found the storefront and house for lease in Kalapuya, where Leah and Micah had moved.

It's difficult being in that place, Leah said in a low voice.

The town or the house? Ned asked.

I don't know. Both. Leah set the pieces of crust on a cloth napkin.

I can imagine, Ned said. He set down his fork and focused on Leah.

Maybe I should leave, she said.

To where?

Maybe I could lease a storefront in Portland.

Do you have that kind of money?

Probably. If not, I could work at a friend's store there.

I don't think you'd enjoy not running your own place, Ned said.

Leah looked up at him. I never thought you'd enjoy working in a cannery.

Ned picked up his fork and took a bite, his eyes downcast. Things change, he said.

You made that change because Micah died, Leah said. I need one too. I just don't know what.

Ned's eyes met Leah's in a look of understanding as Marilyn entered. Leah frowned at her mess. She rose and dumped the mangled crust into the garbage can. How's Tim? she asked.

He's fine, Marilyn said. Their conversation had been brief and mostly one-sided. She thought he'd feel sad or resentful that she was gone one more night, but if he did, he'd hid it well. He was at that age where he needed her but didn't need her, she thought. She thanked Leah for the mini-pie and sat next to her to eat it. The three finished their desserts in silence, each focused inward.

In the morning, when Leah and Marilyn woke, Ned had left for work. They laughed as their fried eggs slid to the side of the skillet, then drove north again toward Lincoln City. The terrain rose above the ocean. Leah drove slowly around the road's curves and along sides of cliffs. Fog made visibility difficult.

First off, encourage them to call or write a letter, Leah said. Phone numbers and addresses are on three-by-five cards in the glove box. Hand them one even if they seem unsure.

I've never been to this part of the coast, Marilyn said.

Never? Leah asked. Her friend hadn't been looking at her, she realized, but past her, over the side of a cliff.

If my family went to the coast when I was a kid, we'd visit my aunt Pearl south of Florence. And Jackson doesn't see the point of traveling up and down the coast when we live on it.

Starting in high school, Leah had hitchhiked from Portland to Seaside or Cannon Beach. Kalapuya was more peaceful than those touristy towns, but she thought Marilyn ought to see at least once Haystack Rock and the Seaside boardwalk.

I'll just watch you talk, Marilyn said, if that's OK.

A gap in the fog revealed a grassy knoll and triangular headland that jetted out above the sea. I love these cliffs, Leah said. In clear weather with the wind blowing, she loved to lie flat on a cliff, poke out her head, and feel mist from the water far below. That's fine, Leah said. I don't mind talking.

I wish we didn't have to be back tonight, Marilyn said.

I wouldn't mind driving all the way up the coast, if that's what you mean.

I'd like to see it. And I don't want to redo that estimate.

We could always break down, Leah said. She remembered her pseudo breakdowns to avoid high school while at the coast as an adolescent.

Leah had hand-drawn maps of the Lincoln City neighborhoods. Marilyn tucked the maps in a notebook to keep them dry. They parked in a church or a school parking lot and walked down streets from house to house. Marilyn held an umbrella. Leah sometimes walked under it, but more often walked ahead. Mist settled like snowflakes in her shoulder-length hair. To keep herself interested, she varied the speech. She asked how the person was, she dipped right into her pitch, or she handed over the three-by-five card and let the person react. She talked to whomever came to the door, whether it was a ten-year-old boy or an eighty-year-old woman hard of hearing. If they can listen and write, they're good candidates, Leah told Marilyn. The more kinds of people the better.

It was difficult for Marilyn to adopt Leah's attitude when some people seemed too rude to deserve cordiality. A lady came to the door in a pink bathrobe. A man opened the door while talking on the phone. A little girl held back a snapping dog by the collar until Leah suggested she step outside and close the door. At first, Marilyn stood beside Leah while she talked; later, she stood curbside while her friend knocked on doors. At the end of each street, Marilyn pulled out the map and checked off each house they'd canvassed. She starred the house if the person had promised to write a letter.

A third of those who promise won't, Leah said, as Marilyn tallied their winnings on the way home.

I need to write one, Marilyn said.

I wasn't sure where you stood on all this.

It's a good bill. She may not be able to preserve her view of the sea, Marilyn thought, but maybe she could help preserve the beaches for her and others to walk on.

Leah slowed around a curve. It was late afternoon. They'd just skirted Yaquina Bay.

I'd love to keep driving, Marilyn said.

I hear you. Driving appealed to me almost as much as canvassing.

When did you learn to drive? Marilyn asked. She herself hadn't learned until she began to visit Jackson.

In the camps.

The logging camps?

Sure.

Your dad teach you?

No, one of the men. They were always trying to teach me something, like I was their surrogate child. Most didn't have cars, as you can imagine, but one man did. I must have been twelve or thirteen, not long before Dad sent me away. That man was a wild one.

Always giving others rides to town and only sometimes coming back himself. Everyone knew he wouldn't last. The men said he'd either be fired or die from an accident or some venereal disease.

One day when I was cleaning up from supper, he asked, How'd you like to learn to drive? Like I said, I was used to the men trying to teach me things, and I said that would be grand. I didn't tell my dad. I'd stopped telling him everything because I thought him too strict. The man—I don't remember his name—gave me lessons on the logging roads. Talk about learning the hard way. If I killed it on a hill, we'd roll backward over tree ruts. But I learned. I heard later he wanted to teach me so I could drive the men to and from town. None of them wanted to pay for a motel or stay sober enough to drive back.

Did you do it?

No. He disappeared. Not dead or fired, I don't think. A lot of men just disappeared. I was used to it. On the job for days or weeks, and one morning, just gone. City customers were like that at The Sweet Seller in Portland. I'd see them every Saturday for months or years, then they'd move, or switch jobs, or lose their job and not spend money at my place anymore. Rarely they'd tell me. They were more part of my life than I was theirs.

Like guests at The Wave, Marilyn said. They'll reserve the same weekend for five years then never come back.

It's different for me here, Leah said. Most of my customers now, I know them well. By the time August rolled around, she yearned for conversations with Kalapuyans. By this time of the year, she was ready to chat with tourists. She liked to feel connected to the world of Kalapuya as well as associate with worlds she knew little or nothing about.

Whatever floats your boat, Marilyn said. She remembered Jackson said that, and rolled her eyes. She didn't mind not knowing most people she serviced and wasn't curious about their lives, either.

Leah pulled curbside in front of her house.

I'm heading out, Marilyn said. She held out the clipboard.

Thanks for the help, Leah said.

Sure thing, Marilyn said.

Leah went inside and locked the door—a habit from her time in a city, which prompted Sandy to call her a city slicker. There's only been two break-ins here in my life, Sandy said. Leah didn't mind the teasing. Although she doubted anyone wanted to steal flour or her cast iron—they were part of her livelihood and important to her.

Leah left the clipboard on the coffee table. In The Sweet Seller, she fished out her notebook from under the register and looked over her baking schedule. She planned a month ahead, then each week adjusted. For Tuesday, she crossed out the words *strawberry and* in the entry *strawberry and orange peel scones.* It had been optimistic to think fresh strawberries would be in season this early.

Leah flipped to the back of the notebook and began to inventory. When she'd opened her shop in Portland, she'd inventoried and bought ingredients on her day off, but she'd learned that not only did she need that day off, but she also got a better feel of the week if she bought some ingredients after the first or second day of it. She used to give a list to Micah, and he'd shop in Newport after his workday, or even as far as Corvallis. Now she closed the shop two hours early and drove up herself.

Leah finished the inventory on three out of eight shelves in the pantry before her stomach growled and she stopped to make food. While she was laying cold chicken on slices of bread, the doorbell rang. Two college students, Nathan and Jane, stood on her porch, holding sleeping bags.

Skipping class? Leah asked.

Don't have another till Wednesday, Jane said. She tucked her hair, very blonde and very straight, behind her ear.

We came by a couple hours ago, Nathan said. Jane wanted to break in. Said you wouldn't mind. I stopped her. He straightened his blue bandana across his forehead.

Jane stepped languorously inside. I was joking, she said. And you're a tattletale.

Leah wouldn't put it past the girl. She'd brought coke to Leah's house once, but when Leah chided her, she said she wouldn't again. Pot was fine, but Leah drew the line at coke. Where'd you go? Leah asked.

Joe's, Jane said.

Some logger was talking sweet to her, Nathan said.

The kids took off their shoes, per her rule, tossed their sleeping bags by the couch, and headed to the kitchen. Some old chocolate chip muffins are on top of the fridge, Leah said.

Old? Jane asked.

I baked them yesterday. They're fine.

The students came back holding glasses of milk and muffins. Jane sat next to the record player, placed her snack on the floor, and pulled out Leah's only Beatles record. Jane was crazy about the Beatles. They taught me what love is, she'd said. Leah wasn't sure whether a nineteen-year-old could understand love, at least not many of its facets, and thought any understanding came more from experience than music. Jane closed her eyes and leaned against the couch and moved her shoulders to the music while Nathan finished his muffin. When he reached for her muffin, she kicked his hand away.

Leah had finished making her sandwich. I need to work in the bakery, she said. You two OK here?

Yeah, Nathan said. He rubbed his kicked hand. We're fine.

Leah ate the sandwich at her favorite table in the corner while an evening fog rolled down her street. She thought about the foggy evening in February when Jane and Laura had knocked on The Sweet Seller door. Although the shop was closed, Leah let in the girls for a snack. After chatting with them, she invited them to crash on her couch and cot. In the morning, the girls helped bake, which culminated in a pantomime of the pie fight between Lucy and Viv from *The Lucy Show.* By the time the shop opened, flour coated the floor and melted chocolate chips clumped on the stove. Leah didn't chide the girls; everything had been too neat since Micah's death. As they were leaving, Leah told them they could visit anytime. They had, and had brought friends.

She didn't know what these kids saw in her or her shop but didn't mind their presence. All her life, most people had liked Leah, partially because she didn't mind whether they liked her or not. In high school, if she hadn't apprenticed in her father's friend's Portland bakery for so many hours, she could have had more friends. After high school, while most of her female peers started families, she started the first Sweet Seller in Portland. This, if nothing else, created small distances between them, but Leah, entrenched in her work, didn't give her unusual lifestyle a second thought. She loved the solitude in the deserted city streets at 2 a.m., in the scent-filled shop at four. She loved the rhythm of regulars, how she could converse or not converse with them, depending on her mood.

Leah rinsed her plate and returned to inventorying. She weighed nuts, flours, sugars, and chocolate chips and wrote the weights in her notebook. She'd ask the kids to write the legislature a letter, she thought, either tonight or in the morning. Jane had expressed interest, and as a college student, she should be able to write a coherent argument. Not that those without a degree weren't as intelligent as those with one. Leah herself had finished high school only to please her father. A gallon of milk had expired. She poured the remaining liquid into the sink and began to make a grocery list.

At The Wave, Marilyn left her suitcase on a chair in her bedroom. From the kitchen wafted the scent of ground elk cooking. It sizzled as she walked down the hall. In the living room, glancing out the window, she saw only fog close against the glass.

Tim stepped from the kitchen, spatula in hand. Hi, Mom, he said.

Hi, dear. She kissed him on the forehead. He wiped off the kiss with the back of his hand. A kind of ritual between them. You do your work today? she asked.

I did it, he said. He pushed the ground meat around the skillet with the spatula. At first, he'd thought the writing question easy. *Summarize your favorite song on the album. Describe why it's your favorite.* He'd chosen "Don't Think Twice It's All Right," but on relistening, he didn't know how to summarize. Someone was leaving, he wasn't sure why. What he liked best was the song's anger and tenderness, but he wasn't going to write that. Instead, he'd picked "Blowing in the Wind" and said it was about growing up.

Marilyn watched him through the cubbyhole window that linked the living room and kitchen. Was he old enough to deserve an explanation for her absence? Not her absence from Jackson; he probably deduced reasons through his parents' quarrels. Her absence from him. She had many reasons for wanting to be away from Jackson, but not any to be away from Tim.

Where's your father? she asked.

Joe's, Tim said. He broke noodles above a pot of boiling water and dropped them in.

Jackson wasn't a heavy drinker, and he never allowed social pleasures to trump his obligations at The Wave. Both in his favor, but to Marilyn his whereabouts reminded her of their stagnant life. She spent all her time at The Wave or The Sweet Seller and he at The Wave or Joe's. They'd never even been to Lincoln City.

Leah and I went to Lincoln City today, Marilyn said. We should go sometime. The twenty miracle miles, they call it.

The twenty miserable miles, you mean, Tim said.

Who said that?

Dad, Tim said. Said the coastal developers made it into a shithole. That the new motels are awful.

Well, they certainly aren't as nice as The Wave, Marilyn said. Had she been around when Jackson said that? She didn't remember. If she was, she would have laughed. She loved his sense of humor, but lately all his jokes had felt at her expense.

I'd rather go to Florence, Tim said. Rent a dune bike. They'd said he wasn't old enough last year, but since Mom had kind of taught him to drive a car this winter, he should be able to manage a four-wheeler on sand.

We'll go there this summer then, Marilyn said, as soon as we have a few days of sun.

Tim smiled.

Marilyn took salad makings from the fridge.

Only two more pounds of elk in the freezer, Tim said.

I'm sure your grandpa will give us more, Marilyn said.

But that's all summer without.

Marilyn was about to say that she was sure Micah would supply them with fish but bit her lip. We'll manage, she said. Maybe become vegetarian.

Gross, Tim said.

Marilyn laughed.

Marilyn and Tim were sitting on the couch, television on and plates full, when Jackson arrived. He walked past, dished up food in the kitchen, then sat next to Tim. He shoveled in a forkful and moved the food from cheek to cheek to rid himself of the beer breath that

Marilyn disliked. By the time he swallowed and took a sip of water, his breath smelled only of spaghetti. It was good spaghetti, too, he thought. Just enough spice. He wondered whether Tim had made it. He didn't like Marilyn teaching the boy women's work, but his skills had come in handy during the last couple busy summers.

The news was showing Saturday's anti–Vietnam War protest again. Jackson had seen images on the television at the bar. Four hundred thousand people had marched from Central Park to the UN. It's as if every person in Portland had marched, Joe had said.

You talked to Sara lately? Marilyn asked. Her eyes didn't leave the screen.

Last week, Jackson said. The boys are fine. Sara, his older sister, had two sons in Vietnam. You heard from Carl? Jackson asked Tim.

Marilyn frowned. We'll hear from them in July when the family stays here, she said. I told Tim Carl's not over there yet.

On television, a boy no older than three sat on his father's shoulders and rested a sign on his father's head. *How many boys have you killed today?* the sign said. What a crazy week, Jackson thought. All the draft card burnings and antidraft demonstrations. The screen flashed images of Stokely Carmichael and Martin Luther King. Jackson stuffed spaghetti into his mouth, chewing once or twice before swallowing. Tim ate in fits and starts. Marilyn hadn't touched her food.

They already showed the names and faces, Marilyn said.

I saw them at Joe's, Jackson said.

Before that, he'd been telling two men at the bar a story. The men leaned toward him, smiling in anticipation at a Jackson punch line certain to come. Jackson sat up straight, happy under their gaze, and said he'd wanted to place a landmark near Little Faithful to make it easier for guests to find. Yesterday evening he'd taken wooden stakes and a hammer to the rocks. The sky was dark and low. Rain dripped off his beard and soaked his flannel shirt. He'd first tried to stake closely around Little Faithful, between rocks. He pounded less than an inch or two into wet sand or mud before he hit more rock. Frustrated, he hit harder and harder until the force of stake against rock toppled him over and the stake flew into the sea. The men laughed at the barnacle cuts on his hands. He was about to describe how he'd solved the problem—he'd staked as high as in grass and as low as in sand and ran a rope boundary on the outside of those firmly rooted stakes—when the news showed the names and faces of the men killed that day in Vietnam. Afterward, the men wouldn't stop talking about the war.

He'd dropped in at the bar to tell someone about the loan before he came home and received flak from Marilyn. He wanted a couple buddies to share his excitement. But after ten minutes of Vietnam talk, he paid his tab and left. Why must Marilyn be against the expansion that had always been his dream? His eyes followed her long nose to her thick lips and pointed chin. He'd told her the plan when they were courting. She seemed encouraging, or at the least indifferent, about it then.

After dinner, he waited for her on the couch as she washed dishes. When she walked past him, he said they needed to talk.

Let's go to the office then, she said. Or better, outside.

She didn't like Tim to hear them argue. Jackson didn't know why; to him, it was a part of life. Fine, he said.

Tim, Marilyn said. She tapped on his bedroom door. Your father and I are going outside. If you hear the bell, go downstairs.

OK, Tim said.

Outside, wind flapped their jackets. Jackson zipped his coat and Marilyn put up her hood. How about the lounge? Jackson asked.

OK, Marilyn said. No, let's go to the rocks.

Marilyn had been so indecisive lately, Jackson thought. Fine, he said. Tonight, he wanted to pick his battles.

Behind the motel, overcast sky dissolved into gray sea. Jagged black rocks led to wet sand. No one walked across the horseshoe-shaped stretch of beach that separated them from town.

Without speaking, they walked to the bench overlooking Little Faithful that Jackson had built as a wedding present. Each summer he'd restained it. He stood behind the bench and ran his finger along the top while Marilyn sat down.

She leaned forward, knees on elbows. Did you rope off the motel land? she asked.

Just Little Faithful. Jackson pressed his thumb into a knot in the wood. Now guests will know where it's at.

Marilyn tucked her hair into her hood. Pointing the direction wasn't enough? she asked.

Not for some, Jackson said.

It doesn't look good, Marilyn said.

Not as bad as if the state gets ahold of it. No plaques yet.

What do you mean? Marilyn asked.

Jackson sat next to Marilyn. I wanted to tell you, he said. I think I'll get the loan. For thirty thousand.

Good Lord. The wind blew off Marilyn's hood. She pulled it back on and cinched it tighter. I thought you'd wait for me, she said.

I didn't want to change the appointment. But I could have used you there.

The overcast sky deepened. Marilyn stood. Looks like rain, she said.

Jackson pulled at his beard. They'll start work after Memorial Day, he said. Be done by Labor Day if all goes well. I'm going to oversee them. Maybe even help out. Jackson remembered working with the builders on the wings when he was sixteen. The scents of sweat and the sea, the rewarding exhaustion after ten hours of manual labor. That summer he'd gained his first real muscle, conquered his fear of heights, and heard about people and places outside of Kalapuya. He smiled in reminiscence as Marilyn walked away from him.

What do you want? Marilyn asked. She turned. Strands of hair swirled. What do you want from me, she said.

Jackson leaned forward. She'd never asked him that. She was his wife for god's sake. Couldn't he just share something without wanting anything from her? But he wanted to answer the question. He rubbed his forehead. He stood up and stepped toward her. I want you to be happy for me, he said.

I don't agree with the loan, she said.

And to keep the finances in line during the project, Jackson said. There, that's what he wanted. Those two requests seemed reasonable.

I don't agree with the loan, she said again.

He walked to her and picked up her red, chapped hands. You can still be happy for me, right? he asked. That this dream's coming true?

She rubbed her thumbs against his hairy knuckles. If I didn't think we'd go bankrupt, I'd be happy, she said.

There's always risk, Jackson said. I've done well so far. She pulled her hands away and went to turn from him, but he grasped her arms above the elbows and looked into her face. She stared at him.

To keep finances in line, she said.

As though she hadn't been in charge of the finances for over a decade, Jackson thought. He wasn't asking her to do anything she wasn't already doing.

Marilyn broke free. She walked in a straight, firm line across the rocks. Jackson didn't follow. She turned. I'm done with that, she said. Hair blew into her mouth. She pushed it aside. I'm done with that until I get paid.

This again, Jackson thought. On one of the most exciting days of his life, she was bringing up this bullshit. You can use money from our account, he said. What do you want to buy anyway?

I want my own account, Marilyn said. Pay me or let me pay myself.

Jackson pulled at his beard. Did Leah give you these ideas? he asked.

Marilyn looked down and muttered.

She did, didn't she? Jackson said.

Marilyn looked up. Good Lord. You think I can't think on my own? Marilyn walked farther away. Fog began to fill the gap between them.

Where are you going? Jackson asked.

Marilyn turned. On a walk.

I'm not going to pay you.

Then I won't manage finances.

Light was fading. To keep warm, Jackson hugged himself and stomped. She mirrored him; they both stomped and stared at each other. Jackson never thought she'd threaten that. What are you going to do around the motel all day? he asked.

Maybe I won't be around the motel at all.

She turned and stepped deftly over and between rocks. Jackson remembered her hesitation the first day they walked on them, how she held his hand as she stepped over or into each crevice. Even then she'd moved gracefully, like a deer, but a young one, knock-kneed, unsure. A walk would settle her anger. She wouldn't carry out either threat. She cared about the motel as much as he did. Her hair swayed as she made a leap, but her steadiness did not falter. He watched her until fog and darkness filled the space between them.

Marilyn knew of a cave you could stay in at high tide and remain dry. She'd never done it alone but supposed she might try. For ten minutes, she walked across rocks in the direction of the cave. Then, realizing her coldness and tiredness, she sat. Shivering, she looked around. Darkness had fallen. The fog limited visibility. She drew her knees to her chin and wrapped her arms around her legs. Her rear was so cold it felt damp. She rocked back and forth. She would stay at Leah's tonight, she thought, and at her parents for the summer, or longer if necessary. If her absence didn't affect Jackson at first, it would when tax season rolled around.

She stood and stalked toward The Wave. Wind pushed her landside shoulder. Tim, she thought. Should she bring him? He was too old to force. He liked Toledo fine, but always while visiting said he missed the ocean. Then for his own good he'd stay. But she'd visit. Or he'd visit somehow. What about his schooling? She'd worry about that in the fall.

Suddenly, she tripped and fell. She lay, the wind knocked out of her. Her breath recovered, she raised herself to all fours, brushed dirt off her hair, and felt around. Her knuckles knocked against a rope. The rope around Little Faithful, she thought. As she grasped it, she laughed. She laughed and laughed and fell against the cold, hard ground, laughing. How insane, she thought. To think it was better to designate this spout with a rope than to find it for oneself.

Inside, Tim sprawled asleep on the couch in front of a still-on television. Marilyn turned it off and leaned over him and straightened his bangs.

Tim, she said. He moved his head. I'm leaving. You think you can hold down the fort?

His eyelids fluttered. Sure thing, he said.

Marilyn smiled. He wasn't really awake. Because he was too large to carry, she raised him to his feet and held him by the armpits and led him to bed. She pulled the covers to his chin and kissed his hands and forehead.

His eyelids fluttered again. Good night, he said.

Goodbye, she said.

He opened his eyes. Where're you going?

To Leah's tonight. To your grandparents in the morning.

Can I come?

You can. But I might be gone awhile.

How long? Tim clutched at the sheets.

I'll visit, Marilyn said. And you can visit me. His darting, confused eyes were almost enough to change her mind. It might only be a few days, she said. Or a few weeks. Your dad and I have some things to figure out.

He grabbed one of her arms, a gesture he hadn't done in years.

How about I call you tomorrow morning from Leah's? Marilyn asked. You can decide whether you want to come then.

His grip loosened and he nodded. Marilyn straightened the sheet and blanket. I love you, she said. She kissed him on the cheek. He wiped off her kiss, blinked rapidly, and closed his eyes. She sat by him until he breathed evenly.

In her room, she threw another pair of jeans into her suitcase, more blouses, another nightgown. If she had two suitcases, she'd have filled them both. Students travel across Europe with only one backpack, she thought, remembering Leah's students' stories. I can survive with one suitcase for the summer. She couldn't decide which jewelry to take so she stuck in the whole box. After tossing in three more dresses, two pairs of shoes, and underclothes, the suitcase bulged. She smashed the top with one hand while she zipped it with the other. She looked around, aware of Jackson's absence. He hadn't been in the office either. She grunted as she lifted the suitcase. She didn't leave a note for her husband on the way out.

Marilyn saw a light in the shop and knocked at its door. Chairs rested upside down on tops of tables. After Marilyn knocked again, Leah, wearing an apron, opened it. Marilyn lugged in her suitcase and stood on the kitchen side of the register. Isn't it late for you to be baking?

Depends on the day, Leah said. She rinsed her hands in the sink, then punched down dough. Just finishing this honey whole wheat. I'll make pastries in the morning. She studied Marilyn. Her friend's hair looked wind-twisted. You want to help? she asked.

Right now I need a shower.

Go ahead. And take the spare room tonight. You're always welcome to it. A couple kids are here but they sleep in the front room.

Thanks. Marilyn pulled the suitcase into the house.

Leah divided the mass of dough into eight piles. She cinched each loaf shut, plopped them into floured cast-iron pans, and placed the pans in the preheated oven. She thought of the spare room, which had been her and Micah's old room, where she'd stopped sleeping after his death. Below all this fog, the sea, she knew, was rising. While they all slept, water would cover the horseshoe of sand, then recede. She opened the door and went into the house to listen to Woody Guthrie with the students while the loaves baked. She left the bakery door open so that they could smell the bread.

PART
TWO

1.

Writing a letter to his son had been more difficult for Elliot than working on his memoir. First, his tone had seemed too businesslike. Then, taking into account their estrangement, it had seemed too casual. He'd wanted to stick to facts but also somehow personalize the letter: he hadn't wanted it to sound like a letter to just any lawyer.

After working the better part of a morning, Elliot had written a draft. *Dear Conrad,* it had begun, *I hope you are well. I trust our strained relationships won't preclude you from doing me a favor and giving me advice.* In the next paragraph, he'd asked Conrad to use his connections to sway those in the legislature. In the final paragraph, he'd asked specific advice on his own piece of land. His son, an estate lawyer, couldn't represent him but could advise him.

Elliot had sent the letter to Conrad over two months ago and had received nothing in return. By now he knew his son didn't intend to reply.

For a couple weeks after Elliot visited The Sweet Seller, the newspapers included nothing on the Beach Bill. One columnist then adopted the issue as his pet cause. Almost every single day, it seemed to Elliot, this man, Matt Kramer, wrote an article. In mid-May, Governor Tom McCall had flown a helicopter up and down the coast, stopping at various beaches to promote the bill. The state house passed the bill, but the senate had deliberated, proposing amendments. Meanwhile, letters flooded the committee hearings. Last Elliot read, they'd received over thirty thousand from supportive citizens.

On a Monday in late June Elliot woke with the intent of driving to Salem. With the state senate's vote imminent, he wanted to try once more to talk to his son. He dressed and took Lana outside. Despite the early hour, the breeze felt warm. June had been dreary, and Elliot was thankful for the sun. The old man and his dog walked south on the rocks and lowered themselves to the beach and walked back north on the sand. Elliot's footprints a straight line along the tide line; Lana's in zigzags, her body following her nose. To the new objects washed onto the wet sand during the night—a jellyfish, a rope of seaweed, a crab shell—Lana gave momentary sniffs. As Elliot climbed a rock toward the lighthouse, Tim ducked into the woods. Lana scrambled above and beyond Elliot, her nose in the air. About to call Tim's name, Elliot called Lana's instead. Time to go inside, girl, he said. She veered from the woods and trotted at his heels. Elliot wanted the ignorant public off his land, not this one local boy. It was the first he'd seen of Tim since the boy came inside the lighthouse. If he trespassed every day that would be a problem.

Elliot made oatmeal on the stove, stirring the simmering oats and water with a wooden spoon. He dished himself up a bowl, then lowered the pan to the side of Lana's water dish, where she slurped up the rest. He would have never served her like that when Darlene was alive, but Lana cleaned the pan better than a spatula, which made less work for him. On top of his oatmeal, he dolloped homemade strawberry freezer jam. His mouth watered as he imagined spreading it across a slice of Sweet Seller bread. He'd enjoyed The Sweet Seller's white bread even more than Darlene's, but he couldn't return to the shop, not without bringing the photo. The couple times he'd seen Leah around town, he'd accelerated his truck and looked away.

After breakfast Elliot shaved and put on the only suit he owned, black with a white shirt and dark green tie. The last time he'd worn the suit was at Darlene's funeral. From a drawer in his desk, he took out the folder where he kept his will. He'd given the property to Conrad. If a request didn't work, he could try a bribe. He hoped his son would want the land for nostalgic purposes if nothing else. Their house near Coos Bay had been on a small island lot; this property opened up the daily wilderness to his son. People changed,

Elliot knew. And although he himself had changed for the better as he aged, he knew not everyone did. But he had hope that Conrad would love this land.

He drove up the coast to Newport, then east past Toledo to the freeway. He thought of Marilyn as he passed Toledo; she was the only person he knew from there. People at Joe's Bar had wondered why she'd left her husband. Adultery was ruled out, because if one citizen were having an affair, every other person in such a small town would know. Neither Jackson nor Marilyn seemed the abusive type, but sometimes it was hard to recognize that kind. Most thought the couple had quarreled over how to run the motel. It's difficult for a couple to run a business together, Joe had said. Ben, the grocery store manager, had guessed that Jackson had given Marilyn too much say and it backfired. Jackson was a favorite around Kalapuya, while Marilyn didn't socialize much, except with Leah. Townsfolk tried to pull details from Leah, who either didn't know or wouldn't spill. Not even Sandy could broach the topic.

None of this concerned Elliot, except that he was fond of Marilyn's boy. He wondered how Tim was dealing with his mother's absence. Elliot wished he would have told the boy more about the light. Tim seemed interested, and soon enough, no one would remember or understand nonautomated lighthouses.

Perhaps, because of the self-imposed gap in Elliot's memoir, the situation also remotely reminded him of himself and Darlene. He'd been surprised she didn't leave when she learned of his cheating. Then again, where would she have gone? She'd have had to admit the situation to a girlfriend in the Coos Bay area if she'd wanted to stay with one of them. They would have told their husbands, and everyone would have known. Her parents were dead, and she hadn't stayed in contact with her aunt and uncle in Astoria.

The affair had been brief—a handful of rendezvous, maybe a dozen. Elliot didn't know why he was involved and despised himself for his involvement, but he knew well enough, through observing other couples, that such entanglements didn't simply stop. His retirement had come up the year before, but at the time, although he'd begun to dream of his book on Oregon lighthouses, he didn't plan to retire for another ten. However, during the affair he'd discovered a house and three acres for sale south of Kalapuya and decided to buy them. Despite Darlene's protest that Conrad wanted to go to high school with his friends, Elliot wouldn't delay the family's move. He lied to Catherine, telling her that Darlene had discovered their affair and that it must end. Then, for his own good, he retired and moved his family seventy-five miles north.

After settling into the old boxy salt house, built by Sandy's grandparents in the 1870s, Elliot threw himself into its maintenance. Despite being in his fifties, it was the first place he'd owned. Whenever he'd wanted to do projects at the lighthouse, he'd had to run them by his superiors. Shingling the roof, refinishing hardwood floors, and making and installing kitchen cabinets distracted him from dwelling on his affair.

The summer after their arrival, Conrad confronted his father. They were standing near an old oak tree, the only deciduous tree on the property. Five years later that spot of ground would hold the lighthouse. Conrad had emerged from the woods to see his father, arms crossed, eyes out to sea. Elliot was thinking of the remodeling he'd accomplished in the months since his retirement, and of the woodworking and writing he could accomplish in the future with his abundant time. It was a content moment for him, and he imagined his son wanted to spoil this contentment.

I know about you and Miss Turner, Conrad said. His fists were clenched, chin raised. I'm going to tell Mom.

Elliot didn't know how his son knew. Maybe someone at school had told him. Maybe he'd heard before the move and had mulled on it all year. He and Conrad hadn't talked much since they'd moved north.

Elliot remembered the boy's broad shoulders but thin body. He'd stepped forward and slapped his son on the face. Twice? Five times? Ten? Once would have been too many. Elliot remembered that he'd bruised him badly. Conrad's cheek puffed, crowding his eye. Elliot remembered the surprise on Conrad's face, even awe. And then anger. His son turned and stomped into the woods, his chin still raised. And he never really came back, although he lived in the same house as Elliot for two more years.

Elliot had walked into the house and confessed to his wife, who had been sewing at the kitchen table. Her bowed head and silence hurt him more than words. She'd had no idea.

The next two years were the unhappiest of Elliot's life. He, his wife, and his son lived in separate, impermeable spheres. The close quarters on the island had sometimes bothered him, but now he remembered that time with fondness: he'd had the solitude of his work as well as the camaraderie of family; now, he felt a forced isolation. He often thought that after Conrad left for college, he might request a divorce. He had a brief wish that after Darlene left, Catherine might join him, but he quenched that thought, knowing Catherine wouldn't commit to him like that, and even if she would, that wasn't what he wanted. He wanted Darlene's trust.

During that period, perhaps as a strange penance, Elliot broke almost all of his early woodworking projects, almost everything he'd constructed from his adolescence through his twenties. A small desk, two chairs, a bureau. A bookshelf, an uneven table, an unstable canoe. In the shed, he hit them with a baseball bat over and over until they contained enough random indents to satisfy him. He chopped them up and threw them in the woodpile. His happiest moment was when the old oak fell in a harsh winter storm. The day after he joyfully chopped it into firewood. It gave him pleasure that the natural world could work like a relationship; that gusts of wind could destroy years of growth. It made him feel less alone.

After Conrad left, Elliot and Darlene's relationship shifted. They picked up Conrad's domestic tasks, such as washing dishes and stacking firewood. She began to watch Elliot more, and he began to watch her. One day when she asked him to peel an orange, a task he enjoyed and she did not, he dared to hope they might be OK. The next year, when the lighthouse was approved and he asked her to help him with the details of the design, and they fell into their usual planning and banter, he knew they would be OK or even better than OK. And until Darlene died, Elliot never ceased to be amazed that they were.

Elliot felt that Conrad had taken his parents' revitalized relationship as a personal affront. When his son saw Elliot and Darlene holding hands at his college graduation, he scowled. Conrad had gone to law school on the East Coast, and when he returned had visited Elliot and Darlene only three times, including when he came to Kalapuya for Darlene's funeral. He allowed Darlene but not Elliot to visit his place in Salem.

Elliot's shoulders relaxed as he exited the freeway. Speeds above forty made him nervous. He looked at the streets before him. Navigating cities had never been a strong point either. He pulled over and unlocked the glove compartment and took out a Salem street map that he'd marked up the night before. He closed the compartment and studied the map and set it on the seat next to him and pulled out the car. His face grimaced in concentration. After a couple miles and almost a dozen turns, he located his son's square, brick office building. He sweated just thinking of parallel parking. Fortunately, a couple of empty, consecutive parking spaces lined the curb, so he easily pulled in. Dozens of suited people walked up and down the sidewalk. He waited for a break in the foot traffic, then stepped from the car. Heat bounced off the pavement. Elliot sweated more. A car honked a few feet from him, and his body cringed.

According to the copper-plated names outside the building, his son worked on the third floor. Inside, he located the stairs and walked up them. The hallway on the third floor was hotter than the street. He stood outside Conrad's office until three people strode past him. None of them looked in his direction. When he knocked, his son said come in.

Elliot watched his son finish writing a sentence at a desk in the deep center of the room. He'd been the kind of boy to complete whatever he was doing before he gave something else his attention. His body had grown into its wide adolescent frame. His shoulders sloped slightly, like his father's. File cabinets lined the wall on one side of the desk, two unfinished bookshelves the other. The homey scent of unfinished wood relaxed Elliot. In the back wall sat a box fan inside a large window. Out it, he could see the street and his car.

The fan's humming had masked Elliot's entrance. When Conrad raised his eyes and saw his father, he dropped his pen. Elliot realized that he'd wanted to surprise Conrad in order to elicit a verbal response from him. Since the family had moved to Kalapuya, the boy had spoken stoically to his father, any joys or sorrows hinted at only by brief facial expressions. Today Elliot saw a standard annoyance, as though a stranger had bumped into him. It faded within seconds.

You've come to discuss the letter? Conrad said.

Yes, Elliot said. He sat in the chair in front of Conrad's desk, then stood because Conrad hadn't invited him to sit. Partly, he said. To feel the direct breeze from the fan, he sat again.

All I know about the bill is what's been in the papers, Conrad said.

Quite a lot, don't you think? Elliot said.

Conrad looked at the sheet of paper and moved it to the side. He folded his hands in the now-empty space. Enough, he asked. But none of it pertains to me.

Elliot looked into his son's eyes. Their strange color reminded him of Leah's. You don't know anyone in the legislature?

I know people. But my voice counts only as much as anyone else who writes a letter or speaks at a hearing.

You're not friends with any of them?

Not really. Even if I were, what could I do? I don't have anything to offer in exchange for their dissension.

Elliot sat straighter, clutching the folder on his lap. The fan's breeze pushed his gray, thin hair backward. Politics was a bargaining game. Conrad was right about that.

Conrad threw a thumb over his shoulder. They have a committee hearing today, he said. Just down the street. Why don't you go talk at that? He wanted his father to leave before his meeting with a client in a half hour.

Sweat gathered in Elliot's armpits, from a feeling of imminent failure as much as the heat. He sucked in air and looked at the fan, longing to move closer to it. He imagined a room crowded with the slick, young people he'd seen on the sidewalk, himself taking the stand and sputtering under their gaze. During training sessions for the Lighthouse Service and Coast Guard, blood rushed to his head whenever he asked a question in front of a group. Someone like Leah could talk in front of all those people, he thought. He could not. And yet his son had said more words to him than he had in years. That itself was a kind of victory.

What about a lawyer? Elliot asked. Do you know someone who could represent me if this passes?

Conrad crossed his arms. Maybe, he said. He'd already said more to his father than he deserved.

What's in it for him? Elliot thought. That's what he wants to know. He handed Conrad the folder that held the will. This affects you, Elliot said, when I'm gone.

Conrad opened it and scanned the document. He gave a thin-lipped smile, amused and cynical.

Elliot squinted, confused.

Why are you leaving it to me? Conrad said. He slapped a hand against the will. Isn't there a lighthouse group somewhere? A Coast Guard friend?

You're my son.

Look, Elliot wanted to say. I'm dying sooner than later. Are we going to resolve this before then or not? There wouldn't be a deathbed reconciliation—that, he knew.

Conrad turned his chair to look out the window. Below, cars and people passed. He recognized a friend of his who, if he wanted to be generous, he could recommend to his father. Hell, the man owed him a favor; his father could consult him for free. He knew the effort Elliot must have made to come into a city. Sometimes, walking into the street after hours of detail work, the incessant activity still startled him.

In his mind as a child, there had been how other men treated women and how his father treated them. Unlike many of his friends' dads, his father never commented on women's looks as though they were some pretty, mediocre, or ugly decoration. He held the door open for them and thanked Darlene when she made supper. Then, at Waldport High School, Catherine Turner's nephew had told Conrad of the affair. After that there was no division between his father and anyone. He'd become like other fathers, or worse.

It's a false childhood dichotomy between good and evil, a girlfriend in Boston had told him. Most people grow out of them. She'd recommended he go to a therapist. To please her, he did. He'd never known anyone who'd gone to a therapist. The ceiling of the office was high, at least twelve feet, and the bookcases' wood looked fake; what he told his girlfriend when she asked how it went. He never went back. Maybe that false dichotomy was still intact, Conrad thought. But it didn't matter. It was like as a child when kids dared each other to swim in the freezing Pacific. To him the thrill and bragging rights weren't worth the certain cold. His life was fine without his father.

Conrad turned his chair and again looked over the will. What would he do with it? He didn't want to vacation in such a remote place; he preferred Seaside or Astoria, where there was better food and shows. He could sell it, he supposed. He could pay off the mortgage on the house he'd just purchased. The Beach Bill controversy had been an advertisement for coastal tourism; the property was probably worth more to developers than before. But if he accepted the offer, his professional integrity demanded that he rephrase this rough, handwritten document. Such rewritings were part of his job and he enjoyed them. But he'd also have to communicate with his father again. And this relationship, so conveniently settled, would bubble like a long-dormant active volcano. But he could handle a few phone calls to pay off his mortgage. They didn't need to do lunch.

This uses imprecise language, Conrad said. You mind if I rephrase it?

Certainly not, Elliot said. His son knew legal language better than he did.

I'll mail the rewrite to you.

Or we could meet for supper?

Conrad looked at him. No, we can't.

Hurt, Elliot stood, then sat again. What about that lawyer? he asked.

Conrad flipped through a card catalog. He wrote a name, address, and phone number on a slip of paper and held it toward his father. Ted Johansson, he said. He's good. Conrad figured he'd save the favor Ted owned him for another time. He'd given his father enough.

Elliot had to stand and lean to reach the held-out paper. He held his back, which ached from too much sitting in the car. You're quite the city slicker now, aren't you? he asked, unable to withhold the dig.

I guess I am, Conrad said. He didn't look up from his paperwork.

Elliot shook his head. He'd insulted his son and his son had agreed with the insult. Maybe that land'll bring you back to your roots, he said.

Maybe.

I'll keep an eye out for the will.

Conrad looked at him. OK, Dad, he said.

Outside, Elliot looked around. He couldn't remember the last time Conrad had called him *Dad*. Across the street, light fell off another brick building. A young couple clasping hands strolled by. Most people walked alone, hurrying for unknowable reasons.

Two other cars boxed in Elliot's. Elliot glared at them. Inside the cab, he debated going to the committee hearing only to listen, but he didn't know where the building was or what time it began, and his back hurt, and he didn't want to be that tottering, lost old man who questioned strangers. A car waiting for his parking spot honked. I'm going when I want to go, he told the rearview mirror. The car drove by. He shrugged out of his suit jacket and laid it on the passenger's seat. He carefully backed up and rolled forward and backed up and rolled forward and backed up and pulled into the street. On Elliot's route to the freeway, he took two wrong turns, and while checking the map at a red light, rolled forward and almost rear-ended someone. As he merged onto I-5, sweat dripped off his face. He drove the freeway in a daze. Why did people drive so fast? he wondered. Where did they need to go that required such hurry?

By the time he passed Toledo, the temperature had dropped and his head had cleared. To neutralize his body odor, he rolled down the window. When he smelled the sea, his whole body relaxed. He decided that his son had showed him a kindness. Conrad may never forgive, but he'd keep the property. And there was that parting *Dad*. Because Elliot thought Conrad had lost any inclination for kindness toward him, the endearment cheered him. The lighthouse would be preserved, Elliot thought. Maybe, as Conrad visited the land, he'd come to know his dad, even if it were after Elliot's death.

When Elliot entered Kalapuya, the sun was nearing the ocean. Relieved to be home, Elliot let out his breath. He turned off 101 and onto the grid of houses and stores. On the street closest to the rocky shoreline, he pulled into the parking lot of Joe's Bar.

      Since Elliot's confrontation with Leah, he'd come into town more regularly, always on weekday afternoons when he might avoid most loggers and tourists. His intent had been to learn more about the Beach Bill. Many—and, after the Tom McCall publicity stunt, even most—locals wanted the bill passed. Most didn't own beachside property, so in supporting the bill, they gained more than they lost. Some who didn't live beachside thought it an infringement on private property rights, but those people became fewer each week. Elliot had listened more than he spoke, because if he talked too much about something he knew so little, he'd lose his self-respect. He ate at Joe's Bar or the adjacent Dame's Fine Chowder where he and Darlene had been regulars. Since Darlene's death, the owners had painted the white interior a dark blue, which made the restaurant less familiar and more bearable.

      Joe's Bar was a hangout for locals, mostly men, many bachelored or retired. Elliot had discovered their elk burger and kept coming back for that. Tonight, tourists had invaded the space: a couple in a corner, a family of five on the deck above the rocks, and a pale young man bandannaed and backpacked, who seemed like a hitchhiker. Elliot sat at the bar, a few seats closer to the window than the young man. He appreciated that Joe had stopped airing news footage of the war. Elliot ordered the usual and looked outside. Above the deck, gulls circled and swooped. Out at sea waves lapped. The sun stretched across clouds on the horizon. Elliot couldn't see his lighthouse, six coves south, but drew a mental line that reached there. He needed to leave soon to turn on the lamp.

Elliot bit into his burger just as Jackson Ryder entered. The drops on Jackson's forehead reminded Elliot of his own dried sweat. After he turned on the lamp, he'd take a bath. Lana, who'd feel neglected because of his absence, might whine and scratch the bathroom door. Despite the crisscross marks she made, Elliot didn't do anything but scold. Jackson sat at the bar, closer to the sea than Elliot and partially blocking his view. He leaned his elbows on the counter and pulled at the neck of his white T-shirt to force a breeze. A sawdust scent bounced off him. He looked sideways at Elliot and they nodded to each other.

Joe gave Jackson a can of Bud. Working on the new units? he asked.

How'd you guess? Jackson said. As usual, Joe's presence calmed him. He cracked the can and took a swig. It's going pretty well. He licked his lips. We're on track to finish by Labor Day.

Good news, Joe said. Or maybe not, he thought, if the new units had caused Jackson and Marilyn's troubles like he suspected. Before Marilyn left, Jackson had described their disagreements to Joe; afterward, he hadn't mentioned her name. Joe figured that for a man like Jackson—who talked to anyone about anything—not to mention her, he must feel the loss deeply. But Joe himself didn't pry; it wasn't his nature. And, surprisingly to him, over the years he'd found that disinterested silence elicited more information than intrusive questions. Can I get you something to eat? he asked.

Nah. This'll be it. Jackson was hungry but didn't want to spend money on bar food.

Joe drifted over to check on the hitchhiker.

How you doing, Elliot? Jackson asked.

Not too bad, Elliot said.

You going on a date or something?

Elliot looked at his clothes. He'd forgotten he was dressed up. A glob of ketchup slid off the burger and onto his thigh. He set down the burger, dunked his napkin in water, and dabbed at his suit pants. I had business in Salem, he said.

Mind if I ask what?

Yes, I do. Elliot again grasped the burger. Ten minutes ago, he would have been more bothered by the question, but the food was pacifying him.

Jackson didn't mind Elliot's terseness; he knew how grouchy the old man could be. I've had to go there twice this month, he said. Not an easy town to navigate.

Not at all, Elliot said. He finished off the burger in three large bites.

Jackson lowered his voice. Joe must hunt out of season, he said. How else does he have elk all summer? In over twenty-five years, I've never seen him turn down anyone for a burger.

I heard you, you gossip, Joe said. He held up his metal spatula. This can do more than flip burgers you know.

Jackson held up his can. I can throw this other places than down my throat. Jackson and Joe laughed. I'm sure Elliot doesn't care, Jackson said. He's the one taking pines from national forest land. He winked at Elliot.

Elliot pushed his empty plate across the counter. To hell with that, he said.

Hey, Joe said, no need to worry. We won't squeal.

I'm within my rights, Elliot said. He kept his eyes on the counter.

How so? Jackson asked.

If this bill passes, the beach belongs to the people. They can collect shells off it. So why can't I cut down trees off national forest land? Doesn't it belong to the people?

That's what my dad said, Jackson said. It makes some sense

but wouldn't hold up in court. National forests belong to the government.

Elliot fixed his dark eyes on Jackson's blue ones. Who is the government, if not the people? he asked. Out the window the day wasn't becoming lighter. He took a sip of water, then placed cash from his wallet on the counter.

No need to run off, Joe said.

I need to turn on the light, Elliot said. Good evening. He nodded and turned and walked to the outer door and opened it and left the bar. He'd never been one to gracefully leave a room.

Lana barked when she heard Elliot's car. He couldn't remember the last time he'd been gone so long from her. He opened the door and squatted. She placed her paws on his shoulders. Gently chiding her, he removed them. He scratched behind her ears and rubbed his hands down the length of her black back and white belly. He let her out front to pee and, in the kitchen, opened a can of chicken and dished half into her bowl. While she ate, he promised that they'd go on a walk as soon as he turned on the light. Although she turned her head toward him, seeming to understand, she whined when he shut the lighthouse door.

Elliot firmly and quickly walked up the steps. A pinkness had settled on the horizon. He flipped on the light. The intense brightness caused the outer world to seem darker. As usual, he admired the grooves in the Fresnel lamp. Built for and installed in Cape Blanco in 1868, this first-order Fresnel had been replaced with a smaller one in 1936. By the time Elliot built his lighthouse, the lens had been in storage for over fifteen years. His friend, Aaron Strom, a former keeper at Cape Blanco, insisted that Elliot use it so that it wouldn't sit around until they both were dead. The two men had wrapped it in twenty blankets, buoyed it by twenty pillows, cinched it down to Elliot's truck bed with rope, and transported it north. Elliot had lovingly cleaned off the dust, sometimes spending an entire morning on one frame.

At Tillamook, he'd lit kerosene lamps. When he served near Coos Bay, the lamp was electrified, like here. Now lamps were automated; no one needed to turn a switch. Lighthouse keepers would go the way of blacksmiths, he thought. They would set up a tent at fairgrounds, sell trinkets, and tell stories of *the good old days*. Only the good old days weren't that good; only someone awash in sentimentality or nostalgia thought that. It was a privilege to live in a time when people who died at sea made the front page of the newspaper instead of the fine print a few pages in. If his pleasure were bittersweet because his services were no longer needed, who could blame him? He turned toward the ocean. The lamp refracted the light's rays as far as twenty miles out to sea.

Elliot had watched light fade into the sea more times than most men alive. The most dismal evenings of his service were on Tillamook Lighthouse, when the dim, foggy, rainy days would fade to dark, rainy nights for months. On rare evenings of colorful winter sunsets, the men would call to each other and stare like children. They'd sent one man from the rock because the winters depressed him. Elliot himself didn't mind the weather. Tillamook's winters weren't as dreary as Aberdeen's. The close quarters and lack of access to the mainland bothered him sometimes. During winters in Aberdeen, he traipsed around the woods despite the coldness.

The sea was very dark. It sloshed against rocks. Elliot exited the light chamber and walked downstairs, a hand holding his aching back. His knees hurt, too. He thought that dying next to the light wouldn't be a bad way to go. He could go out with the sunset or sunrise or, better yet, in the middle of a stormy night. He remembered a Robert Bly poem that ended "All the sailors on deck have been blind for many years." He didn't know what it meant but had always liked it. Maybe he himself had overexplained in his attempts at poems. Lana backstepped when he opened the door. Her nose had been pressed against the crack. When Elliot saw her, his thoughts moved outward.

Come on girl, he said. Let's go for that walk.

Outside, the light of the moon shone off the water. Elliot hadn't noticed when the light had faded. It was impossible, he thought, to pinpoint the exact moment day turned to night.

2.

After Jackson drank one beer, he ordered another and fries. The sky turned pink and orange. The tourists had left, but the bum remained. Joe whispered that, although the kid had been there since four, he'd only ordered one beer and a side of fries.

Sounds like me lately, Jackson said.

Joe smiled. But I know you, he said.

The kid rested his chin on a hand and stared at the liquor shelf or the blank television screen. The news is too depressing, Joe had told Jackson. Not worth the little extra business. Jackson figured the kid just didn't want to pay for lodging. To avoid a slap on the wrist by the cops, he might set up tent on the beach after the sun set and take it down before the sun rose. As long as they didn't leave trash around, Jackson didn't mind such people. His father would have already talked to the kid, invited him to stay at The Wave for a reduced rate. Jackson didn't give out as much charity, although if it were the middle of winter or rainy, he might do the same.

Jackson wondered whether his personality innately differed from his father's or whether he'd been influenced by Marilyn. Soon after they married, a couple of his father's charity cases had stolen bedding from the rooms. Later, when Jackson ran The Wave and suggested offering a reduced rate, she reminded him of her own father's experience and said that most people would be offended at the offer. Plenty of people will accept a reduced rate if they need to, he'd argued. Not decent people, she'd say, and remind him of the thieves. That was only two out of twenty—or more, he'd say. She'd ask whether he wanted to take that risk.

For her it was always about minimizing risk. She'd always paid their bills, fully and on time, and the motel gave them enough income. But Jackson had just turned forty-six, and he'd felt as though he were passing his prime. He wanted to *do* something significant, something that he could enjoy but that would also outlast him. Maybe Marilyn couldn't understand because she was a woman, Jackson thought. She said she wanted to be paid, but why? She rarely spent money on herself. Maybe she just wanted a nest egg independent of their mutual accounts. Maybe with such a fund she'd feel safer. Comfort, safety, and love were what mattered to women.

How's your family, Joe? Jackson asked.

They're fine, Joe said. Joe opened another can of Bud for Jackson. Jackson held up both hands. On the house, Joe said. He didn't mind giving a free one here and there to regulars. Plus, Jackson had cut back on his bar time and Joe had missed him and his casual optimism. Jackson nodded a thank you. With a wet rag, Joe wiped off the section of the counter where Elliot had eaten. Think Betty doesn't like having kids underfoot all day, he said. While they were in school, she'd go to Eugene and sell that catalog makeup to her family and friends. She's trying to do it over the phone now, but the kids keep screeching.

Jackson remembered the thick film of facial makeup that Joe's wife wore. Her eyelashes clumped with mascara. He was glad Marilyn didn't wear makeup every day, and when she did, it didn't look that gaudy. Jackson took a swig and set down the can and twisted its pull tab. He missed seeing Marilyn's face. So far this summer, from forgetfulness, he'd only sporadically kept baked goods in the lounge. When he remembered, or when guests commented on their absence, he usually sent Tim to The Sweet Seller. The couple of times he'd gone, Marilyn wasn't there. He twisted the tab harder. Jackson was almost certain that Marilyn would return any day. The end of June was approaching, and she had to do the second quarter income sheet and balance statement. Before she left, even when she was acting so strange and agitated, she'd finished the first quarter ones. Without them, Jackson wouldn't have been able to secure the loan. If he were wrong, and she didn't come back to do them, she'd return before Tim started school. Her care for The Wave's accounts and her son would trump any feud with him. The tab popped off. Beer sloshed in the can.

Your oldest is what, a fifth grader? Jackson asked.

Joe nodded.

Wait a couple years, Jackson said. She won't even notice he's around. He aimed the tab at the ice bucket half-full of them and tossed. The tab landed on the tiled floor. Jackson scowled.

Joe grabbed the tab and placed it in the bucket, the motion fluid and inconspicuous. We're hoping the bus service'll be running before he goes to junior high, he said.

That would be nice, Jackson said. Too bad it missed Tim. His frown lingered.

What did you work on today? Joe asked. For Jackson, the new units were always a joyful topic.

Jackson felt his sore arm muscles and smiled. Finished framing, he said.

Nice. Congrats.

Jackson remembered the sound of pounding hammers, the salty sweat in his beard, the sandwich and beer the men had shared at their midday meal. The balloon frame felt sturdy and looked good. His smile faded as he remembered the extra expense to get that estimate. He'd taken Marilyn's to the bank to get the loan, but after he received it, he'd hired a contractor to estimate based on the balloon method. And he hadn't added the contractor's fees to the books. In the two months since Marilyn left, he hadn't added dozens of costs to the books; at best, his bookkeeping had been erratic. Even if Marilyn returned tonight, Jackson thought, she couldn't start the second-quarter paperwork without hours of prep. It was her own damn fault. Still, for him to retain the loan, the bank needed a quarterly income sheet and balance statement, so he couldn't get too far behind. He gulped down the rest of the beer.

You OK? Joe asked. Jackson wasn't usually one to ponder.

Yeah, Jackson said. He rubbed his palm across his mouth. I got some work to do.

I'd be the last person to keep you from that.

Sure you would. Jackson's eyes flashed with laughter, then his mouth firmed. He placed cash on the counter. See you later, Joe.

Joe playfully saluted; an old joke between them.

As Jackson walked by the young man, he stopped and rested a hand on the back of his bar chair. You got a place to stay tonight? he asked. I own the motel south of here. You could have a room at a reduced rate. As long as Marilyn was gone, he thought, he might as well take that liberty.

I have a couple places in mind, the young man said.

Jackson withdrew his hand. Good luck with that, he said.

At The Wave, the office was quiet. Jackson slipped a flannel over his T-shirt, and leaving it unbuttoned, went into the closet-office and left the connecting door open. Paperwork from the bank lay on top of the bookkeeping ledger. Receipts filled the tab holder that Vic had gifted Marilyn when she quit his restaurant. Unpaid invoices crisscrossed the desk's center. Jackson sat down and cleared the paperwork off the ledger and placed it on top of the invoices and opened the ledger and pulled a couple receipts off the tab holder. As he tried to focus, his eyelids fluttered. A day of manual labor at forty-six left him twice as exhausted as a day of manual labor at sixteen. When the office phone rang, he rose, relieved.

The Wave, Jackson speaking.

It's Eileen Smith.

Hello, Mrs. Smith, how are you? Jackson sat and opened the scheduling book to the Fourth of July week, the week of the Smith's usual visit.

Not too well, but thank you, she said.

Sorry to hear that.

We're going to cancel our reservation.

Did something come up that week? We have a free room the third and fourth weeks in July.

Our counselor thought we should vary our summer routines. Carl died a month ago.

I—, Jackson coughed. Saying sorry didn't do it justice. Oh, ma'am, he said. I'm so sorry.

May I please speak with Marilyn?

She . . . she's not here right now.

Will you ask her to call me?

Sure.

We'll see you again. Just not this summer. Goodbye.

Goodbye, Jackson said. He placed the phone in its cradle and opened the center desk drawer and pulled out a cigarette and lit it up. Whenever he heard that someone he knew had died, memories flooded him of others closer to him who had died. In his mind's eye, his little sister cried, her frail child body in a ball on a bed upstairs in the kids' shared bedroom. His mother, who had died after weeks in an inhospitable hospital room, toward the end hadn't known where she was. A guest had found his father dead in a reclining chair in front of the TV in the lounge. The area stunk of bodily fluids; Jackson had discarded the chair and corded off the room for a week.

Death was a season that happened over and over in variation. Jackson rested the cigarette in the ashtray and lifted the receiver and set it back down. He stood up and sat down. He leaned his head against his hands. This was a serious and private conversation. If Marilyn wouldn't come to The Wave, he'd ask her to meet up somewhere other than Leah's house. But not tonight. The Fourth of July was less than two weeks away; he had to tell her soon so that she could tell Tim. He sure as hell wasn't doing that. But maybe she'd be back home by then, he thought. Probably, she would.

He looked at the scheduling book again. Hopefully someone else would reserve the room between now and then. That week was usually packed, and he could use the money, especially right now, when one third of the old units were closed because of the construction of the new units on top of them.

In the closet, Jackson placed the receipts back on the holder. In the adjacent laundry room, he squatted and took a small can of stain off a bottom shelf. He popped it open with a quarter from his pocket and stirred the stain with a wooden stake. The scent overpowered the detergent smell of the room. After the oil dissolved, he put the stake on top of an old newspaper, grabbed the can's handle, and stood. Off the top shelf he took a small brush and clean rag.

Outside, in the growing cold and darkness, Jackson walked by the old units. No one had filled the boxes with flowers. He hoped guests chalked up their emptiness to the construction. None of them knew Marilyn had left. To them she was simply out of the office or out of town. The lie worked on guests, since most stayed no longer than a few days. As for him, it seemed as though she'd been gone half a year.

While he walked by the new units, Jackson lifted his nose to smell the sawdust. Beyond the motel, he kneeled next to the bench and in circular strokes wiped off dirt and dust with the rag. His knees and forearms ached. Satisfied the bench was clean, he restained it, starting at the top, his brush strokes firm and straight.

The rhythm focused and calmed him, though the bench itself incited memories. In the early years of their marriage, he and Marilyn had sat on it together in the evenings. Her fascination with the sunsets on the sea had charmed him. These days, motel guests plopped there to watch the sea, but as far as he knew, Marilyn preferred to walk. No, he corrected himself as his brush hit a knot, Marilyn had sat there that night she left, before their argument. Maybe she sat there frequently; he didn't know all of her habits. When he kneeled to restain the bottom of the seat, pain shot up and down his back. Damn, he thought. After this he'd stand without moving or, better yet, lie down. And tomorrow he wouldn't help the construction crew. He'd never consciously been aware of Marilyn's routines until she left. Then he'd discovered that on weekdays he expected her to be in the closet-office in the mornings, inside their apartment in the late afternoons, and walking on the rocks at dusk. On weekends she did bookkeeping or helped Annie clean in the mornings and in the afternoons ran the main desk. Sometimes, on weekends, he turned circles in the office, looking, and once he'd called out to her from the bottom of the office steps. Marilyn, he'd yelled, you going to take over the desk?

Now, only the light from one corner unit and the moon lighted his work, but for Jackson that was enough. Mostly by memory he finished staining the bottom of the bench. He rested the brush across the can and stood up and lit a cigarette and looked toward town. The scent of smoke replaced the stain's fumes. Not moving chilled him. While holding the smoke between his lips he buttoned his flannel. The lights in Joe's Bar were brighter than when he'd left. Maybe loggers had come down for the evening. He wondered whether someone on the deck could see his one, small orange light. Jackson took a drag. Above the rocks strode a hunched-over figure with something on his back. It was that young man from the bar. Jackson almost hadn't recognized him, since the boy now wore a black stocking cap. He raised a hand as the boy neared him. Change your mind? he said.

Maybe, the young man said. It's cold.

Damn right.

Are nights always this cold in June?

Depends on the night, son. Jackson took another drag.

What do you charge?

Thought I'd put you in one of those units for free. Jackson threw a thumb over his shoulder.

For free? Why? The young man squinted.

That the young man was suspicious of generosity seemed promising, Jackson thought. He then scowled, realizing Marilyn had indoctrinated that in him. Those units are closed, Jackson said, for the construction of the second story. You'd need to be out by 7 a.m.

Not a problem, the young man said. Thank you.

Jackson nodded. I'll let you in. He crushed the last of his cigarette under his boot, picked up the can of stain and brush, led the young man up the small incline, and unlocked the corner room. The young man's eyes widened when he saw the kitchenette. You can use it, Jackson said. Just don't make a mess.

Thanks again, the young man said. He held out a grubby hand, which Jackson shook.

Jackson walked back to the laundry room and stowed the can and brush. Realizing he hadn't eaten dinner, he headed upstairs to find food. The office doorbell rang before he reached the apartment. He swung in a circle and stepped back down. Such interruptions were routine and he didn't mind them. The young man, rubbing his red cheek, stood by the desk.

Do you have some toilet paper? he asked. I'll pay you.

You don't need to pay, Jackson said. One second. In the closet he reached to the top shelf but didn't feel anything. He stood on his toes and looked around. Nothing but a slab of board until the wall.

He walked through the laundry room and into the lounge. A closet near the piano kept the toilet-paper overflow. Inside he found extra hand and bath towels, extra paper towels, and two chipped mugs. The closet smelled like bleach. He rubbed the side of his beard. Shouldn't Annie have noticed they were out? Shouldn't she have told him? Probably, but that wasn't her job. Marilyn did toiletries inventory. He shuffled around the items in the closet one more time, just in case, and chuckled as he grabbed a roll of paper towels. Looks like we're out of toilet paper, son, Jackson told the young man as he handed him the roll. This'll have to tide you over.

OK, the young man said.

My wife's been gone awhile. She's the one who did inventory.

I'm sorry for your loss.

She ain't dead, Jackson said. Just on some kind of extended vacation. Things'll right themselves soon enough.

The young man held up the paper towel roll. Well, thanks, he said.

Sure, Jackson chuckled. Good night.

As the young man was leaving, Jackson pulled on his jacket, popping up the collar for warmth. He went to his truck and started it and drove down The Wave's entryway and pulled onto the highway. All the way to the general store he laughed at his incompetence, intermittently slapping the wheel.

While Tim slept, he dreamed. He was in Micah's fishing boat far out in the ocean: he couldn't see shore. A light blue sky arched over deep blue water. Harsh waves produced white caps. The boat rocked agreeably. He was paddling, as though the fishing boat were a canoe. Somehow a normal-size paddle reached the water from the deck. A couple of his elementary-school friends appeared. They began paddling too. One deep-sea sturgeon jumped in front of the boat. Another one jumped to the side. Soon sturgeons jumped all around the boat while the three kids paddled through. Some were as small as Tim's head, others as large as his wingspan. Their black eyes seemed dumb. Rainbows glistened as sunlight fell against their gray, oily skin.

Tim opened his eyes and looked out the window. The sun touched the water; he figured it was past eight. Vaguely thinking of his dream, he rolled off the couch and pulled the plastic covering over it. Dust scattered and he sneezed. From the kitchen counter he snatched his backpack. The room smelled like cocoa. He shut the front door quietly behind him. He froze when he saw Mr. Yager outside the lighthouse's front door. The old man was picking up pinecones around the yard. Every time he kneeled, he held his back. Lana ran from the anteroom, dropped down, and rolled over. Mr. Yager placed the pinecones inside, rubbed her belly, then headed up the long driveway. As the dog stood, she glanced in Tim's direction before following her owner. Tim let out his breath and jogged in the opposite direction, into the forest. He'd napped through suppertime and wanted to hurry home so he could eat.

As the days had become longer and warmer, Tim had visited Mr. Yager's old house more and more. The old man took walks in the early mornings or early afternoons or late evenings, usually later than tonight. Tim avoided those times, so Elliot wouldn't see him. He came in the late mornings, in the midafternoons, sometimes late at night, and slept there. It had become a game to outsmart the old man. As Tim became more familiar with the house, he became more comfortable sleeping there, at least downstairs. Once, in the middle of the night, he'd made a fire in the fireplace.

Jackson's lack of attention made Tim's solo excursions easy to enact. Grab a few starfish, his dad might say, as Tim, backpack bouncing, ran past the units in construction, where his dad was working. But after such an interchange, unless his dad was looking for him to watch the office, Jackson didn't notice whether Tim was gone five minutes or five hours. As long as Tim returned by breakfast, his dad didn't detect that he'd stayed away overnight. Tim enjoyed the freedom until he became lonely and wanted someone to know or wonder where he was.

His mom would have wondered. His first memory was playing on a beach south of The Wave. He'd wandered away from his parents and had fallen asleep a couple inlets away, his cheek resting on warm sand. His mom found him and carried him back to where she and his dad sat. Tim cried at the sand in his mouth.

Now, his mom wasn't near enough to worry. Sometimes she called and asked about his day, what he did and ate. She was happy that his dad was letting him handle motel money. Sometimes she asked him to come to The Sweet Seller on some pretense, such as picking up free baked goods. She never came to The Wave. One time she called and said that a college student had left a record. When Tim saw that it was the newest Dylan, *Blonde on Blonde*, still in its wrapping, he knew his mom had bought it for him. When he told her so, she blushed. Tim blushed as well but didn't know why. After all, he'd thought, she was the one who'd lied. Another time she gave him ten dollars cash. She beamed as she handed the money across the counter. For new clothes, she said. You'll have to show me what you buy. So far, he hadn't bought anything because he hadn't left Kalapuya all summer. Usually, his mom took him on such outings. They should've visited the dunes by now.

The day had been warm, but the evening was cool. Tim jogged until he could walk without shivering. Beyond him, on rocks, a man and two small children leaned over, examining tide pools. Far beyond them, on the other side of the stretch of beach, town lights shone brighter and brighter in the growing darkness. Tim tripped on something and looked down. Finding a rock, he kicked it. It jumped a foot ahead. He kicked it again and again. His stomach growled so he moved on without.

His dad had taken down the rope boundary line. For a week, people had talked about it at the grocery store and The Sweet Seller. Then a couple of guests came into the office one morning and claimed they'd tripped over it the night before. One showed Jackson and Tim his limp, the other his scraped knee. His dad apologized to the guests and took it down, telling Tim that he didn't need a lawsuit. Money would be tight for a couple of years.

His dad spent hours in the closet-office trying to figure out bills and finances. About once a week, he swore over the sound of Tim's records. Tim didn't know whether his dad wasn't as competent as his mom, whether their financial situation had deteriorated because of the new units, or if it was something else entirely.

As Tim passed the bench, he saw his dad kneeling. Jackson had a can next to him and was rubbing against the seat of the bench with a red rag torn from one of Tim's toddler shirts. The scent of stain wafted toward Tim. The sun was now a line of orange light between dark blue sea and dark blue sky. Hadn't his dad said you needed good light while painting? Tim jogged between the units and entered the lounge. No muffins were left so he headed toward the apartment. In the office, a man with dark complexion stood at the desk.

May I help you? Tim said.

Out of toilet paper, the man said.

Tim handed him the last roll from the closet. His stomach growled. He was supposed to refill the shelf with rolls from the lounge, but his mom wasn't here to enforce that rule and his dad didn't notice what he had or hadn't done.

After the man left, Tim took the stairs two at a time. In the kitchen, he made himself a ham sandwich with tomato and mustard. The waves were barely visible between framing for the new units. Since his mom left, he and his dad had gotten into the habit of cooking one kind of meat—a ham, a chicken, or a turkey—picking off that till it was gone, then cooking another.

Tim also ate all the baked goods he could, sometimes two or three a day.

In the living room, Tim turned on the television and plopped on the couch, sandwich in hand. More war footage. Searching for Carl, Tim scanned the young men's faces. Since his mom left, the war had escalated. Or maybe only coverage of the war had escalated. Who knew?

Agates stabbed Tim's bottom. He reached into his back pocket, pulled out three, and set them on the windowsill ledge behind the couch. Across the street, in front of the units, a row of cars was parked. Guests filled nine of the ten available rooms, but this group was relatively quiet. All of his agates lay on the windowsill ledge now instead of in his mom's jewelry box.

When his mom had first called and requested that he visit The Sweet Seller and say hello, he wouldn't go. If you want to say hello, come here, he'd said. He didn't understand why he had to leave The Wave to see her.

A few days later, he discovered that his mom's jewelry box and all of his agates were gone. He became angry and called his mom. You took my agates, he said. I didn't mean to, she said. You can come get them. He didn't know whether she meant to or not. Maybe she'd planned the blackmail all along. That didn't sound like his mom, but leaving just because she and dad didn't agree didn't sound like her either. How long would she be gone, he wondered. Forever? In elementary school, the parents of a friend had divorced. His dad had said, When your mom comes back. . . . But for some reason his dad thought the best would happen. Even Tim knew better than that. He waited until he'd collected more agates and really wanted to compare them to his old ones. When he went to The Sweet Seller, his mom wasn't there. Leah said she was canvassing for the Beach Bill and gave him his agates in a paper bag. Tim threw five of the best into the ocean on the walk home. They shimmered in an arc, plopped, and disappeared.

At his dad's request he'd returned to The Sweet Seller for baked goods. On warm days his mom took him to get ice cream at Lollipops. She'd cup her hand around his chin; she'd chide him for not finishing math problems. Mostly tender, at times severe. That she acted the same seemed strange to him.

Tim had never seen Carl on television. It didn't surprise him; a few hundred thousand troops were over there now. Still, every evening, when he heard the coverage on Vietnam, he thought of Carl. In a little over a week, for the Fourth of July, Carl's family would stay at The Wave. His parents, maybe an uncle or aunt and cousin or two. The cousins were too young for Tim to play with, and anyway, they were girls. He changed channels and finished an episode of *Star Trek*. When he heard his dad on the stairs, he placed his plate in the sink, went into his room, and closed the door. He dropped the needle on *Blonde on Blonde* so he wouldn't hear his dad's movements.

Tim took out his poetry notebook from between his schoolbooks, its hiding place. If you wanted to hide something, he'd heard, you should hide it in an obvious place. No one would rummage in his schoolbooks, and thus no one would find his notebook. Sitting on his bed, he opened the notebook and turned each page, smoothing them as he went, until he came to a blank one. He'd finished his poem on the wind. *Always calling, always crying*, the poem ended, *never dawdling, never dying*. He'd written a couple other poems, but he liked the wind one best. One of the poems he disliked was about his mom. No doubt inspired by Dylan's love song, in it he wondered why she left. He mentioned the lack of her scent around the house. The emotions bothered him. He kept it but tried not to reread it while he flipped through.

Today he wrote the words *sea lions* at the top of a page. The creatures near the lighthouse had become used to him. They didn't turn their heads as he walked by. Just that afternoon he'd sat and dangled his feet off rocks while they burrowed below. The tide came in and they allowed it to pull them out to sea, their huge bodies rolling on the waves. They seemed like lazy creatures, Tim thought. *Soft and rubbery, critters of the sea,* he wrote, and smiled. He felt calm and playful.

In the hallway the phone rang. Tim poised his pen above paper. His father, who was shuffling around the kitchen, answered. When Jackson asked, Do you want to talk to Tim?, Tim knew it was his mom. He put down his notebook, crawled to the other side of the room, and crouched at the window. If his dad put down the phone and walked toward his room, Tim planned to crawl onto the wide second-story eave and drop onto a firewood box.

Tim doesn't need to be around hippies, Jackson said. Then, No. I'm taking care of him, right? His father hung up.

Tim relaxed against the wall. He ran his finger along a grain of wood on the windowsill and looked at the stars, not often visible. Did she invite him to a student gathering? If he didn't have to see his mom, he wouldn't mind going. The students might bring new music. And Leah herself had a record collection that he hadn't explored. He crawled back to his poem. Unable to think of sea lions because his mind had turned to his mom, he closed the notebook and pushed it between schoolbooks. He again looked at the stars, those distant balls of fire. No one had taught him the constellations, maybe because there were so few clear nights in Kalapuya. Maybe he'd learn in high school, but two years to wait seemed so long.

His dad's footsteps approached. Instead of going downstairs, they entered his room. Tim crossed his arms. He wished he had a lock. His dad smiled, pleased to find him. Tim sensed that his dad didn't know whether he'd be there or not.

Come with me, his dad said. I want to show you something.

His dad led him downstairs, out of the office, to the front of the new units. Light shone through a crack in the curtains on the lower story.

Is someone in there? Tim asked.

In the darkness, Tim could barely make out his dad's nod.

Are you letting people stay in it again?

Just for tonight, his dad said. Come to the other side. Tim followed his dad to the ocean side, where he smelled newly coated stain. Jackson plucked at his beard. But we could let people stay in them again, his dad said. We could give a discounted rate. Stain clung to Jackson's hand. Without thinking, he rubbed it against his jeans. They'd been losing money by closing all five units during the peak season, he thought. Sometimes, when he flipped the sign to "No Vacancy," he felt as though he were lying. He'd leave it on "Vacancy" until these rooms were full. Five dollars off sound reasonable? his dad asked.

Tim didn't know and sensed his dad wasn't really talking to him. His mind wandered toward Mr. Yager's house, the rooms he hadn't yet explored. He wanted to spend a night upstairs, to rid himself of fear. He wanted to descend into the basement for the same reason. There was no light switch near the basement door and no ground-level windows to let in light. At first, he'd thought brown recluses, black widows, or rats lived down there. Lately he'd imagined that a tunnel led from basement to sea. Florescent deep-sea creatures swam between basement and ocean, comfortable in both spheres. Slowly the water level would rise, someday reaching the main level of the house. The sea creatures would either take over or die.

For these new rooms we'll charge more, his dad was saying. Tim wasn't sure what he'd missed. I want you here at eight o'clock sharp.

Why? Tim asked.

To help with the new units, like I said.

I don't know anything about construction.

You'll learn. If they need a tool, you'll get it for them.

I can do more than that.

Maybe after you learn the tools. Didn't you just say you didn't know anything about it?

Yessir, Tim said. His first thought had been to get out of it, so he could go to Mr. Yager's house. His second thought was that his dad, by designating him as the gopher, was treating him like a little kid.

You'll work until at least lunchtime, his dad said.

Yessir.

Jackson started toward the office, Tim close behind. There, Jackson thought. Learning construction was more beneficial than whatever Tim would learn at one of Leah's parties. What he really should have told the boy, Carl's death, he'd pushed deep inside him while staining the bench. He hadn't remembered the news until he'd seen the bench again a minute ago, and even then, his thoughts had turned to Marilyn, that telling Tim was her responsibility. He'd tell her soon. He couldn't have tonight, with Tim listening.

Tim returned to his room, while Jackson plopped on the couch. Television noises filled the main room. Tim unlatched the window and pushed it up. He stepped over the sill and turned away without closing the window. He walked with ease along the wide eaves, sat at the end of the row, hanging his legs, then lowered himself onto the lounge's woodbox. An uneven landing from the bulging wood forced him to slide off. In the lounge, a family sat at a table around a board game. A little girl in pigtails stood on her chair while an older boy read the directions out loud. The parents held hands under the table. Tim walked around to the office and back up to his room. He completed this circle three more times, just to see whether his dad would notice.

3.

For the first couple weeks that Marilyn woke at The Sweet Seller, she was unsure of her whereabouts. Then she'd see light out the window on her right, instead of on her left, like at The Wave, and she'd remember. As she'd blink toward the ceiling and the deep blue walls of Leah's guest room, her chest would expand from anxiety and excitement, as though she were in a boat with the sea surrounding her and she were looking into a clear, night sky.

Marilyn assisted Leah's baking on the weekends and ran the register on weekday mornings. The comforting scents and physical labor in baking directed her mind away from her and Jackson's relationship, whereas bookkeeping and accounting had for months been a catalyst for such thoughts. While running the register, she'd encounter townspeople who wanted to know the whys. She'd ignore inquisitive looks and reply to questions by saying no more than, I'm staying with Leah for a while.

In addition to the new tasks and Leah paying her, Marilyn's days differed from those at The Wave in that she could leave anytime. Go on a drive, Leah would say. Didn't you want to see the North Coast? To drive for the sake of driving seemed frivolous to Marilyn, but she often walked along the beach during the day—something unheard of at The Wave—accompanied Leah on Beach Bill work, and even made a few canvassing trips on her own.

Besides short trips from Kalapuya to Toledo to visit her parents or from Kalapuya to Newport or to Florence for supplies, Marilyn had never driven alone. Either Tim sat next to her—as a small child, quiet, then for a half-dozen years, talkative, and now as an adolescent, quiet again—or she sat in the passenger's seat while Jackson drove. While driving alone her mind wandered. She usually checked it and forced herself to rehearse the Beach Bill spiel. But on one particular trip on the last day of June, when she was driving all the way to Astoria, the only town near the coast that she or Leah hadn't canvassed, Marilyn recognized that she knew the spiel by heart and allowed her mind to roam.

Images from Toledo rose: playing with dolls in a tree house, the rope swing over the river's swimming hole, routes through town she walked to school. Her childhood felt more varied than her ten years working at Vic's Café. The repetitive cleaning and inane people. She found few customers remarkable and said as little as possible to most. She loved escaping to the back to do finances. Vic liked that she didn't become involved with customers, but many regulars, citing this aloofness, called her a *bitch*. The word stung, but whenever she worked figures, she forgot insults and became joyfully entrenched. After a few years, she ran the place's accounts and had to train Vic before she left. He was more apathetic about his business than Jackson. This lack of caring bothered her, but he'd also allowed her to spend money how she saw fit. At The Wave, Jackson allowed her to order only toiletries and cleaning supplies.

As she drove along cliffs, around curves, and through fog, she thought of The Sweet Seller, where the person who did the accounts made the financial decisions. She and Jackson, who both ran The Wave, should have a say in both. Assistance on the finances would be useful to her, but right now, Jackson knew so little that he'd get in the way, like Tim before he knew how to cook and wanted to *help*. This analogy gave Marilyn pause. She'd taught Tim to cook. Should she have taught Jackson how to run accounts? But he'd never wanted to learn the nuts and bolts, only for her to give him a summary so he could have his authoritative say. Who was she kidding, Marilyn thought. Since Jackson wouldn't even pay her, why did she imagine they'd ever share such duties?

Fog gave way to low clouds of smoke and steam. A cone-shaped, tree-tall metal furnace on the side of the road blazed with wood scraps. The sounds of the Warrenton mill filled the car. Its scents reminded her of Toledo. As far as she knew, her parents didn't know she'd left Jackson. But Oregon was small, and she expected a call from them any day. Maybe a neighbor of theirs would stay at The

Wave or they'd call The Wave and Jackson would tell them. She was surprised such a scenario hadn't already happened.

Upon entering Astoria, Marilyn pulled her car into a parking lot overlooking the Columbia River and ate her sack lunch. Chicken and mustard between slices of Leah's honey whole wheat bread, a red apple, a Hershey's chocolate bar. She left the radio and heat on. Out the window, beyond blowing knee-high grass, lay a thin stretch of beach. A couple lounged while a small child built a sandcastle. Two older children with rolled-up jeans jumped tiny waves. The whole family wore long sleeves, as did a solitary man farther along the beach. As long as the coast was this cool in summer, the beaches would never be overcrowded, Marilyn thought. That argument against the Beach Bill didn't hold.

Marilyn's indifference toward the bill had morphed into a quiet advocacy. She had initially canvassed for the solitude and to feel the freedom of travel, and although those desires remained, she now spoke with conviction. At first going door to door felt intrusive; while she worked at Vic's Café or The Wave, people had chosen to come to her. And the number of smiles Leah flashed seemed unnatural and unattainable. When Marilyn was a child, everyone had told her to smile. Aren't you having fun? they'd ask at the annual lumberman contest. Don't you like cake? they'd say on her birthdays. You're not smiling. When she waitressed, men waited in vain for her to smile at their jokes about her not smiling. Regulars at The Wave had mentioned her stoicism to Jackson, who, to his credit, made fun of the guests' complaints, not her. Now, to demonstrate the positives in setting aside the beaches, Marilyn thought she should smile. The first time she spoke alone she forgot. As they walked from the house, Leah didn't mention it. After her second house, Leah praised her for remembering coastal history. On her third house, Marilyn tried to smile, but speaking and smiling for her didn't go hand in hand. After that, she didn't try, and no one mentioned it. She had enjoyed learning and responding to the views of different towns' citizens. But now that the issue had gained publicity, the door-to-door visits had become less necessary as well as less challenging, and she looked forward to the legislature's vote.

Marilyn took a street map from the passenger's seat and, laying it across the steering wheel, studied the town. After checking her watch and determining her route, she backed out, crossed a main road, and headed toward neighborhoods. If she hurried, she could hit up a couple hundred residences by suppertime.

The day went quickly. Walking the hills warmed her, and although the sky grew darker, rain held off. She liked that, while canvassing by herself, the aloneness of driving was punctuated by talking to people, but she also liked that most exchanges were brief, since most people had decided one way or another. For those against, Marilyn had learned how to pinpoint who might change their minds. Often they'd have a secondhand opinion, saying something like: Well, my uncle told me about that, and he doesn't like the idea. Or they'd repeat an easily debunked argument. With the resolute ones, Marilyn had learned not to waste her time.

The spires, stateliness, and high ceilings of some of Astoria's Victorian houses filled Marilyn with nostalgia for a discarded daydream. As a child she'd imagined that she, her future husband, and a handful of kids would live in such a house. Marilyn was old enough to know that the life you imagined as a youth didn't always suit the needs or personality of the adult you became. Although she would have liked another kid or two, five would have overwhelmed her, and she wouldn't have wanted to maintain such an old house.

While Marilyn canvassed the final street, the clouds turned dark. Just as the first drops hit her cheek, a younger man invited her inside. Marilyn usually declined such offers, but because the wind was pushing her jacket up her back, she stepped into the entryway and shut the front door.

My name's Marilyn Ryder, she asked. Have you heard of the Beach Bill?

Ryder, he said. Your husband owns that motel, right? The Wave?

It was Conrad Yager, she realized. He looked so much like Elliot. Conrad Yager, right? She held out a hand, and he shook it. You own this place?

No. Some friends invited me up for the weekend.

Marilyn had met Conrad only once, at Darlene's funeral. She'd meant to take Elliot a casserole or two after Darlene died, but maybe because she was busy comforting Leah, she never did.

What brings you up this way? Conrad asked.

Marilyn was bothered but not surprised that she'd run into someone she knew. I'm working on the Beach Bill, she said. She held out a brochure.

Conrad smiled, but not pleasantly. Marilyn withdrew the pamphlet. She remembered Elliot's scene in the shop that Leah had described to her.

Why are you canvassing? Conrad asked. It's not a referendum.

I'm trying to get people to write letters. The legislature has received thirty-five thousand.

Conrad raised his eyebrows, surprised at the amount.

I know your father's opposed, Marilyn said.

I'm not my father, Conrad said.

The boy was estranged from his father, she remembered. But he had seemed pained at his mother's funeral; he must have been close to her. I'm sorry for your loss, Marilyn said.

Conrad remembered the funeral, when people who didn't even know their family had wished him condolences and had remarked on Darlene and Elliot's love.

I don't know why she stayed with him, Conrad said.

Marilyn wasn't sure what he meant but felt like he wasn't really talking to her.

The funeral. You were there?

Marilyn nodded. Rainwater splashed against the long windows on either side of the front door.

Everyone kept praising their relationship, but I knew better. Did you know, when I was kid, he'd cheated on her?

Conrad didn't know why he'd said it. He wanted someone in Kalapuya to know the truth maybe. The memory of people praising their love had grated on him all winter.

Marilyn felt uncomfortable that he'd disclose this information to a relative stranger. I didn't know, she said.

Conrad looked down, maybe embarrassed by her discomfort, and grabbed the handle of an umbrella in a stand.

Marilyn's legs hurt. She wanted to sit in the car, maybe stop at a diner. People gaped at a woman eating alone, but since canvassing, she'd become used to it, and when hungry enough, didn't even notice. She opened the front door. I have a long drive back, she said. Nice to see you again. The rain hadn't stopped, but she didn't care.

Outside, she secured the clipboard against her chest and ran down the sidewalk. In the car, her wet clothes pressing against the seat, she shivered. Elliot the philanderer, she thought. Who would have guessed? She was surprised his wife knew. She'd often seen Elliot and Darlene grocery shopping. Darlene would pretend to sneak chocolate into the cart, while Elliot pretended to sneak beer. Marilyn opened the door and unbraided and wrung water out of her hair before she turned on the car.

Marilyn stopped at a Seaside diner, half-full of locals, half-full of tourists. She ordered a bowl of meat and potato stew and ate while rain pounded against the walls of windows. She wondered how The Wave had fared in such a wet June. According to her predictions based on past years, the number of summer nights with no vacancy would continue to increase regardless of the weather. However, when she'd left, they'd been fully booked for only two weekends of the month. A solo woman nodded at her. Marilyn nodded back. A heightened awareness occurred when in public alone. Marilyn appreciated what she noticed, even as she didn't like the attention. She wondered how Jackson was faring with the finances. He should have done the quarterly reports by now. It had been twenty years since she hadn't taken care of a business's finances, and she missed the work.

She ate every bite, paid, and continued driving south. The heavy rain followed her down the coast. Marilyn focused on the white line and what lay immediately ahead. Around Garibaldi, a logging truck slowed her down, but she didn't risk passing. Fortunately, it turned off. Two hours later, she pulled into The Wave and turned off the car. Her clothes were wrinkled but dry. She sat still, exhausted from driving in such hard rain. Drops against the hood made a hollow sound. She then realized she was in front of the motel office.

She went inside. The room smelled of cigarette smoke. A new pane set in the window frame. The window, for once, was closed.

In the closet-office, papers were strewn across the desk as though they'd been tossed there. Receipts sat in and around the tab holder. A dead bee lay on top of a half-eaten sandwich. Marilyn raised a hand to her mouth. She stepped toward the mess. She could organize some of these papers, she thought. She'd enjoy putting them in order. She bit her lip and stepped back. No, she wouldn't. Working without pay and decision-making authority had placed her in a subservient position for years.

In the outer office, the scheduling book lay open. Weekends were booked through August. The weekdays averaged about half-full. She checked the pages for May and June. Her eyes narrowed when she saw that Jackson had kept track only of reservations, not of how many rooms had been filled each night. So much for making predictions based on this summer.

On a notepad with The Wave name and logo across the top, she wrote: *Do you need a bookkeeper? I know one with fair rates. –Marilyn*

She smiled thinly. Jackson should enjoy that, with all his joking.

Back in the car, Marilyn pulled a U-turn and drove toward the highway. In front of Leah's, she killed the engine. She hadn't even driven the loop and looked at the new construction, she thought. She wanted to see how that was progressing. And why didn't Jackson, Tim, or Annie come to the office when the office doorbell rang? They shouldn't leave it unattended. But neither was her concern, she reminded herself. She wouldn't care until Jackson relented. She sucked in her breath, grabbed the clipboard and her purse, and stepped into the rain, which had settled into a mist. She pushed open Leah's door. Inside, her parents sat on the couch. Leah sat across from them in the recliner.

Leah stood and walked to Marilyn and took the clipboard from her outstretched hands. I said you might be back late because of the weather, Leah said.

Marilyn nodded to them. Let me change, she said. I'll be right out.

In the spare room, she took off her wrinkled skirt and blouse and put on nylons and a dark green housedress. Her body felt numb. She'd expected her parents in the abstract, but not tonight, not now. She ran a brush through her damp, ratty hair. Between running into Conrad and now them, the day seemed to be telling her she couldn't hide any longer. Back in the sitting room, she sat in the rocking chair next to Leah.

Leah had always liked Marilyn's parents, and they had always respected her. Linda had a good sense of humor and enjoyed baking. Richard kept Leah up to date on the insider scoop on the region's logging news, which she craved as one will from time to time crave aspects of childhood.

To Linda, Leah's upbringing was strange but acceptable because she was half-orphan. Her father had done the best he could. Richard had less reverence toward what whites considered a traditional family. If he thought of her upbringing at all, he didn't think it abnormal.

But that evening their conversation had been strained. Both parents had avoided speaking of Marilyn leaving Jackson. Leah's forthright nature disliked this avoidance, but not wanting to discuss the situation with Marilyn's parents before her friend had a chance to do so, she avoided the topic, too. Plus, the Fourth of July rush started tomorrow. Leah hadn't accompanied Marilyn so that she'd have time to plan. Usually able to dismiss work when hosting, tonight Leah kept thinking on it.

When Marilyn sat, Leah stood. After she caught her friend's pleading eyes, she walked toward the kitchen instead of the bakery. Marilyn wanted her to stay. Leah set the teapot on the stove and pushed away the thought of what needed to be baked. Would anyone like tea? she asked.

They all three did so she added water. By the time anyone spoke, Leah felt the heat of the burner against her face.

Leah says you've been canvassing for the Beach Bill, Richard said.

Yes, Marilyn said.

You were, where? Astoria?

That's right.

You must've driven by the mill.

Yes.

Richard spoke of a couple families he knew who worked there, while rubbing together his cracked, chapped hands. He himself had led planks out of the Toledo sawmill for almost forty years, retiring two years ago at age sixty-seven.

Leah set a porcelain pot of peppermint tea next to the record player. Linda lifted her thin hands to the steam rising from the spout. I drink more of this stuff in a winter than most people drink in a lifetime.

I hear you, Leah said. Keeps the dampness from the bones.

Marilyn was holding her hands, fingers interlaced, close to her waist. She wished Leah would continue to talk about something impersonal, like tea. Instead, her friend went to the kitchen, came back with cream-colored porcelain mugs, and poured each person a cup.

Can't do much more than listen now, Leah thought. She'd provided a room for Marilyn, where her friend could stay as long as she wanted, but she couldn't assist in family business, either with Jackson or Marilyn's parents. Leah wished she could communicate these thoughts to Marilyn, who was looking at her tea.

And what're you going to do with yourself now? Richard asked.

Excuse me? Marilyn raised her eyes.

Leah says you're almost done canvassing.

Yes, almost.

What then? You know Vic's Café'll take you back.

Marilyn took a sip and started when she burned her tongue. She surrounded the burn with saliva. She hadn't expected that suggestion. And Toledo held no interest for her now. On the first day after she left, when she woke up at Leah's and recoiled at the thought of going to Toledo and staying with her parents, she'd realized that whether or not she ever returned to The Wave or Jackson, Kalapuya had become her home.

That's so far from Tim, Linda said.

Not so far, Richard said.

Linda frowned and patted her dirty-blonde curls close to her head. She saw the spousal separation as impermanent. Hadn't she and Richard had their rough periods?

Dammit, bring him, too, Richard said. He placed a hand on Linda's knee. Because he'd never liked Marilyn's adopted life,

Richard hoped the separation was permanent. But he had compassion for the boy, and while they'd driven toward the coast, Linda had admonished him to wait and see.

Marilyn took another sip. Tim likes to play with guests, she said, especially in the summer. She looked toward the front door, at her father's boots that he'd owned for a decade. I'm good at accounting, she said, apropos of nothing.

That's true, dear, Linda said. It's a wonder how Jackson gets on without you.

Marilyn thought of the messy closet-office.

Leah said he's expanding, Richard said. Seems a little premature.

Linda squeezed Richard's hand. *It's none of our business*, the squeeze said.

For a moment Marilyn wanted to defend Jackson, to explain his plan for expansion and assert that it could succeed. I'm good at accounting, Marilyn repeated. Maybe I'll offer my services around here. Maybe I'll do that next.

To who, dear? Linda asked.

I don't know, Marilyn said. She drained the tea from the mug and set it on the floor. The warmth dissolved her chills. The idea was just something to say. Maybe it would become a reality. She hadn't thought of it until now.

Entrepreneurial ventures interested Leah. And this one could be perfect for Marilyn, she thought. Sandy needs some advice, Leah said, and that new hotel maybe.

Which hotel? Richard asked.

You passed it on the way in, Leah said. Or you passed the sign. You can't see it from the road.

As Leah described the hotel, Marilyn crossed her arms and relaxed against the rocker, rotating between the balls of her feet and her heels. Finally they were discussing something more impersonal.

But when she thought of working for the hotel, her emotions became complex. It was one thing not to work for The Wave; it was another to assist The Wave's competitor. Such work was like cheating on The Wave. She thought of Conrad's anger that afternoon, of Elliot's cheating. At least Jackson wasn't cheating, Marilyn thought. But that train of thought disgusted her. Marilyn's grade-school friend, whose dad beat her mom, used to say, at least he don't beat her, when she witnessed Marilyn's parents in a spat. That comparison didn't comfort Marilyn then, and this one didn't now. Not once had Jackson contacted her since she left, she thought. He must not want to reach a compromise.

That might be a good business for you, Richard said.

Marilyn stopped rocking. We'll see, she said.

And it'll keep you close to Tim, Linda said.

Yes, Marilyn said.

How is he? Linda asked. We were going to stop by—

He's fine, Marilyn said. And you can.

Leah stood. She cleared the empty teapot and mugs. As soon as possible, she should return to work. The family tableau became more intimate as she rinsed dishes. The three talked of Tim, his health and schooling. Marilyn had no reason to be reticent on these topics.

Outside, a car honked. Any precipitation had stopped. Leah thought of how she hadn't experienced such generational concern. She remembered when she almost ran away with a man at nineteen. A coastal mechanic had courted her on her work breaks in an alley. One day, sitting on a wooden pallet and smoking, he asked her to run away and she assented. She rode behind him on his motorcycle. City dropped away to rolling farmland, then to forests of dense trees. Halfway to the beach, he stopped at a gas station to buy smokes. Two truckers were filling up. When one asked where she was headed, she jumped off the bike and asked for a ride back to town. Although she loved the sea, she didn't love the mechanic. It wasn't time for her to live on the coast. She showed up for work the next morning and no one knew where she'd been. Over ten years later, when she married Micah, her father had met Micah as a formality, not to give approval. Fishing isn't as dangerous as logging, she remembered her father saying. It has that going for it.

Leah remembered seeing a man die after a log fell on him when she was ten. His speech became stilted, his face went ashen. She shook her head to remove the memory, then went to the bakery and came back with her ledger. Marilyn's parents were standing by the outer door. They both hugged Marilyn and raised a hand to Leah. After they left, Marilyn told Leah her parents were headed to visit Tim.

Leah sat on the couch, ledger on her lap. He's welcome here anytime, she said.

Marilyn stood behind the rocking chair. She imagined Tim glaring at her from the other side of The Sweet Seller counter. His monosyllables over the phone. He's upset, she said. I don't think he understands.

How could he? Leah said. No one does completely. Do you?

No, Marilyn said. She grasped two of the rocking chair's wooden bars. I mean, not completely, no.

You could sit him down and—

I could, Marilyn said. Maybe I will. I thought I'd told him enough.

What did you say?

Just that his dad and I have some things to work out. She'd used this line the night she left and also when she called him from Leah's the next morning.

Maybe that's all he needs to know.

Marilyn clenched the bars tighter. But he's upset, she said.

Why wouldn't he be?

He has that right, Marilyn said. I know he wants me there.

But he lived with Jackson and me. He sensed the tension. You think he'd understand I need a break from that. You'd think he'd need a break too.

He's just a kid, Leah said.

I know, Marilyn said. I can't fault him for wanting his mom back.

When Marilyn had moved to Kalapuya, her mom was guardedly happy; although she liked Jackson, she'd hoped Marilyn would find a spouse closer to home. Her dad hadn't understood her desire to live on the coast; his grandma had left the coastal reservation in 1875, when the government allowed white people into the area. She figured if white people were everywhere, she might as well move inland, Richard had told Marilyn more than once. Our family had enough trouble trying to farm the godforsaken coast. Marilyn had wanted too much understanding from her parents, she thought, and she'd wanted too much from her son.

Did you want your parents to understand too? Leah asked.

No, Marilyn said. They hadn't lived with her and Jackson. I simply wanted to respond to my parents' concerns.

And you did.

Marilyn glanced at the ledger. I just want it to feel final, she said. Like bookkeeping or something.

Thinking of Micah, Leah frowned. Memories of him had a startling and unwelcome finality. Nothing in life's final except for death, she said. And that's good. Don't you think?

Marilyn sat down in the rocker. She didn't know whether she agreed with that. Leah flipped open the ledger and examined figures. Marilyn stared past her. One of Leah's neighbors walked a shaggy white dog through the porch light. Finality could come, she thought, but she wanted the feeling of finality without making a final decision. She wanted comfort not backed up by logic; she wanted her feelings to lie.

Leah caught her friend's eye and set down her pen. For a couple months after I married, I dreamed about other men, she said. Did you have that experience?

Marilyn shook her head.

It surprised me. Years before, one of my suppliers in Portland had told me she'd had such dreams right before her marriage. I thought they meant that she wasn't sure about marrying her husband. Then I had similar dreams *after* marriage. And Micah and I were happy.

Men you'd dated before Micah? Marilyn asked.

Yes, them, Leah said, but others, too. Former customers, even loggers from my dad's camp. People I hadn't thought of in years. After maybe three months, the dreams stopped. I came to understand them as a necessary mourning for lives I could have led. They didn't mean I didn't love the life I had. Leah picked up her pen.

Marilyn remembered that after Micah died, Leah hadn't left her house for a week. Relatives and friends from Newport, Portland, and Seattle came bearing food. Each morning and evening, a rabbi led a service in this sitting room, where participants read Psalms and prayers in Hebrew. During the second week, the services and visits ceased, but Leah kept The Sweet Seller closed. Marilyn thought this allowance for grief had enabled Leah to more quickly return to equilibrium. She remembered Phil's funeral: the short service, burial, and the potluck. She and Jackson had returned to work the day after. For months Jackson had grimaced at the television in the lounge, and he eventually moved it to a large unit. Their ceremonies had been similar to the rest of Protestant society's, but they hadn't been enough.

Leah looked up. I've been meaning to ask, would you be interested in working for me full-time between the Fourth and Labor Day? I'm going to need someone.

Marilyn rested her elbows on her knees and leaned forward. Bookkeeping? she asked.

A bit of everything, Leah said. Especially during the peak season, she'd come to rely on Micah for last-minute supply replenishments. And even with his help last summer, she almost hadn't managed.

Marilyn leaned back. She thought of the summer busyness of The Wave. She didn't know how Jackson would handle it alone. This work could help her keep her mind off that. And by September she needed a long-term plan. After Labor Day, Tim should again begin schooling. Sure, she said.

That was easy.

I need something to occupy the time. Marilyn rocked back and forth. I might look into helping Sandy too. You sure she'd like someone to do bookkeeping?

I don't know if *like* is the right word, Leah said. But I've told her she needs to hire someone and she's agreed. She won't turn down someone who approaches her and who lives across the street; I'm sure of that.

Marilyn smiled. What's her story anyway? she asked.

Her story?

Where's she from? Marilyn wanted to continue to think about someone or something other than herself.

From here, Leah said. Why do I know more than you about townspeople? You've lived here longer.

Not by much, Marilyn said. And you care more.

Leah laughed. She couldn't argue with that. Today would already be a late night, she thought, so why not make it a little later? Sometimes people needed stories more than food. She closed the ledger and rested her elbows against it. She told the story of Sandy's great-great-grandparents, who didn't settle in the Willamette Valley like many early pioneers but drove their wagon through the valley, across the Coast Range, and all the way to Kalapuya, to the coast.

4.

It was evening; The Sweet Seller was closed. Marilyn had left with Tim to visit her parents. Leah had opened the back windows and propped open the front door with a chair to allow a cross breeze. She was mixing ingredients for loaves of wheat-germ bread and thinking how well the Fourth of July week had gone. The week of the Fourth was the most profitable week of the year, and The Sweet Seller had made 50 percent more this year than last. Leah took out the electric mixer and plugged it in and turned it on and watched the thick dough swirl around the beaters slower and slower until the dough clotted and she pulled it out with her hand. This recipe needed both thick dough and to use the electric mixer; she'd found no way around it. She and Micah had discussed traveling to the Northeast some fall when they had extra money. Micah wanted to try fresh Eastern seafood, and Leah wanted to see the fall foliage and maybe look up her mother's family. Alone, the trip no longer appealed to her. She wanted to buy a Deepfreeze, she thought, and the oven could use an update. If she stayed around Kalapuya, she'd do that. After extracting the dough from the beaters, she stirred in three cups of wheat germ, then she greased trays and formed the dough into six loaves. She covered the loaves with plastic and set them in the fridge, where they'd sit until the morning, when she'd bake them. As she closed the front door, mist fell on her arms. She set the chair back at its table and wiped the rainwater off with a cloth.

She felt grimy and was thinking of taking a shower as she stepped from shop to house and heard the phone ringing. It was her acquaintance Ethan Lewis, the charismatic leader of the Eugene chapter of Citizens for Oregon Beaches, who said that the bill had been signed into law. Now all the crazies will begin their lawsuits, he said. But it's a law, Leah. It's not going anywhere.

That's great news, Leah said.

Do you want to come to Salem for a party? he asked. Next Friday? A bunch of chapters are meeting there.

I have too much work to do, Leah said. But thanks for the invite.

After she hung up, she sat for a minute in the chair next to the phone table. Light rain splattered against windows. She stepped to the side of the record player, where a glass container full of seashells and a framed photograph of her and Micah sat on a thin wall shelf. She and Micah stood above the sea on the rocks at the end of their street. The wind blew her short hair sideways. As usual, Micah smiled only with his eyes. Micah and college students had given her the shells. The ones toward the bottom of the jar, collected by Micah, were larger and less blemished than the small snail shells toward the top collected by the students. She ran a finger over the shiny, whorled interior of a smaller one and dug out a larger one to hold to her ear and listen to what as a child she'd called the sound of the sea. And now all the seashells would be public land, she thought. It was the first political project in which she'd participated, and if someone had asked for her thoughts, she would have said that she was happy at how many people the bill would affect, both now and especially, for Kalapuya, in the future. The town might have become more isolated if some local beaches were off-limits; now, more people might visit or even move there. But Leah also had a deeper, sinking feeling, as though she'd been exploring a cave and had come to the back wall.

She took out a sand dollar. It was round, but the star in the middle had cracked off, leaving a gap. It was difficult to find whole sand dollars, especially for out-of-town college students who rushed or didn't know where to look. Unlike what she'd told Ethan, work wasn't the reason she wouldn't go to the party. The committee hearings she'd attended in Salem had made her wary of bureaucrats, politicians, and professional activists. They dressed well and talked in a language of their own. Although many didn't know each other, they joked as though they did. And even when they spoke of serious matters, their tone remained casual. Leah didn't know what she'd wear to the party and couldn't have feigned intimacy even if she wanted to. She and they had little in common but something abstract.

She took out a thumb-size snail shell that looked like a small coil of dough and followed the circular shape with her pointer finger. What was she to do now? Work on another cause? But she wasn't interested in any others and didn't see a reason to have a cause just to have a cause. Move to Portland? There, she'd live in a place that wouldn't remind her as much of Micah, and she'd have a larger year-round customer base. She thought of the college students and regulars she'd leave behind, as well as Marilyn and Sandy. She thought of her loneliness when she first moved to the coast. How not having the option to be near a community of people she knew made her feel ill. She placed the shells and sand dollar back in the jar. Wind whistled and whipped between houses. Hoping to dispel her low spirits, Leah called her outspoken friend.

Sandy answered, and Leah told her the news.

Congrats, Sandy said. You calling to invite me to the party?

Party?

You're going to celebrate, right?

I was invited to a party in Salem—

Salem? Those people wouldn't know a party if it showed up at their door.

Leah smiled.

I can host, Sandy said. How about next Friday?

Leah thought of Sandy's house, an extension of her cluttered antique shop. It smelled like cats and cigarette smoke. I can host, Leah said. But maybe you can round up people? Who were you thinking?

Anyone who views this as a victory, Sandy said. Invite those college kids of yours. They make me feel young.

You just want to talk Vietnam, Leah said.

After hanging up, Leah went to the refrigerator, where a piece of paper on which students had collaged their names and numbers hung. Each signature, whether small or large, straight or curved, denoted a distinct personality. She took the sheet to the phone, sat down, and began to dial. Almost everyone she reached said they'd come. At the sound of excited voices, she herself became eager to have a party. Culminations, whether sad or joyful, required gatherings as a kind of cathartic release. Her Jewish heritage should have taught her that. After she'd phoned everyone, she left the sheet on the side table to remind her to re-call the ones who hadn't answered. The rain had quieted. The wind still whistled. As she stood to head to the shower, the phone rang. Expecting Sandy's voice, and a list of those she'd recruited, Leah answered with an enthusiastic hello.

Hello, this is Conrad Yager.

Leah sat from surprise. Elliot's son, right?

That's correct. Is this Leah Tolman?

Yes.

Conrad coughed. I got your number from Ethan Lewis. I hope you don't mind.

Not at all. How may I help you?

I might be able to help you.

How's that?

Well. My father intends to will me his property.

Oh? Leah was surprised.

And I intend to sell it.

Leah didn't respond.

Ethan told me you were interested in new opportunities, Conrad said. I thought you might want to buy.

Can you sell something you don't yet own? Leah asked dryly. She had told Ethan that, hadn't she. She'd said she wanted a different venture, something about wanting to expand her business or move out of town. At the time he'd seemed a safe confidant.

Not officially, Conrad said.

Why don't you contact Jackson Ryder? she asked. The Wave's closer to the lighthouse, and Jackson's expanding.

I don't think Jackson's as discreet. I hoped I could trust you not to tell my father.

Leah hadn't thought of telling Elliot until she was asked not to. She twisted the phone cord on a finger. What could I do with that property? she asked, more to herself than to Conrad.

Any number of things. Bed-and-breakfasts are becoming popular on the coast.

And your father thinks you're keeping it? That's why it needs to be a secret?

Conrad coughed again. Look, I could sell the land to a hotel chain and get more than you could afford to pay.

Then why don't you? Leah asked. His tone sounded like a playground bully's, and she had no patience for that.

I might. You're not interested?

Why not sell it to a chain? What's in this for you?

I want to keep the buildings intact. My father would want that.

Conrad was lying. He'd checked the zoning on the property. High-density residential or commercial structures weren't allowed. Just to tear down the lighthouse might require knowledgeable and connected maneuvering. Ethan had told him that Leah was working on that bill to preserve the coast, and he'd decided to spin his motives toward what he assumed were her sympathies.

From what I hear of you, you wouldn't care to respect your father's wishes, Leah thought, but figured she'd said enough, especially if she were considering the offer. It sounded appealing, but the old man might not die for fifteen or twenty years.

You still there? Conrad asked.

Yes.

I'm well off financially. I won't try to squeeze pennies from you.

I'll think about it, Leah said.

That's great. That sounds promising.

We haven't even talked cost. Leah stood.

Like I said, I'll work with you.

I'd want some kind of contract we could renegotiate every few years. I'm not starting a new business at sixty-five.

Conrad chuckled. My father won't be long now.

Leah crushed the phone cord in her hand. She'd had her own problems with the old man, but she didn't wish him dead. Did Conrad know something that she didn't? Did Elliot have a terminal illness? If I'm open to talking more, I'll let you know in two or three weeks, she said.

Fair enough, Conrad said. Take care.

Leah hung up and headed to the bathroom. She turned on the shower and changed her mind and plugged up the bath. After that conversation, she thought, she needed a nice long soak. She took off her red housedress and black bra and hung them on the peg where Micah used to hang his towel. She kicked her underwear onto the floor, stepped into the hot water, and lowered herself.

Aren't you gonna search me? Tim asked. I brought booze. And pot.

His mom pulled his arm, and he stepped into Leah's house, which right now smelled like her bakery. His mom kissed his cheek.

Tim rubbed off the kiss with the back of his hand. His mom wore a floral dress with a defined waist, her hair in a braid. Her dark eyes looked happy. Tim looked away. Some Beatles song played. In front of him, college students enmeshed in conversations lounged on the floor and couch. A guy wearing a blue bandana looked up and gave him a peace sign. From a girl wearing a loose red jumper, he heard the words *Beach Bill* and *Tom McCall*. In reality, Tim had brought nothing but newly found agates. He stuck his hand in his pocket and rubbed one between his thumb and forefinger. His mom linked his arm in hers and walked him toward the kitchen, where Sandy stood in front of the stove, talking to a man with a reddish-gray beard. They were asking each other which acquaintances they had in common. When Tim and Marilyn walked up, Sandy and Ned turned toward them.

My son, Tim, Marilyn said to Ned.

Ned, the man said. He held out a deeply wrinkled large hand and Tim shook it. Tim liked that Ned offered him a hand as though he were grown, instead of a nod or a pat on the back as though he were a kid. A platter of chocolate chip cookies sat on the counter that separated the kitchen from the living room. Ned followed Tim's eyes, took the platter, and held it out. Tim took a couple. I think that's what the students are here for, Ned said. You too?

Sure thing, Tim said.

Jenny Lee Baker's son's in Vietnam, Sandy said to Ned.

I heard that, Ned said. He took a cookie and set the platter back on the counter.

A tragedy, that's what it is, Sandy said.

Marilyn and Tim turned away. Tim thought of Carl. His mom must have, too, because she asked whether he'd talked to Carl's parents over the Fourth.

No, he said. They're coming the first week of August instead.

Your father talk to them on the phone?

I guess, Tim said. He'd finished the first cookie and started on the second. Each bite increased his hunger. On a low table in front of the couch sat a platter of peanut butter cookies and a bowl of macaroons. As he walked over and reached out, a guy on the couch spoke.

What did you do to help the Beach Bill, kid? he asked.

Tim froze. He couldn't hear or see anything except this guy. It wasn't the student who'd given him the peace sign, but an intent

young man with a pale face and black hair. The guy his dad let stay
for free in the kitchen unit, Tim realized. He'd seen this guy leave
the first morning he'd assisted the construction crew. I live here,
Tim said. Everyone on or near the couch laughed. The scene fell
into focus; Tim again heard music in the background. He grabbed a
macaroon and retreated toward his mom. He hated that he became
tongue-tied among groups of young adults. He wanted to be witty
but instead said something unrelated. His mom stood by the kitchen,
unaware, he thought, of the interchange.

I wonder why Eileen hasn't called me, she said, referring to
Carl's mom.

I dunno, Tim said. Maybe she doesn't know where you are.
He wanted to talk music with the students, but now they probably
thought him stupid. I'm going to the shed, he said. He hadn't looked
at Micah's fishing gear for a couple months.

OK, Marilyn said. She touched his shoulder as he walked by.
She'd heard the student's question and her son's answer. She felt
him feel rejected. He seemed more sensitive than other boys his
age, she thought. Was it the homeschooling? Maybe next year she
should drive him to junior high. Marilyn bit her lower lip. And why
hadn't Eileen called her? As their boys became friendly, she and
Eileen had followed suit. Surely Eileen would have asked Jackson to
ask Marilyn to call. Marilyn had left three months ago, and Jackson
hadn't once contacted her. Why must she always be the one to make
that effort? Still, she'd call and ask about Eileen. Eileen's extended
family always had a reunion the first week of August; why would
they bypass that to stay at The Wave?

Been telling Ned how you're trying to straighten out my
finances, Sandy said.

Marilyn turned.

She's good, Sandy said. She's proving it's not a hopeless cause.

Marilyn smiled faintly. She was used to loud expectations or quiet acknowledgement, not public praise. Sandy's finances had been as messy as her antique shop, but they were falling into place.

Been trying to think of who else you can sell your services to, Sandy said. Ned and I know this family, the McAlisters. They own an inn north of Newport.

The whole town knows they need help, Ned said. But how do you say that without offending?

That's what Marilyn told me, Sandy said. I wasn't offended.

No. Marilyn smiled widely. That's what *you* told *me*. I asked if you needed a few hours of tax prep next winter, and you said, if I died right now, my finances would take months to untangle.

Ned laughed.

Which inn? Marilyn asked.

Blue Beard, Ned said.

Leah emerged from the shop with three bottles of champagne in each hand.

Damn, Sandy said. I forgot to rinse the glasses. Marilyn, can you give me a hand?

After Sandy rinsed out each dusty glass, Marilyn dried it with a dish towel. Maybe she'd ask that family, the McAlisters, she thought. Just drop by—a cold call. Or make an advertisement or letter and send it out. Before she'd canvassed for the Beach Bill, such thoughts wouldn't have crossed her mind. But now, as long as they discussed business, not small-talked, she didn't mind as much initiating conversations with strangers.

Leah had popped the champagne bottles. She asked Ned to hand her the glasses.

A couple weeks ago, when Marilyn had fled to the antique shop to escape the holiday crowds in The Sweet Seller and was going through years of incomplete records in the back room, she'd realized that she truly enjoyed working on someone else's business accounts and that she enjoyed the money she made. She'd decided that she wanted to take on more freelance jobs, to enjoy life more in this way and to earn more money. This concrete desire she could fulfill fueled the foreign happiness that Tim had seen in his mom's eyes.

After Leah filled the glasses, Sandy distributed them. Her large figure teetered as she stepped around chairs and over legs. The students' talk fizzled. The intent young man—the self-appointed deejay—lifted the needle from the record.

Leah raised her glass. To the Beach Bill, she said. And to all of you who made the Beach Bill possible.

The students clicked glasses among themselves. Sandy, Ned, and Marilyn clicked glasses. Leah moved between the groups, raising her glass in individual and group toasts.

Ned and me didn't do a damn thing, Sandy said, once everyone had drunk.

You balance the youth here with your age, Leah said.

And let's toast to Bob Straub and everyone else working against the proposed highway, Laura suggested. Everyone raised their glasses again.

What's this about the highway? Sandy asked.

Some people want to turn the Nestucca Spit into a highway, Marilyn said.

I didn't know they were preserving the beach to build highways on, Sandy said.

That's what I said. Leah returned from the group of students. They proposed it the day after the Beach Bill was passed.

I told you something like this would happen, Sandy said. You gonna work against it?

Not right now, Leah said. She nodded at Marilyn. Marilyn might.

Sandy raised her thick eyebrows at Marilyn, and Marilyn nodded. I'm going to a debate on Monday, she said.

Leah had become upset when she'd read about the proposed spit, and rightly so, Marilyn thought. But her own first thought had been: I knew it couldn't be as simple as one bill. It was like a trigonometry proof that you proved too fast, then noticed you'd neglected to show your steps and had to go back and show them. Marilyn was content to keep working on the beach issue until they'd resolved every loophole.

The deejay dropped the needle onto the record. Laura and Jane came to the counter to refill their glasses. Leah handed them each an almost-full bottle, and holding them, they headed back to the vicinity of the couch.

Thanks for having me, Leah, Ned said.

Leah smiled, relaxed. You're welcome, she said. It was Ned's first visit since he'd come to sit shiva with her. During the winter, she'd thought of having him for supper, but they'd never had a one-on-one relationship. The party was a good excuse to invite him. Did you look at the fishing gear? she asked. It's up for taking. Since Micah's death, she'd in increments moved most of his belongings to the shed.

You know I'm done with all that, Ned said.

You still fish for fun.

He rubbed the back of his red neck. Maybe I'll take a look.

Can you send Tim back in here? Marilyn asked. That boy spent most of his life alone, she thought. Tonight, he needed to take the opportunity to be social.

Ned nodded, then left.

Leah wanted to talk to Marilyn about Conrad's offer, but her friend had arrived back in town only that morning, and they hadn't had a moment alone. The college students were discussing draft-card burnings—who they knew involved, whether or not they'd do it. Leah glanced at the pale-faced young man. Laura had told her that he was a dodger, but right now the girl kept quiet and the boy focused his eyes on a record sleeve. Sandy stepped forward, stepped back, and stepped forward again, within a foot of the students' circle.

How many of you've been part of a protest? she asked.

Leah caught Marilyn's eye and tipped her head toward the kitchen. They stepped inside.

Outside, Tim had finished looking over Micah's stuff. Now, he was in front of the house, searching for ripe cherry tomatoes. He twisted branches up and around, smelling the unique tomato scent. The yard hadn't held any flower or vegetable plants until a month or so ago, when Leah or his mom had planted half-grown flowers and tomato seedlings. At The Wave, until this year, his mom had grown flowers from seeds in the window boxes. He enjoyed watching The Wave's flowers sprout and grow; this kind of immediate garden seemed unnatural. He popped a light red tomato in his mouth and puckered and spit it out.

In the shed, he'd set aside one of Micah's poles for himself. Now that Micah was dead, no one he knew well fished, but the skill seemed worth knowing. What if he needed to strike out on his own like Bob Dylan was always doing? Even if he didn't know how to hunt, with a fishing pole he could find meat on the road. While squatting in sandy crevices, he'd watched The Wave's guests cast their lines off rocks. It didn't seem too hard.

Two more tomatoes he tried were bitter. He thought of writing a poem about The Wave's window boxes. Would he write them empty or full of flowers? He left the tomatoes half-chewed in the dirt and headed inside for more cookies.

What would you do with the place? Tim heard his mom say as he opened the back door.

Not keep the light, Leah said. That's a given. I don't know how to run a lighthouse.

Tim left the door open and crawled on the floor to the side of the counter opposite them.

Conrad suggested a bed-and-breakfast, Leah said. That might be a good challenge.

The offer seems a bit sketchy, Marilyn said.

The door creaked farther open. Leah walked around the counter to close it and saw Tim.

Tim's here, she said to Marilyn. She shut the door and walked toward Sandy and the students. She wondered how much Tim had heard and whether that mattered. Sandy sat on the floor, her breasts pushed against the coffee table. She was telling the students about a fifties commune near Waldport that she'd participated in. Leah took the empty platter to The Sweet Seller kitchen and loaded on the last two dozen. She set it back on the coffee table and stood over the group. She thought of Marilyn's skepticism.

Would you live in a place like that? someone asked. Asked her, presumably. Leah raised her eyes to Jane.

A commune? Leah asked. No, probably not.

Jane ruffled her blonde hair with her hand. It would feel so freeing, she said. To share all possessions.

Leah thought of the logging camps, the cramped sleeping quarters, the lack of privacy. One wants to experience what one hasn't, or can't, she thought. It gets bothersome, she said.

You've done it? Nathan asked. He was looking down while retying his bandana.

Lived in logging camps, Leah said. So, similar.

You just have to go into it with the right mindset, Sandy said. Give and take.

Maybe it takes a certain kind of person, Leah said. To do it long-term at least.

Anyone can do it, Sandy said. You just have to have the right mindset.

That mindset doesn't appeal to me, Leah said. I like to host. She gestured around the room. I like to share. But at the end of the day, I like to have my own space.

These kids aren't so set in their ways, Sandy said.

I'm game, Jane said. I have nothing going on next summer.

I'd rather just stay in my dad's hotel, Laura said.

Which hotel does your dad own? Leah asked.

He's building the one next door, Nathan said.

You dad owns that? Leah asked.

Laura nodded. He promised us we could all crash for a night when it's ready, she said, before it opens for guests.

Isn't he petitioning for rights to the beach?

He's trying for a few feet. We'll see.

Leah looked over her shoulder at Marilyn. Her friend had a hand on Tim's back, and they both walked toward the group. Tim's eyes darted over each student on the couch and floor. His arms were crossed; his body language spoke fear or reluctance. To me the students seem so young, Leah thought. To him they seem remote, experienced.

Laura's father owns the new hotel, Leah said to Marilyn.

Oh, Marilyn said. She and Tim sat on their knees. Marilyn placed a hand on Tim's knee. Tim removed it.

Does he have a bookkeeper? Sandy asked.

I think so, Laura said. Why?

We have a resident bookkeeper right here, Sandy said. Marilyn. If he needs one.

I'll let him know, Laura said.

What's this music? Marilyn asked one of the students, more for her son's benefit than her own.

The Byrds, Tim said. Come on, Mom.

You like music? the pale deejay asked.

Sure thing, Tim said. He rubbed his sweaty palms against his jeans. Maybe this guy would give him a quiz.

Like who?

Bob Dylan.

Cool. I just listened to *Blonde on Blonde* for the first time. "I Want You" is a great song.

I like "Memphis Blues," Tim said. He let out his breath. If they stayed on Dylan albums he could hold his own.

Marilyn was glad the new hotel had an accountant. She had enough work for now, and that option still seemed a betrayal. Marilyn wanted to thank this kid for talking to Tim. And not talking down to him either.

Sandy had moved from communes to women's rights. Or maybe she was still talking about communes, Marilyn thought, and how they gave women rights. Leah had crossed her arms. Marilyn didn't want to be too pessimistic toward Leah regarding Conrad's offer. Unlike Jackson, her friend had a nest egg. But signing a contract before Elliot's death? That seemed risky.

Throughout history men have traded in their women with little repercussion, Sandy said. In communes, women can trade their men too.

Many people don't want to trade at all, Leah said.

That's your experience, Sandy said.

Leah and Micah had agreed that the deepest romantic relationships were between two people. After the early, inevitable misunderstandings, Leah didn't doubt Micah's love, commitment, or good intentions.

Marilyn was thinking of Elliot's affair. Sandy was right: if Darlene knew and had had an affair, their marriage relationship would have deteriorated further. But for Darlene to know and not care? That was worse. Marilyn rang her hands.

Did you hear of Elliot Yager's affair? Marilyn asked Leah.

No, Leah said.

I ran into Conrad while I was canvassing. It seems like he's still mad about it.

Sandy looked in their direction. If his wife had had an affair, she would've been a called a whore and dropped by the man, she said. But he and Darlene stayed together. Women's rights allow women to act like that.

Leah reached out an arm and retracted it. Marilyn stood and stepped to her friend's side. Is that women's rights? she asked Leah quietly.

Sandy's version of them, Leah whispered. I'd rather just call Elliot a whore, too.

Marilyn smiled. I'd like women to receive equal opportunities at work, and even in the home, she said. I'm not so sure about free love.

I agree, Leah said. But the kids love this kind of talk. She waved her hand. They'll have to figure it out for themselves, like we all do.

I didn't mean to dismiss the bed-and-breakfast idea, Marilyn said.

You didn't, Leah said. I needed a different perspective. She thought of Micah, of how they could disagree without it becoming personal. Leah wondered whether Marilyn had this kind of trust with anyone. Had she ever experienced the security and vulnerability possible in a relationship? Jackson must miss your perspective, Leah said.

Have you been by The Wave lately?

No.

Tim says the new units are coming along, Marilyn said. I was probably just holding back Jackson, she thought. But she had valid reasons. Just because she'd adopted his hometown didn't mean she had to agree to every one of his decisions, which affected both of their lives.

Did Marilyn want her to argue for her side? Leah thought. Jackson could be paying Marilyn directly, no doubt about that. But she didn't know their financial situation well enough to make a call on the units.

Someone knocked on the door. Leah stepped over and opened it. Jackson stood on the porch, wearing jeans and a rare button-down.

Tim here? he asked.

Leah waved Marilyn over and stepped aside.

I told you I don't want him at a hippie party, Jackson said.

Marilyn opened the door wide. Does this look like a hippie party? she asked.

A dozen people stood or sat on the couch or the floor. A few cookies remained on a platter. Two empty bottles of champagne sat by the couch. Tim looked at his parents, then away.

It's called polygamy, Sandy was saying.

Jackson raised his eyebrows.

Sandy's the only hippie here, Marilyn said.

Tell Tim he needs to go, Jackson said.

I didn't invite him, Marilyn said. I don't know how he heard.

Jackson didn't know either. But he'd really come to talk to Marilyn, not to fetch Tim. He pulled at his beard.

Marilyn was pleased that, for whatever reason, Jackson had come to her. He tells me the Smiths aren't coming until August? she asked.

Jackson was relieved she'd raised the topic. He reached inside and pulled the door halfway shut. The front bumped against Marilyn's back. Come outside, Jackson said.

Marilyn stepped onto the porch, the pavement cool against her bare feet. A breeze rushed up her dress. She bunched the excess material and held it against her thigh. On the edge of Leah's lot, the tops of pines swayed.

Jackson wouldn't look at her. What? she said. Why are you all dressed up?

Jackson looked down as though someone else had put on his shirt. Oh, he said. I've been helping with the units. It makes me feel gross. I like to wear something nice after.

Marilyn's brow wrinkled. He wasn't one to lie, but he wasn't one to dress up, either. He also smelled like aftershave. Elliot's affair came to mind.

Jackson stepped onto the lawn and motioned to her with his hand. You look nice yourself, he said.

Can't we talk on the porch?

Just come here.

She followed him. They stood in the middle of the lawn. Grass tickled her feet, dirt pushed between her toes. Jackson took one of her hands. Without thinking, she pulled it away. His brow wrinkled.

Carl's dead, he said.

Marilyn grabbed Jackson's arm. What? she said.

Killed overseas. His family isn't coming this year. He removed her hand from his arm and held it again.

You haven't told Tim.

No.

She released his hand. The whole body of the pines swayed now. Her dress flapped. She slapped at the material uselessly.

Eileen wanted you to call her, Jackson said.

When—?

Two or three weeks ago.

Two or three weeks?

Yes, he said. Her long dark hair swirled against her floral-print white dress. Jackson didn't remember that one; maybe it was Leah's? At first, he'd been so sure that she'd return before the end of the quarter. Then, he'd been busy with guests over the Fourth. At the same time, he'd had to do the income statement and balance sheet on his own. It had taken a couple weeks, off and on, and although he'd submitted them to the bank that morning, he wasn't sure he'd done them correctly. Her feet looked beautiful without shoes, he thought, slim and dark in the fading light against the grass. He didn't understand why she hadn't returned.

You haven't told Tim, she repeated.

I thought you could tell him, Jackson said.

Marilyn fixed her eyes on a porch light across the street. A dog barked close by. The wind muffled the sound of the sea.

You're better with that kind of thing, Jackson said.

She looked straight at him. He looked back. His hands were in his pockets.

No, she said.

What?

You need to tell him, Marilyn said. I'll talk to him after, but you need to tell him.

Me? Jackson said. He plucked at his beard. When his father had died, Marilyn had explained death to the boy. When Micah died, Marilyn had broken the news. This situation was a continuation of those ones.

You're bad at that sort of thing, Marilyn said. Now you can get better.

Another porch light came on and Marilyn turned her eyes toward it. The dog barked again. Probably barks when each porch light comes on, she thought. She'd heard him at twilight every night.

I'll just make him upset, Jackson said. Why did his wife keep insisting on not doing what she was good at? What was wrong with her?

I said I'd talk to him after, Marilyn said.

How—?

Have you even gone anywhere this summer? Marilyn shook her head so her hair wouldn't catch in her mouth. Anywhere out of Kalapuya?

I went to Salem for—

With Tim?

No.

He wants to go to the dunes. Take him there. Tell him then. I'll talk to him when you get back.

OK, Jackson said. His chest hurt like heartburn. The cool night felt warm to him. I'll be in touch, he said, and turned away.

Do it soon, Marilyn said.

He turned back around. We'll go tomorrow, he said. Annie can watch the office. Unless you want to?

Marilyn bunched her dress in her hand and looked away.

Jackson unbuttoned the top three buttons of his shirt, walked to the truck, and drove away, windows cracked. As soon as he'd sat, he'd felt tired from the day of manual labor. He'd asked Marilyn once, he thought. He wouldn't ask again. He'd tried to give her as much space and time as she needed, but apparently she needed more.

Marilyn sat on the porch until she thought she'd composed her face. Inside, most eyes focused on Sandy. Tim sat a few feet outside the ring of students. He looked at his mom, then away. Marilyn squatted and placed a hand on his shoulder. Your father's taking you to the dunes tomorrow, she said.

What? Tim said.

Go home and get some sleep.

Really?

Yes. Marilyn stood. Go on.

The guy Tim had talked music with leaned against the couch, his eyes closed. OK, Tim said.

Marilyn kissed Tim on the forehead. He wiped it off.

You want a ride? she asked.

He shook his head and stood.

Be careful on the dunes, she said. She shut the screen door behind him.

Dark gray clouds cluttered the dark blue twilight sky. The wind billowed Tim's shirt. From the shed he took the fishing pole he'd set aside. Through town he ran, then trotted, then walked. He stood on rocks above the Kalapuya River, listening to himself pant. Below him water sloshed. The river flowed parallel to the rocks and ended in the nearby sea. Across the river, sand stretched for a half mile. That beach ended in more rocks, which led to The Wave. This route was quicker than the footbridge, but few took it because you had to ford the river. In summer Tim waded across, except in higher-than-usual high tides, when he swam. Tonight, the river sounded mellow; high tide wasn't for four or five hours. His eyes had adjusted to the darkness. He climbed down the rocks, not once needing to look down. From the river's edge, the lights of Joe's Bar were visible. A couple people sat on the deck. Tim took off his shoes, tied the laces together, strung them around his neck, and stepped into water. The sharp pebbles didn't bother his calloused feet. Toward the middle, water splashed onto his shorts. On the other side, he didn't put on his shoes. He ran across the beach, against the wind, his eyes smarting, his pole bobbing, his shoes bouncing against his chest. Sand collected on his wet feet and legs. He climbed the rocks, careful to avoid barnacles. His first sight of The Wave as he crested the rocks was the partially finished new units, dark above an occupied room, where slivers of light shone through pulled curtains. He liked the new units but felt sadness within his pride, as though he were somehow betraying his mom by his liking them.

The couch bounced. Elliot jolted awake and raised his throbbing head. At his feet crouched Lana, her head tilted, her eyes meeting his. She always tried to sneak on the couch after he'd had too much to drink. He let his head fall back and she nestled into a pillow. He felt like he never wanted to move again.

That afternoon he'd had an hour-long phone conversation with the lawyer, Ted Johansson. As it stood, through the passing of the final version of the bill, Elliot still owned the cove and had to pay taxes, but he also had to allow the public on it and couldn't build there without governmental permission. He wanted to sue the state, asking that the land be reverted back to no public access. Ted said he'd represent him but advised against this course. We'd probably lose, he said. Ted said the best options were to either petition the state for the right to build a specific project that touched the beach or, if he didn't want to pay taxes on the cove, to petition the state to buy the beach outright. Neither option appealed to Elliot. And he doubted he had the money for the long and probably fruitless fight to reverse the bill's stipulations on his land.

Elliot dozed for a couple more hours, then woke up parched. He groaned as he stood. His head felt like a knife was inside it that he needed to rip out. Lana spread out over more of the couch. He shook his head at her audacity, then groaned at his headache.

On the kitchen table sat a glass of whiskey, Leah's framed photo, a newspaper, and a page of notes from his talk with Ted. He poured the remaining whiskey back into his decanter and filled up the glass with water. He sat at the table and leaned his head against his hands. Time passed—a half hour, an hour, two? He didn't know. He opened his eyes to the newspaper's photo, a picture of the same motel in Leah's photo but with the boundary gate and "Keep Out" sign removed. He spread his fingers over it and pressed his nails into the paper and squeezed his hand into a fist while he ripped it out. Leah's frame was in good shape and could be reused, so he carefully unclasped the back and lifted out that photo and reclasped the back of the now-empty frame. On his second try, he stood.

In the living room, Lana eyed him. Get off there, he said. Just get off. She did.

He wanted to burn the photos but didn't see a matchbook anywhere. Without bothering to put on shoes, he stumbled outside. Lana wriggled out after him. They walked to the dark beach. Elliot took off his socks and rolled up his pants to his thighs. Lana brought him a driftwood stick, but he waved her aside and kicked at the ocean. Lana jumped around, mimicking, splashing seawater. We're not playing, he told her. She paddled off. The tide was going out. He waded to his thighs and tore up the photos and tossed the pieces onto the waves. He shivered as he walked back to shore.

5.

Twenty miles south of Kalapuya sat Florence, a town known for logging, fishing, and dairy farming. South of Florence, across the Siuslaw River, sand dunes stretched parallel to the ocean for over thirty miles. For years locals had been fighting the federal government, who wanted the dunes to become a national park. Some citizens didn't want the attention that a national park would garner. Some businesspeople whose livelihood depended on their access to the dunes didn't want to be kicked out.

Jackson and Tim drove to one of these establishments, a general store that rented out dune bikes by the half hour. The ride had been quiet; Jackson was thinking of how to break the news, and Tim had nothing to say to his father. Their route had wound around Cape Perpetua, alongside Heceta Head Lighthouse, and through Florence. The shop where they stopped had a sand dune backyard: an instant desert rising behind and above pines and firs. Tim wanted to drive to the ocean and back. To do that, he figured they'd have to rent for a couple of hours.

This store was the farthest point south that Marilyn and Jackson had traveled together. If Marilyn were there, she'd have been thinking that. Jackson was thinking of the intractable dune bikes he and Marilyn had ridden ten years ago. You sat on a seat a few inches off the ground and leaned back, your pedals directly in front of you. The bikes regularly didn't make it up the dunes. They often crashed on the way down. After an hour, he and Marilyn, panting and covered in sand, dragged the bikes over the final two dunes and into the store. They'd been celebrating something, but he couldn't remember what. A birthday? An anniversary? He'd heard the place rented motorized vehicles now.

The inside of the store smelled like meatballs. Cold sandwiches sat in a display case. Tim stared at them. Although not yet lunchtime, Jackson was hungry, too. They should have packed lunches, he thought. Although he hadn't calculated exactly, they seemed to be spending more on food since Marilyn left. And on a lot of things. He ordered toiletries at the last minute or after they'd already run out. In the latter cases, like with the toilet paper, while he waited for the bulk items to arrive, he had to buy the supplies in small quantities, which cost more. Across the counter, on the wall, a chalkboard listed the prices to rent dune bikes. At the end of a hallway behind the counter, a door was open. From it came a *vrooming* that sounded like a motorcycle. A round-faced man wearing an apron stepped from a back room.

Howdy, he said. How can I help you?

Tim glanced at the clerk, then at the sandwiches.

I'd like to rent an hour on a motorized dune buggy, Jackson said.

Two people on a four-wheeler? the man asked.

Yessir, Jackson said. I'll also take two meatball sandwiches.

Saliva flooded Tim's mouth. Can we go for two hours? he asked his dad. Please.

The clerk looked at Jackson, waiting. Usually, Jackson would be upset that Tim questioned him, especially in public, but the more time on the dunes, the more time he had to tell Tim. Sure, he said. Two hours it is.

Tim smiled. He watched the man roll each sandwich in brown paper. Wanting to remember every detail of such an unordinary day, he looked around. A rack of kites stood by the front door. The past few years Tim had considered kites toys for tourists and little kids, but today he wanted to fly one. Maybe now that he was older he could handle a kite better. Maybe he could predict and prevent its descent. Maybe he could run faster and keep it longer in the sky.

His dad was saying his name. Tim turned. The clerk opened a wooden swinging door that led behind the counter. They all walked down the long hallway and out the back. Dune bikes with pedals sat on one side of the door, four-wheelers on the other. The clerk gave his dad a key, showed them a seat pouch to store their sandwiches, and went inside. An overcast sky muted the usually gold sand.

Can I drive? Tim asked. In his father's current mood anything seemed possible.

Not at first, Jackson said.

Tim thought this answer generous. He straddled behind his father, and after hesitating, placed his arms around his waist.

Jackson turned the key and felt a moment of joy as the motor jumped to life. He hadn't been on a motorized bike since the fifties. This one had four tires, but the anticipation of swift movement through open space felt the same. Joe had offered his motorcycle to Jackson at the potluck after Phil's funeral. You should get away for a couple of days, Joe had said. Jackson drove the motorcycle along the Oregon Coast Highway all the way to Brookings, on the border of California, stayed the rest of the night there, drove north the next morning, and was back at work by the afternoon. He remembered his shirt flapping against his chest. Every time he passed a motel, he slowed down to assess its features. The Wave had held its own, but dozens of motels had sprung up on that route since then, and Jackson didn't know how The Wave would now compare.

His father had signed The Wave over to Jackson five years before he died, but because Jackson continued to consult his father in the lounge, where, before they bought the television, Phil played solitaire or did crossword puzzles, Jackson didn't feel as though he owned the motel until his father died. Since his father had been fading for over a year, his passing had been the opposite of a surprise; afterward, Jackson had to accustom himself as much to acquisition as to loss. He took ownership seriously. When Marilyn accused him of misuse of money, he felt as though she thought he did not.

On their third try, the four-wheeler gained enough traction to climb the dune. Jackson clutched the wheel while sand sprayed from the tires. Feeling the pull of the boy's weight, he tightened his thighs against the sides. He killed the engine as they crested the first dune. Beyond them spread hill after hill of sand. The clouds that had enclosed the valley petered out halfway across the sky to reveal a blue sky and below it, shimmering sand. They couldn't see the sea.

Jackson glanced over his shoulder. Tim's eyes had widened. Jackson was glad he'd brought the kid, regardless of whether he had to share the news. For the moment he'd forgotten that goal.

Hold on, he said. We're going down.

Tim interlaced his fingers and tightened his grip. Jackson guided the four-wheeler to a descent path that didn't seem too steep. He gasped for air as they plunged. Woohoo, Tim yelled. Jackson smiled. Sand crunched between his teeth. When they started up the adjacent hill, he pushed the gas pedal down.

Jackson hadn't told Marilyn where he'd gone on Joe's motorcycle. If she wanted to know, he'd thought at the time, she could have asked. He thought of other incidents that he could have shared: tiffs with her father, his disconnect from Tim when Marilyn started homeschooling, the plans for the new units. He'd told her from the beginning of their relationship that he wanted to build them, but he'd told her the details only when they became pertinent to her life. Why did she need to know beforehand? But maybe she'd wanted to know. She couldn't have asked in this instance, because she didn't even know he was planning. Until that past January, he'd discussed the specifics of the dream only with Joe. If he'd told Marilyn earlier, he'd figured, she'd have become upset about money earlier. With her it was always about money. But not only money, he reminded himself. She cared about The Wave, too. Maybe, if he'd told her years before, and they'd set aside a little money each month, she wouldn't have had the same reaction. But he couldn't do anything about that now.

They'd crested another hill. The magnificent view suppressed Jackson's thoughts. He pulled on his beard and stretched his fingers, cramped from holding on.

Can we go to the ocean? Tim asked.

I don't see any ocean, Jackson said.

I bet we can see it from the top of the next dune.

I'll tell you what. Jackson pointed to a towering dune five hills away. If we can see the ocean from there, we'll go there. If we can't, we won't.

OK. Tim brushed sand off his face and braced himself for the downhill ride. So far his dad had been more lenient than he'd expected. Again, they descended. Before Tim could form a thought, they'd crested another hill. The drop in his stomach reminded him of riding a rope over a ravine behind his uncle Dave's house in Toledo. There, the feeling came as much from the thought that the rope might break as from a sense of flight. His dad didn't stop until they'd crested the large dune. They both panted.

Takes the wind right out of you, Jackson said.

I can see it, Tim said. Far off, the sand dunes relaxed into a beach. A blue line of ocean stretched across the horizon.

Jackson checked his watch. Doubt we'll get there in forty-five minutes, but we'll head in that direction.

Forty-five minutes later, they stopped to eat lunch in a valley. Not as much wind down here, Jackson said. Don't want too much sand in our food.

Tim took the meatball sandwich from his father and plopped in the sand. The ocean was out of reach for a two-hour trip, he knew now, but he didn't feel too bad. The tasty sandwich was the best meal he'd had since his mom left. And this adventure was only half-over.

Jackson stood and leaned against the four-wheeler while he

ate. They were in a bowl between a few dunes. The sky was a light blue with a few cloud wisps. Heat radiated off sand. The purpose of the trip returned to Jackson. He could tell Tim now, he thought. But then he'd have to deal with that the rest of the ride. He could tell him right before they got home—but then he couldn't keep an eye on his reaction. Right before we get in the car, Jackson decided. I'll tell him then. His son's legs sprawled to one side of his body in a way that seemed uncomfortable.

Tim wanted to put this day in a poem. He would start with the sky. No, he would start with the dunes. No, he would start with the wind on his face. He opened the seat compartment and put the paper packaging inside. Can I drive? he asked, still chewing his last bite.

OK. Jackson finished off his sandwich and placed the packaging on top of his son's. You see how I went down the less steep sides of dunes? Do that.

Tim couldn't climb the first dune, so they switched places, then at the top, Jackson sat behind Tim and placed his own hands on the bottom of the wheel inside the boy's. Tim guided the four-wheeler down a gradual decline, at first oversteering, then doing just fine. After Tim climbed up and down five dunes, Jackson's shoulders relaxed. The boy could drive better than he'd expected. And the movement had cooled him. He looked south: he couldn't see the conclusion of the stretch of sand. Patches of long grass adorned the sides or tops of every few dunes. The sky in all directions was blue.

When they crested the second-to-last dune, Jackson placed his hands over his son's and guided the machine to a halt. At the bottom of the far side of the next dune sat the store. A dense forest rose on the other side of the highway.

I need to tell you something, Jackson said. He was glad he couldn't see his son's face.

What? Tim said. Sand swirled in patterns by his feet. He

pulled his toes back and forth, feeling the particles in his shoes. The height of the dune dizzied but challenged him: he wanted to go down a steep slope.

It's why I brought you here.

Tim glanced over his shoulder. Jackson studied a crease in his jeans. Tim looked down the dune again. He was sure they could make it, he thought. His dad didn't bring him here just to ride? The thought saddened him; he didn't know why.

You know Carl? Jackson said.

Tim looked over his shoulder again. Of course he knew Carl. What a silly question.

Jackson wanted his son not to look at him. His family didn't stay over the Fourth because Carl is dead, he said, his eyes downcast. They didn't want to be reminded of him. That didn't come out right, Jackson thought. But it's said now, thank God. He was killed in Vietnam, he added.

Tim looked away. Jackson sighed.

Carl was dead? Tim thought. He hadn't been on the news, had he? Tim watched the news almost every night. Almost, Tim thought. And he'd started that after his mom left. Maybe Carl had died before that.

When? Tim asked. The when seemed important.

When? Jackson said. I don't know.

The boy's body quivered as though reining in tears.

I can find out, Jackson said. Or you can. You could call his mom.

I don't want to call his mom. Tim no longer saw the sky, the forest, the dunes, the four-wheeler, his dad, even his own hands. The outer world had ceased to exist. His head hummed.

Let's get to the store, Jackson said. Our time's up.

Tim's shaking continued.

We can talk in the car, Jackson said.

He hoped Tim wouldn't talk in the car. He'd turn on the radio;

Tim could listen to that. Ever since his son was a baby, music had calmed him.

Come on, Jackson said. He steered the four-wheeler toward the side of the dune. Tim turned it toward the middle of the dune. Jackson, surprised, didn't move. It raced down the steepest part of the hill. Jackson pushed Tim's hands away, killed the engine, and put on the brakes. The four-wheeler skidded into the valley. Tim, who'd let go when Jackson pushed away his hands, flew off and landed on a steep sandy descent. He rolled down it and lay still, breathing hard. The machine halted to the side of him, at the bottom of the same descent. To avoid hitting the hill head-on, Jackson had turned it at the last second. His left leg had smashed between it and the sand.

Tim sat up. His body hurt all over. Dad? he said. It felt like a cup of sand was in his mouth. He spit until he ran out of saliva.

Damn, Jackson said. You OK?

Tim stood and walked to the front of the four-wheeler. He shook out his arms and legs one by one.

Jackson raised his eyes. Go get the clerk, he said.

What's wrong? Tim asked.

My leg, Jackson said. Bring a board . . . some of kind of tourniquet. He was breathing hard. Too much sweat beaded across his forehead.

Tim ran up the dune. After a few steps, he dropped on all fours and scrambled. At the top, he rose to two legs again. Tim ran down the hill, whirring his arms to keep balance. He halted in front of the clerk and two women. They stared at him. He dusted sand off his face.

My dad, he said. We crashed.

Good lord, the clerk said. Is he OK?

His leg's hurt. Broken maybe.

Where's he at?

The other side of this dune.

So much for their safety, one woman said. Right, Clancy?

You're safe if you're not idiots, the clerk said. Excuse me ladies. If you want, help yourself to a pop on the house. He shook his head and muttered. He turned and went inside.

The women still looked at Tim. He averted his eyes and brushed sand off his arms and legs. When they walked around to the front of the store without speaking to him, his body relaxed. Then his stomach convulsed and he dropped on his knees. Just as the clerk came out, Tim spewed meatball pieces into the sand.

Jesus, the clerk said. He carried a towel and first aid kit in one hand, a leg-length one-by-four and rope in the other. Clean that up, he said. There're towels in the bathroom cupboard. He walked past Tim, then turned, squinting through his glasses. And call someone to pick you up. Doubt your dad's going anywhere.

Tim felt more vomit rising. He held it back until he thought the clerk out of earshot, then threw up again. Afterward, he lay in the sand. His mouth felt dry. The fact of Carl's death returned. Tim imagined him being shot. He imagined him sinking in a swamp. He imagined him dying from hunger, lying in the same position as Tim now. And what had his dad said? *This is why I brought you here.* Tim coughed, swallowed, and crinkled his face. The inside of his mouth tasted nasty. He pushed himself to a sitting position and stood. From the cupboard of a bathroom off the hallway, he took two towels. Back outside, he gathered his vomit. He emptied as much as he could into the toilet and flushed. The rest he tried to spray off with a hose. The dirty liquid dripped onto his shoes and sunk in. He thought of calling his mom. He wondered whether she knew about Carl.

Tim dropped the almost-clean, wet towels outside the back door and sat under the store's eaves, legs curled to his chest and his back against the wall. He closed his eyes. The day was too bright and warm. He wanted to be in a cool, dark inside place. When he heard voices, he opened his eyes. His dad and the clerk stood at the top of the dune, a board tied under his dad's hurt leg from ankle to crotch.

The clerk helped him lower to a sitting position. His hurt leg sticking straight out and his face contorting, his dad slid on his bottom and one leg down the dune. The clerk walked backward in front of him, his hands out to break any accidental slide. At the bottom, his dad leaned back on one arm and groaned. He blinked and saw Tim.

You call anyone yet? he asked.

Tim shook his head.

Call your great-aunt Pearl, he said. She'll take you home.

What about you? Tim asked.

Clancy here'll take me to the hospital.

Here, son, lemme show you where the phone is, the clerk said.

Tim followed him into the office.

Your aunt's that Indian who works at the bar downtown, right? the clerk asked. Small world, isn't it? He found her home number in the phone book, pulled the dials, and handed the receiver to Tim. I'll be outside, he said, loading your father into my car.

To Tim, his tone was too friendly compared to his disgust earlier. Maybe his dad told him about Carl, Tim thought. If so, he hated him. He hated them both.

By the time Pearl arrived, Jackson and Clancy had left. Tim was swinging slowly on the porch swing, avoiding the inevitable creaking when he swung too fast. This mindless task was as much as he could focus on. As she drove up, Pearl viewed him as an intent boy on the small side for his age. On the drive to Kalapuya, she tried to converse, but he answered all questions in monosyllables and stared out the window. The boy stunk—of sweat or something else—and she kept the windows down.

At The Wave, before she'd come to a full stop, Tim hopped out of the car. I'll go check on your dad now, she said. And give your mom a call tonight.

OK, Tim said. If she didn't know Mom didn't live there, he wasn't going to tell her.

I can bring him back from the hospital, Pearl said. But Marilyn'll have to find a way to get his truck.

OK, Tim said. He shut the car door.

Annie stood as he entered the office. What happened to you? she asked.

Tim looked at his clothes. Was it that obvious? he thought. He told her.

I was wondering, she said, with you a couple hours late. I need to clean rooms.

Tim said he'd watch over the office. Annie said he wouldn't until he showered. Twenty minutes later, he sat behind the desk, clean clothes on, his dark hair wet and flat against his forehead, bruises scattered across his arms and legs. Sand remained in his ears, in his nostrils, and between his toes.

He flipped the guest book to August. Carl's family wasn't written there. His dad had lied to him. Again, the urge rose to go somewhere and hide, somewhere dark and cool. Heat was accumulating in the office, and the upstairs rooms were even hotter. He thought of the rocks or a dark sea cave. He thought of Elliot's house, surrounded by trees that, right now, in the afternoon, cast shadows across the living room hardwood floor.

An old man and old woman entered, both leaning on canes. For the next couple hours, he was busy, off and on, checking in guests. When he was alone, Tim held the desk tightly, as though he were still holding onto the four-wheeler. Across the small room, a handful of starfish sprawled on the trinket shelf. They were dead, Tim thought, and he was the one who'd killed them. The starfish he'd plucked from the rocks over the years paraded across his mind, all of them so bright until they dried up from lack of seawater and their color faded to a dull version of their alive-selves, like the skin of a corpse. He beat his forehead against the edge of the desk, trying to remove the images.

When Annie returned, she opened the window to let in air. She moved slowly and sweat stained her armpits. Go get some food, she said. I'll take over.

His parents would have told her to go home, that they could watch the office. But at the word *food*, Tim was hungry; he hadn't eaten anything since the meatball sandwich. He took the stairs one at a time, looking at the vomit stains on his shoes. In the kitchen, he made a roast beef sandwich. Everything he picked up seemed heavy. In between bites, he made two more sandwiches. He placed them and four green apples in his backpack. In his bedroom, he put in his notebook, a change of underwear, and pajamas. From the bathroom, he grabbed his toothbrush. He filled his dad's military canteen with water and slipped it across his shoulder. Backpack on and fishing pole in hand, he lowered himself from the roof's eaves onto the bulging woodbox, then onto level ground. The second his shoes touched dirt, he ran—not his usual casual jog, but frantically. He ran below the new units, construction quieted for the day, past the bench his dad had made, and over Little Faithful, which rarely spurted more than a couple feet at this time of year. Running fast hurt his sore muscles, but he liked it because he didn't have a chance to think. When he reached Elliot's house, an hour remained until sunset. He went upstairs for the first time and lay on the spare-room bed. He planned to rest a minute, then to take inventory of the house's supplies and tools. But his breathing became regular, he closed his eyes, and he slept.

Sometime during the night, Micah bent over the bed, his salt-and-pepper beard close to Tim's face. Tim started and sat up. The room smelled like smoked fish. From inside his overall rubber waders, Micah pulled out a brown paper package tied with twine. Tim remembered these gifts, from the first Christmas he could remember up until last Christmas, after Micah's death, when Leah had brought over the package. Tim pulled the twine around the corners and opened the paper. Inside was dark pink smoked salmon. The boy tore his teeth into it, while Micah leaned against the wall, arms crossed, smiling. Beads of water rolled down his waders. They didn't make a puddle on the floor.

When Tim opened his eyes, the curtainless room was full of daylight. He remembered Micah and the fish; he felt full and peaceful. He remembered Carl's death; he buried his face in the pillow. He wanted to lose himself again in sleep, but since the sun was out and the house seemed warm, he must have slept from before darkness until well after dawn, and he doubted he could sleep more.

He slid off the bed and took his things downstairs. His muscles ached. The largest bruise, on his right arm, stretched from shoulder to elbow. The breathless sensation of sailing through the air filled him, then the abrupt and painful thud as he hit sand. He was surprised that he wasn't hurt more, like his dad. But he didn't want to think of his parents. This was his home now.

Downstairs was cooler. He placed the fishing pole by the front door, and the canteen, apples, and sandwiches on the counter. He went through the cupboards thoroughly but found nothing else. At the moment, his lack of food didn't bother him; he was full from the smoked salmon. He sat at the kitchen table and took out his notebook. The lyrics in it made him long for music. It's not as though he could have brought the record player with him, he thought. He'd have to do without music for a while.

At the top of one page, he wrote Carl's name. At the top of the next page, he wrote *Dear Carl*. Why hadn't he thought of writing his friend a letter until now? Surely Carl could have received them during basic. Words halted and rushed across the paper.

Remember that house we spied on last summer? Where the old man and old lady lived? The old lady died and the old man moved. I live there now. You told me that sometimes, when a person gets older, he wants to leave home. I understand that now. But I don't understand why you had to go so far. You could've moved to Kalapuya. We could've lived in this house together.

Tim struggled to breathe, as though someone were strangling him. He heaved and touched his pencil back to paper.

I want to know: Did you see the ocean over there? Does it look or smell different than here? Television makes that place seem mostly jungle.

Tim's hand shook. The next letters were round and wide, unlike his usual tight writing.

How long have you been gone? Why didn't someone tell me? I've been acting normal for days or months while you've been dead.

He dropped the pencil and pushed his notebook forward and banged his forehead on the edge of the table until it bled. He wiped off the blood with his forearm and rested his cheek against the tabletop. It felt cool even as the rest of the nook grew warmer. Tim didn't appreciate the light pushing through his eyelids.

After a half hour of thinking of nothing, he walked toward the basement and opened the door. Light petered out halfway down the stairs. This was a cool, dark inside place. He could stay there until afternoon shadows filled the house. He stepped down and shut the door behind him. His right hand grasped the banister as he walked down the wooden steps. He sat on the final step until his eyes adjusted to the darkness.

The concrete was cool against his bare feet. A dank, underground scent filled the room. Straight ahead sat open shelves lined with Ball jars. Tim stepped to them and picked one up. He brushed off dust and squinted. Something was in there, he wasn't sure what. He twisted the lid open and dipped in his pointer finger, then pushed the cold substance into his mouth. Applesauce.

He sat on the cool cement, the jar between his legs, and dipped in his finger again and again. He ate until the applesauce pushed against his stomach. He dropped his hand and stared at the concrete wall. During the night Micah had given him food. Mrs. Yager had probably canned this applesauce. He felt as though he was being fed by the dead. The thought didn't bother him. Maybe, he hoped, maybe Carl would bring him food, too.

6.

The apartment hadn't been dusted. The dishes had been rearranged. Marilyn didn't feel the need to clean or readjust. She felt like a visitor, and she liked it like that. If she cleaned windowsills or nested pots and pans, she might begin to view the place as home. She might feel the need to stay.

She made tea and took the first sip while looking out the kitchen window. The exteriors of the new units were complete. Banging emanated from the interior. The afternoon sun spread up and out from either side of the center building. Now she must go outside to view the ocean. On a sunny day like today she was OK with that. If she were here in winter, she'd have to bundle up or stay in. An ache of loss emerged as she walked downstairs. Jackson sat in the heirloom chair, left leg in a cast from groin to foot.

They call you back? she asked.

Yes.

Marilyn set her mug on the desk.

They haven't found him, Jackson said.

They talk to that young man in Eugene?

His name's James. He's a draft dodger. Police don't know where he is. Kids don't either.

Are you sure they're telling the truth?

Jackson looked at her, his blue eyes wide, mouth firm, thick beard jutted out. To her, his look said: *don't be difficult.* Marilyn turned away. The office window was open. She didn't shut it. The breeze felt good; it had been a hot day.

I'm going outside, she said. I'll check in before I leave.

I thought, maybe—

No, Marilyn said. How could he think she'd stay? She picked up the cup of tea and walked outside.

The bell jingled as she released the door. Jackson watched her go. She walked like a daydreaming adolescent, he thought, slowly and half-aware of her surroundings.

He wasn't going to ask her to stay; she'd stay when she was ready to stay. He wanted her to look over the invoices stacked on the closet desk. Since he'd submitted the income sheet and balance statement, he hadn't done any bookkeeping. His hospital bills had thickened the pile.

After three days on crutches, his underarms had become raw. Leaning on his casted foot while walking hurt too, but he ate more aspirins than recommended not to notice. At night he couldn't doze until two or three in the morning, then his internal clock, which had worked even through his service overseas, wouldn't wake him for the day at six or seven. When he couldn't sleep, his thoughts focused on Marilyn, and for the first time, he'd admitted that he didn't know when she'd return.

Last night, in and out of restless sleep, he'd recognized that if Marilyn didn't start helping, he'd have to hire someone. Even if he gained the knowledge, he didn't have time, especially with this pain, when he was always tired and everything took twice as long.

He picked up the receiver and pulled the numbers to Laura's house. It wouldn't hurt to reassure the students that he wouldn't hand James over to the police; he just wanted to find his son. Every other route was a dead end.

Glad to be away from Jackson's demeaning look, Marilyn sighed. She supposed she could push through the looks. What are you thinking? she could ask. What does that mean? She supposed she could, if she really wanted to, if she really cared, if she wanted to become enmeshed in that tunnel of drama where she may or may not glimpse light on the other side. Not today, she thought. Not until they found Tim.

She leaned over a window box, picked up a clod of dirt, and sifted it through her fingers. The units seemed less hospitable without flowers in the window boxes. But the interior of the old units and the outer office were, as usual, neatly arranged. From Annie or Jackson's maintenance, she didn't know. Probably Annie's. Jackson was so obsessed with the new units that he'd dragged his cast up the half-finished steps to consult with the crew. At least he'd had enough self-awareness not to ask her opinion. They'd stuck to the topic of Tim, as they should. He'd disappeared a week and a day ago.

Marilyn heard of his disappearance on Monday afternoon; The Sweet Seller was closed. That morning, she'd driven north to Nestucca for a meeting led by Citizens for Oregon Beaches. She and Leah were in the living room; she was checking over Sandy's accounting, and Leah, to estimate what she needed versus what she could afford, was sketching potential furniture into potential bed-and-breakfast rooms. She'd promised Conrad an answer within the week.

Leah answered the call from Jackson. Marilyn accepted the phone reluctantly. Maybe Jackson hadn't told Tim about Carl, and she and Jackson would have another confrontation over that. When he told her Tim was missing, she sucked in her breath. For how long? she asked. Jackson clicked his tongue. About forty-eight hours I think, he said. About *forty-eight hours*, Marilyn repeated. You *think*? She hadn't forgiven him for that, even after she'd seen his cast and heard the story. He'd been home twelve hours before he noticed Tim's absence, twenty-four hours before he worried, and another full day before he called her. All that was unforgivable. She was sure Tim had taken off the moment Annie had dismissed him from the office on Saturday. They'd alerted police from Newport to Coos Bay, from Florence to Eugene, and as far as Brookings, Astoria, Salem, and Portland. No one had seen him.

Hello, Marilyn.

Marilyn looked up. She dropped the dirt from a clenched hand. A tall, heavyset woman stood at her side. Hello, Clara, she said.

How are you?

Marilyn brushed her hands together, transferring dirt particles from one hand to the other. Fine, she said. Just heading on a walk.

Enjoy. As Clara smiled, her cheeks dimpled.

Marilyn picked up her tea from the windowsill and walked past her. Clara was a pleasant woman; a wealthy doctor; one of their only foreign guests, an annual visitor from England. It was so difficult to talk to the regulars this year.

She was headed on a walk, is that what she'd said? Well, she better walk, then. The noise inside the new units grew louder as she passed them.

She brushed her free hand against her skirt and held it up and studied the fingernails. Dirt remained in them. Scratches crisscrossed her palm. She'd been doing yard work for Leah that summer: mowing grass, planting tomato seedlings, trimming the rhododendrons after the flowers wilted, digging up the roots of blackberry bushes encroaching from a neighboring yard. It was the least she could do; Marilyn felt as though she owed Leah so much. Leah, she knew, didn't view it like that. You work, Leah had said, and I pay you. And when Marilyn suggested that Leah might prefer to live alone, Leah had said that she spent enough time alone baking, that she liked to have the option to be around someone while at home. Despite Leah's protests, Marilyn felt her own unsettled life a burden on her friend.

Marilyn placed one hand on the top of the bench, looked at the ocean, and sipped. The low sun shone through patches of clouds that darkened orange and pink rays. Dark blue waves lapped, miles out, until the earth curved from her line of sight. Her chest ached at the immensity. Tim could be floating out there on a boat; he could be a floating dead body; he could have sunk to the bottom of the sea.

She looked away from the water at the bench. Pure speculation, she reminded herself. Tim was smarter than that. The bench had been stained, Marilyn noted. Jackson had kept up on that. For some reason this pleased her.

Tim was missing because she'd left. If this summer had been any other summer—if she'd been working at The Wave and had answered Eileen's phone call, if she'd told Tim the news instead of Jackson, if she'd provided a comfortable home for her son to grieve in. But maybe the not telling instead of the leaving was the clincher; maybe she shouldn't have forced that onto Jackson. She'd been thinking of herself, not Tim, when she'd demanded that of her husband. She'd wanted Jackson to be other than he was. You told him *while* you were on the dunes? she'd interrupted Jackson as he told the story. Not in the car, but *during*? He looked at her, naive. Isn't that what you asked me to do? he said. In that moment Marilyn realized that he wasn't going to change. If she explained why during was dangerous, he might understand, but he wouldn't arrive at that conclusion on his own. Marilyn herself should have come to The Wave and told her son.

A passing middle-aged couple raised their hands, looking altogether too cheery. Agates glittered from the woman's half-open hand. Marilyn raised her hand perfunctorily, then walked on, south, above the rocks. The grass tickled her ankles. For the hundredth time, she tried to think where Tim had gone. Looking for agates? But he was on the run or hiding out somewhere, not on an afternoon adventure. Maybe, while looking for agates, Tim had discovered that cave you could stay overnight in. Maybe he was there. Now that she had a destination, she stopped meandering. She set her mug in a rock crevice, held up her skirt, and glided; her running posture looked like Tim's.

No one could reach their forties without regrets, Marilyn thought. Although, to hear Leah speak, you wouldn't think she had any. No, Marilyn corrected herself. Leah regretted drifting away from her dad. She'd wanted to search out her mother's family. Did she regret not having kids? Leah never mentioned it. Marilyn couldn't imagine not regretting that. She'd wanted at least two, maybe three or four. Jackson hadn't been opposed. Raising them near the sea had seemed healthier than raising them near a mill. She'd wanted to teach them work by having them help around the motel. And then after Tim's birth she couldn't get pregnant again. By the time he was five, she'd given up. She and Jackson had sex less and less, mainly because of her avoidance. Sex was fine; she enjoyed the pleasure and feeling of closeness, but besides that, what was the point? To her, their family had felt incomplete, but not as incomplete as if they had never found Tim.

Her breath labored but she kept running. This week she'd concentrated only on Tim. She'd stopped worrying about the Nestucca Spit and Sandy's finances; she spent hours and too much money driving all over Western Oregon. She prided herself on her work on the beach cause, her freelance accounting, and her thrifty nature, but until Tim was found she'd suspend all that. All her life, after any major life change or catastrophe, within a day or two she'd force herself back to business as usual—but not this time.

When she saw the mouth of the cave, she sprinted, wheezing, her hair flying. The uneven rocks hindered her. To take a more direct route, she splashed through shallow tide pools. Seaweed grazed the sides of her sandaled feet. She stubbed her toes on barnacles. They bled.

She stood above the cave, looking into the mouth where tiny waves lapped. The tide was coming in. She climbed down rocks and stepped into soft sand. The saltwater stung her cuts. Every few waves reached the hem of her skirt. She held it up and ducked into the cave and kneeled and crawled forward. The light from outside lit her way.

Farther in, the ceiling heightened and she stood. The waves' churn and splash outside had a hollow sound. She tried and failed to brush wet sand off her clothes. Tim, she said. Tim! The cave was darkening. She stretched out her hands and walked until she reached a dead end. Thin waterfalls cascaded down hard, bumpy walls. Water pooled in her cupped hands. Tim, she said one last time, then sat, back to rock. Water from wet sand soaked through her skirt onto her underwear and bottom. Light outside the cave seemed distant, even as her eyes adjusted to the inner darkness.

She fished out a handful of agates from a shallow pool where waterfalls gathered. He wasn't there. And if he'd been there and left, the agates would be gone, too. She had no more ideas. Despair returned. She clenched her fingers and threw the agates against the wall. They pinged off and settled in sand. She threw two more handfuls, until she didn't feel any others in the pool.

She gathered her knees to her chest and rocked back and forth. She hadn't felt this vulnerable since Tim's disappearance. In front of Leah and Jackson she remained collected. On her drives, she stuck to main roads or highways where she felt as though other drivers could vouch for her. Going off somewhere remote, alone, had seemed like running away. She wanted to find Tim; she didn't want to run away. She leaned her head against a piece of algae on the rock wall, closed her eyes, and slept.

When she woke, the churn and splash of waves sounded close, not hollow. Water hit her toe. She started and stood.

Jackson had brought her here when they were newlyweds. The waves reach you but don't cover you, he'd said. They'd entered the cave as the tide was coming in and stayed until it was receding. When the tide touched their toes as they sat against the back wall, he held her. I wouldn't risk hurting you, he'd said.

A wave covered Marilyn's foot. Maybe she wasn't at the deepest point. She placed a hand on the back wall and walked alongside it. When it curved into a side wall, she turned and walked in the other direction. The ground remained firm; her sandals never sunk into dry sand.

It was easier to trust in a life-or-death situation than in daily life, Marilyn thought. Of course Jackson didn't want her pulled out by the tide. And if the ocean had pulled her away, he'd have gone, too. Everyone valued staying alive. But in daily life everyone valued different things most. If she moved back to The Wave and no longer saw the ocean from the kitchen window, that lack would hurt her every day. If she moved back to The Wave and had to calculate their debts, especially without pay, that would hurt her, too. As Jackson valued neither ocean views nor being debt-free, he wouldn't understand. Better to drown quickly than slowly. Better not to live there than to live in daily pain.

The wall curved on the other side. A wave splashed over her ankle. The ceiling sloped down, so she couldn't see outside, the expanse of the sea. She sucked in her breath. This is the ocean, she thought. Jackson and I were here fifteen years ago. Who knows what has changed.

Maybe she could swim out. If she jumped in with an outgoing wave she might make it past the cave's opening. As she removed her sandals, blouse, and skirt, she imagined walking into the office, wet and almost naked, while a regular joked with Jackson at the desk. She pushed away the image and, shivering, stepped toward the ice-cold water. Waves hit her calves and knees. Shell shards pierced her skin. When waves splashed against her chest, she felt for a large one to ride out on. One bumped her chin. On its way out she went with it, frantically swimming, hoping not to surface until she ran out of breath or another wave forced her in. The push of a wave came first, much sooner than expected. She raised herself, hoping to see sky. Instead, she glimpsed something open and dark before her head hit the top of the cave and the wave pushed her back. She braced her arms against rock so the water's impact wouldn't crush her. She crumpled to sand, then stood, to avoid swallowing saltwater. A wave hit her thigh. Her head throbbed.

The next wave reached Marilyn's waist. Maybe this happened to Tim, she thought. Him trapped here paralyzed her. He would have screamed and clawed at the back wall before the waves grabbed him. If that had happened, she wanted to join him; she wanted her body floating somewhere, in the same water as his. It's not time to give up, she reminded herself. The agates were here. No one knew where he was.

A wave slapped her shoulder. The water's coldness tightened her chest. She backed against the cave wall, turned, and climbed. Never turn your back on the ocean, she'd told Tim. It's unpredictable. Don't trust it. She slipped and fell into water. The current pulled at her. She grabbed sand. She stood and climbed another part of the wall, in a corner. This one had tiny, natural ledges to hold and step on. She curled there, in a high crevice. For extra support she pushed her hands against the ceiling. How long could she squat on a couple inches of rock?

She closed her eyes. The waves squished, gurgled, and crashed. She didn't want to see the proximity of the water. She had no desire to die, but if she had to, hitting her head on a rock and floating out to sea wouldn't be a bad way to go. Drowning while conscious seemed less pleasant.

She readjusted her hands to push against the walls and thought of her mom and dad. Her mom would be canning overflow from her garden during these weeks of summer, mostly at night to avoid heat. Come late September, she'd arrive at The Wave with two dozen jars as presents. I don't know why you don't have a garden, she'd say. You have enough room. Marilyn would remind her that the salt and wind hindered the growing of vegetables. Her mother had seen Micah's garden and thought she knew better. He's lived on the coast all his life, Marilyn had told her. He knows how to deal with the weather. You're going to live here over half your life, her mom had said. I've mastered flowers, Marilyn said. Flowers won't feed you in winter, her mom said.

A couple years ago, she and her dad woke two hours before dawn to go fishing. The kitchen smelled like tomato sauce from her mom's canning the night before. They hiked to the Yaquina River and sat on a large rock above it. Leaves rustled in the chilly early morning air. She offered a corner kitchen suite at The Wave, if her parents wanted to live nearby when they were older. Her dad shook his head. I'd rather sit by this river than the sea, he said. But when you're less mobile, she said, maybe in ten or fifteen years. Her dad shook his head again. The rising sun sent rays of light through branches. He shielded his eyes with his arm. People who live by the ocean are romantics, he said. They want to live by something they can imagine but never experience. Like Jackson? Marilyn asked. Like Aunt Pearl? Her dad removed his arm and recast his line. Like you, he said.

A scene rose of her, Jackson, Leah, and Micah playing Yahtzee in The Wave's lounge. A cold drizzle fell through the darkness outside. They all wore thick sweaters so they could keep the heat low. Jackson mimicked the stuttering of a finicky old man who stayed at The Wave for a week each fall, using up boxes of wood and stinking of body odor. He broke character after he got Marilyn to laugh. It was a weekday early last November, Marilyn remembered, right before Micah drowned, right before the busyness of the holidays, right before Jackson's proposal to build the new units. For some reason, after that night, everything went to hell.

Marilyn pushed against the ceiling again and opened her eyes. The cave was dark. Water sloshed nearby. She stretched down with her toe to touch it but couldn't reach. Perhaps the tide had turned? Not that she was out of danger if it had; waves going out had more pull than those coming in. She periodically hung her leg off the crevice. When not even her toes felt a splash for minutes at a time, she stepped down. Her feet sunk into wet sand. Her thigh spasmed, her legs collapsed. She sat in inches of water. A wave splashed to her waist. Shouldn't I feel colder? she thought. Isn't the water cold? She felt the urge to doze. She leaned her head against algae, closed her eyes, and opened them. I should sleep at home, she told herself. A seagull squawked near the cave's entrance. With effort, she rose.

Marilyn remembered trying and failing to wade out, the waves too high near the entrance. She remembered walking from the cave, an occasional wave hitting her waist, her weak body wobbling against the water's impact and suction. She remembered seeing the stars and thinking, I must have missed the sunset.

She didn't remember walking on the grass above the rocks or sitting on the bench in front of The Wave. She didn't remember her nonsensical phrases to Clara or Clara walking her to the office past the stare of a guest who was loading firewood from the box to his arms. She didn't remember Jackson saying he didn't need to take her to the hospital. If she's not better in the morning I will, he said. She's just cold.

She's more than cold, Clara said. But it might be faster to care for her here.

Upstairs, Clara took off Marilyn's bra and underwear and wrapped her in blankets on Tim's bed. She told Jackson to lay next to his wife for the body heat. When Jackson hesitated, Clara cursed. What's wrong with you? she said. She asked for a towel and stocking cap. Jackson brought them, and after drying Marilyn's hair with the towel as much as possible, Clara secured the cap on Marilyn's head. She heated up water, poured it into water bottles, and placed the bottles underneath Marilyn's armpits and next to her legs.

After Clara left, Jackson repeated this procedure twice, as Clara had instructed. Marilyn mumbled off and on. While the third round of bottles cooled, he lay next to her, one arm across her chest. He had to lie close to fit on Tim's twin bed. He eased his body onto hers, careful not to let any of the weight from the cast drop on her. She was warm, he thought. That meant she wasn't dead. Of course she wasn't dead. Why would he think that? She'd fallen into a pool of seawater, he surmised from her sandiness and scent, but then why was she so incoherent? And why had she taken off her clothes? Through the contact, his body was warming. Her chest rose and fell against his, her even breath moist against his face. At least she was sleeping peacefully now. Images of them making love flashed through his mind. His dick hardened. He scooted off her, rolled off the bed, and applied two more hot water bottle cycles. He tightened the blankets, mummy-like, around her, and placed one more blanket on top. For the final hours of the night, he dozed in a chair by the window, from which, unknown to him, Tim had escaped.

A half hour after the sun came up, Marilyn opened her eyes. I stayed here, she said. She wiggled her arms out of the cocoon of blankets.

Jackson wanted to tell her that that wasn't what he'd wanted to ask the night before. You stayed here, he repeated. Are you OK?

Kind of cold, she said. She pulled the blankets under her chin.

Good.

Marilyn crinkled her nose. Her head had weaseled its way from the stocking cap, and her hair laid spread in uncombed clumps across the pillow.

Clara said that was a good sign, Jackson said. He retrieved the cap from the floor and set it at her side. He was tired of his and his wife's misunderstandings, and right now, he was just plain tired. Sighing, he pulled at his beard. It had been his second night in a row with almost no sleep. And guests would start checking out soon.

Clara? Marilyn asked.

She brought you in last night, Jackson said.

Marilyn looked to either side. Tim's room, she said.

You want some coffee? Jackson asked.

Marilyn nodded.

While he made coffee, his leg ached. He should have lain next to Marilyn longer, he thought. Lying down took pressure off it. When he returned, she was asleep again. Her breathing was regular. He set her mug of coffee on Tim's nightstand and stood above her, sipping his own. He again wondered where she'd been and what had happened. He imagined her sitting on a rock. A sneaker wave pulled her out to sea. She furiously swam in. He imagined an aerial view: her hair spread in thin strands and floating. Unlikely, he thought. Sneaker waves were so rare.

The office bell rang. Marilyn's eyelids fluttered.

Your coffee, Jackson said. He nodded toward the nightstand.

Marilyn laboriously sat up. The covers slid to her waist. One wide bruise lay between collarbone and breasts. As she reached for the mug, her hand wavered.

The bell, Jackson said.

I'm fine, Marilyn said.

It had been too long since he'd seen her naked, Jackson thought. He watched her take a sip of coffee, then he left.

7.

The Cape Arago Lighthouse was also on an island, but unlike Tillamook Rock, a bridge connected this island to the mainland. People called it the Bridge of Sighs. The first Cape Arago Lighthouse was built in 1866, the second in 1908, and the third in 1933, six years after I moved there. The first two lighthouses had been made of wood; the third was made of concrete, to better withstand storms. My wife, my son—born in 1933—and I lived in the keeper's dwelling, a stone's throw from the lighthouse. While constructing the third lighthouse, the workers lopped off the tower of the second lighthouse and told me I could use the remaining structure as an office. For a few years I used it as a workshop for woodworking. Later I wrote there, too.

During my twenty years on Lighthouse Island, as it was called, the island eroded. Rocks where I showed my young son starfish were ten years later in the sea, or at the very least, submerged by it. This visible shrinking felt sinister and claustrophobic, even to me, who had lived at Tillamook Light, on a much smaller island. Each morning those last couple years, my wife or I checked to see whether the bridge had collapsed. We kept a dory, just in case.

How could he keep his family in such danger? Elliot thought. Lana placed her head on his sock-covered foot and moved it back and forth, nesting. Elliot set down his pen, patted her, then picked up his pen again. It wasn't that dangerous, he argued with himself. They had a dory; the island was only fifty yards from the mainland. The bridge could have collapsed when he was gone, but Darlene was capable: she and Conrad could have evacuated without him. He remembered once, hurrying home from Catherine's to tend to the lamp while an unexpected storm began. Fog had rolled in, and as he walked, Darlene sounded the foghorn. The bridge swayed as he crossed.

In 1936, before the bridge's rapid deterioration, the city had dynamited the 1866 lighthouse. The blast sent Conrad and the family's then-dog, an ugly, tan mutt named Buster, under the bed. Darlene coaxed both out with food. For months after, whenever Conrad heard a gunshot or any other loud noise, he ran around, ears covered with hands, elbows jutted out. Buster followed him, emitting random, low howls. The duo looked so funny that Elliot couldn't help laughing.

He needed to include that dynamited lighthouse. Should he include the city's reasoning and his own impressions while watching the process? Yes, he'd include both. He wouldn't include that memory of Buster and Conrad. No need to share that. But wanting to remember it, he wrote out a description on a separate sheet of paper. *Buster plowed into his thigh. Conrad's elbows knocked a book off the coffee table.* Maybe later he'd try to incorporate the duo into a poem.

Just that year, as Elliot had told Tim, the 1933 lighthouse had been automated. Elliot's chest hurt whenever he thought of it. After he'd read the news in the local paper, he'd written an old Coast Guard friend who he hadn't spoken with in fifteen years. He received a reply from his widow. Many of his former colleagues were sick or dead. Most were or would have been in their sixties to eighties, and the rugged Coast Guard work had accelerated their aging, as had serving in one or both World Wars. Townspeople thought Elliot was grieving for his wife, and despite his inner bravado while talking with Leah, he was, but he also held this other, waxing and waning, less personal grief at the death of his profession. The last chapter of his memoir would be called "The Automation of Lighthouses." Some days he fondled details from the past; other days his mind rushed ahead to this final chapter, where he would describe to his readers, people who probably loved lighthouses, the irreversible changes that had arrived.

Lana trotted to the door and whined. The past week she'd wanted to go out a dozen times a day. At first Elliot thought the tourists, set loose by the passing of the Beach Bill, had arrived. After he'd seen no one, he reconsidered. The weather had been warm; maybe she wanted to roam. When she'd returned tired and wet with nettles in her fur, that theory seemed confirmed.

This time he accompanied her. In the anteroom, he eyed the newspapers, stacked but not read. Since the Beach Bill passed, he hadn't had interest in them. Outside, Elliot followed Lana into the forest on a path that paralleled the long driveway. As he passed the old house, Elliot glanced through the kitchen window. Probably covered in dust, he thought. He needed to air out the place before winter and give away or sell the furniture and Darlene's clothing. If he and Conrad were on better terms, Elliot would ask his son to help organize an estate sale.

Once he and Lana crossed the highway, Elliot took the lead on the southernmost of the half-dozen paths he'd, from frequent walking, whittled from the dense underbrush. This one switchbacked to the top of a hill and followed a ridge. Lana bounded off through ferns and appeared five minutes later, panting. When Elliot reached the old logging road halfway up, he paused. A squirrel ran across, and another followed, chasing it. Knee-high grass grew between tire indents. Rays of light shone through the tree canopy. In the fall, Elliot would drive his truck up and load into the bed sections of trees he'd cut down. Some he chopped into firewood. Others he'd get cut into boards, which Elliot used for woodworking projects. It now dawned on him that he didn't have any winter woodworking projects in mind. Two remained in the queue, but he had wood for them. Maybe he'd cut only enough for firewood this year. He crossed the road and continued upward, his bent shoulders dipping lower to propel himself up the incline.

Elliot had received a letter from Conrad that contained nothing but the revised will. Elliot signed it, sent a copy to his son, and placed the original in his center desk drawer. Each time he opened the drawer for a new piece of paper or pen or pencil and inhaled the inland scents of his son's office, Elliot tried to think of another reason to contact Conrad, but couldn't.

The lawyer, Ted Johansson, had been helpful, even meeting outside Corvallis so that Elliot wouldn't have to drive into downtown Salem. With Ted's assistance, Elliot had petitioned the government to buy up his dry sand, because under the current conditions, he'd rather not own it. Once Elliot knew the outcome of this petition, he'd call his son. After all, whether or not Elliot paid taxes on the adjoining cove affected the heir of the property, too.

At the top of the hill, Lana pawed the trunk of a Douglas fir, then barked into its branches. Elliot messed the fur on her head as he passed. From the ridge, looking south, inlet after inlet of black rocks curved into each other. The massive Cape Perpetua loomed above. North, a few houses perched on the westernmost point in Kalapuya. Below sat Elliot's house, his lighthouse, his stretch of beach, and the ocean.

Elliot's gaze lingered on the beach. He couldn't believe that the legislature could pass such a sweeping rule that regulated hundreds of miles of coast; they should have had a democratic vote. Someone ran barefoot on the wet sand, along the lip of the ocean. Elliot squinted. Tim again. That boy had miles of rocks and beach by his place. Why did he come here? Wet sand flew up behind him. His arms flailed. At one end he halted and leaned over, hands on knees. Seconds later, he sprinted in the opposite direction. He repeated this ritual ten times, then, looking as though he were dry-heaving, Tim dropped to his knees. He lay down, his cheek against the sand. The boy looked defeated, Elliot thought. Was he training for something? If not, why run so fast?

Tim walked along the edge of the surf, kicking the crests of shallow waves, looking as though he wanted to desecrate or hurt the sea. What a strange desire, Elliot thought. With quick and firm strides, he headed back along the ridge. Lana wiggled ahead as they ducked into denser forest and headed downward. A handful of thistles hung off her fur. Lana . . ., Elliot said. The thistles stung him when he plucked them off. At the sound of her name, she tilted her head, then trotted faster. She barked. Elliot shushed her and tried to keep up. He wanted to say something to the boy.

By the time they reached the beach, Tim was gone. Lana looked at Elliot, her tongue lolling. She located a shallow stream leading to the ocean and lapped freshwater. Elliot walked along the boy's tracks. He found an indent where Tim had lain. Kneeling beside it, he deciphered the shape of the boy's head and the curves in his ear. This beach was more isolated than others. Did Tim want to be alone? Elliot was the last person to find that desire strange, but the boy's angry movements had disturbed him.

Elliot went inside the keeper's house, where he cut himself chunks off a block of Swiss cheese and ate them with crackers at the table. He fed a few to Lana who sat beside him, her front legs taut, her nose up. He tried to remember his encounters with Tim. Besides the lighthouse tour, he'd seen Tim only around town. The boy seemed alert but waiflike: Elliot had no other strong impressions. Elliot put away the cheese and went to the stand-alone garage of the old house, where he kept his half-finished projects, tools, and materials. Lana headed to the beach to sniff tide pools.

Inside, Elliot picked up one of the oak boards he had cut for a cabinet. He'd already penciled out pieces to cut joints. He considered working on this project but instead went to his workbench in the back. On it sat pieces for a trinket pine box he'd been making Darlene when she died. She'd collected more jewelry since they'd moved to the mainland and had run out of storage space. He'd seen it sitting there so many times that the association no longer upset him. Now, for the first time since her death, he touched the pieces, then held them. He'd already cut the lid and base sections, as well as the sides and pieces for the interior lining. In comparison to the large oak board, these pieces felt delicate and light.

He sat down, looked over the rough blueprint, and within seconds became absorbed. His elbows resting on the desk, he marked out the sockets on each end of the eight side pieces—four for the base and four for the lid—to prepare for through dovetail joints. He extended the measurements across the edges with a ruler, then on the side pieces marked the desired angles for the tails. He secured each side piece in a vise and cut his marked tails, then removed the waste, which fell onto the workbench and concrete floor. The dust caused him to cough. The sun went behind a cloud. He turned on an overhead lamp, then chiseled out waste from the remaining ends—sixteen in all—and set down the tools and rubbed the back of his neck. His coughing had increased, so he went into the old house to get water.

The kitchen wasn't as dusty as he'd thought. As he opened the cupboard, packaging in the corner caught his eye. He pulled out the store-bought canister of Hershey's hot chocolate and placed it on the counter and crossed his arms. Was some drifter in his house? His dry mouth became drier. He strode through the living room. His gaze swept over the couch and chairs. All dust covers were in place. He stepped up the stairs two at a time. He peeked into his and Darlene's room: it also seemed untouched. Maybe Darlene bought that cocoa, he thought. She liked to try new products. He paused in the hallway, imagining her walking by him, thinking maybe her ghost had dusted the place.

The door to the guest room, Conrad's old room, was half-open. Elliot stepped to it. Inside, Tim lay asleep on his stomach on the made bed, his head facing away from the window, his limbs sprawled. Saltwater from his clothes had darkened sections of the checkered quilt. A square ray of window light cut across the bed and body. Elliot gripped the doorframe. So the boy had come here. He should have suspected; Tim had disappeared too quickly from the beach. Besides the quilt, and maybe the cocoa in the cupboard, everything else in the house seemed untouched. This care pleased Elliot. Still, the boy's presence was trespassing. He'd tell him that, and warn him that if he saw him again on his land or in this house, he'd tell Jackson, who could take a firm hand.

Elliot stepped over to a backpack, which sat next to the bed. He squatted and picked up a notebook from the top of it and tapped it against his knee. He set it down and stood over Tim. A seagull squawked, and Elliot turned his head toward the window. The boy hadn't moved. How deeply children sleep, Elliot thought. In the last few years, any small movement by Darlene or Lana might wake him. Noises, even accustomed ones, startled him or entered his dreams.

Tim, Elliot said. Then, louder: Tim.

Tim jolted. He opened his blue eyes, a contrast to his dark hair and skin. He wiggled backward and pressed himself against the headboard. He noted that his notebook had not been touched.

You're ruining the quilt, Elliot said. Tim's demeanor nettled Elliot. He wasn't some scary stranger. He'd given the boy lunch for god's sake.

Tim slid off the bed. He didn't know what to say. In his notebook, he'd written poems and a dozen letters to Carl, but he hadn't talked out loud to a person in over a week. He sidestepped toward the corner and crouched. He froze after his back hit the wall, then formed fists.

As Tim had stepped through the window light, Elliot had seen that his cheeks were too thin, his eyes too wide. Why was he wearing long sleeves and jeans on such a hot day?

Is that your cocoa downstairs? Elliot asked.

It's empty, Tim said. He'd finished the cocoa on the second day, the applesauce on the third, and his sandwiches by the fourth. He'd tried and failed at fishing. He'd found enough ripe blackberries to hold back his hunger, though he never felt satiated.

Are you hungry? Elliot asked.

Tim nodded. He'd planned to pinch items from the lighthouse cupboard that night, while Mr. Yager and Lana took their evening walk. People were more likely to find him if he wandered into town or hitchhiked somewhere. It was smarter to stay put.

I'll give you some cheeses and crackers, Elliot said. Then you have to go home.

Elliot was at the top of stairs before he realized the boy wasn't following. He went back to the room, where Tim had opened the window. The boy, backpack on, had one leg over the frame. Below him was a two-story drop.

Elliot grabbed the backpack. It slid off the boy's arms. He was about to secure Tim's shoulders from behind when the boy pulled in his leg, turned, and snatched the backpack, holding it tightly against his chest.

What's wrong with you? Elliot said.

Tim put on the backpack. He looked into the hallway. He wasn't going back to The Wave, he thought. He just wasn't.

I saw you on the beach earlier, Elliot said. What were you doing?

Running.

Why?

I was just running, OK? When he ran he didn't think. When he slept he didn't think. The rest of the time he felt hungry or angry, or worse, sad. After that first letter to Carl, he didn't write to him about his death. He reminisced about other summers or wrote out Bob Dylan lyrics and told Carl what he thought they meant. During this writing, a childish voice ding-donged in his thoughts, saying he's dead, he's dead, until he had to put aside his notebook. He also thought of his parents and wondered whether they'd always live separate. He wrote another poem about his mom leaving. For some reason his mom's leaving and Carl's death were connected, almost as though they were the same event. Running or sleep were the only antidotes to these intermingled trains of thought; he did both as much as he could.

Elliot crossed his arms. The boy's eyes looked at him but his mind was elsewhere. People didn't just run, he thought. Do you want food or not? he asked.

Yes, Tim said.

Then follow me, Elliot said. No, you go first. If the boy ran off, so what, Elliot thought, but he didn't want him jumping from a two-story window.

Lana met up with them between house and lighthouse. When Tim petted her, her tail whirred. She'd joined him while he'd picked blackberries, eating them from his palm.

If his beach were overrun with people, she'd be pleased, Elliot thought. Tim petted her for so long that Elliot reminded him to go on, that she'd be in the house too.

Tim sat at the same place at the table as when they'd eaten chili together and leaned his backpack against the legs of his chair. A wet splotch, where Tim's body had pressed against the quilt, covered the front of the boy's shirt. He does not seem OK, Elliot thought. After drinking a glass of water, Elliot took out the block of Swiss cheese and stood at the counter, cutting it. Lana lay on the kitchen floor between the two. Whatever happened, he wasn't going home, Tim thought. If Mr. Yager offered a ride, he'd refuse. If Mr. Yager forced him to take a ride, he'd run off as soon as the old man dropped him off at The Wave.

Elliot gave Tim a plate of cheese and crackers. Saliva flooded Tim's mouth. He pushed in piece after piece until Elliot touched his wrist and he slowed down. Elliot turned away and put the cheese in the refrigerator. The old man wouldn't force him to do anything, Tim thought. He only wanted to be left alone.

Elliot added a cold chicken leg to Tim's plate. Lana sat up, her nose in the air. Tim looked at Elliot, his eyes sparkling with thanks. He ripped off a bite with his teeth, noting ribbons of blood along the bone. He thought of Carl. How mangled was his body? Did they have a closed-casket funeral? Did they have a body at all? It was the first time Tim's mind had strayed to the details of Carl's death since he'd woken up. Can I do something for you? Tim asked, to pay you back.

It's fine, Elliot said. He sat, kitty-corner to the boy. He placed a hand on Lana's head and her tail twitched. Maybe you could wash that quilt. I want to sell that stuff.

Sure thing, Tim said. Right after I eat.

I'm sure the maid at The Wave could do it.

Tim's shoulders cringed. He yanked off another bite of chicken. Talking to someone distracted, Tim thought. He didn't want to imagine Carl's funeral. I only ate five jars of applesauce from the basement, he said. Didn't touch anything else.

Didn't know there was food down there.

My mom doesn't can, he said. Leah does. Did Mrs. Yager can those? He wanted Mr. Yager to talk: to tell him a story; an anecdote; anything he didn't know; anything that would distract.

Elliot scratched behind Lana's ears. It's a nice house, isn't it? he asked. Demanding that the boy never trespass again was a more appropriate topic, but he wanted to wait until the boy calmed down.

Oh yes, Tim said. I wish my house was that big—a first and second story and a basement. Maybe Mr. Yager wasn't talking about his wife because she'd died, Tim thought. Maybe he wanted to be distracted, too. Everyone died, but unlike Carl, Mrs. Yager had lived a long life. He pulled off a large piece, revealing more blood along the bone. A now familiar anger filled him, a rage-pain that started in his stomach and moved to his chest and head. His face flushed. He wanted Mr. Yager to feel this anger too. But it's not very large for a bed-and-breakfast, Tim said.

A bed-and-breakfast?

There are only three bedrooms, so only three guests could stay, Tim said. And then, where would Leah sleep? He looked from side to side before demolishing the rest of the chicken leg. Here, I guess, he said, his mouth full.

Leah? Elliot asked. He looked into Tim's eyes. What're you talking about?

Tim looked at Lana. At the change in her owner's tone, the dog had lowered her body against the floor. Maybe telling Mr. Yager wasn't the best idea, Tim thought, but the property belonged to the old man. It wasn't wrong to tell. He knew that for sure; in fact, maybe it was wrong not to. Tim looked back at Mr. Yager, who had fiercely spread his fingers against the table. Tim's anger dissolved as the old man's grew, as though he were handing over his emotions. He popped the last piece of cheese in his mouth and again looked at Lana, who whined.

Your son's going to sell this place to Leah, Tim said. She wants to turn it into a bed-and-breakfast. Energy filled Tim. For the first time in days, he didn't feel angry, sad, or lethargic. He petted Lana. If I made this place into a bed-and-breakfast, he said, I'd make the area around the light into a room. And charge twice as much—for the view and the light. He imagined making the front room into an office. He'd keep a fire going every day, all year, except maybe in August.

Was it August now? Tim thought. It had to be, or pretty close. His birthday was August 5. What date is it? he asked.

Elliot's hands shook. Don't touch her, he said. Tim looked up. Don't touch Lana, Elliot repeated. Confused, Tim placed his hands in his lap.

How do you know this? Elliot asked.

Leah told my mom.

And your mom told you?

No. I was just there when they talked about it.

Elliot's face flushed.

Tim stood. Thanks for the food, he said.

Sit down, Elliot said. Stay here. His voice was calm and angry at once.

Tim wanted to leave but didn't. When Elliot turned to the office-bedroom, and Lana stood to follow him, Tim snuck a pet of Lana's back. By the time Tim thought of bolting, Elliot was back, holding a folder. Elliot went to the telephone and set the folder on the counter and flipped it open. Lana came to Tim, and he let her lick his greasy fingers.

Elliot looked back and forth between will and phone as he dragged the dials. The thought of all those strangers staying overnight in his house and lighthouse made his head hurt. Maybe Leah would even tear down the existing structures; she had connections. Elliot was angry at Conrad, but on second thought, not surprised. He should have known his son wanted the land only to resell it. He should have known the place held no great memories for him. Elliot had hoped that since he and Conrad couldn't reconcile, perhaps Conrad and the land could reconcile, and this hope for reconciliation had blinded him to his son's desires and character. While the phone rang and rang, he became angry at himself, as angry—or angrier—than he was at Conrad. He spread out his free hand and pushed it against the counter until his fingertips throbbed.

Hello. The voice was garbled, as though the ringing had woken Conrad from a Sunday nap. Elliot had never called his son at home. He had the number only because of Darlene.

It's your father, Elliot said. None of this *dad* stuff, he thought. Even before Conrad was in high school, he'd never been a dad. He'd always been a father; he might as well accept that.

Oh, Conrad said. Hi. You got the will?

I got it right here.

Did you have a question about it?

Why did you lie to me?

What?

I know you mean to sell to Leah.

I don't know what you're talking about.

I have a boy here who can testify to that.

Tim looked up. Did Elliot mean in court? he thought.

A boy? Conrad said. Dad, I didn't lie.

You did, Elliot said.

No. I just didn't tell you what I was going—

You know I wouldn't have willed it to you—

When you give a gift, that's the end of it, Conrad said. You can't tell me what I can and can't do with it.

It was a lie of omission.

That's something Catholic, right?

It was, Elliot thought. He hadn't thought of his Catholic upbringing for years. You know I don't want this place to be overrun with strangers, Elliot said.

A bed-and-breakfast isn't bad. If I sold to a chain hotel, it could look like the miracle mile.

The place isn't zoned for that, Elliot growled. I'm sure you've looked that up.

I didn't know, Conrad lied. I just wanted it to retain its charm.

How do I know you're not lying again?

I wasn't lying before, Dad.

Goddammit, you were.

You have a bad temper, you know. Maybe you should see someone about that.

You're not selling to anyone. I'm getting rid of this will.

Who'd fix it up less than Leah?

Elliot held the receiver with his shoulder. He lifted the will close to the speaker, then ripped it in half.

Just answer my question, Conrad said. Who'd change it less than her? Isn't that what you want: for it to stay the same?

Did you hear that? Elliot asked.

You're being dramatic.

Elliot heard his own breath, raspy and heavy in the phone.

If you change your mind, call me back, Conrad said.

I'm never calling you again.

Lana walked over to sniff the pieces of paper. She licked one experimentally.

Who are you going to will it to now? Conrad asked. His tone was still flat but less calm. Who? he repeated.

Why the hell would you care?

Lana decided she didn't like the taste and returned to Tim's fingers.

Who do you think taught me to lie? Conrad asked. It's not like you're a saint.

No one's a saint. I thought you'd've learned that by now.

Elliot hung up. He looked at Tim, who was scratching Lana behind the ears. He leaned over and picked up the pieces of paper and placed them in the garbage can underneath the sink. He looked over the sink, toward the sea, which was the bright, almost turquoise color of sunny summer days. The incoming tide had obliterated the boy's tracks on the sand.

There were problems everywhere, Tim thought. Problems at home, problems overseas, problems right here. Although none of these problems were his fault, he felt involved in all of them. He couldn't escape; he couldn't run away. His plan had failed. Crying rose and he choked it back. Tears welled. He turned his head and wiped them off. What a sissy. How long would he cry every day? Weeks? Months? Forever? The potential indefiniteness made him want to cry more. When he lowered his hands from his face, Lana licked them. At first he pulled away, then he let her. Her saliva served as a balm to the blackberry scratches that crisscrossed the backsides of his hands.

Elliot heard the boy coughing back sobs. He himself wanted to cry—he didn't know whether from anger or sadness or, more likely, from relief. He composed his face and turned toward the boy. You wanted to hear about the light, didn't you? Elliot asked.

Tim looked at him.

The history of the light? Didn't you ask about it last time you were here?

Yes. Tim hoped Mr. Yager didn't notice he'd been crying.

You want to go up there now? I'll tell you about it.

Tim nodded. He stood. His head hurt. On the way up the lighthouse stairs, he looked at his feet and held hard to the banister, as though at each step he might slip, as though he were climbing for his life.

8.

A tapping sound, like someone pounding a nail, came from outside. Leah opened the door. A two-by-four rested on Sandy's shoulder. Off her other arm hung a tin bucket. Leah smiled.

Remember last year? Sandy asked. All the good ones were out of reach. Why didn't we think to use a board?

Because I don't want to fall into thorns, Leah said. I did that as a kid.

Used a board or fell into thorns?

One led to the other. I'd invite you in, but——. She waved her hand at the board.

I understand. Is Marilyn coming?

She stayed at The Wave last night.

Oh? She and Jackson back together?

Sandy never gave up, did she? Leah thought. Jackson called me this morning, she said. Lyn fell into the ocean and came down with a cold or something. She turned away. I need to grab my hat and pail.

To Leah, blackberry season meant blackberry scones, blackberry tarts, and blackberry pies on The Sweet Seller shelves. For her own kitchen, she canned jam. Most years, she could pick enough for The Sweet Seller's needs; in the rare years of a poor crop on the coast, she bought the berries in bulk from the Willamette Valley. Her customers counted on blackberry goods and she didn't let them down. For months she'd watched the coast's bright green vines. They'd bloomed white flowers, which had morphed into green berries, which had ripened toward a purple, juicy, summer feast: they were in for an early and exceptional crop.

Dew faded as the women walked through town. Although the day would be warm, both wore jeans, long-sleeve shirts, floppy hats, and galoshes. Standard berry-picking clothes; armor against thorns.

Ben, the bald manager of Main Street Grocer's, waved to them, and they waved back. Outside town, they crossed a narrow footbridge over the Kalapuya River. Far to their right and below churned the silver morning ocean, the fog almost off it, the sand and rocks available for anyone to walk on. Already lawsuits had been filed, Ethan had said. And there was that Nestucca Spit business that Marilyn was working on. But Leah felt sure the beaches would allow public access for generations, maybe forever. The outcome of their work would last.

On the other side of the bridge, rocky grass gave way to large black rocks, which gave way to sand. Leah volunteered to carry the board down the embankment. Sandy handed it over, but the pail hampered her balance. She threw it into sand and followed after. After Sandy reached the bottom, Leah lowered the board to her.

Might not make it back up with full pails, Sandy said.

We've made it every other year, Leah said.

Sandy held up the board in contradiction. And I've gained weight.

We can leave the board by the river.

It was one of my display shelves.

Were you going to use it for that after this? Leah asked. She walked toward the river, stepping off sand and into the dirt, weeds, and brambles of an overgrown footpath.

Sandy followed. Why not? she asked.

Leah laughed. She pulled back a branch so Sandy could pass her, squeezed around her friend, and forged the trail inland, pushing aside shrubbery near the ground and branches above. After the Beach Bill celebration, Sandy had caught a ride with students to the Summer of Love in San Francisco. If Marilyn hadn't been so distracted this week, she would have chided her for abandoning the antique shop during peak season. Some branches had been broken recently, Leah noted. Had Tim been here? More likely other blackberry scavengers had broken them.

They'd received the call from Jackson a couple days after the dune accident. First time he's called since I left, Marilyn said, when Leah said Jackson was on the phone. Leah didn't know which was stranger: that a husband wouldn't call his wife or that a wife would keep such tabs. She handed over the phone and returned to her sketches, then was again roused by Marilyn's tense tone. Leah had accompanied her friend to the police station to file a report. That evening Marilyn and Jackson had upended Kalapuya, asking every proprietor and every household whether they'd seen the boy. During the following days, Marilyn had searched what seemed like the whole state.

At first Leah wasn't worried. After hearing about Carl's death, Tim had wanted to run off for a night or two. But now he'd been missing for over a week. Either something had happened to him or he'd found a place to hole up. Marilyn, Leah knew, feared the former. Leah hoped for the latter. Yesterday, when Sandy had returned from San Francisco and heard of Tim's disappearance, she'd suggested calling James, the college student with whom Tim had made a connection.

Leah crushed a blackberry branch underfoot. She looked up. Blackberries scattered across branches on both sides. Here we go, she told Sandy.

Sandy set down the board and came alongside Leah, who had begun picking. Berries plunked in their pails.

Did you know, Sandy said, that I haven't made a profit for years?

I did not, Leah said, though she'd expected as much. The antique shop almost always seemed empty, even during tourist season, and Sandy didn't astutely reprice her goods.

I thought Marilyn might've told you.

She wouldn't discuss a client's finances. Does it bother you?

Wouldn't it bother anyone?

Most. But I thought it might not bother you. Sandy, in addition to living off inherited money, had made tens of thousands from selling her home and property to Elliot Yager and moving to town. She seemed to enjoy collecting antiques for their own sake, not for the reselling and an income.

OK, I've never made a profit, Sandy said. In almost twenty years. That's the truth.

Leah was impressed that Sandy had kept enough records for Marilyn to figure that out.

A few years wouldn't bother me, Sandy said. Hell, if I made a profit one year, I'd consider myself a success. She grinned.

Leah had filled the bottom of her pail. She rewarded herself by popping a couple in her mouth. Every year the sweetness surprised her. Why don't you try next year? she asked.

Next year?

To make a profit.

Oh, Sandy said. She smiled, a large smile with an underbite. Maybe I will. I came close a couple years.

Leah wished all sadness dissolved so easily.

You really have a knack for business, Sandy said.

Thank you, Leah said. A berry-laden branch a couple yards into the bushes caught her eye. I might need the board for that, she said, unless you want to do the honors.

Nope, Sandy said. Be my guest. She moved to the side of the path so that Leah could pass her and pick up the board. Leah squeezed past Sandy and laid the board across the bushes. She picked up her pail and stepped onto it. Each step sunk the board lower. I might weigh a few more pounds than when I was ten, Leah said.

Sandy chucked. Don't we all.

Leah first picked blackberries while living among the logging crew. Her dad, the camp chef, used them in fish dishes or as an oatmeal topping. He didn't enjoy making desserts, but when he saw Leah stuffing sugared blackberries into the middle of biscuits, he taught her how to make a basic piecrust. Within months she'd made so many pies that he increased his orders of lard and flour. The crew loved the pies and told her so. She was glad the men liked them and that she could help her father, but neither their enjoyment nor her ability to assist inspired her to bake. The act of baking itself inspired her—the hours of attention, the scent of the ingredients, the possible experimentations.

Like the Beach Bill, baking improved her life and the lives of those around her, she thought, though each differently. Work on the Beach Bill had looked more to the future, and making baked goods gave a more present pleasure. While she made breads or pies or doughnuts or muffins, or while people ate them, they forgot about everything but the beauty of the object, the smell, the taste. And sometimes forgetting about the future and the past was OK, Leah thought, and maybe the best way to prepare for or recover from either.

Toes at the forest end of the board, she looked to either side. She'd picked every berry within reach. Some had landed on the board, where her shoes had smashed them. Their crushed look reminded her of wine-making; she'd never had blackberry wine. She walked to the other end and hopped off. In her pail, berries jumped and resettled. Blackberry wine, she said. Have you made it?

Oh, yes, Sandy said. We made it at the commune.

Good?

Delicious. Sandy pulled out the board from the bushes, and they continued down the path. Their feet sweated into their boots. The canopy of trees and their hats provided shade.

If I make a profit next year, Sandy said, maybe I'll reward myself by rejoining a commune.

I don't follow.

You should join with me.

Leah shook her head.

They take a couple weeks to get used to, Sandy said. I'll admit that.

I wouldn't be used to them after a couple years. Leah stopped at a patch of blackberries. They plopped a couple berries in their mouths before tossing more in pails.

Don't you ever miss it? Sandy asked.

What?

Sex.

I miss everything about Micah, she said. The close companionship as much as the sex, she thought. That she didn't need to be alone if she didn't want to. The weight of her pail, already two-thirds full, pulled on her arm. They'd have to stop at only one more patch that day. I'm coming back here every day this week, Leah said. In the evenings. You're welcome to join. She set down her pail and stretched out on tiptoe, but still couldn't reach a berry-laden branch. Can you grab that for me? she asked.

Sandy reached up and pulled down the branch. Leah took it from her and stepped on it so she could use both hands to pluck berries.

Wanting to have sex isn't all it takes to like a commune, Leah said. You know I'm not big on free love.

I know. Sandy sighed. Are you going to date?

Not right now.

If I didn't know Micah, I'd think you idealize him.

But you knew him.

Too shy for my liking. But all right.

Leah smiled and released the branch. It bounced upward.

Not that there's many options in Kalapuya, Sandy said.

They walked on. The path dipped toward the water. In summer the river looked more like a creek; if it weren't rocky, you could have waded across in seconds. On the opposite shore a deer eyed them as she drank. When the path veered from the water, it became denser.

Leah broke branches to clear their way. Sandy ran an arm across her forehead, wet with sweat. Up there, she said. She pointed out a patch above the trail.

Leah nodded. They ducked under a fir and around a thistle bush. They began to pick; Sandy reached high, and Leah squatted.

Went to that hotel's restaurant last night, Sandy said. Rooms aren't open yet.

Ocean View's?

Yes. What a terrible name.

Why?

So unoriginal.

Like The Sweet Seller? Leah smiled. Or Sandy's?

I ate supper there. Salmon. On the deck. Guess who served me?

Laura, Leah said. Sandy tossed a blackberry at Leah's head and she looked up.

She was involved in that protest in Eugene, Sandy said. You hear about that?

Yes. Leah stood. My pail's almost full, she said.

Next time something like that happens I'll be there, Sandy said. Your students are my connection.

Leah looked downhill at the river. On the opposite shore a man with tight brown curls cast a line. He raised a hand. Leah was surprised she didn't recognize him. How was the salmon? she asked.

Not as good as what Micah brought in, Sandy said. You want to join me? In the protest?

Not right now, Leah said. I have work to do. I'm thinking of expanding.

Oh good. I've been telling you you should, haven't I?

Leah skirted the thistle bush and ducked under the fir branch.

But to where? Sandy asked. No one around here's selling. You going to use the students to deliver?

Leah couldn't mention the lighthouse to Sandy. She didn't want the whole town to know. She started down the path, Sandy at her heels.

You're thinking of moving? Sandy asked.

No, Leah said. As soon as she'd said it, she thought, no, she wasn't thinking of moving anymore. At least not in the next year.

I remember when I saw you at The Sweet Seller on Alder, Sandy said. Her friend told the story of when she thought she and Leah first met. Leah didn't listen. She'd heard the story a dozen times; she also doubted whether Sandy had been a customer there. Her friend didn't leave the coast much, let alone go as far as Portland. Her San Francisco visit was the first trip farther than Eugene that Leah had seen her take. Trees dropped way to bushes and grass. Wind picked up as they neared where river met sea.

They stood in the sand at the bottom of the steep rocks, looking up. I left the board, Sandy said. At the last place we picked.

I'll get it tomorrow.

But my shelf.

Leah laughed. Just display them on the floor. It won't look much different.

Sandy chuckled. Marilyn says I should organize.

Leah scaled the first large rock. She reached down for Sandy's bucket, held it while her friend scaled the rock, then handed it back.

Sweat soaked through their clothes as they climbed the remaining rocks and walked across the bridge and through town. They parted at Leah's lawn.

If you want to learn to make wine, come over tonight, Sandy said. I'll use these berries.

I'd like that, Leah said. I'll call you.

On the porch, Leah took off her boots. In her bedroom, she took off her hat and long-sleeve shirt. She carried the pail of berries to The Sweet Seller kitchen, placed it on the counter, set the oven to preheat, and tied a full-length apron over her bra. The warm air against her back felt good. Who knew how many more warm days they'd have, she thought. Fall and winter seemed just around the corner.

She poured half the berries from her pail into the colander and rinsed them off. She let the faucet's flow run over her scratched hands. The water stung while it cleansed, then soothed. She shook off water, rubbed her hands against the apron, and took out ingredients for her signature blackberry piecrust: cottage cheese, sugar, flour, baking powder, salt, oil, and butter. She ticked on the radio, usually reserved for winter baking. "Strangers in the Night" flooded her workspace.

Portland's winters were dark and rainy, Seattle's winters were darker and rainier, but the Kalapuyan winters took darkness and rain to a whole other level. Every winter since she'd moved to the coast, the incessant darkness and rain had caused her a handful of disheartening, sometimes paralyzing, days, when the most she could do was listen to records and drink tea. And last winter she'd had more. Before that, when she was having a lonely day and Micah was away fishing or working in the shed, she knew they'd unite later on, that he was there. Last winter, unless she sought out people, sometimes she'd seen no one after her last customers at 10 or 11 a.m. This winter the students would probably be back some days, but she couldn't count on them.

She mixed the cottage cheese, sugar, and oil mixture in a blender and poured it into the flour, salt, baking powder, and butter mixture. She laid three bottom crusts in three pie tins. She placed the tins inside the fridge and ran her hand down the door's cracked handle as she closed it. She'd buy a newer fridge this winter. Once she had more storage space she could expand from this shop, she thought. She could drive her products places instead of sitting around feeling the wetness and darkness. There was no need to wait until the old man died.

In her notebook, she wrote down ideas. Ocean View might need baked goods. A couple of store owners in Waldport and Florence liked her products. She could drive as far as Coos Bay, if places there were interested. And maybe Eugene. Didn't one of the students' fathers own a restaurant there? Bryan's? Yes. She'd call him.

In a large bowl, she folded sugar and a touch of cinnamon into the berries. They shrunk and bled sweet juice as they absorbed the sugar. She took out the pie tins and poured the berries into them, careful to divide them evenly and withhold juice. She rolled out the remaining dough and cut strips for lattice tops. She remembered when such piecrusts had been difficult for her. In Portland, in her apprenticeship, when her dad's friend saw her uneven strips, which he said looked like the crests of waves, he'd assigned her to make only lattice crusts for two full shifts. Now to cut unevenly took effort. She braided the strips over and under one another, pinched the outer edges of the crusts together with her thumb and forefinger, and set the pies in the oven.

Leah wiped her hands on her apron and picked up the shop phone and called Marilyn. The line rang and rang. Leah hung up. Hopefully she was sleeping peacefully, she thought. Hopefully the chill hadn't turned into a fever or pneumonia.

Next, she tried Conrad's number. She was ready to talk. It also rang and rang. Perhaps he'd given her his home phone number and he was at work, she thought. She'd try again later on.

In her house Leah showered and put on a gray skirt and blue blouse that brought out her gray-blue eyes. She considered heels, decided against them, and slid on flats. Ocean View wasn't the Heathman Hotel in Portland, she thought. It may be fancy, but it was still the coast. She blow-dried her hair and put on mascara, lipstick, and blush and checked her figure, front and side, in her bedroom's full-length mirror. Although her breasts and butt sagged more now than when she was young, she'd weighed around one hundred and ten since her early twenties. Back in The Sweet Seller, she took the pies from the oven and set them to cool on the island cutting board. She grabbed her notebook. Best to go before they opened the rooms, Leah thought. That way the management was more likely to be free.

Outside, the day was warm. A cloud covering muted the summer sunlight.

9.

Minutes after daylight, Tim woke on Elliot's couch. The image of his backpack rose. He sat up and looked toward the fire in the fireplace. He looked down. The backpack, still zipped, lay next to the couch. He set it next to him. He shivered and moved with his backpack toward the fire. Out the small front-room window, a muted early morning light filtered through fog, against trees.

After Elliot had explained the light and its history, he'd fed Tim again, this time a meat and potato stew. Afterward, Elliot picked up Tim's bowl and said, You can stay or go. I'll be in the office. Tim had wandered into the front room toward the fire. He'd thrown in twigs and placed a log. Before sunset, he'd fallen asleep.

He must have slept a long time. His mom would have placed a blanket over him, or, as she did on the night before she left, led him to bed. Elliot had let him alone, and Tim liked that. Why be too nice when Tim was just going to leave? But the old man had started the fire this morning, though probably more for himself than for Tim.

Tim jabbed between two logs with a brass poker. Sparks flew out and up. He rubbed his arms. He wore the same shirt as yesterday, the same shirt he'd worn since he left. The water had dried but he still smelled like salt and seaweed.

His eyes roved the framed photos of shipwrecks on the walls, resting on one on Neahkahnie Mountain, on the Northern Oregon Coast. In the foreground was an enormous ship, beached. Two men sat on the railing talking. A woman, hands on hips, looked inland. Were they waiting for rescue? Didn't they have a ladder they could lower over the side? And why did Elliot cover his wall with photos of shipwrecks? Lighthouses would make more sense. Maybe the wrecks inspired him to be a better lighthouse keeper. Maybe, whenever Elliot entered this room, he remembered how many ships had wrecked and vowed, through his profession, to help avoid future wrecks. Like his grandpa Richard, who kept photos of men whose limbs had been cut off while working in mills. He'd shown Tim photos of fingerless, handless, or armless men, saying, you could get hit by slabs, drowned, tangled in chains, crushed by rolling logs, or pounded by machinery. The equipment's a bit safer now, he always added. We made sure the union saw to that. As for him, Tim thought, he'd rather hang photos of tall lighthouses like Heceta Head or Yaquina Bay, or own photos of men standing on floating logs during the Toledo Logging Show. He'd rather think of Carl smiling, his hands full of agates, than see a photo of Carl dead. Such photos served no purpose for him, who couldn't stop the killing, who couldn't in any way help.

Tim shrugged on the backpack and went to the kitchen. On the table lay two green apples, which he slipped in his backpack. Out the window above the sink, a low fog covered the grass and rocks and sea thick as smoke. From under the office-bedroom door, a light shone. Lana whined. Tim left the house, slowly closing the front door, sure he was fooling neither the dog nor her owner. They knew when he woke and when he left. It was a miracle Mr. Yager hadn't found his hiding place until yesterday.

Tim lowered himself down a steep embankment onto the rocks and walked north, toward Kalapuya. Above the inlet in which sea lions often lay, he stopped, squinting. Nothing but fog and more fog. Wind whistled in a crevice. Water lapped against rocks. He hadn't been in these really deep caves yet. He imagined sea lions in there, lounging on top of one another, secure that no humans would bother them because no one could see them. Tim spun in the fog, arms out, daring someone to find him. In a couple months, he remembered, some sea lions would migrate to California for the winter. Tears dribbled. He mashed his fists into his eyes until his eyeballs hurt. But they'd come back, he thought. He could trust them to return, unlike any human being.

He walked near the cave in which he'd almost drowned. He stepped down the rocks, toward the water, with only the barnacles, tide pools, or algae directly in front of his tennis shoes visible. The tide was low and coming in. He knew this fact as well as the poems in his notebook, as well as the tunes on his records, as well as the scent of The Wave's units. Without hesitation he lowered himself into the cave's crevice. Starfish lined the ceiling and sides, their splayed figures outlines in the dim light. Toward the back of the cave, he touched an orange one on the ceiling, then pulled at each of the five legs with his signature gentleness and intentness. As the starfish unattached, its legs curled, reaching for the rock no longer there. Tim took it to the front of the cave, where waves lapped at his shoes, and placed it low on a rock covered by water. He moved five more—two more orange, two purple, and a red.

At the back of the cave were two pools. He squatted, waiting for his eyes to adjust, then spotted agates, which must have been there for years. He dipped in his hand gingerly in order to not disturb sand and cloud his vision. He laid the rocks on the wet sand and separated out the ones he'd keep. The large and shiny ones interested him most, or the smaller ones with irregular shapes. As the agates rolled off his fingers into his pockets, something bunched in the corner of the cave caught his eye.

He turned to the other pool, but the presence of the bunched-up objects distracted him. He went over, picked up one, squeezed out water, and shook it open. A skirt that looked like his mom's. He dropped it and held up the other. Mom's blouse, he thought. It had to be. Water ran down his arm and dripped off his elbow. Forgetting the other pool of agates, he dropped the blouse, grabbed his backpack, and ran from the cave.

He climbed the rocks to a flat grassy embankment and sprinted, his backpack bouncing. He'd check The Wave. He'd check The Sweet Seller. He'd ask his dad and Leah. For a moment he forgot he'd been gone; his absence seemed unimportant compared to his mom's potential drowning. He'd conflated his mom's absence and Carl's death, but now he saw they were so different. His mom, although he hadn't seen her much this summer, had existed, living her life that he may or may not be a part of. To be dead, to not have existence, meant he couldn't wonder what she was doing, because she wouldn't be doing—or feeling—anything. Sobs clogged his throat and he choked them out, coughing. What would he do, he thought, if his mom were dead? As he sprinted, fog moved in clumps and wisps off the sea.

As he neared The Wave, he halted. His mom sat on the bench, a winter coat on, her eyes fixed on the newly visible horizon. Behind her, light peeked over the new units.

Why was she wearing such a heavy coat? Tim thought. He sidled across the grass, far to the side of, then behind the bench. His flushed face deepened in anger. It wasn't fair, he thought. It wasn't fair she'd scared him. He wanted to go to her, for her to hug him, her chin resting on his head as she'd hugged him before he grew too tall, but he held himself back, resenting her because he'd worried about her throughout the summer and especially this morning.

On the front side of the units, he tiptoed up the new stairs and pushed open a door with a doorknob hole but no doorknob. He stood next to a glassless window, hands tucked into his jeans' pockets, a couple dozen feet from his mom's back. The sea and sky were becoming blue. He felt the beauty of the view but knew that the clearness or storminess of the ocean stood independent from him and was indifferent to him. Peaceful weather couldn't calm him; he'd have to find his own peace through his own actions in whatever ways he could. His fingers clutched at agates. He pulled one out, admired it, then hurled it at his mom. It bounced off her thick coat. She didn't flinch. He threw another, aiming at her head. He ducked as she yelped, then ran down the stairs and toward the main road. Once on the highway, he headed toward town, alternating between a sprint, a jog, and a walk. He didn't care who saw him now. He just didn't want his mom to know he'd thrown the rocks. Although he knew she'd know. He wanted her to know, he decided, but he didn't want to see her disappointment.

In town, Tim slurped water from a hose behind the grocer's. Water pooled at his feet and ran downhill, toward the elementary school. Three boys he recognized kneeled near the school fence, shoulders hunched, exchanging marbles from brown leather bags. Next school year they'd be sixth graders. It was fun to be the oldest at the school, he remembered. The little kids thought you knew everything.

Ben stepped out from the back of the store. How many times do I have to tell you kids—, he said. Tim dropped the hose. Tim, he said. Tim took off running. Tim! Ben said again. The voice was fading. Ben wouldn't catch him, Tim thought. He had a beer belly, and everyone knew he'd ruined his back pulling green chain at a mill. Tim ran north, past rows of houses. He wiped water from his lips and breathed deeply. He passed The Sweet Seller's street, a grove of trees, and the sign for the Ocean View Hotel. "Now Open for Dinner," a panel hanging off the bottom advertised. That was new, Tim thought. He'd been gone less than two weeks and the whole town had changed.

He stopped, panting, at a gas station on the outskirts of town, sat on a bench across from the pumps, and pulled out an apple. A logging truck coming from the south pulled in. A dirt cloud and the scent of sawdust drifted toward him. The driver, a pale woman in a flannel shirt and overalls, her dark hair braided, nodded at him as she walked into the store. His mom, Ben, or others would be here soon, Tim knew. Cars were an unfair advantage; he had only legs. He eyed between the logs on the truck. His whole body wouldn't fit there. The woman came out, eating a Hershey's bar. She smiled at him.

Mind if I hitch a ride? he asked.

Hop in, she said.

He climbed into the cab's passenger's side. The driver maneuvered the long truck onto the coastal highway. Tim munched on the apple. He would have loved to tick on the radio. But the woman seemed pleasant, in that she minded her own business. Tim held the core of his apple between his thumb and forefinger.

Throw it out the window, the driver said.

What his dad always said, Tim thought. His mom wanted him to save cores for her compost pile. Tim rolled down the window and chucked the core into the forest.

Where're you headed? the woman asked as they neared Waldport.

Here, Tim said. Waldport. He didn't know why.

Near the business district, the woman pulled onto the highway's shoulder. Here OK? she asked.

Sure thing, Tim said. Thanks. He opened the door and slipped out and down.

Take care, the driver said.

The truck was back on the highway before Tim had gained his bearings. Below him lay Main Street. He walked down an adjacent neighborhood street, avoiding shops and the people in them. Small square houses, similar to Kalapuya's, lined the road. A young, bob-haired woman wearing an apron smoked on a front porch. Beside her, a freckle-faced boy moved his toy boat up and down as though through fierce waves. After a dozen blocks, the street ended in knee-high grass and sand above the Alsea Bay.

Tim walked through the grass and sat in sand with the toes of his dirty tennis shoes inches from lapping waves. Small dunes lay across the water. To his right, a concrete bridge stretched across the inlet between river and bay. He counted two cars in ten minutes, then turned his head the other way, toward the ocean he couldn't see but imagined as gray as the bay right now, as gray as the sky. He pulled the remaining agates from his pockets, spit on them, and rubbed his palms together. When he opened his hands, the rocks shone like the sun bouncing off the sea. Should he throw them in the bay? Instead, he shoved the agates back into his pockets and hugged his knees. For a single morning, he thought, he'd gone a long way.

The abandoned house was off-limits now. The old man seemed more fair than kind, and to be fair the next time he found Tim in the house, he may write him up for trespassing. Tim remembered the old man going on and on the night before when describing lighthouses. The more questions Tim asked, the more Mr. Yager's cheeks flushed. His mom had said that this year for school they'd have a unit on the history of coastal towns. That had to include lighthouses, right? Maybe he could interview Mr. Yager. If Tim visited to ask about lighthouses, the old man wouldn't mind.

But maybe his mom wouldn't be living at The Wave when school started. The first books he was supposed to read, *Tom Sawyer* and *Huckleberry Finn*, had covers—a boy in a cave and a boy on a raft—that looked promising. Maybe he could read those on his own. He didn't need his mom to teach him, except maybe in math.

She certainly knew nothing about music. At the Beach Bill party, she wasn't aware of what kind of music was playing or even that music was playing at all. Once, when someone asked her to choose the next album, she said whatever was fine. Tim couldn't imagine not listening or not having an opinion. Every time an unfamiliar album began, he listened closely, comparing its sound to familiar tunes.

The yearning tone of the song "I Want You" filled Tim. He'd listened to *Blonde on Blonde* after the Beach Bill party, the night before he and his dad went to the dunes, the night before he'd run away. He wanted to be in his room, lying on his bed, listening to music. An ache flooded his chest, a different kind of ache than when he thought of Carl, because concerning music, he could listen again if he wanted. To do so he would only have to go back home.

Tim made his way back into the downtown by a different street. He walked by the junior high playground, where he stopped outside a chin-high, chain-link fence. Kids were lined up in front of an outdoor basketball hoop. Two kids in front held two balls. Most passed the ball to the next person in line once they made a basket, but some gave the ball to the next person without making a basket, then stepped away, to the side. They must be out, Tim thought, but he wasn't sure why. He didn't remember the game from elementary school. Behind the playground stood the brick, two-story school with dark, square windows. One of the boys approached Tim.

Mitch, Tim said. They'd gone to elementary school together.

Hey, Mitch said. Where have you been?

Oh yeah, Tim thought. He was supposed to be missing. Around, he said. Away. I'm back now.

Some people thought you were dead. Mitch itched his sunburned, peeling nose. His dirty-blonde curls had overgrown into his ears.

Tim shrugged. That people would compare his state to Carl's was laughable, he thought.

What're you doing here? Mitch asked.

What?

Mitch grabbed the fence and shook it. Here, he said, in Waldport.

Tim tightened the straps on his backpack. I'm signing up for school, he said. What else could he say, *I'm running away again?* He didn't think he was.

Hey, Mitch, some kid yelled. New game.

See ya, Mitch said.

Tim went to the front of the school. Wide cement steps led to double doors. An American flag flew high on a pole. He thought of the flag burnings on television and wondered whether someone was burning a flag right now. Someone was dying in Vietnam right now. And here no one seemed to care. If to care, Tim thought, meant to stop regular tasks and mourn or to stop regular tasks and protest. But if people stopped their routine every time someone was killed, regular wouldn't be regular anymore. That many deaths happened. Maybe people showed their caring differently. Tim hoped so, but he couldn't imagine how.

He walked up the steps. Inside, the halls were empty. A red-haired lady with a large mouth sat behind an entryway desk, reading a magazine. Tim remembered he hadn't bathed for days and days.

May I help you? she asked, not looking up.

I'd like to sign up for school. Eighth grade.

You new around here?

I'm from Kalapuya. My mom homeschooled me last year.

The lady pulled out a sheet from a file drawer and thrust it at him. You'll need to fill this out, she said. And get one of your parents to sign it.

Tim took it. That's it? he asked.

Yes. She was avoiding looking at him. May I help you with anything else?

No. He unzipped his backpack and stuck the paper in between pages of his notebook.

Back on the highway, standing with a foot on the white line, Tim stuck out a thumb. Gusts rolled down the wooded hill, past him, through town, and onto the beach and the bay. Ten cars passed in an hour. The eleventh, a young couple, picked him up. They volunteered to take him farther than Kalapuya. He imagined himself riding on to Florence, to Reedsport, to Coos Bay, but music on the radio reminded him of his records and he turned them down. Kalapuya's fine, he said. For now, he added to himself. On his ride back, wind tossed beachside trees.

Neither his mom's sedan nor his dad's truck was in The Wave's lot. Tim imagined them out looking for him, his dad dropping by places on a whim, his mom searching store by store and house by house. The thought of his parents held no emotion for him; they were out there and he was in here, and he was sure they'd meet soon enough.

The office and apartment were both empty. He stood over the kitchen sink, eating peanut-butter-filled celery sticks and looking at the new units, the exterior finished except for siding and windows. After, he went to his bedroom, where one of his mom's dresses lay folded on his bed. He set the dress and his backpack on the floor, cued up *Blonde on Blonde,* and sprawled on the bed to listen. The rollicky tune of the first track quieted him. By the end of the third track, he felt saner than he had since he'd heard about Carl. Music was better than running or sleeping, he decided. He could remember while listening without as much pain.

Jackson hobbled into an empty office. He'd left Annie in charge of checkout. Now, during the dead period between checkout and check-in, she was cleaning rooms. He leaned over and checked the book. So far only six units were filled tonight. Six wasn't bad for a weekday in the summer, but he had bills to pay. Maybe some guests would drop in last minute. Probably, they would.

While Jackson had been drinking his morning coffee at the desk, Marilyn, flushed and frantic, had rushed in. Tim had thrown agates at her from the new units, she'd said. She'd seen him. They decided she'd search town while Jackson drove up and down the coast. He'd driven south as far as Florence and north as far as

Newport, stopping at every service station and store. Climbing in and out of his cab with a cast made his leg throb. He should have taken Marilyn's sedan. He wondered why she wasn't back and hoped she'd had better luck. Why was the kid throwing rocks at his mom? Jackson thought. What was he doing, running away and scaring them all half to death? Now that Jackson knew Tim was near, anger surfaced. He and Marilyn had raised him better.

Over the past week, Jackson had become so angry that he didn't recognize himself. On Friday, after a sleepless night, a guest had stalked into the office and complained about the construction noise above his unit. That's why I gave you a discount, dammit, Jackson said. The guest said he couldn't wait until Ocean View's rooms opened. The force in Jackson's voice had startled, then embarrassed him, even as he'd chalked it up to the limitations imposed by his leg. Pain makes ordinary life look divine, Jackson thought. He located an aspirin bottle in the office drawer and forced two down his dry throat. Without two good legs, he felt caged.

The wind whipped at Annie's white dress as she walked across the parking lot. Every few feet she readjusted the cart. The wind had been strong on Jackson's drive, too, sometimes shaking the cab of his truck. He remembered how Marilyn had marveled at such gusts when they were dating. Inland we have wind, she'd said, but not like this. Before that, Jackson hadn't given the wind a second thought. She still avoided going out in it. It doesn't last, she said, when he asked why she waited. She claimed the harsh gusts lasted two hours max, and after studying the wind, Jackson admitted she was right. He'd never noticed that, either. The weather you're used to is normal, Jackson thought now. Not good or bad or something to avoid. Some people say it rains too much here, Jackson's dad had told him. But I think there's too much sun everywhere else.

Jackson clumped up the stairs using the railing for support. In the kitchen, he filled the percolator with water. A knife spotted with peanut butter lay in the sink. Marilyn didn't eat peanut butter, he thought. He set down the pot and dragged himself to Tim's bedroom. The boy lay asleep on top of the covers. He hadn't even taken off his shoes. Jackson stumbled across the room, removed the clicking needle on the record player, and dropped into the chair by the window, where he'd sat the night before and monitored Marilyn, where Marilyn had sat in the evenings when Tim was younger and read to him until he fell asleep.

Seaweed, saltwater, and sweat scents rose off Tim. Dried mud streaked the back of his neck. His hair was oily. Jackson looked away from his son, and Tim's record sleeves caught his eye. All summer the kid had played three or four records over and over. Jackson picked up a sleeve and read the lyrics. They seemed familiar, as they should; he'd heard them a hundred times from a room or two away.

The boy shouldn't have run off. Maybe Marilyn was right, and on a dune wasn't the best place to break the news, but that didn't excuse Tim's leaving. If the boy got away with it, he'd do it again. And throwing agates at his mom was unacceptable.

Wind shook the gutters. Rain pattered against them, then fell harder, plopping and drumming. Marilyn stepped up the stairs. Jackson stood. From premonition or knowledge or just plain luck, she ran straight to Tim's bedroom. From the entryway, she brushed her eyes over Jackson before focusing on Tim. Tim, she said, Tim. She kneeled by the bed and touched his shoulder and cheek.

He woke, startled, then pulled away. When Marilyn moved toward him, Tim relaxed, allowing her to hug him. He stretched his arms around her limply, as though she were a distant relative.

Jackson looked out the window at a guest, who held a newspaper over his head and ran from his car to under an awning.

The man shook water off the paper before unlocking and opening his room's door. Jackson imagined himself running and grimaced. He couldn't remember walking without hurting.

I'm so glad you're safe, Marilyn said. She kissed Tim's cheek and he wiped it off. Marilyn smiled.

Jackson stepped toward the bed. There's no excuse for scaring us like that, he said.

Tim pulled away from his mom. He looked at Jackson's cast and out the window. Avoiding looking in his face, Jackson thought. Look at me, he said.

Not now, Marilyn said. She stood across the bed from Jackson.

Jackson stepped closer to the bed and grabbed the boy's arm. Tim pulled away. Jackson grabbed it again, tighter. The people who stay have to do the work, he said, while you're running around. Jackson looked at his wife, who looked away. He wasn't sure whether he was talking to Marilyn or Tim. The big deal is those who stay, Jackson said, not those who go, leaving others to work and worry. He shook the boy until his body bounced on the bed. He yanked Tim toward him, close enough the boy felt his jagged breathing. I thought you were past whipping age, Jackson said, but this time you deserve it.

Marilyn reached out, then retracted her hand. It's not the time, she said.

Maybe it's time to leave him, like you did, Jackson said.

The boy's muscles tightened. He twisted his arm away and slid by his father and kicked his cast. Jackson cursed and stumbled and caught his fall on the bed. Tim! Marilyn said. Tim looked out the window at the large drops against the pane. A chill filtered through. There was nowhere else to go, he thought, not now, not today. He swung around, made fists, and held them in front of his face.

From the bed, Jackson gasped. Sharp pains waved through his leg. The dull ache the aspirin had suppressed increased. Inside his cast, sharp and dull pains overlapped and competed. He accidentally bit his tongue. He cried out.

Can I get you something? Marilyn asked. She leaned over the bed, raised his casted leg, and pushed a pillow underneath it.

Jackson yelped again. The throbbing felt like the day of the accident. He'd forgotten that feeling and he groaned, oblivious to his wife and son.

Go get a wet rag, Marilyn said to Tim. The boy was watching, eyes squinted, arms crossed. Two rags, she said. Run them under warm water. Tim didn't move. Marilyn looked straight at him. Go, she said.

When Tim was in the hall, the phone rang. He stood by, waiting for one of his parents to tell him to answer. No sound came from his bedroom. One of them will come out, he thought. One of them will answer. Tim, his mom yelled. Hurry up. Marveling at this strangeness—that neither would care about a ringing phone—he went into the kitchen.

In the bedroom, Marilyn asked Jackson whether he needed aspirin. Just took some, he growled. As the pain subsided, he heard the ringing. I'll get it, he said. The moment his foot touched the ground, he swore, then fell back against the bed. You get it, he said. Standing above him, Marilyn shook her head.

The heightening pain overrode any desire but to rid himself of pain. The ringing stopped. Marilyn placed warm rags on his forehead and above his cast. Tim shut the door on his way out. In retrospect Jackson found times of intense pain a relief from the incessant dull ache; like while doing intricate physical labor, his mind focused on the project, not caring about past or future. While living through these minutes, however, he just wanted them to end.

Marilyn moved around the room, rearranging things. She returned to Jackson and moved a rag from his forehead to his chest. It had half-cooled but still felt good. The ache was abating. He opened his eyes. Now he really deserves a beating, Jackson said.

Marilyn unzipped Tim's backpack. She pulled out a notebook, an apple, the canteen, and clean pajamas.

You're not speaking to me? Jackson asked.

I'm speaking.

Jackson didn't have enough energy to repeat himself.

Marilyn pulled a sheet of paper from the notebook. In the parking lot, a car pulled in. Jackson wondered whether a drop-in or reservation had arrived. I sent Tim downstairs to check in guests, Marilyn said.

Relief, anger, and grief filled Jackson. He'd missed these instances, when both he and Marilyn had the same thoughts about the running of The Wave. Hadn't she missed them, too? Sure he won't run off again? he asked.

For now, Marilyn said. Somehow she knew the boy wouldn't leave without his backpack. She waved the sheet of paper. This is from Waldport Junior High, she said. Apparently Tim wants to go there in the fall.

Another car pulled into The Wave. It's up to you, he said. You're in charge of his schooling.

Marilyn crossed her arms, wrinkling the paper. If he'd have done that, she'd have snatched it from him and placed it under a book, Jackson thought. What was wrong with her? Wasn't this part of marriage, this splitting of tasks? She took charge of some and he did the same. Wasn't that one of the best parts of marriage? He thought of the empty window boxes, the muddled accounts since she'd left.

Don't think it'll hurt him, Marilyn said. Better than the no schooling he's getting with me gone. She fished out a pen and signed the paper. Her long hair fell over her shoulder, and she pushed it back. We'll figure out transportation later. She took the rags and headed into the hall, leaving the bedroom door open. In the kitchen, the faucet ran.

He wondered whether she'd leave again. With Tim back, she'd probably stay a few days or take the kid with her if she left. He was surprised she wasn't with Tim now.

She reentered and placed a hot rag high on his thigh. How's it feel? she asked.

Like someone kicked it, he said. Then, Better now.

She paced to the door and back, then stood at the window. Her lids fluttered and she crossed her arms.

She seemed out of place, Jackson thought. And she was. Not only by being in Tim's room, but by being at The Wave. She had no official role here now. If he wanted her to do her old tasks, he'd have to ask. Any chance you can do a little bookkeeping? he asked.

I'll enter figures for the motel accounts but not from the new units.

Well, Jackson said. His shin inside the cast needed to be scratched. He moved an inch or two and gritted his teeth.

They're not separated, are they? Marilyn asked.

Why should they be? Jackson said.

I'll separate them. And give you an estimate on how long it would take.

Like how many hours?

Hours and money, she said. Before he could reply, she left, closing the door behind her.

Marilyn stepped down the stairs. This again, Jackson thought. The more desperate would have to compromise, and that seemed at this moment to be him. He clinched his fists. He could always barter on her estimate, he thought. Halve it to start with, the tactic of the logging companies his father had said. But unlike his father, Marilyn wouldn't estimate higher than her services were worth. If she insisted on her price, he could bluff competition; he could even find real competition, like that guest, an accountant from Salem who came down every August. But did he want to go through all that? He was tired enough. Maybe he'd pay her for this one job. He'd decide when the time came.

His fingers relaxed, and he dropped into the deepest sleep since his accident, an inevitable, physiological sleep relieving his prolonged pain.

While he slept, the drizzle stopped, the sky darkened, and the temperature dropped. Cold seeped through the windows and onto Jackson's bare arms. A few hours later he woke shivering. The phone was ringing. He tossed his legs over the bed and stood. He was pleased that his leg felt OK. He hobbled to the phone on the hallway table.

Joe here, Joe said. Heard Tim's been found.

Yes.

That's great. Every kid needs to run away. It's a rite of passage.

Jackson, feeling his beard, couldn't remember when he'd last trimmed it.

Have you heard the forecast? Joe asked. Supposed to get down to the lower thirties. Cold for summer, isn't it? Thought you'd want to know. I remember you saying you need to clean your flue.

I appreciate it.

Don't be a stranger down here, OK?

I'll be down soon.

Alcohol is the best painkiller.

I know.

Tell Marilyn and Tim hello.

The other line clicked. Jackson hung up. He'd long ago stopped wondering how Joe knew the town's news as well as an accurate forecast. But Tim and the weather were just Joe's excuses to call. Jackson hadn't been to the bar since the accident, and Joe missed him. And Jackson missed Joe as well. Before his accident, he'd never minded being alone in the office—but that was when he'd had two good legs, when Marilyn had been a room or two away or he knew he could take a break and go to the bar. Without either option, solitude had become loneliness. But he was feeling better now, he thought. He'd get down there soon. Maybe today, before supper, after he cleaned the flue.

He hobbled to the front room. The fireplace sat on the other side of Tim's bedroom wall. A mesh curtain hung over the opening. Inches of ash lay under the grate. Jackson took a shovel from a rack next to the fireplace and spread the ashes across the bottom. Black dust drifted up, and Jackson sneezed. His cast bounced, and pain returned. The cleaning supplies were in the shed outdoors, he remembered. Walking down the stairs and back up felt as impossible as running a marathon.

The shooting pains settled into a dull throb. He hobbled to the kitchen and took an aspirin. He grabbed a matchbox from the highest cupboard and opened the closet off the kitchen. Leaning forward, unable to bend his left knee, straining his back, he lit the pilot light. It was early in the year for that, and Marilyn would give him hell, but he didn't care. Still holding the matchbox, he clumped to the television, turned it on, and sat on the couch. His throat felt dry—he should have brought over a cup of water, he thought—but not dry enough to rise again. On television a husband and wife argued while the wife fed a kid in a high chair. He had no idea which show was playing; he never watched television in the afternoon. He struck a match. A bright flame jumped, then dimmed while sizzling down the stick. Right before the fire singed his thumb and forefinger, he blew it out. Again and again, he lit a match, until the box was full of used matches.

Jackson remembered one fall the year before Tim started school; he'd been in the office, Marilyn in the laundry room, washing their personal blankets and comforters. When Tim complained of the cold, Jackson lit the pilot light, but Tim must have felt the apartment was taking too long to warm up, because he put on his coat, went looking for blankets, and when he found none, decided to start a fire. Jackson came upstairs to see firewood stacked on kindling in the fireplace, crushed newspaper in crevices between them. The boy stood on the kitchen counter, looking for matches in the highest cupboard. Fortunately, they were out. Jackson lifted his son down. What have we told you about fire? he growled. The boy looked down. Holding his son's arm with one hand, Jackson grabbed a wooden spoon from a drawer with the other. He hit Tim ten times, hard. When he let him go, the boy went running to his mother, who was mounting the stairs. She saw his red arm and dropped the clean, unfolded laundry on the floor and picked him up. You hit him too hard, she said. Maybe he'll remember to stay away from fire, Jackson said. While his parents argued, Tim slid down his mom, nestled under the still-warm blankets and comforters, and fell asleep. His parents looked ten minutes before they found him. While Marilyn folded the laundry, Jackson used a flimsy match from a motel pack to light the newspapers in the hearth. He sat by the growing fire, and Tim sat next to him and rested his flushed arm on his dad's leg. It was still very red, Jackson thought. Maybe he'd hit him a tad too hard.

The air smelled like sulfur. Jackson leaned against the couch and closed his eyes. Tim's step bounced up the stairs. Jackson's eyelids fluttered. Tim jogged by his father, giving him a sidelong glance. In the kitchen, he filled a glass with water and drank while looking out the window. Looking for all the world like his mother, Jackson thought. As though they both wanted to go somewhere out that window, somewhere else. To Jackson, The Wave was its own world, and he left, even to the bar or the store, with reluctance. So he had money problems. He'd figure them out, not leave and let the place go to hell. What would Marilyn do if he took off like she did? Let the motel run itself into the ground? Tim filled up his glass again, still looking out the window. How far could he see in all this darkness? Jackson thought.

But Marilyn would stay if he left. She liked Kalapuya and running the motel, she just had different ideas on how to run it. She could have gone to Toledo when she'd left The Wave, but she'd stayed in town. If she were running the place alone, she'd leave the new units half-finished or empty until she paid off more of the loans. But like many of her business ideas, that didn't make sense. In order to start receiving revenue, they'd finish the siding and painting, fill the units with furniture, and open them as soon as possible. But the assurance that Marilyn would continue to run The Wave if he left, or more likely died in some accident like on a dune, comforted Jackson.

Tim had noticed the open mesh curtain. You making a fire? he asked.

Jackson stared at the television screen. The flue needs to be cleaned, he said.

Tim set down his glass. When are you gonna clean it?

Jackson tapped his cast. When this thing feels better.

I can clean it, Tim said.

Jackson looked at the boy. His hair flopped in half-dry, silky clumps; he must have taken a bath. He was far past the age where Jackson might say, Not sure whether you're old enough. He'd been old enough to do such tasks for years, Jackson knew. The construction crew said he was careful and precise when they allowed him to use their equipment. Hell, at age four, he'd stacked the kindling and firewood correctly.

OK, Jackson said. The equipment's in the shed. I'll direct you from here.

The boy smiled, rounded the corner into the living room, and stepped down the hallway.

Wait, Jackson said.

Tim stopped, his smile dissolved. What? he asked.

Can you get me a glass of water first?

Tim spun on his heels and headed back to the kitchen. Sure thing, he said.

10.

On a late morning in early September, Elliot played fetch with Lana on his beach. Every place he threw—in the ocean, in streams, in inlets, on rocks—she'd without hesitation hurry toward. Unlike his and Darlene's first dog, Casey, Lana didn't require that Elliot wrestle the driftwood stick from her; wherever he walked, she'd find him and drop it at his feet. If he ignored the stick, she'd pick it up, run ahead, drop it again, and bark once. Today Elliot threw the stick over and over and farther and farther until his arm became sore. September was his favorite month. The tourists were gone, deer-hunting season had begun, and the rain hadn't set in yet.

He and Darlene had found Lana three years after Conrad left for college and a couple months after the completion of the lighthouse. Although they loved dogs, they weren't the kind of people who continually needed a dog underfoot. After one died, they waited until the time seemed right to buy another. Buster, the second dog of their marriage, had died months before they moved north. Elliot, accompanied by Darlene and Conrad, carried the dog across the bridge and buried him on the mainland. In retrospect, standing together as a family with the sounds of the sea behind them was a unifying moment in an otherwise divergent period.

Lana had come from a litter of pups owned by a Coos Bay friend of Darlene's. The bitch was some kind of black lab mix, the father a border collie. In her friend's backyard, Darlene chose the largest and friendliest girl pup from the litter. On the drive home, the pup paced back and forth in the back seat but didn't have an accident. Lana was the first puppy they'd raised. They laughed at her floppy walk, scolded her chewing, and taught her basic commands. The dog became an expression of their deepening love, like some young couples' first child.

Below a blue and cloudy sky, the wind pulled the collar of Elliot's light jacket. After an hour outside he was chilled. Come on,

Lana, he said. Let's go. She cocked her head, then scrambled onto the rocks above him, as though she knew what he wanted. She probably did. She was the smartest dog he'd had.

Early that morning, he'd written the first poem that had pleased him, a poem about his childhood dog. The light brown, short-haired mutt wasn't as smart as Lana but had still followed him everywhere. *Too young to know / No one else would follow me without reason*, the poem had ended, a thought that hadn't occurred to Elliot until he'd written it. The line breaks seemed fine, which felt like a breakthrough in his writing, even though he'd had difficulty finishing his memoir.

Inside, Elliot built up the smoldering fire for Lana and went into the workshop. The place wasn't insulated, and although he'd worn his jacket, after a half hour, he returned to the lighthouse quarters. Fortunately, he'd almost finished the trinket box. He was pleased with how snugly the lining fit in the interior. Only waxing the exterior remained. That, and deciding what to put in it.

As he opened the door, Lana looked at him, then behind him, as though looking for someone else. This gesture, which had begun after Darlene died, hadn't occurred for a few months. Maybe she was looking for Tim. Elliot himself wished the boy would trespass again but in the past month hadn't seen him once. Or maybe Tim reminded Lana of Darlene, and the dog was looking for her dead owner. So many times, since Darlene's death, Elliot had wished he could communicate better with Lana. Describing death to the child-Conrad had been a chore, but being around Lana, who didn't know Darlene was dead, was more difficult than any brief, awkward discussion.

Elliot built up a fire in the kitchen stove—the first of the season there—and on its top cooked himself an elk steak. The scent filled all three rooms, and Lana licked her lips. He ate the steak at the kitchen table with a glass of whiskey and thought of the imminent elk-hunting season. During October he'd hike the forest with his rifle and overnight satchel, never straying more than a half mile from an old logging road. After he killed an elk, he'd quarter it, drag it to the logging road, hike the road out of the woods, and drive in his truck to pick it up. He skinned and butchered the elks himself, and if he wanted the meat ground, he borrowed a friend's grinder.

Right now, before elk-hunting season began, local grocery stores and restaurants would pay him for whatever elk he'd stored. Despite Jackson's claim that Joe never ran out, the bar owner had mentioned he was running low. Elliot decided to offer him and Main Street Grocer's twenty pounds each. He'd never sold meat to Joe, but that summer, he'd come to enjoy the man's presence. The bar owner didn't talk too much, and his conversation didn't focus on himself, and he had an openness that Elliot admired, partially because he himself lacked that quality.

The meat was tender and pink, the gristle minimal. Elliot gnawed just short of the bone and tossed Lana the remains. She retreated to the living room and settled by the hearth, a paw on either side of the bone. Elliot squatted over her and rubbed her. Enjoy that, he said. I'm headed to town.

Joe stood in an empty bar, his elbows on the counter, his eyes on the newspaper. He was smoking and reading about a Vietnam protest and thinking of a conversation with his parents, who lived with him, his wife, and their three kids. His dad had told him at breakfast that he thought he and Joe's mom would both die that winter. Sometime in the early morning, when the tide's going out, his father said. How do you know? Joe asked. Both of you? We want to go at the same time, his mother had said. He'd brushed them off, but the strange conversation returned to him again and again. His parents had always claimed they could predict events, and to his dismay, sometimes their predictions were correct. Too long living on the coast for both of them, Joe thought as a young man, and he found himself a wife inland, from Eugene.

A haze had settled around him. He lit another cigarette and focused on reading. So far, no major protests had plagued Oregon, but Joe figured it was only a matter of time. When he heard a car out front, he buried his half-smoked cigarette in an inch of ash and waved his hand; he thought it unprofessional to smoke in front of customers.

Elliot, upon entering, looked left and right.

Everyone's staying in, Joe said. Too cold—or too early.

Elliot sat on a bar chair.

What would you like? Joe asked.

A Jameson toddy.

Outside, the fog reached as high as the bar's deck. Below the deck, Elliot knew, inside the fog, rocks dropped way to the river and the river flowed into the sea. *The rivers run into the sea*, Elliot thought, *yet the sea is not full.*

Joe placed the steaming glass on the counter. Bet you're glad you don't have to run a real lighthouse in this weather, he said. He kicked himself for using the word *real*, but Elliot didn't seem to notice.

I am, Elliot said. Back in the day, lights and foghorns couldn't always prevent wrecks in this weather. *A light shines in the darkness*, he thought, *but the darkness has not understood it.* More Scripture. But there was truth in that. Some darkness, like darkness filled with fog, was almost impermeable to light.

Especially that Tillamook Light, eh? Joe asked.

Elliot sipped the drink.

I've been reading your lighthouse book, Joe said. He pulled it from a shelf below the counter. And that one seems the worst of them to be a keeper at. They shut it down, right?

Ten years ago, Elliot said. Did it when I was young. Couldn't now. Couldn't even in my forties, I don't think.

You were a keeper there?

Yep.

For how long?

About ten years.

Lord. Why don't you mention it in the book?

It's about lighthouses, not about me.

Wind sucked and whirred as the door opened. Leah stepped inside, Marilyn on her heels. Leah wore a thick black coat but shivered.

This ain't Antarctica, you know, Joe said.

Give it a rest, Joe, Leah said.

It ain't even the East. You'd think with that Eastern blood in you—

My boiler finked out.

As I said—

Repairman can't come till tomorrow. She stepped to the bar, to Elliot's side. I need something warm.

He's drinking a hot toddy, Joe said.

Elliot clutched his drink and clenched his jaw. Leah, that damn snake, he thought.

That's fine, Leah said.

And for you? Joe asked Marilyn.

I'll get the same, Marilyn said.

How you doing, Elliot? Leah asked.

Better, since you're not stealing my property, Elliot said. She smelled like freshly baked bread.

Not stealing, she said, but do what you want with your land. When Leah had finally reached Conrad, Conrad had told her that his father had changed his mind; he wasn't willing him the property. Leah wasn't too put out. So far, two places in Florence had liked her delivery idea. She could expand without Conrad, or Elliot.

You wanted to take more than my cove, you damn sneak, Elliot said.

You want to give that photo back? Leah asked. It won't do any good now.

It's serving a purpose, Elliot growled. You're the one who doesn't need it.

You're right. I don't.

She thought she'd won, didn't she? Elliot thought. Maybe the beach was public, but she'd never get the rest of his property.

Joe had frozen, his back to them. When the conversation didn't progress, he finished the drinks and placed them on the counter. Leah and Marilyn went to a corner table. As the scent of bread faded, Elliot wished he could buy another of those delicious loaves. But he'd never set foot in The Sweet Seller.

The morning after he'd torn the old will, Elliot had written a new will that gave the house, land, and lighthouse to the Coast Guard. After the paperwork was finalized, they'd, in a letter, thanked him for his gift and asked, since he knew so much about lighthouses and coastal history, would he want to give tours of his light? He could start them now and the Coast Guard would continue them after he passed. He'd written back no, he was a writer, not a speaker, but he was glad that the lighthouse would not be destroyed and that someone would educate citizens about it after his death.

Joe wiped the counter below the liquor shelf, then turned and tried the lighthouse angle again. Why don't you write another book about your experiences working at Tillamook Light? he asked. I'd read it.

Geez, Joe, I can feel the cold through glass, Leah said. You'd better do something about that. She and Marilyn moved to another table along the wall but farther from the window.

It'll warm when more people show up, Joe said. If this were Montana, I'd have double panes. Not worth it around here.

If this were Montana, none of us would be here, Leah said. We can't stay away from the ocean, you know?

Joe laughed.

I'm writing a memoir, Elliot said quietly.

Joe raised his eyebrows. On lighthouse keeping? he asked.

On my life, Elliot said. Last week, writing a passage on coastal history had come easily, but the paragraphs that included his family had slowed him down. He'd only wanted to describe how they helped with the running of Lighthouse Island, but even that seemed too intimate, since he kept thinking of how he'd left them alone with the light on the evenings he visited Catherine. He held up his glass. May I have another, please?

Of course.

Elliot listened to the women behind him. Marilyn was saying something about Jackson getting off his cast, then something about Tim kicking Jackson's cast, and Leah was laughing. I suppose it's funny now, Marilyn said. At the time it was tense.

So Tim was at home, Elliot thought. Good.

Joe placed the drink in front of him. It's about your whole life? The memoir?

Yes. Elliot took a sip.

How are old are you?

Sixty-nine.

So you can remember both World Wars and the Depression. What a life.

It's mainly about my work for the Lighthouse Service and the Coast Guard. As Elliot spoke, he desired to make the book even more about work and less about himself and his family. Maybe he should cut those bits from his childhood. Maybe they belonged in poetry.

What do you think of this conflict in Asia? Joe tapped the newspaper spread across the counter.

I don't keep up with it.

Can't blame you. The phone rang. One moment, Joe said, and disappeared into the back.

What did Hemingway write? Elliot thought. That he'd seen the world change, not only the events . . . that he could remember how people were at different times. When Elliot had read *A Farewell to Arms* between the World Wars, he'd agreed with the narrator that the words *sacred, glorious,* and *sacrifice* were embarrassing propaganda that didn't describe real acts, either in war or in civilian life. At that time, not elevating any values was a unique view, especially among Lighthouse Service workers, and he'd had many arguments after reading them that and other passages. But these days, young people had never known those words as anything but embarrassing, and in Elliot's old age, as he read of their protests and hippie festivals, he wanted to tell them how he'd found something sacred after all. Not this incessant war, but incessant love, a concept that no one had discussed when he was a child, a concept that after that ridiculous Summer of Love now seemed inane.

Joe leaned over the counter and lowered his voice. Last summer, Jackson was trying to gain courage to tell Tim one of his friends had died over there, he said. It took me back. It was my friends in World War II.

Elliot had known people who died in World War II, too. One of his best friends had died in the Great War.

He finally told Tim, Joe said. They think that's why the boy ran away.

Tim's face, Elliot realized, his running. It was grief for his friend. The kind of grief you experience only when young, when grief is not yet expected. So maybe a few of the young weren't like those hippies, he thought. Maybe a few thought love and friendship sacred. Elliot remembered writing poem after poem for his friend killed in the Great War, but try as he might, he couldn't replicate those feelings. He remembered that he'd once felt wildly grievous, but he couldn't now empathize with Tim.

Joe was now discussing details of the Asian conflict. I don't want to know, Elliot said sharply.

The women looked toward them.

OK, Joe said. He folded the newspaper and stuck it under the counter.

Elliot looked at the fog, now inches deep on the deck. If Hemingway hadn't killed himself before this conflict escalated, he'd probably kill himself now. Almost ten thousand American troops had died over there in this year alone, Elliot had read, the last article he'd read before he'd stopped following the conflict all together. He had to stay sane somehow.

How you doing over there, ladies? Joe asked.

Just fine, Leah said. She'd unzipped her coat. Marilyn nodded. How many hours? Leah asked Marilyn.

Fifty to sort out basics, Marilyn said. I had to redo the second-quarter paperwork.

And he paid you?

Marilyn shrugged. He had to pay someone. They were a mess. Still are.

The warmth of the drink had spread through Leah. Like my heat, she said. I'd pay almost anyone anything for someone to come tonight.

Did you call inland?

Everyone said tomorrow morning. When will you talk to Jackson? About paying you indefinitely?

Tomorrow.

Maybe you should stay at The Wave tonight. It'll be warmer—

I want to be with Tim anyway, after his first day of school. You could stay with us.

I think Jackson thinks I'm an accomplice in your leaving.

He's the one who invites hobos for free, Marilyn said. You're practically family.

For a minute no one spoke. In the back room, where Joe was unloading a box of beer, bottles clinked. Elliot thought of his fires, probably down to coals. Marilyn thought of how, six months ago, she wouldn't have imagined drinking at a bar when she should be home making supper. She imagined the river below the bar deck that Tim often waded across, the river that ran into the sea.

The new units block the view of the ocean, Marilyn told Leah.

The view from the kitchen?

Yes.

Joe slid a menu onto the table. In case you ladies want something to eat, he said.

Leah ran her eyes down the items. How about fish and chips? Leah said. My treat, cause you're putting me up.

OK. Marilyn smiled. Glad you're coming.

Fish and chips it is, Joe said.

Marilyn took a long drink. I'm thinking of moving back to The Wave, she said. With me driving Tim to school and back, it makes sense, and if Jackson pays me, I'll spend so many hours there during the day.

You'll go back only if he pays you?

Yes. I think, somehow, it'll improve things between us.

Marilyn hoped so anyway. Paying her was a compromise in their ongoing dispute. And once that was resolved, maybe, just maybe, they could again enjoy aspects of each other. Marilyn sipped at her drink and looked out the window. Rocks had been revealed. The fog was lessening, she thought. Good. Driving Tim home from school, while it enclosed the landscape and she couldn't see ten feet in front of the headlights, had been dangerous. She wondered whether she could again fit into The Wave's dailyness, like a missing piece of a puzzle, or if she'd been away too long and changed too much, and she couldn't fit, because her corners were uneven or frayed.

I've always hated doing dishes, Marilyn said. And now, if I go back I'll hate them more.

Have Tim do some, Leah said.

Maybe, Marilyn said.

When Marilyn had suggested that Tim do the dishes, Jackson had said that his son shouldn't do that. If we'd had a girl, she could do them, he'd said. So maybe the new units and paying her to do the accounts weren't the only disputes between them, Marilyn thought. But first she'd get paid. She couldn't take on everything at once.

Leah and Marilyn accidently drank their last swallow at the same time and laughed.

Would you keep working on the Nestucca Spit if you went back? Leah said.

Oh yes, Marilyn said. Though I think Straub and Udall have almost stopped it.

Fish and chips, ladies, fish and chips, Joe said. He set the plate between them. You want another toddy?

I'm fine, Leah said.

I'll take another, Marilyn said.

Leah dipped a piece of the deep-fried cod in tartar sauce while Marilyn ate a fry.

Earlier this year I was thinking of leaving Kalapuya, Leah said. I didn't tell you because I thought you'd try to convince me to stay.

I would have.

Leah briefly smiled. I wanted something different after Micah's death.

But you decided you're better off here?

Not really. I could make a good life in Portland, too. But I decided to stay. I felt better after I made the decision. Once I put my heart into something, I'm happier.

Marilyn nibbled at the fish. Was Leah saying that returning or not returning to The Wave wasn't the issue, but rather making the decision either way?

Every situation's different, Leah said, as though reading Marilyn's mind. But for me it was more difficult to love The Sweet Seller when I kept thinking of being somewhere else. She took a large bite of cod. Really good, Joe, she said. Wish Micah could taste it.

Me too, Joe said. He locked eyes with Leah as he dropped off Marilyn's drink. We miss him around here, he said.

Marilyn placed her hands around the warm glass.

Need any food? Joe asked Elliot.

Do *you* need any food? Elliot countered. Ground elk. I could sell you twenty pounds.

It's that time of the year, isn't it? Joe said. He wiped his hands on his apron. I'll take a dozen. You should talk to Ben, too.

Always do, Elliot said. He gulped the last swig and placed a bill on the counter. I'll bring it later tonight.

Works for me, Joe said.

The women looked up as Elliot stalked to the door. Outside, crystals had formed on the edges of his truck's windows. He stepped inside and turned on the engine and cranked the heat and didn't gear up from first as he drove to the small general store across the way, where cars filled most parking spots. A man examined axes by the outdoor pile of firewood. A woman rounded the corner of the building, a light-blue scarf secured over her head, her face scrunched against the cold. Elliot idled out front until another car honked him on. I'm going, he said, I'm going. He pulled out of the lot and onto Highway 101, toward home. He'd drop by with the meat tonight, he thought, when the store had settled down. He could count on Ben to buy a dozen pounds.

Back home, only wisps of smoke rose from both chimneys. Elliot killed the engine and hurried inside. The living room was cool and dim. Lana hadn't come to the door. He glanced first toward the fire, where coals shimmered under the grate, then the kitchen. His office-bedroom door was closed. He stepped back into the front room, toward the fireplace. The black dog huddled in the late-afternoon shadow of the couch. Her eyes opened, rolled toward him, then closed. By her shoulder lay the steak bone, a finger-size sliver torn off.

Goddammit, Elliot said. He dropped to his knees. He couldn't feel anything in her mouth. He pulled her body away from the couch. When she didn't struggle, his throat clogged with fear. He lay on the rug close behind her and placed a hand-covered fist underneath her ribs. The first time he pulled against her she opened her eyes. The second time she whined. The third time she coughed out the bone.

Elliot rested his hands on the dog's fur. Her stomach rose and fell against him. Coals sizzled from stray raindrops. The sea, as always, lapped on. Elliot pushed himself up and stood. Lana stood too. She sniffed toward the expelled bone. Christ, Lana, Elliot said. Jesus Christ. He swiped both bones from the floor, and in the kitchen threw them away, double-checking that the cupboard door was latched closed. He stood over the sink, at the window, looking out to sea. Lana sat next to him, her chin on his shoe. Splotches of silver-and-white waves shone.

Lana's water dish by the stove was empty. Elliot filled it. Lana lapped up the water. Elliot filled it again and again. Lana drank two more bowlfuls, then drifted toward the living room. Elliot went to the garage for firewood, his shoulders slouching more than usual. After five trips, he'd accumulated a pile. Still wearing his jacket, he sat on the brick ledge of the fireplace and fed wood to the coals. Lana crouched low on the rug next to him. He placed a hand on her head. The wood crackled and flames caught. Warmth and light filled the room.

PART
THREE

1.

Tim's last cross-country meet had been cancelled because of a flash flood. The teams were supposed to run along the Siuslaw River, which had overflowed onto the path. Instead of hitching a ride or calling his mom to pick him up, he decided to walk, or run, home. All day, while thinking of the race, he'd stored energy, which now threatened to bust out. The drizzle was only intermittent, and his parents didn't expect him home until past suppertime. He'd always wanted to explore the stretch of coast between Waldport and Kalapuya.

After his final class he pulled his light green raincoat from his locker and put it on, hood up. He left his backpack at school. Not many teachers had assigned homework that weekend, and those that had he'd already done or didn't mind not doing. Tim waved goodbye to Mitch, hopped down the long front steps, jogged through town, and stepped onto a trail that led through the woods to the beach. A moss-covered fallen cedar had been cut in half to clear the path, its scent strong because of its wetness. The path popped out above a driftwood graveyard. The petrified wood looked like giant slugs, their boughs tentacles. Tim swung or climbed over them, grasping available knobs or branches. By the time he'd cleared them he was breathing hard. He looked down the wet beach. It was only two cross-country races long, he thought. And he didn't have to run the whole length.

As he walked, he swung his arms high and in random waves and circles. Without his backpack his body felt light. He trotted and sidestepped, making zigzagging trails in the sand. He giggled at his ridiculousness. Oh well, he thought, he was alone. He mimicked the cry of seagulls. They replied, swooped toward the sea. It was nice to be alone. Now that he was in school and his mom was home, opportunities to be alone had become rarer. Maybe a few minutes before bed, when he'd drop on a record and fall asleep to it, maybe an hour or two for exploring on the weekends, between a cross-county race and chores.

At school, Tim didn't raise his hand much and found more situations funnier than most kids. Other boys wanted to sit with him at lunch or train with him at practice. Last weekend, after attending a birthday party where only three other boys were invited, he'd realized he was more well-liked than he'd imagined. Not that he'd imagined much about school; he'd only had a vague desire to go.

He'd been upset that his mom had gone through his backpack to find the permission paper, something she wouldn't have done before he ran away, he'd thought, or maybe before she'd gone away; he wasn't sure. His anger receded when he saw that she'd signed the form. She dropped him off at school in the mornings and picked him up after practice in the evenings, or if he had a meet, he found a ride home. If she'd become more intrusive in some ways—going through his backpack or sometimes, during the day, cleaning and rearranging his room and records—she'd become less intrusive in others. On car rides she didn't ask questions about his day or schooling. He'd vowed to talk as little as possible to this person who had left once and might leave again, but for some reason her silence made him want to share. When he talked, she'd tilt her head and reply with an insight or question.

Tim jumped over a winding-toward-the-sea stream. As he landed, his heel hit the edge of the bank and under it sand collapsed. He stumbled forward twice and straightened himself into a walk. His socks and feet were damp but no need for them to be waterlogged. As a kid, he'd worried gangrene would grow on wet feet, something his grandpa Richard had jokingly told him might happen if he played too much in the wet outdoors. He'd imagined gangrene as a mosslike substance that started at the toes and traveled upward. He still wasn't sure what it looked like. But he couldn't catch it from stepping in a stream; he now knew better than that.

His mom was working long hours during the day in the closet-office. At night she slept on the couch. Each morning, the moment he woke, or during the night if he got up to pee, he'd make sure she was there. His concern felt childish, but, he thought, it was her own fault. Sometimes she'd open his bedroom door to look at him when she thought he was asleep or when he was listening to records. This, he realized now, was her way of checking on him, of making sure he hadn't run off again either. He was glad he'd come back. Although he missed Mr. Yager's old house, his life now was better than foraging for food or spending time with an interesting but strange old man. Was his mom glad she'd come back? he wondered.

A subdued pink and orange light glowed on the ocean. The days were short now. Darkness would come before he reached home. This beach had no caves and thus, probably, no agates. Although Tim hadn't searched for the rocks since he'd run away, he identified where they might be. His own agates still sat on the windowsill behind the couch. His mom hadn't offered her jewelry box as a storage space and he hadn't asked. She hadn't mentioned Tim throwing the rocks at her, and his dad hadn't mentioned Tim kicking him. That first night home, Tim cleaned the flue. The next day his mom had informed him that she was driving him to school in the fall, and that was that.

He was passing Ocean View now, while intentionally making deep footprints in the sand that the hotel had advertised as private property. Only four of the two dozen rooms facing the sea had lights on. Off-season, Tim thought, and began to jog, his pose casual, his feet sure. The mist had stopped. He was only a couple miles from home. He'd go through town and over the bridge, he thought, not down the rocks and through the river. He pushed down his hood and sped up his steady pace. Pacing himself had become an art form, and he was good at it. Running was now a means of concentration instead of a means of escape.

Tim had dropped a card in the mail for Carl's family. A generic card, which said, *I'm sorry for your loss*. He'd simply signed his name. His mom told him Carl's mom had said thank you. The women had talked on the phone.

Light shone off buildings as he jogged through town. These minutes, the minutes before structures and trees became dark silhouettes, had become his favorite part of the day. He'd run through the transition many times that fall. Each time he tried to predict the exact second when color would fade, like when, as a kid, he'd tried to predict the exact moment when a wave would curl. Five, four, three, two, one, he counted. And again: five, four, three, two, one. Outside the bar, Joe's oldest boy waved to him, and Tim waved back, then the light was gone. He'd been wrong tonight, as he was often wrong. Only by chance could he predict the moment when light became darkness.

The driveway into The Wave was dim. Tim didn't notice Mr. Yager's truck until he'd opened the office door. He shut it and headed to the lounge to hide. What did Mr. Yager want? To tell his parents that he'd trespassed? Why had he waited so long? He hadn't washed the comforter, Tim remembered. That must be it. All Mr. Yager wanted was for him to wash that comforter.

Through the window, in the lounge, Tim saw Mr. Yager sitting across from his parents. Tim turned to go, then turned back. Who cares what Mr. Yager tells them, Tim thought. They should know he was nearby instead of in Florence or Eugene, like they thought. He'd outsmarted them once and could again.

As Tim opened the door, his mom said his name. He avoided eye contact with anyone and sat on the arm of the couch. The air smelled like sawdust. His dad's left leg jutted out, knee locked, as though it were still in a cast. A small wooden box set on the coffee table.

Mr. Yager tells us you've taken a liking to his lighthouse, his dad said.

Tim didn't raise his eyes.

I told them you'd dropped by on your exploring, and I'd explained the history, Mr. Yager said.

Tim squinted at Mr. Yager. The old man leaned forward, elbows on knees, hands clasped. His sparse white hair was brushed away from his face.

I've been there, Tim said.

He waited for Mr. Yager to tell them that he'd hidden in the old house. That the old man had fed him, and that he didn't have enough gratitude to wash a comforter. A guest came through and nodded toward Jackson. Jackson nodded back.

I told them that I thought you'd be a good tour guide, Mr. Yager said.

Surprised, Tim looked in Mr. Yager's deeply lined face. Tour guide for what? he asked.

I'd like to give tours of my lighthouse, starting in spring. I don't want to give them personally, but I want it to be open to the public one afternoon a week. Mr. Yager picked up the box and set it on his knee. I'd pay you, he added.

I told him it was fine with me, his dad said. You're old enough to have a job.

His mom was looking across the room, at the guest who was pulling out *Reader's Digest* books. Tim wanted to know what she thought, but true to form lately, she seemed uninterested.

I've never talked to a crowd, Tim said.

Wouldn't be more than ten people per tour, Mr. Yager said. Maybe only five. Not much space by the light, as you know.

You've dealt with five people at a time in the office, Jackson said.

Tim nodded. I could do that.

Great, Mr. Yager said. I thought you could come over once a month, and I'd teach you more history to prepare. Maybe the stories of those shipwrecks on the walls.

OK, Tim said.

How about tomorrow to start? Sometime in the afternoon?

Sure. Tim still thought Mr. Yager would mention his hiding spot.

See you tomorrow then. The old man stood. I brought this as a thank you. Thought you might need a place to store your agates. You still collect those?

Kind of, Tim said. Thanks.

His mom turned her eyes to the box. She reached out a hand and let it drop.

Here, Mom, Tim said. Take a look.

She took the shiny box from him and slid the top in and out of its grooves.

That's it then, Elliot said. Good evening.

I'll walk you out, Jackson said. Want to hear how your hunting's going. He winked at Elliot, who remained stoic.

Tim's mom handed him the box. It's well-made, she said. And good timing. Those agates are collecting dust.

Tim took off the lid and ran his fingers over the smooth interior.

There's stew on the stove, his mom said. Feel free to help yourself. She stood and walked by him, her skirt brushing his jeans. Tim opened his mouth to say something—anything—to her, but instead coughed. She paused at the door, facing the exterior. When she heard him breathing normally, she went out.

He wanted her near, but her quiet distance held him back. Since she'd returned, her movements were fluid and peaceful, as though she were choosing to do work around The Wave instead of it being a chore. The foreign happiness in her eyes returned sometimes, but muted, like sun behind clouds. She was like his science teacher, Mrs. Kelly, who knew the answer to any science-related question and became animated whenever she went on tangents, but didn't show interest in the actual lessons, and because of that, her students never formed an interest in them, either. His mom seemed more content than happy, Tim decided, but maybe contentment was better than happiness because it took longer to fade.

Inside, he tossed the agates from the windowsill into a metal strainer and rinsed them off in the sink. Across the way, a line of light from one of the new units shone between black curtains. The windows on that side were only a couple feet square and usually curtained, but once, last weekend, a curtain had been pulled back and Tim had seen a couple kissing. They'd moved out of sight, to the bed, he assumed. A motel, he knew, was often a place where couples came to have sex. A couple hours later, when he went to watch Little Faithful at high tide, they were walking hand in hand on the grass above the rocks.

Tim hurriedly ate two bowls of stew over the counter. The beef broth warmed his chest. He dried the stones and rolled them off his fingers into the box. They filled a third. If he held off gathering agates all winter, he thought, looking for them only in early spring, he could probably fill the rest of the box in one trip. Satisfied, he slipped on the lid, placed the box on his bedside table, and kneeled to flip through his record collection.

His dad, he knew, was also waiting for spring. Business on the new units would pick up at spring break and especially in summer, his dad had told his mom more than once. His mom usually said, OK, we'll see. Tim didn't think she cared. But hadn't she hated the idea of building? If Tim had hated it, he'd want no one to use them; he'd want them to fail. He picked out a Byrds album, set the needle, and sat on his bed, his legs crisscrossed. The music kicked on at the same time as a drizzle.

The actions of adults contradicted their words and even their previous actions. Take Elliot, who had opposed the Beach Bill because he didn't want strangers on his land. And now he was going to host strangers every week, not only on his land but in his house. What sense did that make? Though Lana would like it, Tim thought, as he blinked his eyes in tiredness. And he himself would like it, or at least wouldn't mind it, especially since he'd get paid. He was saving up to buy a guitar. He wanted to learn how to play, to turn his poems into lyrics.

And not only adults, Tim admitted, shaking his head to stay awake. Wasn't he the one who wanted friends, and now that he had them, he wanted to be alone? Mitch had invited him trick-or-treating in Waldport next week, and Tim had surprised himself by saying no. The past couple years, he'd watched a movie on television and handed out candy to the kids who ventured as far south as The Wave. He'd wanted to do that again. If you'd rather watch a movie, come on over, he'd said. Mitch said he'd think on it. It was nice to have the option to hang out with someone, Tim thought. If he didn't have that option, he might not like being alone.

The rain hammered as he flipped the record. When the mist had cleared on his walk, he'd thought the rain was finished for today. You should know better than to predict coastal weather, he told himself, something his grandpa Phil had told guests.

His grandpa Phil was dead. Like Carl. Like, it came to him now, Mr. Yager would soon be, too. Their deaths and the memories of them happened in the same world as music, a world separate than the one in which he did chores and went to school. When he ran away, the dead Carl had spilled into the other world, and it had scared him even as he'd wanted it. Now the worlds were separate, always separate. Was one in his mind, the other out? No, it was more complicated than that. Music was literally outside his mind, as was the card he sent Carl's family. Although he did math in his head, it was part of the school world. Could he combine the worlds without him crying or running haphazardly across a beach or hurting so badly that he wanted to jump out a window? He didn't know. Maybe becoming an adult meant combining them? No. Not all adults lived at once in both worlds. Maybe Leah did. She could talk about Micah while selling baked goods without being stoic or breaking down. When she spoke of music you knew she felt it. The record ended and he slid off the bed to pick another. It unsettled him that Leah functioned like that; he'd always thought her a little strange. Maybe you had to be strange to live at once in both worlds. If so, he wasn't sure he wanted it. After all, it could be the difference between choosing to be and having to be alone.

Tim set the needle on *The Freewheelin' Bob Dylan* and leaned against his pillow, eyes closed. For now, it felt good to simply ask questions. Or, he thought, as "Blowin' in the Wind" began, let Dylan ask questions that he himself hadn't thought to ask. He wasn't even in high school yet. Maybe the answers would come.

2.

Elliot wanted to extract himself from Jackson. Ever since Lana's accident, he'd locked her in his office-bedroom whenever he left. The space was so small that he didn't like to leave her long. And Jackson was trying to pump him on hunting spots. He could find his own, thank you very much. Jackson was the kind of man who mistook energy and knowledge for competence, and Elliot had no patience for that. And then Jackson was trying to cut a deal with him on what—on firewood?

Lose your supplier? Elliot asked.

Just shopping around.

I'm not sure I've cut enough for myself this winter.

Unusual, isn't it? Don't you always have extra? Jackson rubbed his beard and smiled.

How did Jackson know that? Elliot thought. I need to go home, Elliot said. If you want a few pounds of elk, Tim can let me know.

I'll have him do that. Glad you dropped by.

Elliot opened his truck door, hoping Jackson would take the hint.

Showing the lighthouse will be a great first job for Tim, Jackson continued. Marilyn has some notion he should go to college but I'm not sure. He needs to start working. I had him help out with the construction but not for pay. Jackson was leaning sideways, his weight resting on his right foot.

Elliot stepped into the truck bed. Good evening, he said, and shut the door before Jackson could speak again. As he drove down The Wave's long driveway and glanced in his rearview mirror, he saw Jackson turn and limp toward the office. The old man relaxed against the seat. Talkers, he thought. He could handle them better when young. Welcomed them, in fact, some days when he worked at Tillamook Light. Like Thomas Anderson. He could beat you at chess without ceasing his chatter, which became a pleasant background noise when the radio was down. Elliot had forgotten about Thomas. He'd insert a paragraph about him in the memoir.

Ever since Elliot had talked to Joe about his memoir, writing it had become easier. Instead of wondering how many scenes he should include from his family life, he'd cut that aspect all together. In the first chapter, he deleted the descriptions of his immediate family and elongated the passage on Grays Harbor Lighthouse. In the third chapter, "Transition," he didn't mention Darlene. He'd just finished the penultimate chapter, in which he described his own lighthouse. The final chapter would be an overview of the history of lighthouse keeping, using the types of lighting—kerosene, electric, and automatic—as focal points. The last few paragraphs would detail how automation caused the death of the lighthouse keeper.

He stopped the truck at the mailbox, off the highway above the lighthouse. He sniffed as he stepped from the cab. Not done raining today, he thought. He'd received two letters, one from the Coast Guard, the other from his old friend Aaron Strom. He set the letters on the kitchen table while he let out Lana, rubbed her down, and fed her, cutting up leftover bacon to mix with beans. Spoiling her, he knew, but when he'd almost lost her, he'd finally admitted to himself that he didn't mind his solitude only because she was there. He turned on the lighthouse light, built up the smoldering fire in the living room, and ate a cold salmon sandwich on the couch while reading. Lana dropped next to him, her head on his sock-covered foot.

Aaron's letter was only a half-page. Apparently, the keeper's dwelling at Cape Blanco had been demolished. *I thought you might want to know for your book,* Aaron had written. *I feel confident that one of Cape Blanco's items won't be destroyed any time soon. I'd like to come up and see it. Are you around all winter? If so, I'll drive up some Sunday afternoon. Anyway, they won't be automating Cape Blanco's light quite yet. That's something.*

Elliot scratched Lana's neck. He felt sadness at yet another demolition, then his eyes flashed with mischievousness. Aaron wanted to come see the first-order Fresnel lens in Elliot's lighthouse. The lens had been in Elliot's possession for so long that most days, he forgot they'd stolen it. For their actions they could be jailed. But Elliot had hosted men from the Coast Guard who'd seen the lens and made no comment. At this point, he figured they knew but didn't care. And the lens would return to the Coast Guard's keeping after his death.

The envelope from the Coast Guard contained brochures and speeches that tour guides used at other lighthouses along the coast. Elliot had told the Coast Guard that he'd changed his mind and decided to give tours, and even though he'd written an entire book on lighthouses, for some reason, they thought that this literature would be useful. He tossed the papers and the envelope in the fire.

Some days he doubted his decision to will his place to the Coast Guard. They'd probably automate the light and let the public climb all over it. But most days Elliot figured it was better for his lighthouse to be trampled on than for it not to exist, or for it to exist in disrepair, without at least one person enjoying it.

The idea for Tim to give tours had come to Elliot while he had removed the soiled comforter from the spare room and thought of the boy's desperate expressions. Now that Elliot knew they came from grief, his tone and words toward the boy pained him. He'd imagined Tim sprinting along his own stretch of beach or running away again, this time farther and maybe to an unsafe place. Elliot had too much pride to withdraw his prohibition, but how else would the boy come back? Then he thought of the tours. At first he imagined himself giving them and Tim attending. But he didn't like talking to groups, and he didn't have the patience to repeat himself or answer ignorant questions. Then he thought of asking the boy to give tours. That way, if Tim agreed, the boy could visit again and again.

Today, when he saw Leah's muffins in The Wave's lounge, he'd had another idea: to ask Tim to bring him loaves of Leah's bread. If Tim agreed, Elliot would be able to enjoy her product without interacting with her.

Outside, the wind picked up and rain fell. Gusts came down the chimney, pushing around flames and half-burnt papers. Elliot thought of the wind, how he'd only written about it technically, in reference to his lighthouse work. Maybe he should explore it through poetry. He scratched Lana's back and fed her his sandwich crusts. He went to the kitchen and poured a glass of Jameson from his clear decanter. Out the window, shore pines leaned inland.

He again remembered Thomas, who'd come from the East Coast. How can you stand the winter weather? Thomas had asked him once. The constant gray skies and storms? Elliot hadn't thought of it as negative. And there were more gray days where I grew up, in Aberdeen, he'd said. Thomas looked at him like he was crazy. Why would anyone live there? he asked.

The increasing whitecaps filled Elliot with energy. Water jumped onto rocks and drizzled off. He thought of Tim, who'd said the new units would block his view of the sea. The boy looked better today, his cheeks flushed, his eyes alert, not vacant. And his mom had returned, quiet as usual. Elliot was glad he'd given the kid Darlene's jewelry box. The box was meant for valuables. And although agates wouldn't bring in more than pennies at a pawnshop, they were valuable to Tim.

The rocks and waves looked as though they were merging; soon high tide would cover the beach. Because the government hadn't yet reviewed Elliot's offer to sell his dry sands, last week he'd again met with Ted. After Elliot promised a bonus, Ted said he'd call in a favor, but warned Elliot that ultimately these things just took time. Elliot told Ted that he was glad he wouldn't be around in fifty years to see what a mess the government became. From 1939, he'd said, when the Lighthouse Service had dissolved into the Coast Guard, until his retirement in 1950, work meetings had become longer, training sessions had become longer, and paperwork had become more complicated, without him learning a goddamn thing. He'd taken the option to remain a civilian instead of becoming part of the military, but he still resented the transition. Everything was becoming more unified and federalized and bureaucratized, resulting in inefficiency and a loss of individual freedom.

Ted had told him that Citizens for Oregon Beaches weren't satisfied. Because so many hotels and other business had petitioned the government for use of their dry sands, the group wanted to pass a constitutional amendment that would allow the government to buy all of the dry sand from current owners, effectively blocking such petitions. They planned to collect signatures to place such a measure on the 1968 ballot.

Passing such a measure would assist Elliot in his own goal, but he listened with growing frustration. Such land-use rights along the beach should be decided on a case-by-case basis. Ted agreed and said the revised section in the Beach Bill had helped it pass in the legislature. He doubted this amendment would pass, or if it would even acquire enough signatures to reach the ballot, but then again, a whole year remained between now and the election.

Elliot added a log to the living room fire and built one in the kitchen's woodstove. He settled into the straight-backed chair in the office-bedroom, leaving the door open for warmth. Lana lay flat on her side underneath the desk.

Elliot hadn't felled many trees that fall. He had enough firewood for himself and Lana. Same with deer, and although elk season had just begun, he planned to also curtail that supply. He probably wouldn't cut a deal with Joe or Main Street Grocer's next fall. Stocking up on firewood and meat no longer appealed to him. One of these winters I'm going to die, he'd thought. When that happens, I want others to pillage as little as possible. Let them do their own damn work.

He flipped to the section of his memoir on Tillamook Light and scribbled a few sentences on Thomas. He'd gone back East after two years, Elliot remembered, since he couldn't acclimate to the weather. Elliot set aside the memoir and took up a compilation, *Modern European Poetry.* The poems were different than anything he'd read, maybe because he'd read only modern American poetry. He wasn't sure where the difference lay, but if someone had pressed him, he'd have said that these poets were more concerned that they described something well than that they held a particular stance. At least he'd received that impression from the first section, French poetry. He was reading the second section, German poetry. Greek, Italian, Russian, and Spanish poetry were to come.

Elliot had written more poems that fall, mostly on domestic scenes he'd considered placing in his memoir. *Under the bed the boy quivered / As though the world had ended,* began one. *Orange peel under her fingernails* / *Juice stains across our bed*, began another. When Elliot's thoughts wandered over the intimate moments in his poetry, he felt as though he'd lived a long, rich, and various life. Maybe he'd share one or two anecdotes with a person close to him, like Joe or Tim, he thought. But sharing private details with every Tom, Dick, or Harry through his memoir would have cheapened them.

Outside, a branch cracked. Lana seemed to go from lying to standing. She barked. It's OK, girl, Elliot said. Brush was probably falling all over the yard. Tomorrow he'd pick it up. Tonight, the Coast Guard would be extra alert. Forty years ago, on nights like tonight, lighthouse keepers had to be, too. Now boats had better interior mechanisms to gauge distance, his own lamp wasn't going out, and he had no lifesaving duties. Still, such storms raised his adrenaline. He listened to the repeated *crack* of large waves crashing. If caught, no one could resist the pull of such a current. Winter storms were coming and he was glad.

Lana sat. He continued to read. He liked the German poems, especially Rilke, particularly "Sense of Something Coming," the only Rilke poem in the collection that Robert Bly, his favorite modern poet, had translated. *I already know the storm, and I am as troubled as the sea*, it ended, *And spread myself out, and fall into myself,* / *And throw myself out and am absolutely alone* / *In the great storm.*

The poem championed and unsettled him. Lana at his heels, he went to the kitchen and poured more whiskey. He opened the window above the sink, then the outer door. Leaves swirled and branches flailed. Wind sometimes seemed like someone crying haphazardly, he thought, like someone grieving. Lana hung back, whining. Elliot thought of an old, querulous man in Aberdeen who traipsed through the woods during the harshest storms. As boys, he and his friends had dared each other to follow him. He himself wouldn't go out tonight, Elliot thought. He hadn't yet lost all his common sense. He closed the door and left the window open and sat at the kitchen table. A strong gust shook the panes. Lana cowered under the office-bedroom's desk.

Elliot picked up his whiskey and climbed the four flights to the top of the tower. By the lamp's light, he could see lashing raindrops and choppy sea and whitecaps. Outside the reach of his light, the world was darkness. Elliot imagined himself on the one storm-filled night at Tillamook Light when he'd had no assistance. One guy was on emergency shore leave, Thomas was too sick to stand. After he turned on the lamp, he stood in the lighthouse tower, wondering whether the huge waves would reach him, alone in the growing storm.

3.

After Elliot left, Marilyn drove to Florence to buy groceries. Jackson chopped firewood and ate the stew alone and checked on the kid, who'd fallen asleep clothed and on top of the bedcovers. He pulled the needle off the record player and turned off the lights but didn't guide Tim under the covers as Marilyn would have. He turned on the television and turned up the volume to hear over the pounding rain. That weekend, anti-war protestors planned to march on Washington, DC. Already over ten thousand had gathered. He turned it off and spread the firewood across the grate and rinsed out the stew bowls so they'd be ready for cereal the next morning.

When Marilyn first returned, she and Jackson tiptoed around one another, talking as little as possible. By the time talking came naturally, the family had tacitly formed new routines: Jackson and Tim made food or washed dishes when Marilyn, for whatever reason, didn't. Jackson wanted to ask why, but after she'd been away so many months, it was pleasant simply not to make all the meals and not go grocery shopping, and he kept his mouth shut.

Jackson drank a can of Bud while looking at the new units out the kitchen window. To save money, Marilyn had wanted to paint the new units' interiors herself. Jackson agreed with that one. She'd painted their living room and was so damn careful it looked like the work of a professional. Also, to save money, Marilyn suggested letting Annie go during winter months. And that's supposed to make her want to come back for the summer? Jackson said. Marilyn wanted to at least ask. It turned out that Annie was happy to leave during winters. I'd make more waitressing at my sister's restaurant, she said, and took off to Salem. Marilyn, Jackson, and Tim were picking up the slack.

Jackson smashed the can before he trashed it and took out another and turned on the radio. The room was getting cold. If Marilyn had said I told you so—hell, if her eyes had even said that—Jackson would have started a fight. But their discussions centered on facts, and her demeanor was so professional. Too professional. Every Friday he wrote her a check for her bookkeeping hours. Every night she slept on the couch. When either of them left for a few hours or the day, they pecked each other on the lips out of habit. Jackson drank the second beer while sitting with his elbows on the table. The last fire embers died. The radio said a tree had fallen across Highway 101 near Newport. It predicted the storm would let up by midnight.

Jackson began to worry. The section of 101 south of them, on which Marilyn was traveling, the radio didn't mention. Once, when she'd driven to Florence, a tree had fallen across the highway. Marilyn intended to walk to the closest house and phone Jackson, but two snapping sea lions wouldn't let her out of her car. Whenever she tried to open a door, they playfully pushed back. After a couple hours the beasts padded back to the sea and she escaped. When Jackson arrived, Marilyn handed the bags of groceries across the fallen trunk and crawled over. Something like that didn't happen twice to the same person, Jackson thought. Surely she'd be home any minute.

He was almost finished with the second beer when he heard her car. He started up and stepped down the stairs, holding so tightly to the banister that it bowed under his weight. His leg had been out of a cast a few weeks, but it was still stiff. Outside, he strode around puddles and reached her car as she was stepping out. His worry seemed foolish. The rain was too common to mention. I came to help with the bags, he said.

Oh, she said. Thanks. Her hair was wetter than it should have been after an hour's drive in a heated car. She pushed a strand behind her ear, got out, and handed him a bag from the trunk. He opened his arm for a second one, then, remembering his leg, retracted it. She hoisted two bags into her arms and they walked upstairs. After a second trip, they silently put away the food. Rain pattered against gutters.

I had to stop the car, Marilyn said. The rain was coming down so hard I couldn't see. She filled the teapot with water and set it on the stove.

Where'd you stop at? Jackson asked. He'd returned to his beer at the table.

Past Cape Perpetua, right above Devil's Churn, Marilyn said.

It's a rough night to drive along those cliffs.

Do you want tea?

Jackson shook the almost-empty can. Sure.

Marilyn poured hot water over peppermint tea bags. She brought the mugs to the table and sat facing the living room, kitty-corner from Jackson. She stared toward the window above the couch. The darkness reflected back her face.

She was dazed, Jackson thought. Why else would they be sitting together, having tea? He picked up the mug and sipped. The heat warmed his hands.

How long did you wait? he asked.

She looked again at the dark window. The reflection mirrored details down to her tangled hair. I waited longer than I had to, she said. I wanted to see what Devil's Churn looked like in a storm.

You hiked down there?

Yes. She broke the tangles in her hair by running her fingers through it.

Such a hike didn't seem like her, Jackson thought. Not like Marilyn the cautious. But maybe she wasn't always cautious. She'd never told him what had happened to cause her hypothermia.

Why? he asked. It was dark. You couldn't see.

I took a flashlight, Marilyn said.

No one from the coast would be so foolish.

Maybe not.

Jackson drained the mug. Steam poured from his mouth. I was worried, he said. You were taking so long.

Surprised, she looked at him. I didn't think you'd notice.

These simple and honest words hurt Jackson. I did.

I didn't mean to worry you.

Jackson nodded and stood. I guess I'll head to bed. He stepped toward the hallway and turned back around and took his can and mug and went into the kitchen and placed them next to the sink.

Good night, he said as he passed the table.

Good night, Marilyn said. Her hands clasped the mug as though grasping for warmth. Jackson remembered that her hands became icy as the temperature dropped.

In the bedroom, he stripped down to his boxers and slipped under the covers. Starting at the top and moving downward, he massaged his bad leg. Soon Marilyn would come in to change clothes. On the rare nights that Jackson hadn't dozed off before she entered the room, he feigned sleep so as not to disturb her.

Tonight he was listening for the storm to end. It should have already ended. The wind was tapering off; maybe the rain would soon too. His body was so tensely alert that he forgot to close his eyes as Marilyn entered. The light from the hall shone on him. He dropped his lids too late.

Nothing you haven't seen before, Marilyn said.

Jackson kept his eyes closed. He listened to her unzip her skirt and unclasp her bra. He opened his eyes as she slipped a white, sleeveless cotton nightgown over her head. Marilyn still had a slim figure, though both of them had loosening skin. When she sat on the side of the bed and turned to him, he started. Underneath the fabric her breasts bounced.

I don't bite, she said.

Maybe if they'd had more kids, Marilyn would have gained a stomach pouch, he thought. And yet she'd wanted more children. Maybe the pouch didn't matter to her. But she should be glad they hadn't had more, with the finances in such poor shape now.

I think I'm beginning to see the light, Marilyn said.

With what?

The finances.

Do we have to talk about that now?

Marilyn stood. No. Just wanted to share the good news.

Jackson pulled himself to a sitting position. It is good news, he said. He gestured toward the bed. I didn't mind . . .

She sat back down. Again, her breasts bounced. Sometime, when Jackson hadn't been listening, the rain had stopped. Without that sound the world lacked something. He strained to hear the *whoosh* of the sea. When he heard it, his shoulders relaxed. I'd like to separate business time from family time, he said.

What family time? Marilyn asked.

You know what I mean.

That's fine. We can discuss business details downstairs. But can't I say one comment up here?

You can. That was fine.

Outside, a car pulled into the lot. They both waited for the ring of the office doorbell. Instead, a door slammed across the way.

A guest, Jackson said.

See, you're talking business right now. Marilyn rose until Jackson leaned forward and grabbed her cold hand. She sat back down. What? she asked.

Do you want to be married? Jackson asked.

Marilyn pulled away. Why else would I have come back?

Tim, he said. To earn money. He had thought through this. It was possible, probable even, that he had nothing to do with her return. He took her hand again.

I could earn money without working here, she said slowly. But yes, for Tim.

This place then. The place, not the money.

Yes, that was part of it.

You can work here, even if we're not married. You can see Tim. Jackson rubbed the top of her hand with his thumb.

You want to get a divorce?

No. But you seem to want one.

I don't.

Jackson leaned forward and took her other hand and held them both. If we're married, why don't we act married? he asked.

Marilyn leaned forward and kissed him. Not a damn peck but a real open-mouthed kiss. Something of the storm resided in her, something of the wind. He kissed her. Her damp hair fell against his neck. His hands moved from her hands to her waist to her back. They stopped kissing so she could take off her nightgown. He lay back and she moved on top of his chest. Soon, he rolled her over. He kissed her neck and her stomach and her breasts. Her sounds were as welcome and familiar to him as the coastal rain.

Afterward, she lay pressed against his side. Since his question, neither had spoken. As he dozed, she pulled herself away. She found her underwear and nightgown and put them on.

Where're you going? he asked.

To the couch.

What? He opened his eyes.

I have to get up early. I don't want to wake you. She tied her hair in a knot at the nape of her neck.

Where're you going? He rolled his head to the side and looked at her.

She had a hand on the doorknob. I told you I needed tomorrow off.

But where're you going?

Eugene.

Why?

For a speech.

Whose?

Bob Straub's.

Who? He caught her eye.

The state treasurer.

Why d'ya wanna hear him? The name had been in the newspaper recently, but Jackson couldn't remember why.

She kissed his cheek. Good night, she said.

If she didn't want to talk, she didn't have to. How else could he keep the peace? Good night, he said, good night again.

He listened to her open the door to Tim's room, then he listened to her situate herself on the couch. He thought he could hear her steady sleep-breathing but wasn't sure. He raised himself to an elbow and glanced at a porch light across the parking lot. The lack of rain had woken him.

Where did Marilyn say she was going? To Bob Straub's speech? Was it something to do with the beach business? He wondered whether someone who knew them would see her. Was that your wife listening to Bob Straub? someone at Joe's might ask him. Yeah, yeah, he'd say. You know women. They think a small group of citizens can outwit an existing state policy.

He smiled and pulled himself to a sitting position and opened and closed his bad leg. It felt fine. They could have had sex last week.

And they should have had more sex last spring, before Marilyn left. When was the last time? February, March? Too long ago either way. He hoped this wasn't a one-time romp. He could ask again why they weren't acting married—not to guilt her but as a fact. Even if they couldn't have another kid, didn't she enjoy the pleasure and closeness?

Jackson threw his legs off the bed and stood. He wanted another beer but he didn't want to wake Marilyn. He'd go to Joe's. After all, he also wanted to discuss Elliot with someone. First, the old man wanted to provide tours to the public and asked Tim of all people to give them. Then, he didn't chop extra wood for the winter. Jackson pulled on pants and buttoned up a black-and-red checkered flannel. What did that mean? Did he know he was going to die soon or something? It seemed like that. He wondered what Joe thought.

Jackson stepped slowly down the stairs. The days when he had eaten aspirin were as vague as a dream. The stabbing pains were now gone, but he felt different than before the accident, as though he'd gone through a rite of passage like puberty or marriage. In the office he put on his cap and coat. Outside, the air smelled like rain.

He unlocked the truck, paused, relocked the truck, and pocketed his keys. A walk to Joe's would take less than fifteen minutes. And once in a while, everyone, even him, needed to walk.

From the highway, he turned to enjoy the view. In the bottom story of The Wave's center building lay the motel's accounts, almost in order, and on the top story lay his wife and his son. Around that building stretched the angular horseshoe of the motel units, the new units a beautiful second story. He imagined that the adult Tim might construct a second story on the other two sides. Beyond the motel was darkness.

Sure, he had his troubles, like anyone, but he couldn't imagine a life much better than this one. He touched the cracking "Vacancy" sign, noting that it needed to be replaced. As he walked toward town, he was careful to place equal weight on both his good leg and his bad.

4.

Leah reached the outskirts of Florence just as the rain stopped. On either side of the road sat houses, their windows dark. Streetlamps illuminated rainwater along curbs. She rubbed one shoulder, then the other, alternating hands on the wheel. The drive down the coast in the downpour and darkness had tensed her. She could see hardly anything, yet had to pay attention to everything. One of the wood railings on a cliff ledge had been broken. Twice, logging trucks going north had passed, splashing gallons of water onto her windshield. She hadn't wanted to pull over and wait out the storm, lest she be late for her first deliveries.

She pulled off the highway, into the business district, where shops and their wide porches lined both sides of the street. The last store along the main row was Dune Bakery, the first of Leah's two stops. If she looked closely through the front windows, she could see light shining under a door in the back. Leah pulled into the dirt alley behind the store. After so much darkness, the porch light blinded her. When she could see again, a heavyset, aproned man stood smoking under the light on a wood slab.

Leah rolled down her window. OK if I park here? she asked.

Perfect, the man said.

Leah placed the car in gear and stepped outside.

How was the drive? the man asked.

You get rain here?

A little.

We had a storm, Leah said.

You need a hand?

That would be nice, thanks.

The man stubbed his cigarette under his boot and brushed it aside. I'm Fred. He stepped off the porch and extended a hand.

Leah clasped it, then unlocked and opened the trunk. I'd like to buy a van, she said. And build in shelves. She handed Fred a cardboard box and took one herself. Three dozen loaves of cinnamon raisin, she said.

Perfect, Fred said.

For Leah the night had already been a long one. After closing up shop and making herself dinner, she'd tried to rest. She listened to records and read the newspaper but couldn't fall asleep. At 7:30 p.m. she'd made herself coffee and begun to bake. By midnight she'd finished the three-dozen loaves for Dune Bakery and the dozen apple pies that an ice-cream shop had requested. When she returned home, she'd bake for The Sweet Seller.

Through the door, in the kitchen, a woman and a girl mixed dough. Chocolate chip cookie dough in the girl's bowl, Leah saw. She couldn't tell what was in the woman's.

My wife, Mary, Fred said. Daughter, Suzy. This is Leah Tolman.

Nice to meet you, Leah said. The girl looked young to her until she remembered that she'd worked at the Portland bakery at an even younger age.

Nice to meet you, Leah, Mary said. The girl just smiled.

The air smelled more sugary than in her own bakery. Fred had told her his specialty was doughnuts and cookies, not bread. Leah followed him to the front of the store, where he placed the cardboard box on the counter. She followed suit.

What do I owe you? he asked.

She rustled through her box and pulled out an invoice. He paid in cash from a drawer below the register.

These'll sell out by Sunday morning, Fred said. I've spread the word.

Leah asked him what he'd like for the next weekend.

Dozen more cinnamon raisin. A dozen sourdough and a dozen white.

I can do that.

Do you want the boxes back?

Leah waved her hand. No need.

How about some coffee?

Coffee would be nice.

She followed Fred back to the kitchen, where he poured her a cup. The heat and steam immediately warmed her hands and face. While she drank, he told her about the shop's origins. The girl dolloped spoonfuls of dough onto a cookie sheet, and the woman dropped dough in a pan of sizzling oil on the stove.

Leah grew more alert. She held up the empty mug. Thanks, she said.

Fred took the mug. Hope you don't get caught in more rain, he said.

I think it's over for tonight.

The ice-cream shop, Eats and Sweets, was off the highway on the south side of town. Leah found the key under the welcome mat and let herself in. She placed the pies in a row on the front counter and took an envelope of money from beneath the jar of taffy closest to the door. The shop didn't open until 11 a.m. She pulled off the taffy jar's lid and breathed in the scent. It reminded her of Micah. Sadness overcame her, the type of emotion that rose only when she was wide awake but very tired. She dropped into the closest chair. Her body wanted to fold in on itself. Instead, she looked out the window. Across the highway a man was locking up a bar. She saw his wide shoulders and red jacket but no facial features.

Did Micah know he was going to die, that the storm was too much for him, or did his boat jolt and he hit his head and that was the end of it? She couldn't imagine that he considered impending death. He was the rare kind of person who took each moment as it came, who didn't try to manipulate the world to his own desires. He hadn't found a shop in Portland that sold taffy, he told her, so he brought a bag of his own to munch on and when he stopped at the shop, shared them with her. It was she who suggested selling them, who wanted to move sea candy inland to make a profit.

And what would he have thought of her work on the Beach Bill? she wondered. He wouldn't have meddled; he wasn't meddlesome. When she returned home late from campaigning, her head full of ideas and people, he would have listened to her thoughts, then asked about the weather. There was a storm up the coast wasn't there? he might have said. He would have seen it from his boat or felt it in the wind. Who owned the ocean was important to him. Compared to that, the beaches were like long fingernails, an ornament. He knew and enjoyed his place in the world, as she did hers, although through the Beach Bill, she had avoided it.

Leah remembered her own kitchen, the baked goods to be made before sunrise. She stood and turned toward the door. At the same moment, a man entered the shop and leveled a shotgun at her. He had jowls, a mustache, and wide shoulders; he wore a red jacket. The guy who'd locked up the bar, Leah thought. She dropped the envelope on the tiled floor and held up her hands.

What're you doing in Abe's store? the man asked.

Leah tilted her head toward the counter. Those are my pies, she said. Abe wanted to sell them.

And you had to deliver at 2 a.m.? the man asked. What's in the envelope? He kept the gun pointed at Leah as he leaned down. His jowls bounced. The barrel brushed her waist. The man opened the envelope and eyed the bills, then Leah. You stay there, he said. I'll give Abe a call. He sidled behind the counter, gun still leveled. Hands on your head, he said. There you go.

Leah kept her eyes on the man and his gun. He didn't sound drunk. She supposed that would be worse. She could tell him she had a key, but he seemed intent on calling. That the man wanted to defend his friend's shop was admirable. She imagined that she and Micah would have laughed over her situation when she got home.

The phone rang a dozen times before someone answered. She heard a tired voice on the other end but not what it said. The man reluctantly lowered the shotgun as he hung up. Looks like your story checked out, he said.

Only that, Leah thought. No apology. She supposed he had to keep his dignity. She was amused. I have a key to lock up, she said. Shall we?

The man watched her lock up and place the key under the mat. She had to ask him for the envelope of money. He stood on the mat while she stepped into her car and was still standing on the mat when she looked through her rearview mirror as she drove away. Legs wide, eyes on her car, arms cradling the shotgun. Beyond him, covered in darkness, was the highway and the river and the forest and the dunes and the sea. He looked as though he were guarding not only the shop but also the road south.

Leah turned on the radio and allowed herself to smile. She then laughed, soon so hard that tears fell. By the time she reached the north end of Florence, she was crying at the scene of her telling Micah, how he'd chuckle while she rocked back and forth and slapped her knee. It means your first deliveries were a success, Micah might have said. And what would've unsuccessful deliveries looked like? Leah might have asked. He could have taken the money, Micah might have said. Or you could have been shot. There was nothing for Leah to do except to drive and cry. The storm had come inside; the car couldn't keep out this kind of rain. She choked and coughed and cried until she'd cried herself out. Then there was only the dark, windy highway and the sounds of the engine, the radio, the wind, and her labored breathing. She placed a palm against her cheek to feel the heat and wetness.

If you entered Kalapuya at night from the south, driving out of the depths of the forest, the first brightness you'd see was the sign at

The Wave. It flashed with the urgency of a lighthouse beacon. Well before Leah passed, the sign grasped her attention. It blinded her; she couldn't see the motel behind it. She looked into trees on the other side of the highway, and her eyes adjusted back to darkness. As she rounded the corner before town, right before the lights of the business district, more brightness caught her eye—a white T-shirt, worn by Jackson, who hobbled on the other side of the road, in the other direction, presumably toward The Wave. He dragged his bad leg as though he'd just broken it. Leah drove passed him, then pulled a U-turn. As she slowed, he stepped farther from the highway. She leaned across the car and rolled down the passenger-side window. The cold air startled her.

You want a ride? she asked.

I'm fine, he said.

At that rate it'll take you an hour to get home.

I'm not in a hurry. Jackson looked down the road. As she rolled up the window, he stepped toward the car. OK, OK, he said.

He grimaced as he sat and used both hands to lift his bad leg inside. His arms were red, his eyes glistening as though faintly inebriated. He set a flannel in his lap. Where the hell you coming from? he asked.

Florence. I'm doing deliveries there now.

Been meaning to take some flyers down there. Advertisements for the new units. He massaged his leg.

You OK?

Oh yeah. Don't think I could've walked to town and back before I broke the thing. I'm getting old. He smiled.

Leah had thought he'd be in a foul or subdued mood, that maybe a spat with Marilyn had instigated this uncharacteristic walk. But he seemed upbeat, almost euphoric. Unlike Marilyn, his moods radiated off his face. She pulled into The Wave's long driveway.

You doing in-town deliveries? he asked.

No.

Maybe you could make an exception for The Wave?

Doesn't it make more sense for Marilyn to pick up however many you need each day, instead of estimating beforehand? Leah idled by the office.

Was thinking it'd be one less thing for Marilyn to do. I'll ask her.

OK, Leah said. Good night.

Good night and good morning, Jackson said.

Leah circled the center building and drove the driveway and pulled onto the highway, focused on home. In her house she washed her face, changed clothes, shrugged on an apron, made coffee, and settled into chopping apples into both thin slivers and small chunks on the island cutting board. The known morning routines calmed her.

While she baked, repeating recipes she'd made hundreds of times, the strange night began to seem a dream, a dream somewhere between familiar and unfamiliar on the trajectory of dreams she'd had in the almost year since Micah died. She'd dreamed of capsized boats and sea dragons and loaves of bread as large as her house. She'd dreamed of her and Micah sitting on her grandparents' Victorian porch, and him leaning his chair back until it tipped over and he cracked his head. She'd dreamed of herself buried in sand up to her neck and herself running along the tide line and herself working in a kitchen foreign to her while her father stood on a counter, overseeing. Compared to some of those dreams, this dream-night had been tame. But she'd made money off it, she reminded herself. She halted in her baking to make bookkeeping notes. Nothing so tangible came from a dream.

By the time the muted morning lightened The Sweet Seller's hardwood floors, an array of baked goods lay in the case: apple scones, apple pies, apple muffins, sourdough and white loaves, sugar and jam-filled cookies, and basic, round doughnuts. Leah brushed her hair, made herself more coffee, and unlocked the door. She smiled at the sound of the bell as a regular trucker entered.

5.

Marilyn woke to the ring of her alarm clock. She stretched her arm down from the couch and turned it off. A dream returned to her; Jackson had been kissing her back. She loved it when he kissed her back. Last night had been nice, too, though rather short. Baby-making or no baby-making, it had been too long. She removed her blankets and stood and folded her blankets and piled them by the side of the couch and placed the alarm clock on top. She turned to see Tim standing there, hair tousled, pajama pants on, no shirt. His arms were thin, even as his shoulders had filled out.

He squinted. Where're you going? he asked.

To Eugene, she said. I told you that.

He cocked his head.

Maybe she hadn't told him, she thought. Did I not tell you that? she asked. She walked past him and into the kitchen. I meant to. She spooned coffee grounds into the percolator. I'm going to listen to a speech.

Tim swung one leg so that he again faced her. Can I come? he asked.

You have to meet with Elliot, she said. She put the spoon in the sink and filled the percolator with water.

You won't be back by then? Tim asked.

Maybe, but probably not. Go back to bed. It's early. She went to him and smoothed his hair. We'll do something together tomorrow, you and I, she said. She'd felt his presence in the living room some nights, making sure she was there. She wanted him to know that they had a future together here, that she was always coming back. She kissed his forehead.

He wiped off the kiss with the back of his palm. OK, he said. She touched his back as he turned but didn't walk him to bed.

While the coffee percolated, Marilyn changed into the cream-colored blouse and navy skirt she'd ironed and laid across a chair the evening before. She poured herself coffee and went downstairs and unlocked the office's outer door and, with a black Sharpie, crossed out yesterday's square on the wall calendar. She flipped the reservation notebook to Saturday, October 21. So far, they had five reservations for this evening. She slipped on Jackson's boots and heavy coat, and holding the mug, walked out into fog. She passed the still-empty flowerpots and clomped down the path between unit buildings and stepped across the dewy grass to the bench. She checked that Jackson's coat separated her skirt from the moist slats of wood as she sat down. Little Faithful spouted five feet high twice, then burped splashes. Below the rocks and fog, splotches of a gray and green sea were visible.

Every morning since she'd returned to The Wave, she'd sat on this bench. During rain, she brought an umbrella or allowed the water to sink through her clothes. The morning view from the bench replaced her former view from the kitchen. Even if new units hadn't blocked her view, she might have started this tradition. These days the kitchen view might have been too far away from the ocean or too close to her daily tasks. Here, she could experience solitude before plunging into daily intimacies. For now, this was better than being away or feeling enmeshed.

After her mornings outside on rainy days, Jackson gave her wetness a glance but didn't comment on it. Unrelated to the business, he didn't ask why she did anything anymore. Perhaps her leaving and returning had caused this behavior. For the most part, Marilyn liked this benign neglect. They both needed to learn to not care.

Today, Marilyn thought of the evening before. Near the wide crevice of Devil's Churn, her flashlight had illuminated splashes fifteen feet high. The mist from them had touched her face and settled in her hair. She'd crouched and listened and internally cheered the storm's waves.

The hike down to Devil's Churn had been a test. She'd planned to approach the sea without it almost drowning her or her wanting to drown. She'd wanted to explain her actions to Jackson, but for him to begin to understand, he'd have to know about her night in the cave, and she wasn't ready to talk to him about that.

Little Faithful spouted again—eight feet, three feet, then two burps. Jackson had wondered whether the government would designate these rocks as a natural wonder now that they were public land. The spouting is too erratic for Little Faithful to become popular, Marilyn had told him. And where would people park? His face relaxed when she'd said that; as usual, he latched on to positive possibilities as though they were facts. It wasn't always a bad trait, she thought now, to be easily persuaded that life would work out in your favor. She found it attractive, this competent, grown man with such childlike hope.

Because of his hope, she'd realized, he'd allowed her to go away while hoping she'd come back. What if he had cut her off, if he'd said that if she left once, she left for good? The option of return had been necessary. If he hadn't allowed that, she would either be at The Wave, unhappy, or permanently separated from him and her life here without being sure that she wanted that. He was sometimes open to her in ways she wasn't open to him or even to herself.

Marilyn remembered the foreignness and familiarity in the kiss she'd initiated. Kissing was key. Deep kisses were sometimes more intimate than sex. No man probably thought that, she thought, Jackson least of all.

She wondered about Tim, when the sensuality in his life wouldn't be confined to songs. Maybe it already wasn't. She didn't know everything about her son. When she'd asked where he'd run away, he'd said only that he'd hid out somewhere. Threatening punishment had no effect, and she didn't have the heart to follow through. With everything going on, she didn't blame him for running away. She would have run away, too. She did in fact *run away*, although she preferred the morally ambiguous term *leaving*. She hoped Tim wouldn't feel the need to run away again before he left. Less than five years and he'd be gone. To college, she hoped. She didn't want him eaten by the draft. She was saving half the money Jackson paid her to fund Tim's college education. The other half she saved in another account with the money she earned from her freelance jobs. For the thousandth time, Marilyn pushed away the guilt she felt at saving money when The Wave was in such debt. Sacrificing Tim's education and her nest egg would cause resentment, in this case worse than guilt. Maybe a day would come when she'd feel neither. She hoped so.

The fog was rising off the ocean. In the growing light, the water appeared more blue green than green gray. Marilyn drained the coffee and stood and turned from the view. Back in the office, she changed from Jackson's coat and boots to her own jacket and flats. Driving away from The Wave, she glanced in the rearview mirror. Smoke swirled from their chimney. Tim or Jackson? she wondered. Probably Tim.

Marilyn planned to pick up Sandy at The Sweet Seller, where she'd also buy baked goods for The Wave. She'd arrange the treats in the motel lounge on their way back south. Once in Eugene, Marilyn would drop Sandy off at a Vietnam protest, then attend Bob Straub's speech at a local church. Although Sandy knew the streets of Eugene better than Marilyn, Marilyn had volunteered to drive. When Marilyn had sat in the passenger's seat while Jackson drove, curvy roads had resulted in nausea. While canvassing for the Beach Bill, she'd discovered that curves didn't bother her half as much when she herself drove.

Marilyn pulled her sedan against the curb. Bright red leaves from a neighbor's maple peppered Leah's yard. Inside, Leah sat across the corner table from Ned. They both were laughing. When Leah saw Marilyn, she stood. Lyn, she said. She hugged her. Although surprised at the unusual gesture, Marilyn returned the hug. Leah wiped tears from her bloodshot eyes. Ned decided not to fish this morning with that storm last night, Leah said. So he's gracing us with his presence.

I thought you worked in a cannery? Marilyn said.

Used to, Ned said. I'm back to fishing now. Can't stay away from it.

Are you OK, Leah? Marilyn asked. Your eyes . . .

Kind of red, right? Leah said. I've been up all night. Out on my first deliveries. Laura'll be over at nine. I'll sleep then. What can I get you?

I don't want to interrupt . . .

Leah touched Marilyn's arm on her way behind the counter. It's my job, she said. She smiled. How many do you need?

Ten is fine, Marilyn said. You can pick them out.

I'll give you a dozen for the price of ten.

You spoil me, Marilyn said. She looked out the front window. I'm supposed to meet Sandy here. You seen her?

For that protest, right? She won't stop talking about it. I'm sure she'll be over. Leah finished loading the bags and handed them over. Coffee? she asked.

No thanks.

After Marilyn paid, she sat between Ned and Leah, the bags on her lap, her body facing the window. Leah repeated the story of the holdup. She and Ned laughed as heartily the second time, but Marilyn, worried for her friend, only smiled with her lips.

There're people like that everywhere, Marilyn said.

I hope so, Leah said.

Marilyn wanted to tell Leah about her hike to Devil's Churn, but it was too sacred a story to tell with an acquaintance present.

Sandy traipsed down the walkway to the shop. A low ponytail held her long, thin hair. She wore a long cotton skirt and baggy T-shirt, not tucked in.

Marilyn stood. Don't want to be late, she said. Thanks for the extras, Leah.

Anytime, Leah said.

Marilyn met Sandy on the stoop. Good morning, she said. Are you ready?

I want to buy a doughnut, Sandy said.

Marilyn held up the bag. I have extras, she said. You can have one.

Sandy popped her head in the store. They're expecting over thirty thousand at the Pentagon march today, she said to Leah. Sure you don't want to do your part in Eugene?

Not today, Leah said. I've been up all night.

I'll yell enough for both of us, Sandy said.

During the drive down the coast, Marilyn turned inward. She and Sandy had had few conversations that didn't center on the finances of the antique shop. For a month or two, the shop had functioned independently from Sandy's inherited wealth. Around month three, Sandy stopped keeping track of purchases: she'd find a necklace in Newport or a teapot in Lincoln City and dip into her own money. Marilyn hesitantly told her that if she couldn't do basic bookkeeping, she'd no longer work with her. Sandy laughed and with a wave of the hand dismissed Marilyn's services. This is just who I am, Sandy said. To accept who you were, without apology, without sadness or guilt, was enviable to Marilyn. But she didn't envy Sandy her business acumen.

Marilyn's interactions with Sandy had forced her to reevaluate Jackson. If she took into account the entire spectrum of business owners, he didn't seem so bad. He saved receipts, although he didn't place them in the log. He intended to pay off the debt, although not as quickly as she would.

They were almost through Florence. When Marilyn turned on the road toward Eugene, Sandy spoke as if on cue. What I can't believe is that we leave Cuba alone, a communist country not ninety miles from our border, but go halfway around the world to fight communism in Vietnam.

It does seem strange, Marilyn said. She couldn't compete with Sandy on either knowledge or conviction. Especially the escalation, she added.

That damn Gulf of Tonkin. Not that Kennedy and Eisenhower didn't increase troops. But that's a blank check, a damn blank check.

Hatfield wouldn't have voted for it if he were a senator then, Marilyn said cautiously.

Damn right he wouldn't have. We need a few dozen like him in office. Not that we'll get them.

Marilyn rolled down her window. There's always a moment driving east when you can't smell the ocean anymore, she said. She crested a hill, then dipped down and around a curve. There, she said, it's gone.

I've never been anywhere where I can't smell the ocean, Sandy said.

What do you mean?

I've never been away from the coast for longer than a day. Sandy pulled out the side of her shirt and flapped it. The scent stays on my clothes.

Marilyn lowered her chin to smell her own blouse. The saltwater scent had remained. You're right, she said. She smiled.

The problem with Americans is that we think we can fix things, Sandy said. We haven't had enough trouble in our country.

Don't forget the Civil War.

OK, the Civil War. Sandy waved a hand. But who alive

remembers that? Europeans, who've had more recent wars on their home soil, know you can't fix problems, you can only alleviate them. Will Americans ever learn?

I don't know. Marilyn had to distance herself from Sandy before she could objectively ponder what she said. Marilyn left the window down. She was enjoying the ocean scent inside the car but not out.

As they entered town, wind and rain flung yellow leaves across the road. Sandy instructed Marilyn which ways to turn. The march is near the university, she said. Your speech is downtown. She muttered about the poor planning of having the protest and speech on the same day.

A few blocks from the college, they spotted a young woman and young man holding signs. One read *Bring Our Boys Home*, the other *Stop the War*.

Let me out here, Sandy said. I can walk.

Marilyn pulled against a curb. She offered Sandy an umbrella. Sandy shook her head and plunged outside without. Marilyn watched Sandy greet the students before she drove away.

Marilyn found the white and steepled church without trouble and parked in the back lot. At the front door, a man and a woman passed out pamphlets detailing the proposed amendment. *Bond Issue to Acquire Ocean Beaches*, the front read. Marilyn lowered her umbrella and took a pamphlet and walked down the center aisle to the third row from the front, where she sat. The back was less conspicuous, but Marilyn had learned to sit as close as possible, because some speakers spoke quietly. Unlike Leah, Marilyn didn't consider her affinity or lack of it with the other people gathered. She was there solely for the issue.

Voices muffled the rain until a man took the stage and the crowd quieted. Marilyn could hear it again, louder now, against the roof and the stained-glass windows on either side. The man introducing Bob Straub had trouble speaking above it, but Straub's voice overpowered the rain. He spoke about land-use laws and taxes and gathering signatures, directing his listeners to specific pages in the pamphlet. Marilyn hadn't known that they had the option to petition for signatures following the meeting.

At the end of the speech, four people rose to hand out petitions and take a collection. As Straub reminded the crowd that developers would fund the fight against the proposed ballot measure, the sound of rain increased, competing with his voice. Marilyn imagined the Kalapuya River, swollen by last night's storm, flowing into the ocean. The ocean accepted the freshwater even while it pushed against it. Since she had hours before Sandy would be ready to leave, Marilyn accepted a clipboarded petition. She opened her beige pocketbook and fingered a five-dollar bill that she'd brought for emergencies. When the collection basket first passed her, she didn't donate. On its second time around, she did.

When she turned to leave, she was surprised at the church's fullness. Pews were packed and dozens stood. She preferred to wait until the crowd had thinned, but people pushed, and after tucking the clipboard under her arm, she stepped into the flow. She walked shoulder to shoulder until she reached the front door, where the crowd jammed closer before people were spit out one by one onto the streets and into the rain, like boats crossing a sandbar between river and sea.

Acknowledgments

Thank you to Jason Frantz; to Arsen Kashkashian, Conor Moran, and Collin Tracy; to Marc Bruchet, Emily Crum, and Abby Freeland; to Alex Berge, Heather Frese, Charity Gingerich, and Rebecca Thomas; to Alan Good, Michael Jauchen, Phoebe Mogharei, Meredith Pangrace, and Anne Trubek; to David Berney Needleman, Gary Custis, and Chris VanVechtan; to Mark Brazaitis, Kevin Oderman, and Mary Ann Samyn; to Henry Alley, James Boren, Francis Cogan, John Gage, Tom Glenn, Emily Mitchell, Paul Peppis, and Glenn Taylor; and to Amelia Benson, Chris Benson, Heather Benson, Leo Benson, Sam Benson, Robert Kendrick, Virginia Kendrick, Jeanne Kendrick King, Andrew King, Dodie King, Gordon King, Gordon J. King, and Abigail Oladele.

The following books were important to me in my research: *The Oregon Companion* by Richard G. Engeman, *Sentinels of the North Pacific* and *Tillamook Light* by James A. Gibbs, *Lighthouses and Life-Saving on the Oregon Coast* by David Pinyerd, *More Deadly Than War: Pacific Coast Logging, 1827–1981* by Andrew Mason Prouty, and *Fire at Eden's Gate* by Brent Walth. I also studied newspaper microfilm at the Oregon Historical Society Library and digitized newspapers through the Multnomah County Libraries website.

The sentence, "Sometimes people needed stories more than food," comes from a sentence in *Crow and Weasel* by Barry Lopez: "Sometimes a person needs a story more than food to stay alive." The title *People Along the Sand* comes from the first line of the poem "Neither Out Far Nor In Deep" by Robert Frost.

Although the Beach Bill was an actual piece of legislation, this novel is a work of fiction, and names, characters, places, businesses, events, and incidents are either the products of my imagination or used fictitiously. Any resemblance to actual persons, living or dead, is coincidental.

About the Author

Rachel King was educated at the University of Oregon and West Virginia University. Her short stories have appeared in *One Story*, *North American Review*, *Green Mountains Review*, *Northwest Review*, and elsewhere. She lives in her hometown of Portland, Oregon.

CPSIA information can be obtained
at www.ICGtesting.com
Printed in the USA
LVHW021026161121
703348LV00006BA/133

9 781950 843480